Leon

01/07

SLAN & SLAN HUNTER

A. E. VAN VOGT AND KEVIN J. ANDERSON

SLAN & SLAN HUNTER

SFBC
SCIENCE
FICTION

SLAN Copyright © 1940, 1945, 1951, 1968 by A.E. Van Vogt
Introduction Copyright © 2007 by Kevin J. Anderson

SLAN HUNTER Copyright © 2007 by Wordfire, Inc. and Lydia van Vogt, Executrix for the Estate of A.E. Van Vogt

First SFBC Science Fiction Printing: June 2007

Published by arrangement with:
Tom Doherty Associates, Inc.
175 Fifth Avenue
New York, NY 10010

Visit The SFBC online at http://www.sfbc.com

ISBN 978-0-7394-8491-3
Printed in the United States of America.

CONTENTS

SLAN

TO MY WIFE
E. Mayne Hull

INTRODUCTION

by Kevin J. Anderson

His mother's hand felt cold, clutching his." For my money, *Slan* has one of the greatest opening scenes in classic science fiction: young Jommy Cross and his mother being tracked by slan hunters, trying to stay alive in the mean streets, knowing they are special, knowing they are hated.

I read *Slan* in college and quickly turned to other great van Vogt works, such as *The World of Null-A, The Weapon Shops of Isher, The Silkie, The Changeling*. A. E. van Vogt was one of a few writers—mainly groomed by *Astounding Stories* and its influential editor John W. Cambell—who can be credited with creating the true "golden age" of science fiction.

A. E. van Vogt was born on April 26, 1912, in Canada; he moved to the United States in 1944. A voracious reader as he grew up in various towns in Saskatchewan and Manitoba, he had interests that ran the gamut from science fiction to westerns, mysteries, adventures, and historicals, as well as the classics. He did not excel in science in school, but made up his mind early that he wanted to be a writer. He took a correspondence course, but also taught himself most of what he needed to know.

At the age of twenty-six, he encountered an issue of *Astounding Stories* that contained the first publication of the now-classic story "Who Goes There?" (basis for the film versions of *The Thing*), which had been written by John W. Campbell, the magazine's editor, under a pen name. Van Vogt struck up a correspondence with Campbell and a year later—in July 1939—published his own first story, "Black Destroyer," about a horrifying alien creature that seeks to kill a space crew and steal their ship. ("Black Destroyer" has been acknowledged as the foundation for the film *Alien* and its sequels.)

That same year van Vogt began work on his first novel-length story, *Slan,* about persecuted mutants being rounded up and killed by normal humans. Because they were different, because they were superior, slans were perceived as a threat. Interestingly, *Slan* was published the very year that the Nazis opened Auschwitz. As he wrote his novel for Campbell at *Astounding Stories* at the end of 1939, did van Vogt know that the persecution he described in *Slan* would very soon be taking place among Jews, gypsies, and homosexuals in Germany?

The basic idea of mutants living among us, persecuted supermen who have the key to saving humanity, has been used as a springboard for many subsequent stories and variations, including the popular *X-Men* comics and films. But van Vogt was the original.

The serialization of *Slan* was an immediate sensation among the readers of the magazine. Science fiction fans perhaps felt a special kinship with slans, who had interests that set them apart from "mundane" humans, and yet were "persecuted" (teased, rather than being hunted down and killed). "Fans are slans" was actually a slogan used by fledgling SF fandom in the 1940s, a group of whom founded their own cooperative housing development in Battle Creek, Michigan. They dyed streaks—surrogate tendrils—in the hair at the back of the head and moved into an eight-room house that they called the "Slan Shack."

Van Vogt's novels may seem thin to modern readers of "doorstop books," but each chapter is packed with sense-of-wonder ideas, any one of which another author might spend whole books exploring. He was not a fast writer, usually laboring nearly a year on each novel, and he did not plan his stories in advance. In a 1947 essay, van Vogt stated, "Ever since I started writing for the science fiction field, it has been my habit to put every current thought into the story I happened to be working on. Frequently, an idea would seem to have no relevance, but by mulling it over a little, I would usually find an approach that would make it usable."

His concepts are sometimes difficult to grasp and his plots and connections are sometimes difficult to follow or believe, but that is part of the charm and challenge of reading a van Vogt novel. His work is full of energy and imagination. As a writer, A. E. van Vogt was like a crazy Technicolor popcorn maker of ideas. Very few others would dare to put a surprise ending on an entire novel—and yet van Vogt did it, again and again.

He created worlds that can only be called "old-fashioned futuristic"—definitely the product of a man writing in the 1940s and filtering his far-future imagination through the lens of what he saw around him. Though the stories are set centuries or millennia from now, and perhaps halfway across the galaxy, the reader has a sense that the cars still have hood ornaments and wide white-walled tires, that the characters wear fedoras and drink martinis (and not the modern fru-fru ones). *Slan* has an innocence, an optimism, and a confidence, along with some politics that may be either inconceivable or horrifying to a politically correct audience.

Van Vogt's other works have a similar scope, chock-full of super-men and mental advances, rather than the nuts-and-bolts hard science of his contemporaries Asimov and Heinlein. In 1996 A. E. van Vogt was given "Grand Master" status by the Science Fiction Writers of America.

I met Van once at a science fiction awards banquet in the late 1990s, after I had established myself as a reasonably successful SF author. Remembering how much enjoyment his works had brought me, I made a point of bringing my leather-bound copy of *Slan*. I found Van at a banquet table with his lovely wife, Lydia. I had intended just to ask politely for an autograph, but instead I turned into a gushing fan, telling him how much I admired his novels, his stories, his ideas. Lydia quickly intercepted me, helped her husband to sign the book, and invited me to come to their house someday to get other books signed. Van himself said little, mumbled a thank you, and concentrated fiercely on writing his name.

I didn't know at the time that van Vogt was suffering from severe Alzheimer's disease, that very little of the man—the mind—I had admired so much was still there. Nor did I know that he would pass away soon thereafter, in 2000, at the age of eighty-eight.

In the last years of his life, starting in 1984, van Vogt had returned to *Slan,* starting a sequel that he felt would complete his great story. Editor David Hartwell expressed his enthusiasm for the unwritten novel for Tor Books, but unfortunately Van couldn't finish the project. A working outline and a hundred pages or so of draft manuscript were all he completed before he became incapable of the concentration and focus necessary to keep writing. His Alzheimer's had progressed to the point where he could no longer work.

That manuscript remained untouched for more than fifteen years, before a mutual friend put Lydia van Vogt in contact with me. Lydia asked if I would look at the partially finished manuscript and consider completing her husband's last work. I still had my treasured leather-bound copy of *Slan,* signed by both Van and Lydia, and I was very honored to be looking at a grand master's final project. After I read the material she sent, and reread the original novel, I wholeheartedly agreed to bring *Slan Hunter* to completion. David Hartwell, the editor who had originally talked with van Vogt about the sequel more than twenty years ago, is also the editor on the completed book. The story comes full circle: *Slan* was van Vogt's first published novel in 1940, and *Slan Hunter* will be his last, in 2007.

Van Vogt's prose may seem somewhat dated to modern readers, but the adventure and the ideas and the characters certainly captivated me when I was in college twenty years ago, and no doubt they'll captivate another generation of readers. Turn the page, open your mind, extend your tendrils if you have them, and get ready for a roller-coaster ride into the future.

ONE

His mother's hand felt cold, clutching his.

Her fear as they walked hurriedly along the street was a quiet, swift pulsation that throbbed from her mind to his. A hundred other thoughts beat against his mind, from the crowds that swarmed by on either side, and from inside the buildings they passed. But only his mother's thoughts were clear and coherent—and afraid.

"They're following us, Jommy," her brain telegraphed. "They're not sure, but they suspect. We've risked once too often coming into the capital, though I did hope that this time I could show you the old slan way of getting into the catacombs, where your father's secret is hidden. Jommy, if the worst happens, you know what to do. We've practiced it often enough. And, Jommy, don't be afraid, don't get excited. You may be only nine years old, but you're as intelligent as any fifteen-year-old human being."

Don't be afraid. Easy to advise, Jommy thought, and hid the thought from her. She wouldn't like that concealment, that distorting shield between them. But there were thoughts that had to be kept back. She mustn't know he was afraid, also.

It was new and exciting, as well. He felt excited each time he came into the heart of Centropolis from the quiet suburb where they lived. The great parks, the miles of skyscrapers, the tumult of the throngs always seemed even more wonderful than his imagination had pictured them—but then size was to be expected of the capital of the world. Here was the seat of the government. Here, somewhere, lived Kier Gray, absolute dictator of the entire planet. Long ago—hundreds of years before—the slans had held Centropolis during their brief period of ascendancy.

"Jommy, do you feel their hostility? Can you sense things over a distance yet?"

He strained. The steady wave of vagueness that washed from the crowds pressing all around grew into a swirl of mind clamor. From somewhere came the stray wisp of thought:

"They say there are still slans alive in this city, in spite of all precautions. And the order is to shoot them on sight."

"But isn't that dangerous?" came a second thought, obviously a question asked aloud, though Jommy caught only the mental picture. "I mean a perfectly innocent person might be killed by mistake."

"That's why they seldom shoot on sight. They try to capture them and then examine them. Their internal organs are different from ours, you know, and on their heads are—"

"Jommy, can you feel them, about a block behind us? In a big car! Waiting for reinforcements to close in on us from in front. They're working fast. Can you catch their thoughts, Jommy?"

He couldn't! No matter how hard he reached out with his mind and strained and perspired with his trying. That was where her mature powers surpassed his precocious instincts. She could span distances and disentangle remote vibrations into coherent pictures.

He wanted to turn around and look, but he didn't dare. His small, though long, legs twinkled underneath him, half running to keep up with his mother's impatient pace. It was terrible to be little and helpless and young and inexperienced, when their life demanded the strength of maturity, the alertness of slan adulthood.

His mother's thoughts stabbed through his reflections. "There are some ahead of us now, Jommy, and others coming across the street. You'll have to go, darling. Don't forget what I've told you. You live for one thing only—to make it possible for slans to live normal lives. I think you'll have to kill our great enemy, Kier Gray, even if it means going to the grand palace after him. Remember, there'll be shouting and confusion, but keep your head. Good luck, Jommy."

Not until she had released his hand, after one quick squeeze, did Jommy realize that the tenor of her thoughts had changed. The fear was gone. A soothing tranquillity flowed from her brain, quieting his jumping nerves, slowing the pounding of his two hearts.

As Jommy slipped into the shelter made by a man and a woman walking past them, he had a glimpse of men bearing down on the tall figure of his mother, looking very ordinary and very human in her slacks and pink blouse, and with her hair caught up in a tightly knotted scarf. The men, dressed in civilian clothes, were crossing the street, their faces dark with an expression of an unpleasant duty that had to be done. The thought of that unpleasantness, the hatred that went with it, was a shadow in their minds that leaped out at Jommy. It puzzled him even in this moment when he was concentrating on escape. Why was it necessary that he should die? He and this wonderful, sensitive, intelligent mother of his! It was all terribly wrong.

A car, glittering like a long jewel in the sun, flashed up to the curb. A man's harsh voice called loudly after Jommy. "Stop! There's the kid. Don't let that kid get away! Stop that boy!"

People paused and stared. He felt the bewildering mildness of their thoughts. And then he had rounded the corner and was racing along Capital Avenue. A car was pulling away from the curb. His feet pattered with mad speed. His abnormally strong fingers caught at the rear bumper. He pulled himself aboard and hung on as the car swung into the maze of traffic and began to gather speed. From somewhere behind came the thought, "Good luck, Jommy."

For nine years she had schooled him for this moment, but something caught in his throat as he replied, "Good luck, Mother."

The car went too fast, the miles reeled off too swiftly. Too many people paused in the street and stared at the little boy clinging so precariously to the shining bumper. Jommy felt the intensity of their gazes, the thoughts that whipped into their minds and brought jerky, shrill shouts to their lips. Shouts to a driver who didn't hear.

Mists of thought followed him then, of people who ran into public booths and telephoned the police about a boy caught on a bumper. Jommy squirmed, and his eyes waited for a patrol car to swing in behind and flag the speeding auto to a halt. Alarmed, he concentrated his mind for the first time on the car's occupants.

Two brain vibrations poured out at him. As he caught those thoughts, Jommy shuddered, and half lowered himself toward the pavement, prepared to let go. He looked down, then dizzily pulled himself back into place. The pavement was a sickening blur, distorted by the car's speed.

Reluctantly, his mind fumbled into contact again with the brains of the men in the car. The thoughts of the driver were concentrated on his task of maneuvering the machine. The man thought once, flashingly, of a gun carried in a shoulder holster. His name was Sam Enders, and he was the chauffeur and bodyguard of the man beside him—John Petty, chief of the secret police of the all-powerful Kier Gray.

The police chief's identity penetrated through Jommy like an electric shock. The notorious slan hunter sat relaxed, indifferent to the speed of the car, his mind geared to a slow, meditative mood.

Extraordinary mind! Impossible to read anything in it but a blur of surface pulsations. It wasn't, Jommy thought, amazed, as if John Petty could be consciously guarding his thoughts. But there was a shield here as effective in hiding true thoughts as any slan's. Yet it was different. Overtones came through that told of a remorseless character, a highly trained and brilliant brain. Suddenly there was the tail end of a thought, brought to the surface by a flurry of passion that shattered the man's calm. "I've got to kill that slan girl, Kathleen Layton. That's the only way to undermine Kier Gray—"

Frantically, Jommy attempted to follow the thought, but it was gone into the shadows, out of reach. And yet he had the gist. A slan girl named Kathleen Layton was to be killed so that Kier Gray might be undermined.

"Boss," came Sam Enders's thought, "will you turn that switch? The red light that flashed on is the general alarm."

John Petty's mind remained indifferent. "Let them alarm," he snapped. "That stuff is for the sheep."

"Might as well see what it is," Sam Enders said.

The car slackened infinitesimally as he reached to the far end of the switchboard; and Jommy, who had worked his way precariously to one end of the bumper, waited desperately for a chance to leap clear. His eyes, peering ahead over the fender, saw only the long, bleak line of pavement, unrelieved by grass boulevards, hard and forbidding. To leap would be to smash himself against concrete. As he drew back hopelessly, a storm of Enders's thoughts came to him as Enders's brain received the message on the general alarm.

"—all cars on Capital Avenue and vicinity watch for a boy who is believed to be a slan named Jommy Cross, son of Patricia Cross. Mrs. Cross was killed ten minutes ago at the corner of Main and Capital. The boy leaped to the bumper of a car, which drove away rapidly, witnesses report."

"Listen to that, boss," Sam Enders said. "We're on Capital Avenue. We'd better stop and help in the search. There's ten thousand dollars' reward for slans."

Brakes screeched. The car decelerated with a speed that crushed Jommy hard against the rear end. He tore himself free of the intense pressure and, just before the car stopped, lowered himself to the pavement. His feet jerked him into a run. He darted past an old woman, who clutched at him, avarice in her mind. And then he was on a vacant lot, beyond which towered a long series of blackened brick and concrete buildings, the beginning of the wholesale and factory district.

A thought leaped after him from the car, viciously. "Enders, do you realize that we left Capital and Main ten minutes ago? That boy— There he is! Shoot him, you fool!"

The sense of the man Enders drawing his gun came so vividly to Jommy that he felt the rasp of metal on leather in his brain. Almost he saw the man take aim, so clear was the mental impression that bridged the hundred and fifty feet between them.

Jommy ducked sideways as the gun went off with a dull *plop*. He had the faintest awareness of a blow, and then he had scrambled up some steps into an open doorway, into a great, dark-lit warehouse. Dim thoughts reached out from behind him.

"Don't worry, boss, we'll wear that little shrimp out."

"You fool, no human being can tire a slan." He seemed to be barking orders then into a radio. "We've got to surround the district at Fifty-seventh Street. Concentrate every police car and get the soldiers out to—"

How blurred everything was becoming! Jommy stumbled through a dim world, conscious only that, in spite of his tireless muscles, a man could run at least twice as fast as his best speed would carry him. The vast warehouse was a dull light-world of looming box shapes, and floors that stretched into the remote semidarkness. Twice the tranquil thoughts of men moving boxes somewhere to his left impinged on his mind. But there was no awareness of his presence in their minds, no knowledge of the uproar outside. Far ahead, and to his right, he saw a bright opening, a door. He bore in that direction. He reached the door, amazed at his weariness. Something damp and sticky was clinging to his side, and his muscles felt stiff. His mind felt slow and unwieldy. He paused and peered out of the door.

He was staring into a street vastly different from Capital Avenue. It was a dingy street of cracked pavement, the opposite side lined with houses that had been built of plastic a hundred or more years before. Made of virtually unbreakable materials, their imperishable colors basically as fresh and bright as on the day of construction, they nevertheless showed the marks of time. Dust and soot had fastened leechlike upon the glistening stuff. Lawns were ill-tended, and piles of debris lay around.

The street was apparently deserted. A vague whisper of thought crept forth from the dingy buildings. He was too tired to make certain the thoughts came only from the buildings.

Jommy lowered himself over the edge of the warehouse platform and dropped to the hard concrete of the street below. Anguish engulfed his side, and his body had no yield in it, none of the normal spring that

would have made such a jump easy to take. The blow of striking the
walk was a jar that vibrated his bones.

The world was darker as he raced across the street. He shook his
head to clear his vision, but it was no use. He could only scamper on
with leaden feet between a gleaming but sooty two-story house and a
towering, streamlined, sea-blue apartment block. He didn't see the
woman on the veranda above him, or sense her, until she struck at him
with a mop. The mop missed because he caught its shadow just in time
to duck.

"Ten thousand dollars!" she screamed after him. "The radio said
ten thousand. And it's mine, do you hear? Don't nobody touch him.
He's mine. I saw him first."

He realized dimly that she was shouting at other women who were
pouring out of the tenement. Thank God, the men were away at work!

The horror of the rapacious minds snatched after him as he fled
with frightened strength along the narrow walk beside the apartment
building. He shrank from the hideous thoughts and flinched from the
most horrible sound in the world—the shrill voice clamor of people
desperately poor, swarming in their dozens after wealth beyond the
dreams of greed.

A fear came that he would be smashed by mops and hoes and
brooms and rakes, his head beaten, his bones crushed, flesh mashed.
Swaying, he rounded the rear corner of the tenement. The muttering
mob was still behind him. He felt their nervousness in the turgid
thoughts that streamed from them. They had heard stories about slans
that suddenly almost overshadowed the desire to possess ten thousand
dollars. But the mob presence gave courage to individuals. The mob
pressed on.

He emerged into a tiny backyard piled high with empty boxes on
one side. The pile reared above him, a dark mass, blurred even in the
dazzle of the sun. An idea flashed into his dulled mind, and in an instant he was climbing the piled boxes.

The pain of the effort was like teeth clamped into his side. He ran
precariously along over the boxes, and then half lowered himself, half
fell into a space between two old crates. The space opened all the way
to the ground. In the almost darkness his eyes made out a deeper darkness in the plastic wall of the tenement. He put out his hands and fumbled around the edges of a hole in the otherwise smooth wall.

In a moment he had squeezed through and was lying exhausted on
the damp earth inside. Pieces of rock pressed into his body, but for the
moment he was too weary to do anything but lie there, scarcely breathing, while the mob raged outside in frantic search.

The darkness was soothing, like his mother's thoughts just before she told him to leave her. Somebody climbed some stairs just above him, and that told him where he was—in a little space underneath back stairs. He wondered how the hard plastic had ever been shattered.

Lying there, cold with fear, he thought of his mother—dead now, the radio had said. Dead! She wouldn't have been afraid, of course. He knew only too well that she had longed for the day when she could join her dead husband in the peace of the grave. "But I've got to bring you up, Jommy. It would be so easy, so pleasant, to surrender life; but I've got to keep you alive until you're out of your childhood. Your father and I have spent what we had of life working on his great invention, and it will have been all for nothing if you are not here to carry on."

He pushed the thought from him, because his throat suddenly ached from thinking of it. His mind was not so blurred now. The brief rest must have helped him. But that made the rocks on which he lay more annoying, harder to bear. He tried to shift his body, but the space was too narrow.

Automatically, one hand fumbled down to them, and he made a discovery. They were shards of plastic, not rocks. Plastic that had fallen inward when the little section of the wall had been smashed and the hole through which he had crawled was made. It was odd to be thinking of that hole and to realize that somebody else—*somebody out there*—was thinking of the same hole. The shock of that blurred outside thought was like a flame that scorched through Jommy.

Appalled, he fought to isolate the thought and the mind that held it. But there were too many other minds all around, too much excitement. Soldiers and police swarmed in the alleyway, searching every house, every block, every building. Once, above that confusion of mind static, he caught the clear, cold thought of John Petty.

"You say he was last seen right here?"

"He turned the corner," a woman said, "and then he was gone!"

With shaking fingers Jommy began to pry the pieces of shard out of the damp ground. He forced his nerves to steadiness, and began with careful speed to fill the hole, using damp earth to cement the pieces of plastic. The job, he knew with sick certainty, would never stand close scrutiny.

And all the time he worked he felt the thought of that other person out there, a sly, knowing thought, hopelessly mingled with the wild current of thoughts that beat on his brain. Not once did that somebody else stop thinking about this very hole. Jommy couldn't tell whether it was a man or woman. But it was there, like an evil vibration from a warped brain.

The thought was still there, dim and menacing, as men pulled the boxes half to one side and peered down between them—and then, slowly, it retreated into distance as the shouts faded and the nightmare of thoughts receded farther afield. The hunters hunted elsewhere. For a long time Jommy could hear them, but finally life grew calmer, and he knew that night was falling.

Somehow the excitement of the day remained in the atmosphere. A whisper of thoughts crept out of the houses and from the tenement flats, people thinking, discussing what had happened.

At last he dared wait no longer. Somewhere out there was the mind that had *known* he was in the hole and had said nothing. It was an evil mind, which filled him with unholy premonition, and urgency to be away from this place. With fumbling yet swift fingers, he removed the plastic shards. Then, stiff from his long vigil, he squeezed cautiously outside. His side twinged from the movement, and a surge of weakness blurred his mind, but he dared not hold back. Slowly he pulled himself to the top of the boxes. His legs were lowering to the ground when he heard rapid footfalls—and the first sense of the person who had been waiting there struck into him.

A thin hand grabbed his ankle, and an old woman's voice said triumphantly, "That's right, come down to Granny. Granny'll take care of you, she will. Granny's smart. She knew all the time you could only have crept into that hole, and those fools never suspected. Oh, yes, Granny's smart. She went away, and then she came back and, because slans can read thoughts, she kept her mind very still, thinking only of cooking. And it fooled you, didn't it? She knew it would. Granny'll look after you. Granny hates the police, too."

With a gasp of dismay, Jommy recognized the mind of the rapacious old woman who had clutched at him as he ran from John Petty's car. That one fleeting glimpse had impressed the evil old one on his brain. And now, so much of horror breathed from her, so hideous were her intentions, that he gave a little squeal and kicked out at her.

The heavy stick in her free hand came down on his head even as he realized for the first time that she had such a weapon. The blow was mind-wrecking. His muscles jerked in spasmodic frenzy. His body slumped to the ground.

He felt his hands being tied, and then he was half lifted, half dragged for several feet. Finally he was hoisted onto a rickety old wagon, and covered with clothes that smelled of horse sweat, oil, and garbage cans.

The wagon moved over the rough pavement of the back alley, and above the rattling of the wheels Jommy caught the old woman's snarl.

"What a fool Granny would have been to let them catch you. Ten thousand reward— Bah! I'd never have gotten a cent. Granny knows the world. Once she was a famous actress, now she's a junk woman. They'd never give a hundred dollars, let alone a hundred hundred, to an old rag and bone picker. Bah on the whole lot! Granny'll show them what can be done with a young slan. Granny'll make a huge fortune from the little devil—"

TWO

There was that nasty little boy again.

Kathleen Layton stiffened defensively, then relaxed. There was no escape from him where she stood at the five-hundred-foot battlements of the palace. But it should be easy, after these long years as the only slan among so many hostile beings, to face anything, even Davy Dinsmore, age eleven.

She wouldn't turn. She wouldn't give him any intimation that she knew he was coming along the broad, glass-enclosed promenade. Rigidly, she held her mind away from his, maintaining the barest contact necessary to keep him from coming upon her by surprise. She must keep right on looking at the city, as if he weren't there.

The city sprawled in the near distance before her, a vast reach of houses and buildings, their countless colorations queerly shadowed now and subdued, seemingly dead in the gathering twilight. Beyond, the green plain looked dark, and the normally blue, gushing water of the river that wound out of the city seemed blacker, shiningless, in that almost sunless world. Even the mountains on the remote, dimming horizon had taken on a somber hue, a grim moodiness that matched the melancholy in her own soul.

"Ya-a-ah! You better take a good look. It's your last."

The discordant voice rasped on her nerves like so much senseless noise. For a moment, so strong was the suggestion of completely unintelligible sounds, the meaning of the words did not penetrate to her consciousness. And then, in spite of herself, she jerked around to face him.

"My last! What do you mean?"

Instantly, she regretted her action. Davy Dinsmore stood there less than half a dozen feet away. He had on long green silken trousers, and a yellow shirt open at the neck. His little boy's face with its "I'm-a-tough-guy" expression, and his lips twisted into a sneer, reminded her forcibly that even noticing him was a victory for him. And yet—what could have made him say a thing like that? It was hard to believe that he'd have thought of such words himself. The brief impulse to investigate further in his mind seized her. She shuddered, and decided against it. Entering that brain in its present state would sicken her outlook for a month.

It was a long time, months and months, since she had cut herself off from mental contact with the stream of human thoughts, human hopes, and human hates that made a hell of the palace atmosphere. Better to scorn the boy now, as she had in the past. She turned her back on him, and her slightest of slight connections with his brain brought her the overtones of the rage that surged through him at the action. And then there was his jangling voice again.

"Ya-a-ah, the last time! I said it, and I mean it. Tomorrow's your eleventh birthday, isn't it?"

Kathleen made no answer, pretending she hadn't heard. But a sense of disaster pierced her unconcern. There was too much gloating in his voice, too much certainty. Was it possible that dreadful things had been going on, dreadful plans made, during these months that she had kept her mind insulated from the thoughts of these people? Was it possible she had made a mistake in locking herself away in a world of her own? And now the real world had smashed through her protective armor?

Davy Dinsmore snapped, "Think you're smart, don't you? Well, you won't feel so smart when they're killing you tomorrow. Maybe you don't know it yet, but Mamma says the word is going around the palace now that when they first brought you here, Mr. Kier Gray had to promise the cabinet that he'd have you killed on your eleventh birthday. And don't think they won't do it, either. They killed a slan woman in the street the other day. That shows! What do you think of that, smarty?"

"You're—crazy!" The words were forced from her lips. She hardly realized she had uttered them, because they weren't what she thought. Somehow, she did not doubt that he spoke the truth. It fitted in with their mass hatred. It was so logical that she seemed, suddenly, always to have known it.

Oddly enough, it was the mention of his mother having told Davy that held Kathleen's mind. It took her memory back three years to a day when this boy had attacked her under the benevolent eyes of his mother, thinking to bully a small girl. What a surprise, what a screaming and kicking with fear there had been as she held him aloft, until his outraged parent had rushed forward, uttering threats of what she was going to do to "a dirty, sneaking little slan."

And then, suddenly, there had been Kier Gray, grim and tall and powerful, and Mrs. Dinsmore cringing before him.

"Madam, I wouldn't lay a hand on that child if I were you. Kathleen Layton is a property of the State, and in due course the State will dispose of her. As for your son, I happened to observe the entire proceedings. He got exactly what every bully deserves, and I hope he has learned his lesson."

How she had thrilled at his defense of her! And after that she had put Kier Gray in a different category in her mind from that occupied by other human beings, in spite of his ruthlessness, in spite of the terrible stories about him. But now she knew the truth, and that he had meant no more than he said. "The State will dispose of her."

With a start, she emerged from her bitter reverie and saw that in the city below a change had taken place. The whole great mass had donned its nighttime splendor with a billion lights twinkling in far-flung panorama. Wonder city now, it spread before her, a vast, sparkling jewel, an incredible fairyland of buildings that reared grandly toward the heavens and blazed a dream picture of refulgent magnificence. How she had always longed to go into that mysterious city and see for herself all the delights her imagination had built up. Now, of course, she would never see it. An entire world of glory would remain unseen, untasted, unenjoyed.

"Ya-a-ah!" came Davy's discordant voice again. "Take a good look. It's the last time."

Kathleen shivered. She couldn't stand the presence of this—this wretched boy another second. Without a word, she turned and went down into the palace, down to the loneliness of her bedroom.

Sleep would not come, and it was late. Kathleen knew it was late, because the clamor of outside thoughts had dimmed, and people were long gone to bed, except for the guards, the nervous, and party-goers.

Funny she couldn't sleep. Actually, she felt easier, now that she knew. The day-to-day life had been horrible, the hatred of the servants and most of the other human beings an almost unbearable strain. She must have dozed finally, for the harsh thought that came to her from outside did twisting things to the unreal dream she was having.

Kathleen stirred restlessly. The slan tendrils (thin strands like burnished gold glinting dully in the semilight against the dark hair that crowned her finely molded, childish face) lifted clear of her hair and waved gently, as if a soft breeze had caught them. Gently yet insistently.

Abruptly, the menacing thought those sensitive antennae drew out of the night-enveloped palace of Kier Gray penetrated. Kathleen awakened, quivering.

The thought lingered in her mind for an instant, distinct, cruel, cold-bloodedly murderous, shocking the sleep from her like a douche of ice water. And then it was gone, as completely as if it had never existed. There remained only a dim confusion of mind pictures that washed in a never ending stream from the countless rooms of the vast palace.

Kathleen lay very still, and from the depths of her own mind there came the realization of what this meant. Somebody was not waiting until tomorrow. Somebody doubted that her execution would take place. And he intended to present the council with an accomplished fact. There could be only one such person, powerful enough to face any consequences: John Petty, the head of the secret police, the fanatic antislan—John Petty, who hated her with a violence that, even in this den of antislans, was dismaying. The assassin must be one of his henchmen.

With an effort, she quieted her nerves and strained her mind out, out, to the limit of her powers. The seconds dragged, and still she lay there groping, searching for the brain whose thoughts had for a brief flash threatened her life. The whisper of outside thoughts became a roar that shook her brain. It was months since she had explored that world of uncontrolled minds. She had thought the memory of its horrors had not dimmed. Yet the reality was worse than the memory. Grimly, with an almost mature persistence, she held herself in that storm of mind vibration, fighting to isolate each individual pattern in turn. A sentence came.

"Oh, God, I hope they don't find out he's cheating. Today, on the vegetables!"

That would be the wife of the assistant chef, wretched God-fearing woman, who lived in mortal terror of the day when the petty thievery of her husband would be discovered.

Briefly, Kathleen felt sympathy for the tortured little woman lying awake beside her husband there in the darkness. But not too much sympathy, for that little woman had once, on sheer, vicious impulse, paused as Kathleen was passing her in a corridor and without preliminary mental warning slapped her hard in the face.

Kathleen's mind pressed on, driven now by a mounting sense of urgency. Other pictures flitted through her brain, a veritable kaleido-scope, brushed aside almost at the moment of entry as unwanted, un-related to the menace that had awakened her. There was the whole world of the palace with its intrigues, its countless personal tragedies, its hard ambitiousness. Dreams with psychological implications were there, from people who tossed in their sleep. And there were pictures of men who sat scheming far into the night.

Abruptly, then, it came, a wisp of crude purpose, the hard deter-mination to kill *her!* Instantly, it was gone again, like an elusive butter-fly, only not like that at all. The deadliness of it was like a spur that roweled her to desperation. For that second flash of menacing thought had been too powerful for it to be anything but near, terribly, danger-ously near.

Amazing how hard it was to find him again. Her brain ached, her body felt cold and hot by turns; and then a stray picture came for a third time—and she had him. And now she understood why his brain had evaded her so long. His thoughts were so carefully diffused, delib-erately flashing to a thousand different subjects, seeming simply over-tones to the confusion of mind noises all around.

He must have practiced it, but even so, he wasn't a John Petty or a Kier Gray, either of whom could hold rigidly to a line of reasoning without once slipping up. Her would-be assailant, in spite of all his cleverness, had given himself away. As soon as he entered the room she would—

The thought broke off. Her mind soared toward disintegration with the shock of the truth that showered in upon her. The man was inside her bedroom, and was at this very instant creeping on his knees toward her bed.

A sense of time suspension came to Kathleen as she lay there. It grew out of the darkness, and the way the blankets held her down, cov-ering even her arms. There was the knowledge that the slightest move would rustle the stiff sheets. He'd rush her then before she could move, pin her down under the blankets, and have her at his mercy.

She couldn't move. She couldn't see. She could only feel the gather-ing excitement that pulsed through the mind of the killer. His thoughts were quicker, and he had forgotten to diffuse them. The flame of his murderous purpose was a burning thing within him, so fierce and pow-erful that she had to turn part of her mind away, because it was sud-denly like a physical hurt.

And in that full revelation of this thought, Kathleen read the story of the attack. This man was the guard who had been posted outside her door. But it wasn't the usual guard. Odd she hadn't noticed the change.

They must have been switched while she slept. Or else she had been too upset by her own thoughts.

She caught his plan of action as he rose up on the carpeted floor and bent over the bed. For the first time her eyes caught the dim flash of the knife as his hand drew back for the plunge.

Only one thing to do. Only one thing she *could* do! With a swift, firm heave, she flung the blankets up over the head and shoulders of the startled man. Then she was sliding out of the bed—a shadow among the shadows of the room.

Behind her, the man uttered a faint cry as the blankets, flung by her small, extraordinarily strong arms, enveloped him. There was dismay in that low yell, and the first fear of what discovery would mean.

She caught his thoughts, heard his movements as he leaped the bed in a single jump and began flailing out with his arms, searching the dark reaches of the room. Queerly, then, it seemed to her that she shouldn't have left the bed. If death were to come tomorrow anyway, why delay it? But she knew the answer in the surging will to live that swept her; and in the thought, for the second time, that this midnight visitor was proof that someone who wanted her dead feared there would be no execution.

She drew a deep breath. Her own excitement was submerging in the first formulation of contempt for the clumsy efforts of the assassin. "You fool," she said, her child's voice hot with disdain, yet immensely unchildlike in its stinging logic, "do you actually believe that you can catch a slan in the darkness?"

It was pitiful the way the man leaped in the direction from which her words came and beat with his fists in every direction. Pitiful and horrible because his thoughts were ugly now with terror. There was something unclean in such fear that made Kathleen shiver where she stood in her bare feet at the opposite side of the room.

Once more she spoke in her high, childish voice. "You'd better leave before somebody hears you stumbling around. I won't report you to Mr. Gray if you leave right away."

The man didn't believe her, she saw. There was too much fear in him, too much suspicion and, suddenly, cunning! With a muttered curse he stopped searching for her, and flung himself recklessly toward the door, where the light switch was located. She felt him draw a gun as he groped for the switch. And realized that he preferred to take the chance of attempting to escape the guards who would come running at the sound of a gunshot, to meeting his superior with a confession of failure.

"You silly fool!" said Kathleen.

She knew what she must do, in spite of never having done it before. Soundlessly she slid along the wall, fingers searching. Then she had opened a paneled door, slipped through it, locked it behind her, and raced along a dimlit private corridor to a door at the end. It opened at her touch onto a large, luxuriously furnished office room.

In sudden fright at the boldness of her action, Kathleen stood in the doorway, staring at the powerful-looking man who sat at a desk writing by the light of a shaded desk lamp. Kier Gray did not look up immediately. She knew after a moment that he was aware of her presence and she took courage from his silence to observe him.

There was something magnificent about this ruler of men that held her admiration even now, when the fear of him lay like a weight inside her. The strong features of the man formed a noble countenance, now thoughtfully bent over the letter he was writing.

As he wrote, she was able to follow the surface of his thought, but nothing else. For Kier Gray, she had found out long ago, shared with that most hateful of men, John Petty, the ability to think in her presence without deviation, in a manner that made mind reading a practical impossibility. Only those surface thoughts were there, the words of the letter he was writing. And her excitement and impatience overrode any interest in his letter. She burst out, "There's a man in my room. He tried to kill me."

Kier Gray looked up. His face held a harder expression now that it was turned full upon her. The noble qualities of the profile were lost in the determination and power of that lean, strong jaw. Kier Gray, master of men, stared at her coldly. When he spoke, his mind moved with such precision, and voice and mind were so closely co-ordinated, that she wasn't sure whether or not he had actually uttered any words.

"An assassin, eh? Go on."

The story poured from Kathleen's lips in a trembling stream of words that covered everything that had happened from the time Davy Dinsmore had mocked at her on the battlements.

"So you think John Petty is behind it?" he asked.

"He's the only one who could have done it. The secret police control the men who guard me."

He nodded slowly, and she sensed the faintest tension in his mind. Yet his thoughts were deep and calm and slow. "So it's come," he said softly. "John Petty's bid for supreme power. I almost feel sorry for the man, he is so blind to his own shortcomings. No chief of secret police has ever held the confidence of a people. I am worshiped and feared; he is only feared. And he thinks that all-important."

Kier Gray's brown eyes looked gravely into Kathleen's. "He intended to kill you in advance of the date fixed by the council because I could do nothing about it once it was done. And my helplessness to act against him, he knew, would lower my prestige with the council." His voice was very low now, as if he had forgotten Kathleen's presence and was thinking out loud. "And he was right. The council would only be impatient if I tried to force an issue over the death of a slan. And yet, they would take no action as proof that I was afraid. Which would mean the beginning of the end. Disintegration, a splitting into groups growing gradually more hostile to each other as the so-called realists sized up the situation and picked the probable winner, or started that pleasant game known as playing both ends against the middle."

He was silent for a moment, then he continued. "As you can see, Kathleen, a very subtle and dangerous situation. For John Petty, in order to discredit me with the council, has been very assiduous in spreading the story that I meant to keep you alive. Accordingly, and this is the point that will interest you"—for the first time a smile broke over the bleak lines of Kier Gray's face—"accordingly, my prestige and position now depend upon my ability to keep you alive in spite of John Petty."

He smiled again. "Well, what do you think of our political situation?"

Kathleen's nostrils dilated with contempt. "He's a fool to go against you, that's what I think. And I'll help you all I can. I *can* help, with reading minds and things."

Kier Gray smiled a broad smile that lighted up his whole countenance and erased the harsh lines from his face. He said, "You know, Kathleen, we human beings must seem very queer at times to slans. For instance, the way we treat you. You know the reason for that, don't you?"

Kathleen shook her head. "No, Mr. Gray. I've read people's minds about it, and nobody seems to know why they hate us. There's something about a war between slans and human beings long ago, but there were wars before that, and the people didn't hate each other afterward. And then there are all those horrible stories too absurd to be anything but dreadful lies."

He said, "You've heard what slans do to human babies?"

"It's one of the silly lies," Kathleen said contemptuously. "They're all dreadful lies."

He chuckled. "I can see you have heard about it. And this may shock you. Such things do happen to babies. What do you know about the mental outlook of an adult slan, whose intelligence is two to three hundred percent higher than that of a normal human being? All you know is that you wouldn't do such things, but you're only a child. Anyway, never mind that now. You and I are in a fight for our lives. The assassin has probably escaped from your room by now, but you just have to look into his mind to identify him. We'll have our showdown now. I'll get Petty here, and the council. They won't like being awakened from their beauty sleep, but to hell with them! You stay here. I want you to read their minds and tell me afterward what they thought during the investigation."

He pressed a button on his desk and said curtly into a little boxlike instrument, "Tell the captain of my personal guard to come to my office."

THREE

It wasn't easy to sit under the dazzling lights that had been turned on. The men looked at her too often, their thoughts a mixture of impatience and mercilessness, and no pity for her anywhere. Their hatred weighed upon her spirit, and dimmed the life that throbbed along her nerves. They hated her. They wanted her dead. Appalled, Kathleen closed her eyes and turned her mind away, and tried to flatten herself back into her chair as if by sheer willpower she might make her body invisible.

But there was so much at stake, she dared not miss a single thought or picture. Her eyes and mind jerked open, and there it was again—the room, the men, the whole menacing situation.

John Petty stood up abruptly and said, "I object to the presence of this slan at this meeting on the grounds that her innocent, childlike appearance might influence some of us to be merciful."

Kathleen stared at him wonderingly. The chief of the secret police was a heavily built man of medium height, and his face, which was rather more corvine than aquiline, and the slightest degree too fleshy, showed not a trace of kindliness. Kathleen thought: Did he really believe *that*? Any one of these people merciful, for any reason!

She tried to read behind his words, but his mind was blurred deliberately, his dark, powerful face expressionless. She caught the faintest overtone of irony, and realized that John Petty understood the situation perfectly. This was his bid for power; and his whole body and brain were alert and deadly with the tremendousness of the knowledge.

Kier Gray laughed dryly, and suddenly Kathleen caught the glow of the man's magnetic personality. There was a tigerish quality about the leader, immensely fascinating, a flamelike aura that made him alive as was no one else in the room. He said, "I don't think we have to worry about—about our kindly impulses overpowering our common sense."

"Quite right!" said Mardue, minister of transport. "A judge has to sit in the presence of the accused." He stopped there, but his mind carried the sentence on. "Especially if the judge knows in advance that the judgment is death." He chuckled softly to himself, his eyes cold.

"Then I want her out," snarled John Petty, "because she's a slan, and, by heaven, I won't have a slan sitting in the same room with me!"

The answering surge of collective emotion to that popular appeal struck Kathleen like a physical blow. Voices rose up, raging.

"You're damned right!"

"Put her out!"

"Gray, you've got an almighty nerve waking us up in the middle of the night like this—"

"The council settled all this eleven years ago. I didn't even know about it until recently."

"The sentence was death, was it not?"

The hail of voices brought a grim smile to Petty's lips. He glanced at Kier Gray. The two men's eyes crossed like rapiers preliminary to a deadly thrust. It was easy for Kathleen to see that Petty was trying to confuse the issue. But if the leader felt himself losing, it was not visible in his impassive face; nor did a ripple of doubt flicker into his mind.

"Gentlemen, you are under a misapprehension. Kathleen Layton, the slan, is not on trial here. She is here to give evidence against John Petty, and I can well understand his desire to have her out of the room."

John Petty's amazement then was a little overdone, Kathleen analyzed. His mind remained too calm, too icily alert, as his voice took on a bull-like roar.

"Well, of all the damned nerve! You've awakened all of us out of our sleep to pull a two-o'clock-in-the-morning surprise trial on me—on the evidence of a slan! I say you've got an almighty nerve, Gray. And, once and for all, I think we should settle right now the juridical problem of whether a slan's word can be taken as evidence of any kind."

There it was again, the appeal to basic hatreds. Kathleen shivered before the waves of answering emotion that swept out from the other men. There was no chance for her here, no hope, nothing but certain death.

Kier Gray's voice was almost stolid as he said, "Petty, I think you should know that you're not talking now to a bunch of peasants whose minds have been roused by propaganda. Your listeners are realists, and, in spite of your obvious attempts to befuddle the issue, they realize that their own political and perhaps physical lives are at stake in this crisis which you, not I, have forced upon us."

His face hardened into a thin bleak line of tensed muscles. His voice took on a harsh rasp. "I hope that everyone present will wake up from whatever degree of sleep, emotionalism, or impatience controls him to realize this. John Petty is making this bid to depose me, and no matter who wins between us, some of you are going to be dead before morning."

They weren't looking at her now. In that suddenly still room, Kathleen had the sensation of being present but no longer visible. It was as if a weight had been removed from her mind, and she could see and feel and think for the first time with normal clarity.

The silence in that fine oak-paneled room was mental as well as sonal. For a moment the thoughts of the men were blurred, diminished in intensity. It was as if a barrier had been flung up between her mind and theirs, for their brains worked on deep, deep inside them, exploring, gauging chances, analyzing the situation, tensing against a suddenly realized, deadly danger.

Kathleen grew abruptly aware of a break in the blur of thoughts, a clear, sharp, mental command to her. "Go to the chair in the corner, where they can't see you without twisting their heads. Quick!"

Kathleen flung one glance at Kier Gray. She saw his eyes almost glaring at her, so fierce was the blaze in them. And then she slipped off her chair without a sound, obeying him.

The men didn't miss her, weren't even aware of her action. And Kathleen was conscious of a glow as she realized that Kier Gray, even in this moment of strain, was playing his cards without missing a trick. He spoke aloud.

"Of course, there is no absolute necessity for executions, provided John Petty once and for all gets out of his head this insane desire to replace me."

It was impossible now to read the thoughts of the men as they stared speculatively at Kier Gray. For the moment each man was intent; briefly, all their minds were as controlled as were John Petty's and Kier Gray's, their whole consciousness concentrated on what they *should* say and *should* do.

Kier Gray went on, the faintest tinge of passion in his voice. "I say insane because, though it may seem that this is simply a squabble for power between two men, it is more than that. The man who has supreme power represents stability and order. The man who wants it must, the moment he attains power, secure himself in his position. This means executions, exiles, confiscations, imprisonment, torture—all, of course, applied against those who have opposed him or whom he distrusts.

"The former leader cannot simply step down into a subordinate role. His prestige never actually vanishes—as witness Napoleon and Stalin—therefore he remains a permanent danger. But a would-be leader can simply be disciplined and put back on his job. And that is my plan for John Petty."

He was, Kathleen saw, appealing to their cautious instincts, their fear of what change would involve. Her thoughts broke off as John Petty sprang to his feet. For a moment he was off guard, but so great was his rage that it was as impossible to read his thoughts as if he were in full control of his mind.

"I think," he burst out, "I have never heard such an extraordinary statement from a presumably sane man. He has accused me of befuddling the issue. Gentlemen, have you realized that he has as yet produced no issue, no evidence? All we have are his statements, and the dramatic trial which he has sprung on us in the middle of the night, when he knew that most of us would be drugged with sleep. I must confess that I'm not fully awake, but I am, I think, awake enough to realize that Kier Gray has succumbed to that gnawing disease of dictators of all ages, the persecution complex. I have no doubt that for some time past he has read into our every word and action some threat against his position.

"I can hardly find words to express my dismay at the thought of what this means. With the slan situation so desperate, how could he even suggest that one of us would precipitate disunion? I tell you, sirs, we cannot afford even the hint of a split at the present time. The public is on edge over the monstrous worldwide activity of the slans against human babies. Their attempt to slanize the human race, with its resultant horrible failures, is the greatest problem that has ever confronted a government."

He turned to Kier Gray, and Kathleen felt a chill at the perfection of his acting, his apparent sincerity. "Kier, I wish that I could forget what you have done. First, this trial, then the threat that some of us will be dead before morning. Under the circumstances, I can only suggest that you resign. You no longer have my confidence, at least."

Kier Gray said with a thin smile, "You see, gentlemen, we now come to the core of the problem. He wants my resignation."

A tall, thin, youngish man with a hawklike face spoke up harshly. "I agree with Petty. Your actions, Gray, have shown that you are no longer a responsible person. Resign!"

"Resign!" cried another voice, and suddenly it sounded like a bedlam chorus. "Resign! Resign! Resign!"

To Kathleen, who had been following John Petty's words with concentrated attention, the words and the harsh accompanying thoughts sounded like the end. A long moment passed before she realized that four of the seated ten had done all the shouting.

Her mind straightened painfully. So that was it. By crying "Resign!" over and over, they had hoped to stampede the doubtful and the fearful and, for the time being, had failed. Her mind and her eyes flashed toward Kier Gray, whose very presence had kept the others from yielding to panic. Just looking at him brought a return of courage. For there he sat, a little straighter in his chair now, looking taller, bigger, stronger; and on his face was an ironical, confident smile.

"Isn't it odd," he asked quietly, "how the four younger men rally to the support of young Mr. Petty? I hope that it is obvious to the older gentlemen present that here is advance organization, and also that there will be firing squads before morning because these young firebrands are transparently impatient of us old fogies—for, in spite of my being in their age level, they do regard me as an old fogy. They're wild to throw off the restraint we have exercised, and are, of course, convinced that by shooting the oldsters they will only hasten by a few years what nature would, in any event, manage to do in the course of time."

"Shoot 'em!" snarled Mardue, the oldest man present.

"The damned young upstarts!" snapped Harlihan, airways minister.

There was a muttering among the older men that would have been good to hear if Kathleen hadn't been so acutely aware of the impulses behind the words. Hatred was there, and fear, and doubt and arrogance, frustration and determination—all were there, a tangle of mental squalor.

The faintest bit pale, John Petty faced that muttering. But Kier Gray leaped to his feet, eyes blazing, fists clenched. "Sit down, you unutterable fool! How dare you precipitate this crisis now, when we may have to change our entire slan policy? We're losing, do you hear? We haven't got a scientist to match the superscientists of the slans. What wouldn't I give to have one of them on our side! To have, say, a slan like Peter Cross, who was stupidly murdered three years ago because the police who caught him were tainted by the mentality of the mob.

"Yes, I said 'mob.' That's all people are these days. A mob, a beast we've helped build up with our propaganda. They're afraid, mortally afraid for their babies, and we haven't got a scientist who can think objectively on the matter. In fact, we haven't got a scientist worthy of the name. What incentive is there for a human being to spend a lifetime in research when in his mind is the deadening knowledge that all the discoveries he can hope to make have long since been perfected by the slans? That they're waiting out there somewhere in secret caves, or written out on paper, ready for the day when the slans make their next attempt to take over the world?

"Our science is a joke, our education a mass of lies. And every year the wreck of human aspirations and human hopes piles higher around us. Every year there's greater dislocation, more poverty, more misery. Nothing is left to us but hatred, and hatred isn't enough. We've either got to terminate the slans or make terms with them and end this madness."

Kier Gray's face was dark with the passion he had put into his words. And all the time, Kathleen saw, his mind was calm, watchful, cautious. Master of demagoguery, ruler of men, when he spoke again his voice seemed flat in comparison, his magnificent baritone clear and soft.

"John Petty has accused me of wanting to keep this child alive. I want you all to think back over the past few months. Has Petty at any time ever remarked to you, laughingly perhaps, that I intended to keep her alive? I know that he has, because it came to my ears. But you see what he's been doing, subtly spreading the poison. Your political minds will tell you that he has forced me into this position. By killing her, I will seem to have yielded, and thereby will lose prestige.

"Therefore I intend to issue a statement saying that Kathleen Layton will not be executed. In view of our lack of knowledge of slans, she will be kept alive as a study subject. I, personally, am determined to make the best of her continued presence by observing the development of a slan to maturity. I have already made a tremendous body of notes on the subject."

John Petty was still on his feet. "Don't try to shout me down!" he snarled. "You've gone too far. Next thing you'll be handing over a continent to the slans on which they can develop these so-called superinventions of which we have heard so much but never seen. As for Kathleen Layton, by heaven, you will keep her alive over my dead body. The slan women are the most dangerous of all. They're the breeders, and they know their job, damn them!"

The words blurred for Kathleen. Into her mind, for the second time, had come an insistent question from Kier Gray. "How many present are for me unconditionally? Use your fingers to indicate."

One startled look she sent him, and then her mind skewered into the welter of emotions and thoughts that flooded from the men. It was hard, for there were many thoughts, there was much interference. And besides, her brain began to weaken as she saw the truth. Somehow, she had believed the older men were all for the leader. And they weren't. In their minds was fear, a growing conviction that Kier Gray's days were numbered, and they had better play along with the young, strong group.

At last, dismayed, she held three fingers up. Three out of ten in favor, four definitely against him and with Petty, three wavering.

She couldn't give him those last two figures because his mind didn't ask for anything more. His attention was concentrated on her three fingers, his eyes the faintest bit wide and alarmed. For the barest moment it seemed to her that anxiety flickered through his thoughts. And then the impassivity closed over his mind and countenance. He sat in his chair, like a figure of stone, cold and grim and deadly.

She couldn't take her eyes off the leader.

The conviction came that here was a cornered man, racking his brain, searching back into his experience for a technique to turn the imminent defeat into victory. She struggled to penetrate that brain, but his iron grip on his thoughts, the very lucid, straightforward motion of his mind, remained an unshakable barrier between them.

But in those surface thoughts she read his doubts, a queer uncertainty that yet held within it no fear, simply hesitation as to what he should do, *could* do, next. That seemed to mean that he had not really foreseen a crisis of such proportions, an organized opposition, a smoldering hatred of himself awaiting only the opportunity to overthrow and destroy him.

Her thought ended as John Petty said, "I think we ought to take a vote on this matter now."

Kier Gray began to laugh, a long, deep, cynical laugh that ended on a note of surprisingly good humor. "So you'd like to vote on an issue that a moment ago you said I hadn't even proved to be existent! Naturally I refuse to appeal to the reason of those present any longer. The time for reason has passed when deaf ears are turned, but just for the sake of the record, a demand for a vote at this time is an implicit admission of guilt become openly arrogant, the result, no doubt, of the security engendered by the support of at least five, possibly more, of the council. Let me put one more of my cards on the table. I have known of this rebellion for some time and have prepared for it."

"Bah!" said Petty. "You're bluffing. I've watched your every move. When we first organized this council we feared eventualities such as one man dispensing with the votes of the others, and the safeguards then set up are still in force. Each of us has a private army. My own guards are out there, patrolling the corridor, and so are the guards of every member of the council, ready to rush at each other's throats when the word is given. We are quite prepared to give it and take our chance of being killed in the battle that results."

"Ah," said Kier Gray softly, "now we're out in the open."

There was a shuffling of feet among the men, a chilling spray of thoughts; and then, to Kathleen's dismay, Mardue, one of the three she had thought in unconditional support of Kier Gray, cleared his throat. She caught the thought of his weakening resolve just before he spoke.

"Really, Kier, you're making a mistake in regarding yourself as dictator. You're only elected by the council, and we have a perfect right to elect someone in your place. Someone, perhaps, who will be more successful in organizing the extermination of the slans."

It was turncoating with a vengeance. The rats were deserting the sinking ship and trying desperately now, Kathleen saw, to convince the new powers that their support was valuable.

In Harlihan's brain, too, the wind of thought was blowing in a new direction. "Yes, yes. Your talk about making a deal with the slans is treason—pure treason. That's the one untouchable subject so far as the mo—the people are concerned. We must do something to exterminate the slans, and perhaps a more aggressive policy on the part of a more aggressive man—"

Kier Gray smiled wryly; and still that uncertainty was in his brain—what to do, what to do? There was a vague suggestion of something else, a tensing to the situation, a darkening resolution to take a chance. But nothing tangible, nothing clear, came to Kathleen.

"So," Kier Gray said, still in his soft voice, "you would turn the chairmanship of this council over to a man who, only a few days ago, allowed Jommy Cross, nine years old, probably the most dangerous slan alive today, to escape in his own car."

"At least," said John Petty, "there's one slan who won't escape." He stared malevolently at Kathleen, then turned triumphantly toward the others. "Here's what we can do—execute her tomorrow; in fact, right now, and issue a statement that Kier Gray was removed from office because he had come to a secret agreement with the slans, and his refusal to kill Kathleen Layton was proof of it."

It was the strangest thing in the world to be sitting there, listening to that death sentence and feeling no emotion, as if it weren't herself they were talking about. Her mind seemed far away, detached, and the murmur of agreement that rose up from the men also had that odd distortion of distance.

The smile faded from Kier Gray's face. "Kathleen," he said aloud sharply, "we might as well stop playing. How many are against me?"

She stared at him blurrily and heard herself replying tearfully, "They're all against you. They've always hated you because you're so much smarter than they are, and because they think you've kept them down and overshadowed them, and made it seem as if they're not important."

"So he uses her to spy on us," John Petty snarled, but there was triumph in his rage. "Well, at least it's pleasant to know that we're all agreed on one thing—that Kier Gray is through."

"Not at all," said Kier Gray mildly. "I disagree so violently that all eleven of you will face firing squads within ten minutes. I was undecided about taking such drastic action, but now there is no alternative and no going back because I have just taken an irrevocable action. I have pressed a button advising the eleven officers in command of your guard, your most trusted advisers, *and your heirs,* that the hour has come."

They stared at him stupidly as he went on.

"You see, gentlemen, you failed to allow for a fateful flaw in human nature. The desire of underlings for power is as great as your own. The solution to such a situation as came up today was suggested to me some time ago when Mr. Petty's chief aide approached me with the offer that he would always be willing to replace Mr. Petty. I made it a policy then to explore the matter further, with very satisfying results, and saw to it that the men were on the scene for Kathleen's eleventh birthday—Ah, here are the new councilors!"

The door burst open and eleven grim young men with drawn revolvers came in. There was a great shout from John Petty. "Your guns!" And a wailing cry from one man. "I didn't bring one!" And then the crash of revolver shots filled the room with an echoing, re-echoing roar.

Men writhed on the floor, choking in their own blood. Through a blur, Kathleen saw one of the eleven still standing, smoking gun in hand. She recognized John Petty. He had fired first. The man who had thought to replace him was dead, a motionless figure on the floor. The chief of the secret police held his gun steady, pointed at Kier Gray, as he said, "I'll kill you before they can get me unless you make a deal. I'll co-operate, naturally, now that you've turned the tables so neatly."

The leader of the officers glanced inquiringly at Kier Gray. "Shall we let him have it, sir?" he asked. He was a lean, dark man with an aquiline face and a sharp baritone voice. Kathleen had seen him around the palace occasionally. His name was Jem Lorry. She had never tried to read his mind before, but now she realized that he also had a power of control over his thoughts that defied penetration. However, there was enough of his character on the surface of his mind to show him for what he was, a tough, calculating, and ambitious man.

"No," Kier Gray replied thoughtfully. "John Petty will be useful. He'll have to agree that the other men were executed as a result of the investigations of his police disclosing secret arrangements with the slans.

"That will be the explanation—it always works on the poor, bewildered mass of fools outside. We owe the idea to Mr. Petty himself, but I think we were capable of thinking of it ourselves. However, his influence will be valuable in putting it over. In fact," he said cynically, "I believe the best method is to give Petty credit for the executions. That is, he was so horrified at his discovery of their perfidy, he acted on his own initiative, and then threw himself on my mercy, which, in view of the serious evidence he produced, I naturally granted at once. How's that?"

Jem Lorry came forward. "Good stuff, sir. And now there's one thing I'd like to make clear, and I speak for all of the new councilors. We need you, your terrific reputation, your brains, and we're willing to help make you a god to the people—in other words, to help consolidate your position and make it unassailable—but don't think you can make arrangements with our chief officers to kill *us*. *That* won't work again."

Kier Gray said coldly, "It's hardly necessary to tell me anything so obvious. Clear this carrion out, and then—we've got some planning to do. As for you, Kathleen, go to bed. You're in the way now."

As she hurried off, shaking now from reaction, Kathleen wondered. In the way? Did he just mean— Or did he mean— After the murders she had witnessed, she couldn't be sure of him, of anything. It was a long, long time before sleep came.

FOUR

For Jommy Cross there were long spells of darkness and mental blankness that merged finally into a steely gray light through which vague thoughts at last wove a web of reality. He opened his eyes, conscious of great weakness.

He was lying in a little room, staring up at a smeared, dirty ceiling, from which some of the plaster had fallen. The walls were an uneven gray, splotched with age. The pane of the single window was cracked and discolored; the light that forced its way through fell across the end of the iron bedstead in a little pool and lay there as if exhausted from the effort.

Its wan brightness revealed bedclothes that were remnants of what had once been gray blankets. At one edge, straw stuck out from the old mattress, and the whole thing stank with a stale, unaired odor. Sick though he still was, Jommy flung the foul coverings from him and started to slip out of bed. A chain rattled menacingly, and there was sudden pain in his right ankle. He lay back, panting from the exertion, and stunned. He was chained to this loathsome bed!

Heavy footsteps aroused him from the stupor into which he had fallen. He opened his eyes to see a tall, gaunt woman in a formless gray dress standing at the door, her black eyes gleaming down at him like bright beads.

"Ah," she said. "Granny's new boarder has come out of his fever, and now we can get acquainted. That's good! That's good!"

She rubbed her dry hands together raspingly. "We're going to get along beautifully, aren't we? But you've got to earn your keep. No slackers can leech off Granny. No, sir. We'll have to have a heart-to-heart talk about that. Yes, yes," she leered at him over clasped hands, "a heart-to-heart talk."

Jommy stared up at the old woman in repelled fascination. As the thin, slightly stooped creature sank with a grunt onto the foot of the bed, he drew his legs up against his body, withdrawing as far from her as the chain would allow. It struck him that he had never seen a face that more nearly expressed the malignant character that lay behind the mask of old flesh. With rising disgust, he compared her thin, lined, egg-shaped head with the mind inside; and it was all there. Every twisted line in that wrecked face had its counterpart in the twisted brain. A whole world of lechery dwelt within the confines of that shrewd mind.

His thought must have shown in his face, for she said with sudden savagery, "Yes, yes, to look at Granny you'd never think she was once a famous beauty. You'd never suspect that men once worshiped the white loveliness of her. But don't forget that this old hag saved your life. Never forget that, or Granny may turn your ungrateful hide over to the police. And how they'd love to have you. How they would love it! But Granny's kind to them that's kind to her and does as she wants."

Granny! Was there ever a term of affection more prostituted than by this old woman calling herself Granny?

He searched her mind, trying to find in its depths her real name. But there was only a blur of pictures of a silly, stage-struck girl, profligate of her charms, ruined, degraded to the level of the street, hardened and destroyed by adversity. Her identity was buried in a cesspool of the evil she had done and thought. There was an endless story of thieving. There was the dark kaleidoscope of more loathsome crimes. There was murder committed—

Shuddering, immeasurably weary now that the first stimulus of her presence was fading, Jommy withdrew from the abomination that was Granny's mind. The old wretch leaned toward him, her eyes like gimlets drilling into his.

"It's true," she asked, "that slans can read minds?"

"Yes," Jommy admitted, "and I can see what you're thinking, but it's no use."

She chuckled grimly. "Then you don't read all that's in Granny's mind. Granny's no fool. Granny's smart; and she knows better than to think she can force a slan to stay and work for her. He has to be free for what she wants him to do. He's got to see that, being a slan, this will be the safest place for him until he grows up. Now, isn't Granny clever?"

Jommy sighed sleepily. "I can see what's in your mind, but I can't talk to you now. When we slans are sick—and that's not often—we just sleep and sleep. My waking up the way I did means that my sub-conscious was worried and forced me awake because it thought I was in danger. We slans have a lot of protections like that. But now I've got to go back to sleep and get well."

The coal-black eyes grew wide. The lustful mind recoiled, briefly accepting defeat in its main purpose of making immediate wealth from its prey. Greed yielded momentarily to violent curiosity, but there was no intention of letting him sleep.

"Is it true that slans make monsters out of human beings?"

Fury burned through Jommy's brain. Weariness fell away from him. He sat up, in rage.

"That's a lie! It's one of those horrible lies that human beings tell about us to make us seem inhuman, to make everybody hate us, kill us. It—"

He sank back, exhausted, rage evaporating. "My mother and father were the finest people alive," he said softly, "and they were terribly un-happy. They met on the street one day, and saw in each other's minds that they were slans. Until then they'd lived the loneliest of lives, they'd never harmed anyone. It's the human beings who are the criminals. Dad didn't fight as hard as he could have when they cornered him and shot him in the back. He could have fought. He should have! Because he had the most terrible weapon the world has ever seen—so terrible he wouldn't even carry it with him for fear he might use it. When I'm fif-teen I'm supposed to—"

He stopped, appalled at his indiscretion. For an instant he felt so sick, so weary, that his mind refused to hold the burden of his thought. He knew only that he had given away the greatest secret in slan history, and if this grasping old wretch turned him over to the police in his present weakened condition, all was lost.

Slowly, he breathed easier. He saw that her mind hadn't really caught the enormous implication in his revelation. She hadn't really heard him at the moment when he mentioned the weapon—for that rapacious brain had already been too long away from its main purpose. And now, like a vulture, it swooped down on prey it knew to be exhausted.

"Granny's glad to know that Jommy's such a nice boy. Poor, starv-ing old Granny needs a young slan to make money for her and him. You won't mind working for tired old Granny, will you?" Her voice hardened. "Beggars can't be choosers, you know."

The knowledge that his secret was safe acted like a drug. His eye-lids drooped. He said, "Really, I can't talk to you now; I've got to sleep."

He saw that she wasn't going to let him go. Her mind had already realized what could agitate him. She spoke sharply, not because she was interested, but to keep him awake.

"What is a slan? What makes you different? Where did slans come from in the first place? They were made, weren't they—like machines?"

Funny how that could bring a surge of responsive anger when his mind saw that that was her purpose. Dimly he realized that bodily weakness had taken normal restraints from his mind. He said in a dull rage, "That's another one of the lies. I was born just like anybody else. So were my parents. Beyond that, I don't know."

"Your parents must have known!" the old woman prodded him.

Jommy shook his head. His eyes closed. "No, Mother said Dad was always too busy to investigate the mystery of the slans. But now, leave me alone. I know what you're trying to do and I know what you want, but it's dishonest and I won't do it."

"That's stupid," the old woman snapped angrily, on her subject at last. "Is it dishonest to rob people who live by robbery and cheating? Shall you and Granny eat crusts of bread when the world is so rich that every treasury bulges with gold, every granary bulges with wheat, and honey flows in the streets? Bah for your honesty! That's what Granny says. How can a slan, hunted like a rat, talk of being honest?"

Jommy was silent and not only because of his need for sleep. He had had thoughts like that himself. The old woman pounded on.

"Where will you go? What will you do? Will you live in the streets? What about winter? Where in all this world can a little slan boy go?"

Her voice sank, in an attempt at sympathy. "Your poor, dear mother would have wanted you to do what I'm asking. She had no love for human beings. I've saved the paper to show you how they shot her down like a dog when she tried to escape. Would you like to see it?"

"No!" said Jommy, but his mind whirled.

The harsh voice pressed on. "Don't you want to do everything you can against a world that's so cruel? Make them pay? Make them regret what they've done? You're not afraid?"

He was silent. The old woman's voice took on a whine. "Life's too hard for old Granny—too hard. If you won't help Granny, she'll have to go on doing other things. You saw in her mind about them. But she promises not to do that anymore if you'll help her. Think of that. She'll stop all the wicked things she's had to do for a living in this cold, cruel world."

Jommy felt beaten. He said slowly, "You're a rotten, miserable old scoundrel, and some day I'll kill you!"

"Then you'll stay until that 'some day,' " Granny said triumphantly. Her wrinkled fingers rubbed together like dry scaled snakes crawling over each other. "And you'll do as Granny says, too, or she'll turn you over to the police so fast— Welcome to our little home, Jommy. Welcome. You'll be better the next time you waken, Granny hopes."

"Yes," Jommy said weakly. "I'll be better."

He slept.

Three days later, Jommy followed the old woman through the kitchen toward the back door. The kitchen was a bare little room, and Jommy closed his mind against the dirt and untidiness. He thought: The old woman was right. Horrible as the life promised to be, this shack, sunk here in the oblivion of poverty, would make an ideal retreat for a slan boy who had to wait at least six years before he could visit the hiding-place of his father's secrets; who had to grow up before he could hope to carry out the great things that had to be done.

The thought flew as the door opened and he saw what lay beyond. He stopped short, stunned by the vista that opened up before him. Never in all the world had he expected to see anything like *this*.

First was the yard, piled with old metal and junk of every description. A yard barren of grass or trees, without beauty; a discordant, jangling stretch of sterility enclosed by a rusting, twisted fence of rotten wood and wire. A small ramshackle barn tottered precariously at the farthest end of the yard. The blurred mind pictures of a horse came from inside. The horse itself was vaguely visible through the open door.

But Jommy's eyes flashed past the yard. His passing glance picked up the unpleasant details; that was all. His mind, his vision, reached beyond the fence, beyond that rickety barn. Beyond, there were trees, little groups of them; and grass—a green, pleasant meadow that sloped toward a broad river, gleaming dully now that the rays of the sun no longer touched it with their shining fire.

But even the meadow (part of a golf course, he noted absently) held his gaze for an instant only. A land of dream began on the opposite shore of the river, a veritable fairyland of growth, a gardener's paradise. Because of some trees that blocked his vision, he could see only a narrow stretch of that Eden, with its sparkling fountains and its square mile on square mile of flowers and terraces and beauty. But that narrow, visible area contained a white pathway.

A pathway! Jommy's mind soared. Unutterable emotion choked his throat. The path was visible, running in a geometrically straight line away from his gaze. It ran into the dim distance, a gleaming ribbon that faded into the mist of miles. And it was there, at the ultimate limit of his vision, far beyond the normal horizon, that he saw the palace.

Only part of the base of that tremendous, that incredible structure reached up from the other side of the skyline. A thousand feet it reared and then it merged into a tower that soared another five hundred feet into the heavens. Stupendous tower! Half a thousand feet of jewel-like lacework that seemed almost fragile, sparkling there with all the colors of the rainbow, a translucent, shining, fantastic thing, built in the noble style of the old days; not merely ornamental—in its very design, its fine-wrought magnificence, it was ornament in itself.

Here in this glory of architectural triumph the slans had created their masterpiece, only to have it fall to the victors after the war of disaster.

It was too beautiful. It hurt his eyes, hurt his mind with the thoughts that it brought. To think that he had lived so close to this city for nine years and had never before seen this glorious achievement of his race! His mother's reason for not showing it to him seemed mistaken, now that he had the reality before him. "It'll make you bitter, Jommy, to realize that the palace of the slans now belongs to Kier Gray and his ghoulish crew. Besides, there are special precautions against us at that end of the city. You'll see it soon enough."

But it wasn't soon enough. The sense of something missed burned bright and painful. It would have given him courage in his blacker moments to know of this noble monument to his people.

His mother had said, "Human beings will never know all the secrets of that building. There are mysteries there, forgotten rooms and passages, hidden wonders that even the slans no longer know about, except in a vague way. Kier Gray doesn't realize it, but all the weapons and machines the human beings have searched for so desperately are buried right in that building."

A harsh voice jarred his ears. Jommy tore his gaze reluctantly from the grandeur across the river and became aware of Granny. He saw she had hitched the old horse to her junk wagon.

"Quit your daydreaming," she commanded. "And don't get any funny ideas into your head. The palace and palace grounds are not for slans. And now, get in under these blankets, and keep your mind still. There's a busybody policeman up the street who'd better not find out about you yet. We've got to hurry."

Jommy's eyes turned to the palace for one last, lingering look. So that palace wasn't for slans! He felt a queer thrill. Someday he'd go over there to look for Kier Gray. And when that day came— The thought stopped; he was trembling with rage and hatred against the men who had murdered his father and his mother.

FIVE

The rickety old cart was downtown now. It rattled and shook over the uneven pavement of the back alleys until Jommy, half lying, half crouching in the back, felt as if he would be shaken out of his clothes. Twice he attempted to stand up, but each time the old woman poked at him with her stick.

"You stay down! Granny doesn't want anyone to see those fine clothes of yours. You just keep covered up with that robe."

The tattered old robe stank of Bill, the horse. The stench brought Jommy moments of nausea. At long last the junk wagon stopped.

"Get out," snapped Granny, "and go into that department store. You'll find big pockets I've sewn inside your coat. Just fill them with stuff so they won't bulge."

Dizzily, Jommy climbed down to the concrete. He stood there swaying, waiting for the swift flame of his strength to drive away that abnormal weakness. He said then, "I'll be back in about half an hour."

Her rapacious face bent toward him. Her black eyes glittered. "And don't get caught, and use your common sense in what you take."

"You needn't worry," Jommy replied confidently. "Before I take anything, I'll throw my mind around to see if anyone is looking. It's as simple as that."

"Good!" The thin face broke into a grin. "And don't worry if Granny isn't here when you come back. She's going over to the liquor store for some medicine. She can afford medicine now that she's got a young slan; and she does need it—oh, so much—to warm her cold old bones. Yes, Granny must lay in a supply of medicine."

Outside fear came rushing in to him as he breasted the throngs that washed in and out of the skyscraper department store; abnormal, exaggerated fear. He opened his mind wide, and for one long moment kept it that way. Excitement, tenseness, dismay, and uncertainty—an enormous, dark spray of fear caught at him and twisted his mind along into the swirling stream of it. Shuddering, he pulled himself clear.

But during that plunge he had caught the basis of that mass fear. Executions at the palace! John Petty, the head of the secret police, had caught ten councilors making a deal with the slans, and killed them. The crowd didn't quite believe. They were afraid of John Petty. They distrusted him. Thank heaven Kier Gray was there, solid as a rock to protect the world from the slans—and from the sinister John Petty.

It was worse inside the store. There were more people. Their thoughts pounded at his brain as he threaded his way along the aisles of shining floor displays, under the gleam of the ceiling lights. A gorgeous world of goods swelled all around him, and taking what he wanted proved easier than he had expected.

He passed the end of the long, glittering jewelry department and helped himself to a pendant marked fifty-five dollars. His impulse was to enter the department, but he caught the thought of the salesgirl. Annoyance was in her mind, hostility at the idea of a small boy entering the jewelry section. Children were not welcome in that world of magnificent gems and fine metals.

Jommy turned away, brushing past a tall, good-looking man who whisked by without so much as a glance at him. Jommy walked on for a few paces, and stopped. A shock such as he had never known before stabbed through him. It was like a knife cutting into his brain, it was so sharp. And yet it was not unpleasant. Astonishment, joy, amazement flashed through him as he turned and stared eagerly after the retreating man.

The handsome, powerfully built stranger was a slan, a full-grown slan! The discovery was so important that, after the first realization sank in, his brain reeled. The basic calm of his slan-steady mind was not shattered, nor was there the sinking into emotionalism that he had noticed when he was sick. But his mind soared with a sheer, wild eagerness unequaled in his past experience.

He began to walk rapidly after the man. His thought reached out, seeking contact with the other's brain—recoiled! Jommy frowned. He could still see that the being was a slan, but he could not penetrate beyond the surface of the stranger's mind. And that surface reflected no awareness of Jommy, not the faintest suggestion that he was conscious of any outside thoughts at all.

There was mystery here. It had been impossible a few days before to read beyond the surface of John Petty's mind. Yet there had never been any question of Petty being anything but a human being. It was impossible to explain the difference to himself. Except that when his mother guarded her thoughts from intrusion, he had always been able to make her aware with a directed vibration.

The conclusion was staggering. It meant that here was a slan who couldn't read minds, yet guarded his own brain from being read. Guarded it from whom? From other slans? And what manner of slan was it that couldn't read minds? They were out in the street now; and it would have been easy, there under the brilliant lights that blazed from the street lamps, to break into a run that would have brought him up to the slan in a few moments. In all those rushing, selfish crowds, who would notice a little boy running?

But instead of narrowing the gap that separated him from the slan, he allowed it to widen. The entire logical roots of his existence were threatened by the situation presented by this slan; and the whole hypnotic education that his father had imprinted upon his mind rose up and prevented precipitant action.

Two blocks from the store, the slan turned up a wide, side street; puzzled, Jommy followed him at a safe distance—puzzled because he knew this was something of a dead-end street, not a residential section. One, two, three blocks they went. And then he was certain.

The slan was heading for the Air Center that, with all its buildings and factories and landing-field, sprawled for a square mile at this part of the city. The thing was impossible. Why, people couldn't even get near an airplane without having to remove their hats to prove that they were minus slan tendrils.

The slan headed straight toward a big, blazing sign: *Air Center*—vanished without hesitation into the revolving door under the sign.

Jommy paused at the door. *The Air Center, which dominated the entire aircraft industry on the face of the globe!* Was it possible that slans worked here? That in the very center of the human world that hated them with almost unimaginable ferocity slans actually controlled the greatest transportation system in the entire world?

He pushed through the door, and along the corridor of marble that stretched ahead of him, countless doors leading off it. For the moment there was not a person in sight, but little thoughts trickled out to feed his growing amazement and delight.

The place swarmed with slans. There must be *hundreds!*

Just ahead of him, a door opened, and two bareheaded young men came out and walked toward him. They were talking quietly to each other, and for a moment did not see him. He had time to catch their surface thoughts, the calm and magnificent confidence of them, the lack of fear. Two slans, in the very prime of maturity—and bare-headed!

Bareheaded. That was what finally penetrated to Jommy above everything else. Bareheaded—and without tendrils.

For a moment it seemed to him that his eyes must be playing him tricks. His gaze searched almost frantically for the golden strands of tendril that should have been there. Tendrilless slans! So that was it! That explained why they couldn't read minds. The men were only ten feet away from him, and simultaneously, they became aware of him. They stopped.

"Boy," said one, "you'll have to get out. Children are not allowed in here. Run along now."

Jommy drew a deep breath. The mildness of the reproof was reassuring, especially now that the mystery was explained. It was wonderful that, by the simple removal of their telltale tendrils, they could live and work securely in the very center of their enemies! With a sweeping, almost melodramatic gesture, he reached up to his cap, and removed it. "It's all right," he began. "I'm—"

The words blurred on his lips. He watched the two men with fear-widened eyes. For after one uncontrolled moment of surprise, their mind shields closed tight. Their smiles were friendly. One said, "Well, this is a surprise!"

And the other echoed, "A damned pleasant surprise. Welcome, kid!"

But Jommy was not listening. His mind was swaying from the shock of the thoughts that had exploded in the brains of the two men in that brief period when they saw the glittering golden tendrils in his hair.

"God," the first one thought, "it's a snake!"

And from the other came a thought utterly cold, utterly merciless. "Kill the damned thing!"

SIX

For Jommy, from the moment he caught the thoughts of the two slans, it was not a question of what he should do but whether he had time to do it. Even the devastating surprise of their murderous enmity did not basically affect his actions or his brain.

He knew, without even thinking about it, that to run back along the corridors, trying to cover the hundred yards of straightaway marble floors, would be suicide. His nine-year-old legs could never match the tireless endurance of two able-bodied slans. There was only one thing to do, and he did it. With a boy's agility, he twisted to one side. There was a door there, one of the hundreds that lined the corridor.

Fortunately, it was unlocked. Before his battering rush it opened with surprising ease, yet so careful was his control that the actual opening he allowed himself was only barely large enough for him to slip through. He had a glimpse of a second, lighted corridor, empty of life; and then he was shutting the door, his strong, brown, sensitive fingers fumbling at the lock. The latch and the lock clicked home with a sharp, thrilling sound.

The very next instant there was a violent thud as two adult bodies dashed themselves against the barrier. But the door did not even tremble.

Jommy realized the truth. The door was of solid metal, built to withstand battering rams, yet so wonderfully balanced that it had appeared weightless to his fingers. For the moment, he was safe!

His mind relaxed from its concentration and reached for contact with the minds of the two slans. At first it seemed as if their shields were too tightly held, then his exploring brain caught the overtones of chagrin and an anxiety so terrible that it was like a knife hacking at the surface of their thoughts.

"God Almighty!" one whispered. "Sound the secret alarm! If the snakes find out we control Airways—"

Jommy wasted not another second. Every atom of curiosity in him was driving him to stay, to solve the bewildering hatred of the tendrilless slan for the true slan. But before the dictates of common sense, curiosity retreated. He ran at top speed, sure of what he must do.

He knew that by no logic could that gauntlet of corridor be considered safe. At any moment a door might open, or wisps of thought warn him of men coming around some bend. With abrupt decision, he slowed his headlong rush and tried several doors. The fourth door yielded to pressure, and Jommy crossed the threshold with a sense of triumph. On the far side of the room was a tall, broad window.

He pushed the window open and scrambled out onto the wide sill. Crouching low, he peered over the ledge. Light came dimly from the other windows of the building, and by its glow he could see what appeared to be a narrow driveway wedged between two precipices of brick wall.

For an instant he hesitated and then, like a human fly, started up the brick wall. The climbing was simple enough; enormously strong fingers searched with swift sureness for rough edges. The deepening darkness, as he climbed, was hampering, but with every upward step his confidence surged stronger within him. There were miles of roof here and, if he remembered rightly, the airport buildings connected on every side with other buildings. What chance had slans who could not read minds against a slan who could avoid their every trap?

The thirtieth, and top, story! With a sigh of relief, Jommy pulled himself erect and started along the flat roof. It was nearly dark now, but he could see the top of a neighboring building that almost touched the roof he was on. A leap of two yards at most, an easy jump. With a loud *clang!* the clock in a nearby tower began to intone the hour. One—two—five—ten! And on the stroke, a low, grinding noise struck Jommy's ears, and suddenly, in the shadowy center of that expanse of roof opposite him yawned a wide, black hole. Startled, he flung himself flat, holding his breath.

And from that dark hole a dim, torpedolike shape leaped into the star-filled sky. Faster, faster it went; and then, at the uttermost limit of vision, a tiny, blazing light sprang from its rear. It flickered there for a moment, then was gone, like a star snuffed out.

Jommy lay very still, his eyes straining to follow the path of the strange craft. A spaceship. By all the heavens, a spaceship! Had these tendrilless slans realized the dream of the ages—to operate flights to the planets? If so, how had they kept it secret from human beings? And what were the true slans doing?

The scraping noise reached him again. He crept to the edge of the roof and peered across. He could only vaguely see the yawning blackness lessen as the two great metal sheets slid together and the roof was whole again.

For a moment longer Jommy waited, then he bunched his muscles and sprang. Only one purpose was in his mind now—to get back to Granny quickly and by as devious a way as possible. Back alleys, side streets, must be his route. For this ease of escape from *slans* suddenly seemed suspicious. Unless, of course, they didn't dare set up safeguards for fear of betraying their secret to human beings.

Whatever the reason, it was only too obvious that he still needed desperately the security of Granny's little shack. He had no desire to tackle a problem so complicated and murderous as the slan/human/tendrilless slan triangle had become. No, not until he was full-grown and capable of matching the sharp brains that were fighting this unceasing and deadly battle.

Yes, back to Granny and, by way of the store to get some peace offerings for the old wretch, now that he was certain to be late. And he'd have to hurry, too. The store would close at eleven.

At the store, Jommy did not venture near the jewelry counter, for the girl who objected to little boys was still at work. There were other richly laden counters, and he swiftly skimmed the cream of their smaller merchandise. Nevertheless, he made a mental note that, if he came into this store in future, he would have to be on the scene before five o'clock, when the evening staff arrived for their shift. Otherwise that girl could prove a nuisance.

Sated at last with stolen goods, he headed cautiously for the nearest exit, then stopped as a man, a middle-aged, paunchy person, walked by thoughtfully. The man was the chief accountant of the store, and he was thinking of the four hundred thousand dollars that would be in the safe overnight. In his mind, also, was the combination of the safe.

Jommy hurried on, but he was disgusted with his lack of foresight. How foolish to steal goods that would have to be sold, with the risks at both ends enormous compared to the simple business of taking all the money he wanted.

Granny was still where he had left her, but her mind was in such turmoil that he had to wait for her to speak before he could understand what she wanted.

"Quick," she said hoarsely, "get in under the blankets. A police-man was just here warning Granny to move on."

It must have been at least a mile farther on that she stopped the cart and tore the blanket off Jommy with a snarl. "You ungrateful wretch, where have you been?"

Jommy wasted no words. His contempt was too great for him to speak to her more than he had to. He shivered as he watched the eagerness with which she snatched at the treasure he dumped into her lap. Swiftly she evaluated each item, and stuffed it carefully into the false bottom that had been built into the cart.

"At least two hundred dollars for old Granny!" she said joyously. "Old Finn will give Granny that much. Oh, but Granny's smart, catching a young slan. He'll make not ten thousand but twenty thousand a year for her. And to think they offered only ten thousand dollars' reward! It should be a million."

"I can do even better than that," Jommy volunteered. It seemed as good a time as any to tell her about the store safe, and that there was no need for more shoplifting. "There's about four thousand in the safe," he finished. "I can get it tonight. I'll climb up the back of the building, where it's dark, to one of the windows, cut a hole in it— You've got a glass cutter somewhere?"

"Granny can get one!" the old woman breathed ecstatically. She rocked back and forth with joy. "Oh, oh, Granny's glad. But Granny can see now why human beings shoot slans. They're too dangerous. Why, they could steal the world. They tried to, you know, in the beginning."

"I don't—know—very much about that," Jommy said slowly. He wished desperately that Granny knew all about it, but he saw that she didn't. There was only the vaguest knowledge in her mind of that misty period when the slans (so human beings accused) had tried to conquer the world. She knew no more than he did, no more than all this vast ignorant mass of people.

What was the truth? Had there ever been a war between slans and human beings? Or was it just the same propaganda as that dreadful stuff about what slans did to babies? Jommy saw that Granny's mind had jumped back to the money in the store.

"Only four thousand dollars!" she said sharply. "Why, they must make hundreds of thousands every day—millions!"

"They don't keep it all in the store," lied Jommy, and to his relief the old woman accepted the explanation.

He thought about the lie as the cart rattled on. He had uttered it in the first place almost automatically. Now he saw that it was self-protection. If he made the old woman too rich, she would soon begin to think of betraying him.

It was absolutely imperative that during the next six years he live in the security of Granny's shack. The question therefore became: How little would she be satisfied with? Somewhere he must strike a mean between her insatiable greed and his necessity.

Just thinking about that enlarged its dangers. In this woman was an incredible selfishness, and a streak of cowardice that might surge up in a panic of fear and destroy him before he could properly realize his danger.

No doubt about it. Among the known imponderables overhanging the precious six years separating him from his father's mighty science, this gaunt rascal loomed as the most dangerous and the most uncertain factor.

SEVEN

The acquisition of money corrupted Granny. She disappeared for days at a time, and he gathered from her disjointed conversation afterward that she was at last frequenting the pleasure resorts she had always longed to go to. When she was at home, her bottle was her almost inseparable companion. Because he needed to have her around, Jommy prepared meals for her, and so kept her alive despite her excesses. It was necessary—when she ran out of money—to make occasional forays with her, but otherwise he kept effectively out of her way.

He used his considerable spare time to gain an education—something which was not easy to do. The area was poverty-stricken in the extreme, and most of its inhabitants were uneducated, even illiterate, but there was a scattering of people with alert minds in it. Jommy discovered who they were and what they did and how much they knew by asking them and by asking about them. To them, he was Granny's grandson. Once that was accepted as fact, many difficulties were resolved.

There were people, of course, who were wary of a junk dealer's relative, considering him untrustworthy. A few individuals, who had felt the sting of Granny's sharp tongue, were quite antagonistic; but their reaction was to ignore him. Others were too busy to bother with either Granny or himself.

From some he aggressively, though as unobtrusively as possible, compelled attention. A young engineering student called him "a damned nuisance," but explained the science of engineering to him. Jommy read in his mind that the student felt that he was clarifying his own thoughts and understanding of his subject, and that he occasionally boasted that he knew engineering so well that he could make the principles clear to a boy of ten.

He never guessed how precocious this boy was.

A woman who had traveled widely before her marriage—but was now in poor circumstances—lived half a block down the street, and fed him cookies one at a time while she talked eagerly of the world and its people as she had seen them.

It was necessary to accept the bribes because she would have misunderstood if he refused the cookies. But no teller of tales actually ever had a more attentive pair of ears to talk to than Mrs. Hardy. A thin-faced, bitter woman whose husband had gambled away her possessions, she had wandered over Europe and Asia, and her sharp eyes had recorded an immense amount of detail. More vaguely, she knew about the past of those countries.

At one time—so she had heard—China had been heavily populated. The story was that a series of bloody wars had long ago decimated the more densely inhabited areas. These wars, it seemed, were definitely not of slan origin. It was only in the last hundred years that the slans had turned their attention to babies of Chinese and other Eastern origin—and so turned against them people who had hitherto tolerated the slans' existence.

As explained by Mrs. Hardy, it seemed like one more senseless action of the slans. Jommy listened and recorded the information, convinced that the explanation could not be as stated, wondering what the truth was, and determined that some day he would bring all these deadly lies out into the open.

The engineering student, Mrs. Hardy, a grocer who had been a rocket pilot, a radio and TV repairman, and Old Man Darrett—these were the people who educated him, unknowingly, during the first two years he spent with Granny. Of the group, Darrett was Jommy's prize. A big, stocky, lonely, cynical man of seventy-odd years, he had once been a professor of history—but that was merely one of the many subjects about which he had an almost inexhaustible fund of information.

It was obvious that sooner or later the old man would bring up the subject of the slan wars. It was so obvious that Jommy allowed the first few casual mentions of it to pass, just as if he weren't interested. But early one winter afternoon, there it was again, as he had expected.

And this time he said, "You keep talking about wars. There couldn't have been wars. Those people are just outlaws. You don't fight wars with outlaws; you just exterminate them."

Darrett stiffened. "Outlaws," he said. "Young fellow, those were great days. I tell you a hundred thousand slans practically took over the world. It was a beautiful job of planning, carried out with the utmost boldness. What you have to realize is that men as a mass always play somebody else's game—not their own. They're caught in traps from which they cannot escape. They belong to groups; they're members of organizations; they're loyal to ideas, individuals, geographical areas. If you can get hold of the institutions they support—there's the method."

"And the slans did *that*?" Jommy asked the question with an intensity that startled him; it was a little too revealing of his own feelings. He added quickly in a subdued tone, "It sounds like a story. It's just propaganda to scare us—like you've said so often about other things."

"Propaganda!" said Darrett explosively. And then he was silent. His large, expressive black eyes were half hidden by his long, dark eyelashes. He said at last slowly, "I want you to visualize this, Jommy. The world was confused and bewildered. Everywhere human babies were being subjected to the tremendous campaign of the slans to make more slans. Civilization began to break down. There was an immense increase in insanity. Suicide, murder, crime—the graph of chaos rose to new heights. And, one morning, without knowing quite how it was done, the human race woke up to discover that overnight the enemy had taken control. Working from within, the slans had managed to take over innumerable key organizations. When you learn to understand the rigidity of institutional structures in our society, you'll realize how helpless human beings were at first. My own private opinion is that the slans could have gotten away with it except for one thing."

Jommy waited, silent. He had an unhappy premonition of what was coming. Old Man Darrett went on.

"They continued ruthlessly trying to make slans out of human babies. It seems a little stupid in retrospect."

Darrett and the others were only the beginning. He followed learned men around the streets, picking at the surface of their minds. He lay in concealment on campus grounds, telepathically following lectures. Books he had in plenty, but books were not enough. They had to be interpreted, explained. There were mathematics, physics, chemistry, astronomy—all the sciences. His desire had no limit.

In the six years between his ninth and fifteenth birthdays, he acquired the beginning of what his mother had prescribed as basic knowledge for an adult slan.

During those years, he watched the tendrilless slans cautiously from a distance. Nightly, at ten, their spaceships leaped into the sky; and the service was maintained on precision time. Every night at two-thirty, another shark-shaped monster plunged down from space, silent and dark, and dropped like a ghost into the top of the same building.

Only twice during those years was the traffic suspended, each time for a month, and each time when Mars, following her eccentric orbit, teetered on the farthest side of the Sun.

He stayed away from the Air Center, because almost every day his respect for the might of the tendrilless slans grew. And it seemed increasingly clear that only an accident had saved him that day when he revealed himself to the two adults. An accident and surprise.

Of the basic mysteries of the slans he learned nothing. To pass the time he indulged in orgies of physical activity. First of all, he must have a secret way of escape, just in case—secret from Granny as well as the world; and second, he couldn't possibly live in this shack as it was. It required months to build hundreds of yards of tunnel, months also to rebuild the interior of their home with fine, paneled walls, shining ceilings, and plastic floors.

Jommy sneaked the furniture in at night, past the junk-laden yard and the unchanged, unpainted exterior. But that required nearly a year in itself—because of Granny and her bottle.

His fifteenth birthday. At two in the afternoon, Jommy laid down the book he had been reading, took off his slippers, and put on his shoes. The hour for decisive action had come. Today he must go into the catacombs and take possession of his father's secret. Because he did not know the secret slan passageways, he would have to risk going in through a public entrance.

He gave scarcely more than a surface thought to the possibility of danger. This was the day—long ago it had been planted in his mind, hypnotically set by his father. It did seem important, however, that he slip out of the house without the old woman's hearing him.

Briefly, he let his mind contact hers, and without the slightest sense of disgust sampled the stream of her thought. She was wide awake and tossing on her bed. And through her brain poured freely and furiously a welter of astoundingly wicked thoughts.

Jommy Cross frowned abruptly. Into the veritable hell of the old woman's recollection (for she lived almost completely in her amazing past when she was drunk) had come a swift, cunning thought. "Got to get rid of that slan. Dangerous for Granny now that she's got money. Mustn't let him suspect . . . keep it out of my mind so . . ."

Jommy Cross smiled mirthlessly. It was not the first time he had caught the thought of treachery in her brain. With sudden purposefulness he finished tying the shoelace, stood up, and went into her room.

Granny lay, a sprawling shape under the sheets that were stained brown with liquor. Her deeply sunken black eyes stared dully out of the wrinkled parchment of her face. Gazing down at her, Jommy Cross felt a quiver of pity. Terrible and vicious as had been the old Granny, he preferred her as she had been then to this weak old soak who lay like some medieval witch miraculously deposited in a blue and silver bed of the future.

Her eyes seemed to see him for the first time, clearly. A string of bloodthirsty curses reeled from her lips. Then: "Waddya want? Granny wants to be alone."

The pity drained out of him. He gazed at her coldly. "I just wanted to give you a little warning. I'm leaving soon, so you won't have to spend any more time thinking of ways to betray me. There aren't any safe ways. That treasured old hide of yours wouldn't be worth a nickel if they caught me."

The black eyes gleamed up at him slyly. "Think you're smart, eh?" she mumbled. The word seemed to start a new trend of thought that it was impossible for him to follow mentally. "Smart," she repeated gloatingly, "smartest thing Granny ever did, catching a young slan. Dangerous, though—got to get rid of him."

"You old fool," Jommy Cross said dispassionately. "Don't forget that a person who harbors a slan is automatically subject to death. You've kept that mud-turtle-complexioned neck of yours well oiled, so it probably won't squeal when they hang you, but you'll do plenty of kicking with those scrawny legs."

The brutal words spoken, he turned abruptly and went out of the room, out of the house. On the bus, he thought: "I've got to watch her, and as soon as possible leave her. Nobody who thinks in probabilities could trust anything valuable to *her*."

Even downtown the streets were deserted. Jommy Cross climbed off the bus, conscious of the silence where usually there was bedlam. The city was too quiet; there was a very absence of life and movement. He stood uncertainly at the curb, all thought of Granny draining from him. He opened his mind wide. At first there was nothing there but a wisp from the half-blank mind of the driver of the bus which was disappearing now down the otherwise carless road. The sun glared down on the pavement. A few people scuttled hurriedly past, in their minds simply a blank terror so continuous and unvarying that he could not penetrate beyond it.

The silence deepened, and alarm crept into Jommy Cross. He explored the buildings around him, but no clamor of minds came from them, nothing whatever. The clatter of an engine burst abruptly from a side street. Two blocks away a tractor emerged, pulling a tremendous gun that pointed menacingly into the sky. The tractor clattered into the center of the street, was unhooked from the gun, and bellowed off into the side street from which it had come. Men swarmed around the gun, preparing it, and then stood by, looking up at the sky, waiting tensely.

Jommy Cross wanted to walk closer, to read their minds, but he didn't dare. The sense of being in an exposed and dangerous position grew into a sick conviction within him. Any minute a military or police car might roll past and its occupants ask him what he was doing in the street. He might be arrested, or told to take off his cap and show his hair and the golden threads that were his tendrils.

Something big was definitely up, and the best place for him was the catacombs, where he'd be out of sight, though in a different kind of danger. He started hurriedly toward the catacomb entrance that had been his goal ever since leaving the house. He was turning into a side street when the loud-speaker at the corner blared into life. A man's voice roared hoarsely.

"Final warning—*get off the street!* Get out of sight. The mysterious airship of the slans is now approaching the city at terrific speed. It is believed the ship is heading toward the palace. Interference has been set up on all radio waves, to prevent any of the slan lies from being broadcast. Get off the streets! *Here comes the ship!*"

Jommy froze. There was a silver flash in the sky, and then a long, winged torpedo of glittering metal hurtled by straight above. He heard a staccato roar from the gun down the street, and the echo of other guns, and then the ship was a distant sparkling point, heading toward the palace.

Curiously, the sun's glare hurt his eyes now. He was conscious of confusion. *A winged ship!* Scores of nights during these past six years he had watched the spaceships soar up from the building in the tendrilless slan Air Center. Wingless rocket ships, and something more. Something that made great metal machines lighter than air. The rocket part seemed to be used only for propulsion. The weightlessness, the way they were flung up as if by centrifugal force, *must* be antigravity! And here was a *winged* ship, with all that that implied; jet engines, rigid confinement to Earth's atmosphere, ordinariness. If this was the best the true slans could do, then—

Sharply disappointed, he turned and walked down the long flight of stairs that led to the public washroom. The place was as empty and silent as the streets above. And it was a simple matter for him who had passed through so many locked doors to pick the lock of the steel-barred door leading to the catacombs.

He was conscious of the tenseness of his mind as he stared through the bars of the door. There was a vague foreground of concrete beyond, then a blur of darkness that meant more stairs. The muscles of his throat tightened, his breath became deep and slow. He hunched his slim length forward, like a runner getting ready for a sprint. He opened the door, darted inside, and down the long reach of dark, dank steps at top speed.

Somewhere ahead, a bell began ringing monotonously, set off by the photoelectric cells whose barrier Jommy had crossed on entering the door—a protection put up years ago against slans and other interlopers.

The bell was just a short distance away now, and still there was no mind stirring out of the corridor that yawned before him. Apparently none of the men working or on guard in the catacombs was within hearing range. He saw the bell, high up on the wall, a glimmering piece of metal, *brrring* noisily. The wall was smooth as glass, impossible to climb, the bell more than twelve feet from the floor. On and on it clanged, and still there was no clamor of approaching minds, not the faintest wisp of thought.

"No proof that they're not coming," Jommy thought tensely. "These stone walls would quickly diffuse thought waves."

He took a run at the wall, and leaped with desperate strength, up, up, toward the instrument. His arm strained, his fingers scraped the marble wall, a full foot below the bell. He fell back, knowing his defeat. It was still ringing as he rounded a bend in the corridor. He heard it grow fainter and fainter, fading into the distance behind him. But even after the sound was gone, the ghost of it went on ringing in his mind, an insistent warning of danger.

Queerly, the sense of a warning buzz in his brain grew stronger, until suddenly it seemed to him that the bell was actually there again, faint with distance. The feeling grew stronger, until abruptly he realized that there was another bell, clanging as noisily as the first one. That meant (he felt appalled) there must be a long line of such bells sending out their alarms, and somewhere in that vast network of tunnels there must be ears to hear them, men stiffening and looking at each other with narrowed eyes.

Jommy Cross hurried on. He had no conscious knowledge of his route. He knew only that his father had hypnotized a picture of it into his mind, and that he need but follow the promptings of his subconscious. It came abruptly, a sharp mental command. "To the right!"

He took the narrower of the two forks—and came at last to the hiding-place. It was all simple enough, a cleverly loosened slab in the marble wall that slid out under the pressure of his strength, revealing a dark space beyond. He reached in; his groping fingers touched a metal box. He pulled it to him. He was shaking now, his fingers trembling. For a moment he stood very still, fighting for self-control; striving to picture his father standing here before this slab hiding his secrets for his son to find if anything went wrong with his own personal plans.

It seemed to Jommy that this might be a cosmic moment in the history of slans, this moment when the work of a dead father was passed on to a fifteen-year-old boy who had waited so many thousands of minutes and hours and days for this second to come.

The nostalgia fled from him abruptly as a mist of outside thought whispered into his mind. "Damn that bell!" somebody was thinking. "It's probably someone who ran down when the slan ship came, trying to get away from expected bombs."

"Yeah, but don't count on it. You know how strict they are about these catacombs. Whoever started that bell is still inside. We'd better turn in the alarm to police headquarters."

A third vibration came. "Maybe the guy's lost."

"Let him explain that," said the first man. "Let's head toward the first bell and keep our guns ready. Never know what it might be. With slans flying around in the sky these days, there could be some of them coming down here, for all we know."

Frantically, Jommy examined the metal box for the secret of its opening. His hypnotic command was to take out the contents and put the empty box back in the hole. In the face of that order, the thought of grabbing up the box and running never entered his head.

There seemed to be no lock and no catch. And yet, there must be something to fasten the lid down—Hurry, hurry! In a few minutes the approaching men would be passing directly by the spot where he was standing.

The dimness of the long concrete and marble corridors, the dank odors, the consciousness of the thick cords of electric wires that ran by overhead feeding millions of volts to the city above, the whole world of the catacombs around, and even memories of his past—these were the thoughts that raced through Jommy's mind, as he stared down at the metal box. There was a thought of drunken Granny, and of the mystery of the slans, and it all mixed together with the approaching footsteps of the men. He could hear them plainly now, three pairs of them, clumping toward him.

Silently, Jommy Cross tore at the cover of the box, his muscles tensed for the effort. He nearly lost his balance, so easily did the unfastened cover lift up.

He found himself staring down at a thick rod of metal that lay on top of a pile of papers. He felt no surprise at its being there. There was, instead, a faint relief at discovering intact something he had *known* was there. Obviously, more of his father's hypnotism.

The metal rod was a bulbous thing about two inches wide at the center but narrowing down at the ends. One of the ends was roughened, unmistakably meant to give the hand a good grip. There was a little button at the foot of the bulb part, convenient for the thumb to press it. The whole instrument glowed ever so faintly with a light of its own. That glow and the diffused light from the corridor were just bright enough for him to read on the sheet of paper beneath.

This is the weapon. Use it only
in case of absolute necessity.

For a moment, Jommy Cross was so intent that he didn't realize the men were upon him. A flashlight glared.

"What the—" one of the men roared. "Hands up, you!"

It was his first real, personal danger in six long years, and it felt unreal. The slow thought crept into him that human beings were not very quick in their reflexes. And then he was reaching for the weapon in the box before him. Without conscious haste, he pressed the button.

If any of the men fired, the action was lost in the roar of white flame that flashed with inconceivable violence from the mouth of the tube of force. One moment they were alive, rough-built, looming shapes, threatening him; the next, they were gone, snuffed out by that burst of virulent fire.

Jommy looked down at his hand. It was trembling. And there was a sickness in him at the way he had smashed three lives out of existence. The blur before his vision straightened slowly, as his eyes recovered from the fiery dazzlement. As his gaze reached farther out from him, he saw that the corridor was completely empty. Not a bone, not a piece of flesh or clothing remained to show that there had ever been living beings in the vicinity. Part of the floor was hollowed out, where that scorching incandescence had seared a concavity. But the slight depression it made would never be noticed.

He forced his fingers to stop trembling; slowly the sick feeling crept out of him. There was no use feeling badly. Killing was a tough business, but these men would have dealt death to him without compunction, as men already had to his father and mother—and to countless other slans who had died miserably because of the lies these people kept feeding to each other, and swallowing without the slightest resistance. Damn them all!

For a moment, his emotions were violent. He thought: Was it possible that all slans grew bitter as they became older, and ceased feeling compunctions about the killing of human beings, just as human beings had no compunctions about murdering slans?

His gaze fell on the sheet upon which his father had written:

. . . the weapon. Use it only
in case of absolute necessity.

Memory flooded him, of a thousand other instances of his parents' noble quality of understanding. He could still remember the night his father had said, "Remember this. No matter how strong the slans become, the problem of what to do with human beings remains a barrier to occupation of the world. Until that problem is settled with justice and psychological sanity, the use of force would be a black crime."

Jommy felt better. There was proof. His father hadn't even carried with him a replica of this weapon that might have saved him from his enemies. He had taken death before he would deal it.

Jommy Cross frowned. Nobility was all very well, and perhaps he had lived too long with human beings to be a true slan, but he couldn't escape the conviction that fighting was better than dying.

The thought stopped, alarm replacing it. There was no time to waste. He had to get out of here, and quickly! He slipped the gun into his coat pocket, swiftly caught up the papers in the box, jammed them into his pockets. Then tossing the now empty, useless box back into its hole, slid the stone into place. He raced down the corridor, along the way he had come, up the steps, and stopped short within sight of the washroom. A little while before, it had been empty and silent. Now, it was packed with men. He waited, poised yet indecisive, hoping their numbers would dwindle.

But men came in, and men went out, and there was no lessening of the crowd, no diminishing of the bedlam of noise and thought. Excitement, fear, worry; here were little men in whose brains thundered the realization that big things were happening. And the echo of that realization poured through the iron bars of the door to where Jommy waited in the dimness. In the distance, the bell was still ringing. Its unrelenting *brrr* of warning finally dictated the action he must take. Clutching the weapon in his pocket with one hand, Jommy stepped forward gingerly, and pushed the door open. He shut it behind him softly, tensed for the slightest sign of alarm.

But the packed mass of men paid him not the least attention as he shoved his way through them and went up to the street. The pavement level was alive with people. Crowds pressed along the sidewalks and on the thoroughfares. Police whistles shrilled, loudspeakers blared, but nothing could stem the anarchism of the mob. All transport was at a standstill. Sweating, cursing drivers left their cars standing in the middle of the street and joined listeners before the street radios that kept up a machine-gun barrage.

"Nothing is known for certain. No one knows exactly whether the slan ship landed at the palace or dropped a message and then disappeared. No one saw it land; no one saw it disappear. It is possible that it was shot down. Then again it is possible that at this moment the slans are in conference with Kier Gray at the palace. Rumor to that effect has already spread, in spite of the noncommittal statement issued a few minutes ago by Kier Gray himself. For the benefit of those who did not hear that statement, I will repeat it. Ladies and gentlemen, the statement of Kier Gray was as follows:

" 'Do not be excited or alarmed. The extraordinary appearance of the slan ship has not altered the respective positions of slans and human beings in the slightest degree. We control the situation absolutely. They can do nothing anywhere except what they have been doing, and that within rigid limitations. Human beings outnumber slans probably millions to one; and, under such circumstances, they will never dare come out in an open, organized campaign against us. So be easy in your hearts.'

"That, ladies and gentlemen, was the statement issued by Kier Gray after the momentous event of today. The council has been in continuous session since that statement was issued. I repeat, nothing more is known for certain. It is not known whether the slan ship landed. No one from the city saw it disappear. No one except the authorities know exactly what happened, and you have just heard the only statement on the matter, given out by Kier Gray himself. Whether the slan ship was shot down or—"

The chatter went on and on. Over and over the statement of Kier Gray was repeated, the same accompanying rumors were given. It became a drone in the back of Jommy's head, a senseless roar from loudspeaker after loudspeaker, a monotony of noise. But he stayed on, waiting for some additional information, eager with the burning eagerness of fifteen long years of wanting to know about other slans.

Only slowly did the flame of his excitement die. Nothing new was reported, and at last he climbed aboard a bus and headed for home. Darkness was settling over the hot spring day. A tower clock showed seventeen minutes past seven.

He approached the little junk-laden yard with his usual caution. His mind reached inside the deceptive, tumbled-down-looking cottage, and touched Granny's mind. He sighed. Still drunk! How the devil did that wrecked caricature of a body stand it? So much liquor should have dehydrated her system before this. He pushed open the door, entered, and shut it behind him—and then stopped short!

His mind, still in casual contact with Granny's mind, was receiving a thought. The old woman had heard the door open and shut, and the sound had jogged her mind briefly.

"Mustn't let him know I phoned the police. Keep it out of my mind . . . can't have a slan around . . . dangerous to have a slan . . . police'll have the streets barred—"

EIGHT

Kathleen Layton clenched her fists into small, firm, brown knobs. Her slim young body quivered in revulsion as she recognized the thoughts that came at her from one of the corridors. Seventeen-year-old Davy Dinsmore was searching for her, coming toward the marble parapet where she stood staring out at the city, which was wrapped in the soft mists of the humid, hot, spring afternoon.

The mists shifted in ever changing design. They became like fleecy clouds that half hid buildings, then smeared into a haze that held locked within its flimsy texture the faintest tinge of sky blue.

Queerly, the looking hurt her eyes without actually being unpleasant. The coolness of the palace breathed out at her from all the open doors, and beat back the heat of the sun. The glare remained, however.

The wisps of thought from Davy Dinsmore grew stronger, nearer. He was, she saw in his mind, going to try again to persuade her to be his girlfriend. With a final shudder, Kathleen shut out his thoughts, and waited for the youth to appear. It had been a mistake to be polite to him, even though she had saved herself a lot of trouble during her early teens by having his support against the other young people. Now, she preferred his enmity to the type of love thoughts that permeated his brain.

"Oh," said Davy Dinsmore, emerging from a door, "here you are."

She stared at him without smiling. Davy Dinsmore at seventeen was a gangling youth, resembling in face his long-jawed mother, who always seemed to be sneering even when she smiled. He came up with an aggressiveness that reflected his ambivalent feelings toward her, on the one hand the desire for a physical conquest, and on the other a genuine eagerness to hurt her in some way.

"Yes," said Kathleen curtly, "here I am. I was hoping I'd be left alone for a change."

There was a toughness, she knew, in the fiber of Davy Dinsmore's makeup that made him immune to such remarks. The thoughts erupting from his brain penetrated to her at this close range, informing her that "this dame is pulling the same coy stuff. But I'll thaw her out yet."

A mind-curdling experience lay behind that calm conviction. Kathleen closed her brain a little tighter to shut out the details of recollection that floated up from the complacent depths of the youth.

"I don't want you coming around me anymore," Kathleen said with cold deliberation. "Your mind is like a sewer. I'm sorry I ever spoke to you when you first came ogling up to me. I should have known better, and I hope you realize I'm speaking to you plainly because otherwise you wouldn't believe I meant it. Well, I do—every word. Particularly the sewer part. Now, go away."

Davy's face had a bleached quality, but there was a rage in it and an intensity behind it that beat into her shielded mind. Instantly, she closed her brain still tighter, cutting off the vituperation that poured from him. It struck her abruptly that there was no fazing this creature unless she could absolutely humiliate him.

She snapped, "Beat it, you miserable, dough-fleshed thing!"

"Yaaah!" he said. And leaped for her.

For a second her surprise at his daring to pit himself against her superior strength held her stunned. Then, lips compressed, she grabbed at him, easily evading his flailing arms, and jerked him off his feet. Too late she realized that he had counted on her doing that. His rough fingers caught at her head, then clutched a handful of hair, and all the silk-thin tendrils that lay there in golden, glittering threads.

"Okay," he exulted. "Now I've got you. *Don't let me down!* I know what you'd like to do. Get me down, grab my wrists, and squeeze till I let go. If you lower me as much as an inch, I'll give such a tug on those precious tendrils that some of them will tear loose. I know you can hold me up without getting tired—so hold!"

Dismay held Kathleen rigid. "Precious tendrils," he had said. So precious that for the first time in her life she had to throttle a scream. So precious that in some unthinking way she hadn't expected that anyone would dare to touch them. A half swoon of her fright closed over her like a night of wild and terrible storm.

"What do you want?" she gasped.

"Now you're talking," said Davy Dinsmore. But she didn't need his words. She had his mind now, flooding into her.

"All right," she said weakly. "I'll do it."

"And be sure to lower me slowly," the youth said. "And when my lips are touching yours, see that the kiss lasts at least a minute. I'll teach you to treat me like dirt."

His lips were swimming above hers against the hazy background of his sneering face and avid eyes, when a sharp, commanding voice rapped out in surprise and rage from behind her, "What's the meaning of this?"

"Huh!" stammered Davy Dinsmore. She felt his fingers leave her hair and tendrils, then with a gasp she flung him down. He staggered, then caught himself and stammered, "I—I beg your pardon, Mr. Lorry. I—I—"

"Beat it, you miserable hound!" said Kathleen.

"Yes, go!" said Jem Lorry curtly.

Kathleen watched Davy go stumbling off, his mind sending out thoughts of pure fright at having offended one of the great men of the government. But when he disappeared, she did not turn to face the new-comer. Instinctively, she was aware of her muscles stiffening, as she kept her gaze and face averted from this man, the most powerful councilor in the cabinet of Kier Gray.

"And what was all that?" came the man's voice, not unpleasant, from behind her. "Apparently it was lucky I came up."

"Oh, I don't know," Kathleen replied coldly. She was in a mood for utmost candor. "Your attentions are equally repulsive to me."

"Hmm!" He came up beside her and she caught a glimpse of his strong jawline, as he leaned over the railing.

"No difference, really," Kathleen said persistently. "You both want the same thing."

He stood silent for a moment, but his thoughts had the same elusive quality as Kier Gray's. The years had made him a master of evading her special powers of mind-reading. When he finally spoke, his voice was changed. It held a harder quality. "No doubt your outlook on these matters will change after you become my mistress."

"That will be never!" snapped Kathleen. "I don't like human beings. I don't like you."

"Your objections are of no concern," the young man said coldly. "The only problem is how can I take possession of you without subjecting myself to the accusation that I am in secret alliance with the slans. Until I have thought of a solution to that, you may go your way."

His certainty sent a shudder through Kathleen. "You're quite mistaken," she said firmly. "The reason your intentions will inevitably fail is very simple. Kier Gray is my protector. Even you don't dare go against him."

Jem Lorry pondered that. Finally: "Your protector, yes. But he has no morals in the matter of a woman's virtue. I don't think he'll object if you become my mistress, but he will insist on my finding a propaganda-proof reason. He's become quite antislan these last few years. I used to think he was proslan. But now he's almost fanatic on the subject of having nothing to do with them. He and John Petty are closer on the subject now than they ever were. Funny!"

He mused on that for a moment; then: "But don't worry, I'll find a formula. I—"

A roar from a radio loudspeaker cut off Lorry's voice. "General warning! An unidentified aircraft was seen a few minutes ago, crossing the Rocky Mountains, headed eastward. Pursuing machines were rapidly outdistanced, and the ship seems to be taking a straight-line course toward Centropolis. People are ordered to go home immediately, as the ship—believed now to be of slan origin—will be here in one hour, according to present indications. The streets are needed for military purposes. Go home!"

The speaker clicked off, and Jem Lorry turned to Kathleen, a smile on his handsome face. "Don't let that arouse any hopes of rescue. One ship cannot carry important armaments, unless it has a mass of factories behind it. The old-style atomic bomb, for instance, could not possibly be manufactured in a cave, and besides, to be quite frank, the slans did not use it in the slan-human war. The disasters of that century, and earlier, were caused by slans, but not in that way."

He was silent for a minute, then: "Everybody thought those first bombs had solved the secret of atomic energy—" He stopped. Then: "It looks to me as if this trip was designed to give the more simple-minded human beings a scare, preliminary in an attempt to open negotiations."

An hour later, Kathleen stood beside Jem Lorry as the silver ship slanted toward the palace. Closer it came, traveling at enormous speed. Her mind reached out toward it, striving to contact the slans who must be inside.

The ship zoomed lower, nearer, but still there was no answering thought from the occupants. Suddenly a metallic capsule dropped from it. The capsule struck the garden path half a mile distant, and lay glinting like a jewel in the afternoon sun.

She looked up, and the ship was gone. No, there it was. Briefly she saw a silvery brilliance in the remote heights almost straight above the palace. It twinkled for a moment like a star. And was gone. Her straining eyes retreated from their violent effort; her mind came back from the sky; and she grew aware of Jem Lorry again.

He exulted. "Whatever else this means, it's what I've been waiting for—an opportunity to present an argument that will enable me to take you to my apartment this very night. There'll be a council meeting immediately, I imagine."

Kathleen drew a deep breath. She could see just how he might manage it, and the time had, therefore, come to fight with every weapon at her command. She spoke with dignity, her head flung back, her eyes flashing.

"I shall ask to be present at the council meeting on the grounds that I was in mental communication with the captain of the slans aboard the ship." She finished the lie calmly. "I can clarify certain things in the message that will be found in the capsule."

She thought desperately. Somehow she'd read in their minds what the message was, and from that she could build up a semireasonable story of what the slan leader had told her. If she was caught in the lie, there might be some dangerous reactions from these slan haters. But she had to prevent them from consenting to give her to Jem Lorry.

As she entered the council room, a conviction of defeat came to Kathleen. There were only seven men present, including Kier Gray. She stared at them one by one, reading as much of their minds as she could, and there was no help for her.

The four younger men were personal friends of Jem Lorry. The sixth man, John Petty, gave her one brief glance of icy hostility, then turned away indifferently.

Her gaze fastened finally on Kier Gray. A little anxious tremor of surprise whipped along her nerves, as she saw that he was staring at her with a laconic lifting of his eyebrows, and the faintest sneer on his lips. He caught her gaze and broke the silence.

"So you were in mental communication with the slan leader, were you?" He laughed harshly. "We'll let that pass for the moment."

There was so much incredulity in his voice and expression, so much hostility in his very attitude, that Kathleen was relieved when his cold eyes flicked away from her. He went on addressing the others.

"It's unfortunate that five councilors should be in the far corners of the world. I do not personally believe in roaming too far from headquarters; let subordinates do the traveling. However, we cannot delay discussion on a problem as urgent as this one. If the seven of us agree on a solution, we won't need their assistance. If we're deadlocked, we shall have to do a considerable amount of radiotelephoning.

"Here is the gist of the contents of the metal capsule dropped by the slan ship. They claim that there are a million slans organized throughout the world—"

Jem Lorry interrupted sardonically, "Seems to me that our chief of secret police has been falling down on the job, despite his much-vaunted hatred of the slans."

Petty sat up and flashed him a cold glance. He snapped, "Perhaps you would exchange jobs with me for a year, and see what you can do. I wouldn't mind having the soft job of minister of state for a change."

Kier Gray's voice cut across the silence that followed Petty's freezing words. "Let me finish. They go on to say that not only does this organized million exist but there is, in addition, a vast total of unorganized men and women slans, estimated at ten millions more. What about that, Petty?"

"Undoubtedly there are some unorganized slans," the secret-police chief admitted cautiously. "We catch about a hundred a month all over the world, who have apparently never been part of any organization. In vast areas of the more primitive parts of the Earth, the people cannot be aroused to antipathy to slans; in fact, they accept them as human beings. And there are no doubt large colonies in some of these remote places, particularly in Asia, Africa, South America, and Australia. It is years now since such colonies have actually been found, but we assume that some still exist, and that over the years they have developed self-protection to a high degree. I am prepared, however, to discount any activity from these remote sources. Civilization and science are built-up organisms, broadly based on the achievements, physical and mental, of hundreds of millions of beings. The moment these slans retreat to outlying sections of the Earth they defeat themselves, for they are cut off from books, and from that contact with civilized minds which is the only possible basis for a greater development.

"The danger is not, and never has been, from these remote slans but from those living in the big cities, where they are enabled to contact the greatest human minds and have, in spite of our precautions, some access to books. Obviously, this airship we saw today was built by slans who are living dangerously in the civilized centers."

Kier Gray nodded. "Much of what you surmise is probably true. But to get back to the letter, it goes on to say that these several million slans are only too anxious to end the period of strain which has existed between them and the human race. They denounce the ambition for world rule which actuated the first slans, explaining that ambition as due to a false conception of superiority, unleavened by the later experience that convinced them that they are not superior but merely different. They also accuse Samuel Lann, the human being and biological scientist who first created slans, and after whom slans are named—Samuel Lann: S. Lann: Slan—of fostering in his children the belief that they must rule the world. And that this belief, not any innate desire for domination, was the root of the disastrous ambitions of the early slans.

"Developing this idea, they go on to point out that the early inventions of the slans were simply minor improvements of already existing ideas. There has been, they claim, no really creative work done by the slans in physical science. They also state that their philosophers have come to the conclusion that the slans are not scientifically minded in any true sense of the word, differing from present-day human beings in that respect as widely as the ancient Greeks and Romans, who never developed science, as we know it, at all."

His words went on, but for a moment Kathleen heard with only half her mind. Could that be true? Slans not scientifically minded? Impossible. Science was simply an accumulation of facts, and the deduction of conclusions from those facts. And who better could bring divine order from intricate reality than the mighty-brained, full-grown, mature slan? She saw that Kier Gray was picking up a sheet of gray paper from his desk, and she brought her mind back to what he was saying.

"I'm going to read you the last page," he said in a colorless voice. " 'We cannot emphasize too strongly the importance of this. It means that slans can never seriously challenge the military might of human beings. Whatever improvements we may make on existing machinery and weapons will not decisively affect the outcome of a war, should such a disaster ever take place again.

" 'To our minds, there is nothing more futile than the present stalemate which, solving nothing, succeeds only in keeping the world in an unsettled condition and is gradually creating economic havoc from which human beings suffer to an ever increasing degree.

" 'We offer peace with honor, the only basis of negotiation to be that slans must hereafter have the legal right to life, liberty, and the pursuit of happiness.' "

Kier Gray laid the paper back on his desk, coldly flicked his gaze from face to face, and said in a flat, harsh voice, "I'm absolutely against any compromise whatever. I used to think that something could be done, but no longer! Every slan out there"—he waved his hand significantly to cover half the globe—"must be exterminated."

The room, with its subdued lights and paneled walls, seemed dimmer to Kathleen, as if a shadow had fallen across her vision. In the silence even the pulsation of thoughts from the men was a quiet vibration in her brain, like the beat of waves on a remote, primeval shore. A whole world of shock separated her mind from the sense made by those thoughts—shock at the realization of the change that had taken place in Kier Gray.

Or was it change? Was it not possible that this man was as remorseless in his outlook as John Petty? His reason for keeping her alive must be exactly as he had said, for study purposes. And, of course, there was the time when he had believed, rightly or wrongly, that his political future was bound up in her continued existence. But nothing else. No feeling of compassion or pity, no interest in a helpless young creature for the sake of that creature. Nothing but the most materialistic outlook on life. This was the ruler of men whom she had admired, almost worshiped, for years. This was her protector!

It was true, of course, that the slans were lying. But what else could they do in dealing with people who knew only hate and lies? At least it was peace they offered, not war; and here was this man rejecting, without any consideration, an offer that would end four hundred or more years of criminal persecution of her race.

With a start, she grew aware that Keir Gray's eyes were fixed on her. His lips curled in sarcastic mirth as he said, "And now, let us hear the so-called message you received in your—er—mental communication with the slan commander."

Kathleen looked at him desperately. He didn't believe a word of her claim, and in the face of his scathing skepticism she knew better than to offer anything but the most carefully thought out statement to the mercilessly logical brain of this man. She needed time.

"I—" she began. "It was—"

She suddenly realized that Jem Lorry was on his feet. He was frowning. "Kier," he said, "that was pretty sharp tactics, offering your unqualified opposition to a matter as important as this, without giving the council a chance to discuss it. In view of your action, I am left no alternative but to state—with qualifications, however—that I am in favor of accepting this offer. My main qualification is this—the slans must agree to be assimilated into the human race. To that end, slans cannot marry each other, but must always marry human beings."

Kier Gray stared at him without hostility. "What makes you think there can be issue from a slan-human mating?"

"That's something I am going to find out," said Jem Lorry in a voice so casual that only Kathleen caught the intensity in it. She leaned forward, holding her breath. "I've decided to take Kathleen here as my mistress, and we shall see what we shall see. Nobody objects, I hope."

The younger men shrugged. Kathleen didn't need to read their minds to see that they hadn't the slightest objection. She noticed that John Petty was paying no attention to the conversation at all, and Kier Gray seemed lost in thought, as if he hadn't heard, either.

With a gasp, she parted her lips to speak. Then shut them. A thought was suddenly in her brain. Suppose that intermarriage was the only solution to the slan problem. Suppose the council accepted Jem Lorry's solution! Even though she knew it to be based entirely on his passion for her, could she dare defend herself from him if there was the slightest possibility of those other slans out there agreeing to the plan, and thus ending hundreds of years of misery and murder?

She sank back in her chair, vaguely conscious of the irony of her position. She had come to the council chamber to fight for herself, and now she didn't dare utter a word. Kier Gray was speaking again.

"There is nothing new in this solution offered by Jem. Samuel Lann himself was intrigued by the possible result of such a mating and persuaded one of his granddaughters to marry a human being. No children were born of the union."

"I've got to prove that for myself!" said Jem Lorry doggedly. "This thing is too big to depend on one mating."

"There was more than one," Kier Gray said mildly.

Another man cut in impatiently. "The important thing is that assimilation does offer a solution, and there is no doubt that the human race will dominate the result. We're more than three and a half billion to, say, five million, which is probably a closer estimate than theirs. And even if no children can result, our ends are served in that, within two hundred years—figuring their normal life span at a hundred and fifty—there would be no slans alive."

It struck Kathleen with a shock that Jem Lorry had won his point. She saw in the vague, surface part of his mind that he had no intention of bringing the matter up again. Tonight he would send soldiers for her; and no one could say afterward that there had been any disagreement in the council. Their silence was consent.

For several minutes she was conscious only of a blur of voices, and of even more blurred thought. Finally, a phrase caught her mind. With an effort she turned her attention back to the men. The phrase "could exterminate them that way!" brought an electrifying awareness of how far they had gone from the original plan during those few minutes.

"Let us clarify this situation," said Kier Gray briskly. "The introduction of the idea of using some apparent agreement with the slans for exterminating them seems to have struck a responsive chord which—again—apparently seems to have eliminated from our various minds all thought of a true and honest agreement based on, for instance, the idea of assimilation.

"The schemes are, briefly, as follows. Number one. To allow them to intermingle with human beings until everyone has been thoroughly identified, then clamp down, catch most of them by surprise, and track the others down within a short time.

"Plan number two. Force all slans to settle on an island, say Hawaii, and once we've got them there surround the place with battleships and planes and annihilate them.

"Plan number three. Treat them harshly from the beginning; insist on fingerprinting and photographing them, and on a plan for reporting to police at intervals, which will have both an element of strictness and fairness in it. This third idea may appeal to the slans because, if carried out over a period of time, it will seem to safeguard all except a small percentage which will be calling at police headquarters on any particular day. Its strictness will have the further psychological value of making them feel that we're being hard and careful, and will therefore, paradoxically, gradually ease their minds."

The cold voice went on, but somehow the whole scene lacked reality. They couldn't be sitting there discussing betrayal and murder on such a vast scale—seven men deciding for all the human race on a matter of more than life and death.

"What fools you are," Kathleen said bitingly. "Do you imagine for one minute that slans would be taken in by your silly schemes? Slans can read minds, and besides, the whole thing is so transparent and ridiculous, every one of the schemes so open and barefaced, that I wonder how I could ever have thought any of you intelligent and clever."

They turned to stare at her silently, coldly. A faint, amused smile crinkled the lips of Kier Gray.

"I'm afraid you are at fault, not we. We assume that they are intelligent and suspicious, and therefore we do not offer any complicated idea; and that, of course, is the first element of successful propaganda. As for the reading of minds, we here shall never meet the slan leaders. We shall transmit our majority opinion to the other five councilors, who will conduct negotiations under the firm conviction that we mean fair play. No subordinate will have any instructions except that the matter is to be fairly conducted. So you see—"

"Just a minute," said John Petty, and there was so much satisfaction in his voice, such an exultant ring, that Kathleen turned toward him with a start. "Our main danger is not from ourselves but from the fact that this slan girl has overheard our plans. She has said that she was in mental communication with the commander of the slans on board the ship which approached the palace. In other words, they now know she is here. Suppose another ship comes near; she would then be in a position to inform our enemies of our plans. Naturally, she must be killed at once."

A mind-shattering dismay burned through Kathleen. The logic of the argument could not be gainsaid. She saw the gathering realization of it in the minds of the men. By trying so desperately to escape the attentions of Jem Lorry, she had walked into a trap that could end only in death.

Kathleen's gaze continued in fascination upon John Petty's face. The man was aglow with a deep-rooted pleasure that he could not hide. There was no doubt that he had not expected such a victory. Surprise made the thrill all the greater.

It was with reluctance that she turned from him and concentrated on the other men. The vague thoughts that had already come from them came now in a more concentrated form from each in turn. And there was no doubt about what they thought. Their decision gave no particular pleasure to the younger men who, unlike Jem Lorry, had no personal interest in her. But their conviction was an unalterable thing. Death.

It seemed to Kathleen that the finality of the verdict was written in the face of Jem Lorry. The man's manner, as he turned on her, showed his dismay.

"You damned little fool!" he said. With that he started to chew viciously on his lower lip, and sank back in his chair, staring moodily at the floor.

She was dazed now. She stared for a long moment at Kier Gray before she even saw him. With horror she watched the startled frown that creased his forehead, the unconcealed, thunderstruck expression in his eyes. That gave her an instant of courage. He didn't want her dead or he wouldn't be so alarmed.

The courage, and the hope that came with it, vanished like a star behind a black cloud. His very dismay showed that he had no solution to the problem that had dropped into the room like a bombshell. Slowly his expression changed to impassivity, but she felt no hope until he said, "Death would perhaps be the necessary solution if it were true that she was in communication with a slan aboard that ship. Fortunately for her, she was telling a lie. There were no slans on the plane. The ship was robot-propelled."

A man said, "I thought robot-propelled ships could be captured by radio interference with their mechanism."

"So they can," said Kier Gray. "You may remember how the slan ship darted straight upward when it disappeared. The slan controllers shot it off like that when they suddenly realized we were tampering successfully with their ship."

The leader smiled grimly. "We fought the ship down into the

swampland a hundred miles south of here. It was pretty badly wrecked, from all reports, and they haven't got it out yet; but it will be taken in due course to the great Cugden machine works, where, no doubt, its mechanism will be analyzed." He added, "The reason it took so long was that the robot mechanism was on a slightly different principle, requiring a new combination of radio waves to dominate it."

"All that is unimportant," John Petty said impatiently. "What counts is that this slan has been here in the room, has heard our plans to annihilate her people, and may therefore be dangerous to us in that she will do her best to inform other slans of what we contemplate. She must be killed."

Kier Gray stood up slowly, and the face he turned to John Petty was grim. His voice, when he spoke, held a metallic note. "I have told you, sir, that I am making a sociological study of this slan, and I will thank you to refrain from further attempts to execute her. You have said some hundred slans are caught and executed every month, and the slans claim that some eleven million others still exist. I hope"—and his voice was edged with sarcasm—"I hope I shall be permitted the privilege of keeping alive one slan for scientific purposes, one slan whom, apparently, you hate more than all the others put together—"

John Petty cut in sharply. "That's all very well, Kier. What I'd like to know is, why did Kathleen Layton lie about being in communication with the slans?"

Kathleen drew a deep breath. The chill of those few minutes of deadly danger was oozing out of her, but there was still a choked-up sensation of emotion. She said shakily, "Because I knew Jem Lorry was going to try to make me his mistress, and I wanted you to know that I objected."

She felt the tremor of thoughts that swept out from the men, and saw their facial expressions—understanding, then impatience.

"For heaven's sake, Jem," one exclaimed, "can't you keep your love affairs out of our council meetings?"

Another said, "With all due respect to Kier Gray, there is something intolerable about a slan objecting to anything that a human being with authority may plan for her. I am curious to see what the issue would be from such a mating. Your objections are overruled; and now, Jem, have your guard take her up to your apartment. And I hope that ends this discussion!"

For the first time in her seventeen years, it struck Kathleen that there was a limit to the nervous tension that a slan could endure. There was a tautness inside her, as if somewhere something vital was at the breaking point. She was conscious of no thought of her own. She just sat there, painfully gripping the plastic smoothness of the arms of her chair. Abruptly, she grew aware of a thought inside her brain, a sharp, lashing thought from Kier Gray.

"You little fool! How did you get yourself into this mess?"

She looked at him then, miserably, seeing for the first time that he was leaning back in his chair, eyes half closed, lips drawn tight.

He said finally, "All this would be very well if such matings needed testing. They don't. Case histories of more than a hundred slan-human attempts to reproduce children are available in the file library under the heading 'Abnormal Marriages.'

"The reasons for the sterility are difficult to define because men and slans do not appear to differ from each other to any marked degree. The amazingly tough musculature of the slan is due, not to a new type of muscle, but to a speeding up of the electro-explosions that actuate the muscles. There is also an increase in the number of nerves to every part of the body, making it tremendously more sensitive.

"The two hearts are not really two hearts, but a combination, each section of which can operate independent of the other. Nor are the two together very much larger than the one original. They're simply finer pumps.

"Again, the tendrils that send and receive thoughts are growths from formerly little-known formations at the top of the brain, which, obviously, must have been the source of all the vague mental telepathy known to earlier human beings and still practiced by people everywhere.

"So you see that what Samuel Lann did with his mutation machine to his wife, who bore him the first three slan babies—one boy and two girls—over six hundred years ago, has not added anything new to the human body, but changed or mutated what already existed."

It seemed to Kathleen that he was talking to gain time. In that one brief mental flash from him, there had been overtones of a complete understanding of the situation. He must know that no amount of reasonable argument could dissuade the passions of a man like Jem Lorry. She heard his voice go on.

"I am giving you this information because apparently none of you has ever bothered to investigate the true situation as compared to popular beliefs. Take, for instance, the so-called superior intelligence of the slan, referred to in the letter received from them today. There is an old illustration on that point which has been buried by the years; an experiment in which Samuel Lann, that extraordinary man, brought up a monkey baby, a human baby, and a slan baby under rigidly scientific conditions. The monkey was the most precocious, learning within a few months what the slan and the human baby required considerably longer to assimilate. Then the human and slan learned to talk, and the monkey was hopelessly outdistanced. The slan and the human continued at a fairly even pace until, at the age of four, the slan's powers of mental telepathy began painfully to operate. At this point, the slan baby forged into the lead.

"However, Doctor Lann later discovered that by intensification of the human baby's education, it was possible for the latter to catch up to, and remain reasonably level with, the slan, particularly in quickness of mind. The slan's great advantage was the ability to read minds, which gave him an unsurpassable insight into psychology and readier access to the education which the human child could grasp only through the medium of ears and eyes—"

John Petty interrupted in a voice that was thick and harsh. "What you're saying is only what I've known all along, and is the main reason why we can't begin to consider peace negotiations with these—these damned artificial beings. In order for a human being to equal a slan, he must strain for years to acquire what comes with the greatest of ease to the slan. In other words, all except the minutest fraction of humanity is incapable of ever being anything more than a slave in comparison to a slan. Gentlemen, there can be no peace, but rather an intensification of extermination methods. We can't risk one of the Machiavellian plans already discussed, because the danger of something going wrong is too great."

A councilor said, "He's right!"

Several voices echoed the conviction; and there was suddenly no doubt which way the verdict would go. Kathleen saw Kier Gray glance keenly from face to face.

He said, "If that is to be our decision, then I should consider it a grave mistake for any one of us at the present time to take this slan as mistress. It might give a wrong impression."

The silence that followed was the silence of agreement, and Kathleen's gaze leaped to Jem Lorry's face. He met her eyes coolly, rising languidly to his feet as she stood up and made for the door. As she passed he fell into step at her side.

He opened the door for her and spoke in a low voice. "It won't be for long, my lady. So don't build up false hopes." And he smiled confidently.

But it was not of his threat that Kathleen was thinking as she walked slowly along the corridor. She was remembering the thunderstruck expression that had come into Kier Gray's face at the moment John Petty had asked for her death.

It didn't fit. It didn't fit at all with his suave words of a minute later, when he had informed the others that the slan ship was robot-propelled and had been brought down in the marshes. If that were so, then why had he been startled? And if it weren't so, then Kier Gray had taken the terrible risk of lying for her and was probably even now worrying about it.

NINE

Jommy Cross stared urgently yet thoughtfully down at the human wreck that was Granny. There was no rage in him at her betrayal of him. The result was disaster, his future abruptly blank, unplanned, homeless.

His first problem was what to do with the old woman.

She sat blithely in a chair, an extravagantly rich and colorful dressing gown swaddled jauntily around her ungainly form. She giggled up at him. "Granny knows something; yes, Granny knows—" Her words trailed into nonsense, then. "Money, oh, good Lord, yes. Granny's got plenty of money for her old age. See!"

With the trusting innocence of a drink-sodden old soak, she slid a bulging black bag from inside her dressing gown, then with ostrichlike common sense jerked it back into hiding.

Jommy Cross was conscious of shock. It was the first time he had actually seen her money, although he had always known her various hiding places. But to have the stuff out here now, with a raid actually in progress—such stupidity deserved the furthest limits of punishment.

But still he stood undecided, becoming tenser as the first faint pressure of men's thoughts from outside the shack made an almost impalpable weight against his brain. Dozens of men, edging closer, the snub noses of their submachine guns protruding ahead of them. He frowned blackly. By all rights, he should leave the betrayer to face the rage of the baffled hunters, to face the law which said that every human being, without exception, who was convicted of harboring a slan must be hanged by the neck until dead.

Through his mind ran the nightmare picture of Granny on the way to the gallows, Granny shrieking for mercy, Granny fighting to prevent the rope from being placed around her neck, kicking, scratching, slobbering at her captors.

He reached down and grabbed her naked shoulders where the dressing-gown was loosely drawn. He shook her with a cold, deadly violence until her teeth rattled, until she sobbed with a dry, horrible pain, and a modicum of sanity came into her eyes. He said harshly, "It's death for you if you stay here. Don't you know the law?"

"Huh!" She sat up, briefly startled, then abruptly slipped off again into the cesspool of her mind.

Hurry, hurry, he thought, and forced his brain into that squalor of thought to see if his words had brought any basic balance. Just as he was about to give up he found a startled, dismayed, alert little section of sanity almost buried in the dissolving, incoherent mass that was her thoughts.

" 'S all right," she mumbled. "Granny's got plenty of money. Rich people don't get hung. Stands to reason."

Jommy stepped back from her, indecisive. The weight of the men's minds was a heavy, dragging thing on his brain. They were drawing ever nearer, drawing an ever tighter circle. Their number appalled him. Even the great weapon in his pocket might be useless if a hail of bullets swept the flimsy walls of the shack. And only one bullet was needed to destroy all his father's dreams.

"By God," he said aloud. "I'm a fool! What will I do with you even if I get you out? All highways out of the city will be blocked. There's only one real hope, and that will be almost hopelessly difficult even without a drunken old woman to hinder me. I don't fancy climbing a thirty-story building with you on my back."

Logic said he should abandon her. He half turned away; and then, once more, the thought of Granny being hanged came in all its horror. Whatever her faults, her very existence had made it possible for him to remain alive. That was a debt which must be paid. With a single snatching movement he tore the black bag from its hiding-place under Granny's dressing-gown. She grunted drunkenly, and then awareness seeped into her as he held the bag tantalizingly before her eyes.

"Look," he taunted, "all your money, your whole future. You'll starve. They'll have you scrubbing floors in the poorhouse. They'll whip you."

In fifteen seconds she was sober, a hot, burning soberness that grasped essentials with all the clarity of the hardened criminal.

"Granny'll hang!" she gasped.

"Now we're getting somewhere," Jommy Cross said. "Here, take your money." He smiled grimly as she grabbed it from him. "We've got a tunnel to go through. It leads from my bedroom to a private garage at the corner of 470th Street. I've got a key to the car. We'll drive down near the Air Center and steal one of—"

He stopped, conscious of the flimsiness of that final part of his plan. It seemed incredible that the tendrilless slans would be so poorly organized that he would actually be able to get one of those marvelous spaceships which they launched nightly into the sky. True, he had escaped from them once with absurd ease, but—

With a gasp, Jommy set the old woman down on the flat roof of the spaceship building. He collapsed beside her heavily and lay there panting. For the first time in his life he was conscious of muscular weariness contracted from exertion at the full of vibrant health.

"Good heaven," he breathed, "who'd have thought an old woman would weigh so much?"

She was snarling in retrospective terror from that frightful climb. His brain caught the first warning of the burst of vituperation that was rising to her lips. His weary muscles galvanized instantly. One swift hand clamped over her mouth.

"Shut up," he said, "or I'll drop you over the edge like a sack of potatoes. You're the cause of this situation, and you've got to bear the consequences."

His words acted like cold water. He had to admire the way she recuperated from the terror that had racked her. The old creature certainly had staying powers. She pulled his hand from her mouth and asked sullenly, "What now?"

"We've got to find a way into the building in as short a time as possible and—" He glanced at his wrist watch and, dismayed, leaped to his feet. Twelve minutes of ten! Twelve minutes before the rocketship took off. Twelve minutes to take control of that ship!

He snatched Granny up, flung her lightly over his shoulder, and raced off toward the center of the roof. Not only was there no time to search for doors but such doors would obviously be wired, and there was even less time to study and nullify the alarm system. There was only one way. Somewhere there must be the runway up which the ships were projected when they were launched toward the remote regions of interplanetary space.

He felt the difference beneath his feet, a vague rise, a gentle bulbousness. He stopped short, teetering on his toes, unbalanced by the violent ending of his racing flight. Carefully, he felt his way back to the

beginning of the bulbous section. That would be the edge of the runway. Swiftly he tore his father's atomic gun from his pocket. Its disintegrating fire flamed downward.

He peered through the four-foot-diameter hole into a tunnel that
sloped to depths at an angle that must have been a tight sixty degrees.
A hundred, two hundred, three hundred yards of glittering metallic
wall, and then the ship gradually took on outline as Jommy's eyes grew
accustomed to the dim light. He saw a torpedo-pointed nose, with forward blast tubes distorting the smooth, streamlined effect. It seemed a
deadly thing, silent and motionless now, yet menacing.

He had the illusion of staring down the barrel of a vast gun, at the
shell that was about to be fired. The comparison struck him so sharply
that for a long moment his mind refused to hold the thought of what
he must do. Doubt came. Did he dare slide down that glass-smooth
slipway when any second a rocketship would come smashing up toward
the sky?

His body felt cold. With an effort, he lifted his gaze from the paralyzing depth of tunnel and fixed his eyes, at first unseeing, then with
gathering fascination, on the distant, looming splendor of the palace.
His thought paused abruptly; slowly his body lost its tension. For long
seconds he just stood there, drinking in the glory of the immense, exquisite jewel that was the palace by night.

It was plainly visible from this height between and beyond two
great skyscrapers; and it glowed brilliantly. There was no mind-
staggering, eye-dazzling glare to it. It glowed with a soft, living, wonderful flame that was never the same color for more than an
instant—glorious, lambent fire that flickered and flashed a thousand
combinations, and each combination was subtly, sometimes startlingly,
different. Not once was there an exact repetition.

On and on it sparkled, and *lived!* Once, for a long moment, chance
turned the tower, that translucent five-hundred-foot fairy tower, a
glowing turquoise blue. And for that instant the visible part of the
palace below was nearly all a deeply glowing ruby red. For one
moment—and then the combination shattered into a million bursting
fragments of color—blue, red, green, yellow. No color, no possible
shade of color, was missing from that silent, flaming explosion.

A thousand nights he had fed his soul on its beauty, and now he
felt again the wonder of it. Strength poured from it into him. His
courage came back like the unbreakable, indestructible force it was.
His teeth clenched; grimly he stared down into the depths so sharply
angled, so smooth in the promise of madly swift passage to the distant,
steel-hard bottom.

The danger of it was like a symbol of his future. Blank future, less predictable now than it had ever been. It was only good sense to believe that the tendrilless slans were aware that he was here on this roof. There must be alarm systems—there *must* be.

"What do you keep staring down that hole for?" Granny whined. "Where's the door we want? Time is—"

"Time!" said Jommy Cross. His watch said four minutes to ten, and that seemed to shock every nerve in his body. Eight minutes actually gone, *four* minutes left in which to conquer a fortress. He caught Granny's thought then, her abrupt awareness of his intention. Just in time his hand slapped at her mouth, and her shriek of dismay was stifled against his palm. The next second they were falling, committed irrevocably.

They struck the tunnel surface almost gently, as if they had suddenly entered a world of slow motion. The slipway felt, not hard, but yielding beneath his body, and there was only the vaguest sense of motion. But his eyes and mind were not fooled. The blunt nose of the spaceship plunged up at them. The illusion of the ship roaring toward them in full blast was so real that he had to fight a wild impulse to panic.

"Quick!" he hissed at Granny. "Use the flat of your hands—*slow down!*"

The old woman needed no urging. Of all the instincts in her misused body, that of survival was strongest. She couldn't have screamed now to save her soul, but her lips blubbered with fear even as she fought for life. Her bead-like eyes glistened with a moist terror—but she fought! She clung at the gleaming metal, bony hands spread out flat and hard, her legs squeezed against the metal surface; and pitiful though the result was, it helped.

Abruptly, the nose of the ship loomed above Jommy Cross, higher than he had expected. With a desperate strength, he reached up at the first thick ring of rocket chambers. His fingers touched the corded, seared metal, skidded—and instantly lost their hold.

He fell back, and only then did he realize that he had risen to the full stretched-out height of his body. He fell hard, almost stunningly, but instantly, with the special strength of slan muscles, he was up again. His fingers caught one of the big tubes of the second ring of fire chambers with such unbreakable hold that the uncontrollable part of the journey ended. Sick from the strain of overeffort, he let go, and it was as he half sat there shaking the dizziness out of his head that he grew aware of the patch of light farther under the immense body of the machine.

The ship was curving so sharply now toward the tunnel floor on which it rested that he had to bend double as he made his way painfully toward it. He was thinking: An open door, here, now, a few short seconds before the great ship is due to leave. It is a door! An opening, two feet in diameter, in a foot-thick metal hull, with the hinged door leaning inward. He pushed up into the opening unhesitatingly, his terrible gun alert for the slightest movement. But there was no one.

In that first glance he saw that this was the control room. There were some chairs, an intricate-looking instrument board, and some great, curved, glowing plates on either side of it. And there was an open door leading to the second section of the ship. It took but a moment to leap inside and pull the panicky old woman after him. And then, lightly, he jumped for the connecting door.

At the threshold he paused cautiously and peered in. This second room was partly furnished with chairs, the same deep, comfortable chairs as were in the control room. But more than half the space was filled with chained-down packing-cases. There were two doors. One led to what was obviously a third section of the long ship. It was partly open, with more packing-cases visible beyond and, vaguely, a door leading into a fourth compartment. But it was the second door in the second room that made Jommy Cross freeze motionless where he was.

It was on the side beyond the chairs and led outside. A blaze of light poured from the great room there into the ship, and there were figures of men. He opened his mind wide. Instantly a thought wash from many brains came to him, so many of them that the combined leakage from behind their defective shields brought dozens of half thoughts, menacingly alert thoughts, as if scores of tendrilless slans out there were waiting for something.

He cut the thought off, whirled toward the instrument board that dominated the whole front part of the control room. The board itself was about a yard wide, two yards long, a metal-mounted bank of glowing tubes and shining mechanisms. There were more than a dozen control levels of various kinds, all within reach of the finely built chair facing them.

On either side of the instrument board were the great, curved, glossy, semimetallic plates he had already noticed. The concave surface of each towering section glowed with a subdued light of its own. It would be impossible to solve the alien control system in the few moments at his disposal. Tight-lipped, he sprang forward into the control chair. With swift, deliberately crude purpose, he activated every switch and lever on the panel.

A door clanged metallically. There was an abrupt, wonderful sense of lightness; swift, almost body-crushing forward movement, and then a faint, throbbing bass roar. Instantly the purpose of the great curved plates became apparent. On the one to the right appeared a picture of the sky ahead. Jommy could see lights and land far below, but the ship was mounting too steeply for the Earth to be more than a distortion at the bottom of the plate.

It was the left visiplate that showed the glory, a picture of a city of lights, so vast that it staggered the imagination, falling away behind the ship. Far to one side he caught the night splendor of the palace.

And then the city was gone into distance behind them. Carefully, he shut off the mechanisms he had actuated, watching for the effect of each in turn. In two minutes the complicated board was solved and the simple machinery under control. The purpose of four of the switches was not clear, but that could wait.

He leveled off, for it was no part of his intention to go out into airless space. That demanded intimate knowledge of every screw and plate in the machine, and his first purpose must be to establish a new, safe base of operations. Then, with his ship to take him where he willed to go—

His brain soared. There was in him suddenly an extravagant sense of power. A thousand things remained to be done, but at last he was out of his cage, old enough and strong enough, mentally and physically, to live a secure, defensive existence. There were years to be passed, long years that separated him from maturity. All his father's science must be learned, and used. Above all, his first real plan for finding the true slans must be carefully thought out and the first exploratory moves made.

The thought ended as he grew abruptly aware of Granny. The old woman's thought had been a gentle beat against his mind all these minutes. He was aware of her going into the next room, and deep in his mind was developing a picture of what she was seeing. And now—just like that—the picture went dead slow, as if she had suddenly closed her eyes.

Jommy Cross snatched his gun and simultaneously whirled and leaped to one side. There was a flash of fire from the doorway that seared across the place where his head had been. The flame touched the instrument board, then winked out. The tall, full-grown tendrilless slan woman standing in the doorway whipped the muzzle of her little silver gun toward him—then her whole body went rigid as she saw his weapon pointing at her. They stood like that for a long, frozen moment. The woman's eyes became glittering pools.

"You damned snake!"

In spite of anger, almost because of it, her voice was golden in its vibrant beauty, and abruptly Jommy Cross felt beaten. The sight of her and the sound of her brought sudden poignant memory of his glorious mother, and he knew with a sense of helplessness that he could no more blast this marvelous creature out of existence than he could have destroyed his own mother. In spite of his mighty gun threatening her as her weapon threatened him, he was actually at her mercy. And the way she had fired at his back showed the hot determination that burned behind those gleaming gray eyes. Murder! The mad hatred of the tendrilless slan against the true slan.

Dismayed though he was, Jommy studied her with growing fascination. Slimly, strongly, lithely built, she stood there, poised, alert, leaning forward on one foot a little breathlessly, like a runner tense for the race. Her right hand, holding the weapon, was a slender, finely shaped thing, beautifully tanned and supple-looking. Her left hand was half hidden behind her back, as if she had been walking briskly along, arms swinging freely, and then had frozen in mid-stride, one arm up and one swung back.

Her dress was a simple tunic, drawn in snugly at her waist; and what a proudly tilted head she had, hair gleaming dark brown, bobbed, and curled. Her face, below that crown of brown, was the epitome of sensitive loveliness, lips not too full, nose lean and shapely, cheeks delicately molded. Yet it was the subtle shaping of her cheeks that gave her face the power, the sheer intellectual forcefulness. Her skin looked soft and clear, the purest of unblemished complexions, and the gray of her eyes was darkly luminous.

No, he couldn't shoot; he couldn't blast this exquisitely beautiful woman out of existence. And yet—yet he must make her think that he could. He stood there, watching the surface of her mind, the little half thoughts that flicked across it. There was in her shield the same quality of incomplete coverage that he had already noticed in the tendrilless slans, due probably to their inability to read minds and therefore to realize what complete coverage actually meant.

For the moment he could not allow himself to follow the little memory vibrations that pulsed from her. All that counted was that he was standing here facing this tremendously dangerous woman, his weapon and her weapon leveled, every nerve and muscle in their two bodies pitched to the ultimate key of alertness.

The woman spoke first. "This is very foolish," she said. "We should sit down, put our weapons on the floor in front of us and talk this thing over. That would relieve the intolerable strain, but our positions would remain materially the same."

Jommy Cross felt startled. The suggestion showed a weakness in the face of danger that was not indicated anywhere in that highly courageous head and face. The fact that she had made it added instantly to the psychological strength of his position, but he was conscious of suspicion, a conviction that her offer must be examined for special dangers. He said slowly, "The advantage would be yours. You're a grown-up slan, your muscles are better coordinated. You could reach your gun faster than I could reach mine."

She nodded matter-of-factly. "That's true. But actually you have the advantage in your ability to watch at least part of my mind."

"On the contrary"—he spoke the lie smoothly—"when your mind shield is up the coverage is so complete that I could not possibly divine your purpose before it was too late."

The uttering of the words brought him awareness of how incomplete her coverage really was. In spite of his having kept his mind concentrated on danger and out of the trickling stream of her thought, enough had come through to give him a brief but coherent history of the woman.

Her name was Joanna Hillory. She was a regular pilot on the Martian Way, but this was to be her last trip for many months. The reason was that she had recently married an engineer stationed on Mars, and now she was going to have a baby—so she was being assigned to duties that put less strain on her system than the constant pressure of acceleration to which she was subjected in space travel.

Jommy Cross began to feel easier. A newlywed expecting a child was not likely to take desperate chances. He said, "Very well, let us put our guns down simultaneously and sit down."

When the guns were on the floor, Jommy Cross glanced across at the slan woman, puzzled by the faintly amused smile that twisted her lips. The smile became broader, more distinctly ironic. "And now that you have disarmed yourself," she said softly, "you will prepare to die!"

In utter dismay, Jommy Cross stared at the tiny gun that glittered in her left hand. She must have held the toy-sized weapon concealed there all those tense moments, awaiting with a mocking certainty the opportunity of using it. Her golden-rich voice, beautiful as music, went on.

"So you swallowed all that about my being a poor little bride, with a baby coming and an anxious husband waiting! A full-grown snake wouldn't have been so credulous. As it is, the young snake I'm looking at will die for his incredible stupidity."

TEN

Jommy Cross stared at the little gun held so firmly, so unwaveringly by the tendrilless slan woman. Through his shock and dismay he became suddenly aware of a background to his chagrin, the smooth-flowing enormously swift movement of the ship. There was no acceleration, simply that tireless, hurtling pace, the mile on mile of headlong flight with no indication whether they were still in Earth's atmosphere or in free space.

He stood there dismayed. His mind was free of terror, but it was also totally empty of any plan. All thought of action had been driven from his mind for the moment by the startling realization that he had been completely outwitted. The woman had used her very defects to defeat him.

She must have known her thought shield was faulty, and so, with almost animal cunning, she had allowed that pathetic little story to leak through, designed to show him that she would never, oh, never, have the courage for a fight to the finish. It was easy to see now that her courage was of a chilled-steel quality that he could not hope to equal for years.

He moved obediently to one side as she gestured menacingly, and then watched her alertly as she bent to pick up the two weapons on the floor, first her own, then his. But not for the barest instant did her eyes shift from him, and there was not a quiver of weakness in the way her gun pointed at him.

She put away the small weapon that had tricked him, kept her larger gun in her right hand, and, without a glance at his gun, locked it in a drawer beneath the glowing instrument board.

Her alertness left no hope that he might trick her into turning her weapon aside. The fact that she had not shot him immediately must mean that she wanted to talk to him first. But he could not leave that possibility to chance.

He said huskily, "Do you mind if I ask you a few questions before you kill me?"

"I'll ask the questions," she replied coolly. "There can be no purpose in your satisfying any curiosity you may have. How old are you?"

"Fifteen."

She nodded. "Then you are at a stage of mental and emotional development where you will appreciate even a few minutes' reprieve from death; and, like an adult human being, you will probably be pleased to know that so long as you answer my questions I will not pull the trigger of this electric-energy gun, though the final result will be death just the same."

Jommy Cross wasted no time in even thinking about her words. He said, "How do you know I'll tell the truth?"

Her smile was confident. "Truth is implicit in the cleverest lies. We tendrilless slans, lacking the ability to read minds, have been forced by necessity to develop psychology to the utmost limits. But never mind that. Were you sent to steal this ship?"

"No."

"Then who are you?"

Quietly he gave her a brief history of his life. As his story developed, he grew conscious that the woman's eyes were narrowing, lines of surprise gathering on her forehead.

"Are you trying to tell me," she cut in sharply, "that you are the little boy who came into the main offices of Air Center six years ago?"

He nodded. "It was a shock to find a crew so murderous that even a child must be destroyed forthwith. It—"

He stopped because the woman's eyes were aflame. "So it's come at last," she said slowly. "For six long years we've discussed and analyzed, uncertain whether we were right in letting you escape."

"You—let—me—escape!" gasped Jommy Cross.

She ignored him, went on as if she hadn't heard. "And ever since we've waited anxiously for a follow-up from the snakes. We were pretty sure they wouldn't betray us because they wouldn't want our greatest invention, the spaceship, to fall into the hands of human beings. The main question in our minds was, what was behind that first exploratory maneuver? Now, in your attempted theft of a rocketship, we have the answer."

Startled into silence, Jommy Cross listened to the mistaken analysis. Dismay grew in him. Dismay that had nothing to do with his personal danger. It was the incredible insanity of this slan-versus-slan war. The deadliness of it was almost beyond imagination. Joanna Hillory went on in her vibrant voice, tinged now with triumph.

"It's good to know for sure what we have so long suspected, and the evidence is almost overwhelming now. We have explored the Moon, Mars, and Venus. We have gone as far afield as the moons of Jupiter, and not once have we seen an alien spaceship or the faintest sign of a snake.

"The conclusion is inescapable. For some reason, perhaps because their revealing tendrils make it necessary for them to be ever on the move, they have never developed the antigravity screens that make the rocketship possible. Whatever the reason, the chain of logic points inexorably to the fact that they do lack space travel."

"You and your logic," said Jommy Cross, "are beginning to be very tiresome. It seems unbelievable that a slan could be so wrong. For just one second, take a reasonable attitude and assume, just assume, that my story is true."

She smiled, a thin smile that barely touched her lips. "From the beginning, there were only two possibilities. The first one I have already outlined. The other—that you actually have had no contact with slans—has worried us for years.

"You see, if you were sent by the slans, then they already knew we controlled Airways. But if you were an independent slan, then you had a secret that sooner or later, when you did contact the snakes, would be dangerous to us. In short, if your story is true, we must kill you to prevent you at some future date from apprising them of your special knowledge, and because it is our policy to take no chances whatsoever with snakes. In any case, you are as good as dead."

Her words were harsh, her tone icy. But far more menacing than her tone, Jommy realized, was the fact that neither right nor wrong, truth nor untruth, mattered to this slan woman. His world was shattering before the thought that if this immorality was slan justice, then slans had nothing to offer the world that could begin to match the sympathy, kindliness, and pervading gentleness of spirit that he had seen so often in the minds of the lowly human beings. If all adult slans were like this, then there was no hope.

His mind hovered over the fearful, dizzying gulf of the senseless feud between slan, human being, and tendrilless slan, and a thought more dark and terrible than night swept him. Was it really possible that his father's great dreams and greater works were to be blotted out in a solitary waste of nothingness, destroyed and ruined by these insane fratricides? The papers of his father's secret science, which he had removed from the catacombs such a short time before, were in his pockets; they would be used and abused by the cruel, merciless tendrilless slans if this woman carried out her desire to kill him. In spite of logic, in spite of the certainty that he could not hope to catch a full-grown slan off guard, he must stay alive in order to prevent that from happening.

His gaze narrowed on her face, conscious of the shadowy lines of thought in her forehead, a thoughtfulness that yet did not interfere with her alertness.

The lines smoothed as she said, "I have been considering your special case. I have, of course, authority to destroy you without consulting our council. The question is, does the problem you present merit their attention? Or will a brief report be sufficient? It is not a question of mercy, so allow yourself no hope."

But hope did come. It would take time to take him before the council, and time was life. He said urgently, yet conscious of the need for calm words, "I must admit my own reason is paralyzed by the feud between slan and tendrilless slan. Don't your people realize how tremendously the entire slan position would improve if you would co-operate with the 'snakes,' as you call them? Snakes! The very word is a proof of intellectual bankruptcy, suggestive of a propaganda campaign, replete with slogans and emotion words."

The gray fire came back into her eyes, but there was scathing mockery in her voice. "A little history may enlighten you on the matter of slan co-operation. For nearly four hundred years there have been tendrilless slans. Like the true slans, they're a distinct race, being born without tendrils, which is the only differentiation from the snakes. For security's sake, they formed communities in remote districts where the danger of discovery was reduced to a minimum. They were prepared to be completely friendly with the true slans against the common enemy—human beings!

"What was their horror, then, to find themselves attacked and murdered, their carefully built up, isolated civilization destroyed by fire and weapon—by the true slans! They made desperate efforts to establish contact, to become friends, but it was useless. They finally discovered that only in the highly dangerous, human-controlled cities could they find any safety. There the true slans, because of their revealing tendrils, dared not venture.

"Snakes!" The mockery was gone from her voice. Only a hard bitterness remained. "What other word can possibly fit? We don't hate them, but we have a sense of utter frustration and distrust. Our policy of destroying them is pure self-defense, but it has become a ruthless, unyielding attitude."

"But surely your leaders could talk things over with them?"

"Talk things over with whom? In the last three hundred years we have never located a single hiding-place of the true slan. We've captured some that attacked us. We've killed a few in running fights. But we've never discovered anything about them. They exist, but where and how and what their purpose is we haven't the faintest idea. There is no greater mystery on the face of the Earth."

Jommy Cross interrupted tensely. "If this is true, if you're not lying, please, madam, let your shield down for a moment so that I can be sure that your words are true! I, too, have thought this feud insane ever since I first discovered that there were two kinds of slans, and that they were at war. If I could become absolutely convinced that the madness is one-sided, why, I could—"

Her voice, sharp as a slap in the face, cut across his words. "What would you do? Help us? Are you under the impression that we would ever believe such an intention, and allow you to go free? The more you talk, the more dangerous I consider you. We have always made the assumption that a snake, by reason of his ability to read minds, is our superior, and therefore must not be given time to effect an escape. Your youth has saved you for ten minutes, but now that I know your story I can see no purpose in keeping you alive. Furthermore, there seems no reason why your case should be brought before the council. One more question—then you die!"

Jommy Cross stared angrily at the woman. There was no friendliness in him now, no sense of any kinship between this woman and his mother. If she were telling the truth, then it was the tendrilless slans he should sympathize with, not the mysterious, elusive true slans who were acting with such incomprehensible ruthlessness. But sympathy or no, every word she had spoken showed more clearly how dangerous it would be to allow the mightiest weapon the world would ever know to fall into this seething hell's brew of hatred. He must defeat this woman, must save himself. *Must.*

He said swiftly, "Before you ask that last question, consider seriously what an unprecedented opportunity has come to you. Is it possible that you are going to allow hatred to distort your reason? According to your statement, for the first time in the history of tendrilless slans you have caught a tendriled slan who is absolutely convinced that the two types of slans should cooperate instead of fight."

"Don't be silly," she said. "Every slan we've ever caught was willing to promise anything."

The words were like so many blows, and Jommy Cross shrank from them, feeling beaten, his argument smashed. In his deepest

thoughts, he had always pictured adult slans as noble creatures, digni-
fied, contemptuous of captors, conscious of their marvelous superiority. But—willing to promise anything! He hurried on, desperately
anxious to retrieve his position.

"That doesn't change this particular situation. You can verify practically everything I've said about myself. About my mother and father
being killed. The fact that I had to flee the home of the old junk
woman in the next room, whom you hit over the head, after I had lived
with her ever since I was a child. Everything will fit in to prove that I
am what I claim to be—a true slan who has never had any relationship
with the secret slan organization. Can you lightly ignore the opportunity offered here? First, you and your people must help me find the
slans, then I shall act as liaison officer, establish contact for you for the
first time in your history. Tell me, have you ever learned why the true
slans hate your people?"

"No." She spoke doubtfully. "We've had ridiculous statements
from captured slans to the effect that they are simply not tolerating the
existence of any variation of slan. Only the perfect result of Samuel
Lann's machine must survive."

"Samuel—Lann's—machine!" Jommy Cross felt abruptly almost
physically torn, his thread of thought ripped out by the roots. "Are you
actually—do you mean it's true that slans were originally machine-
made?"

He saw that the woman was staring at him, frowning, her brows
sharply knit. She said slowly, "I'm almost beginning to believe your
story. I thought every slan knew of Samuel Lann's use of a mutation
machine on his wife. Later, during the nameless period that followed
the slan war, use of the mutation machine produced a new species, the
tendrilless slans. Didn't your parents find out anything about such
things?"

"That was supposed to be my job," Jommy Cross said unhappily.
"I was to do the exploring, the contacting, while Dad and Mother prepared the—"

He stopped in angry self-annoyance. This was no time to make an
admission that his father had devoted his life to science and wouldn't
waste a single day on a search he had believed would be long and difficult. The first mention of science might lead this acutely intelligent
woman to an examination of his gun. She obviously believed the instrument to be a variation of her own electric-energy weapon. He
went on.

"If those machines are still in existence, then all these human accusations that slans are making monsters out of human babies are true."

"I've seen some of the monsters." Joanna Hillory nodded. "Failures, of course. There are so many failures."

It seemed to Jommy Cross that he was past shock. All the things that he had believed for so long, believed with passion and pride, were tumbling like so many card houses. The ugly lies were not lies. Human beings were fighting a Machiavellian scourge almost inconceivable in its inhumanity. He grew aware that Joanna Hillory was talking.

"I must admit that, in spite of my conviction that the council will destroy you, the points you have raised do constitute a very particular situation. I have decided to take you before them."

It required a long moment for the meaning of her words to penetrate; and then—a wild, surging relief leaped along his nerves. It was like an intolerable weight lifting, lifting. There came an extravagant sense of buoyancy. At last he had what he needed so desperately: time, precious time! Given time, pure chance might aid him to escape.

He watched the woman as she moved cautiously over to the great instrument board. There was a click as her finger pressed a button. Her first words reached up, to the heights where his hopes poised, and dragged them to the uttermost low.

She said, "Calling the members of the council. Urgent. Please tune in at once to 7431 for immediate judgment on a special slan case."

Immediate judgment! He felt angry at himself for having had hope at all. He should have known that it wouldn't be necessary to take him physically before the council, when their radio science canceled all dangers from such delay. Unless the council members understood a different logic than Joanna Hillory, he was through.

The waiting silence that followed was more apparent than real. There was the continuous thin, beating roar of the rockets, the fainter hiss of air against the outer shell which meant that the ship was still flying through the thick sheaf of Earth's atmosphere. And there was the insistent thought stream of Granny—the whole combining into anything but silence.

The impression smashed into fragments. Granny. Granny's active, *conscious* thought stream. Joanna Hillory, in meeting first his resistance, then pausing to question him instead of killing him instantly, had given Granny time to recuperate from the blow, which the slan woman had—obviously now—designed for temporary purposes only, to gain a silent approach on his rear. A killing blow might have made a distinct thud for ears as sensitive as his. The light one had not been effective for long. The old scoundrel was awake. Jommy opened his mind wide to the flood of Granny's thought.

"Jommy, she'll kill us both. But Granny's got a plan. Make some sign that you've heard her. Tap your feet. Jommy, Granny's got a plan to stop her from killing us."

Over and over came the insistent message, never quite the same, always accompanied by extraneous thought and uncontrollable digressions. No human brain as ill trained as Granny's could hold a completely straightforward thought. But the main theme was there. Granny was alive. Granny was aware of danger. And Granny was prepared to cooperate to desperate lengths to avert that danger.

Casually, Jommy Cross began to tap his feet on the floor, harder, louder, until—

"Granny hears." He stopped his tapping. Her excited thought went on. "Granny really has two plans. The first is for Granny to make a loud noise. That will startle the woman and give you a chance to leap on her. Then Granny will rush in to help. The second plan is for Granny to get up from the floor where she's lying, sneak over to your door, and then jump in at the woman when she passes near the door. She'll be startled, and instantly you can leap for her. Granny will call 'One,' then 'Two!' Tap your feet after the plan number you think best. Think them over for a moment."

No thought was required. Plan One he instantly rejected. No loud noise would really distract the calm nerves of a slan. A physical attack, something concrete, was the only hope.

"One!" said Granny into his mind. He waited, ironically aware of the anxious overtones in her thought, the forlorn hope that he would find Plan One satisfactory and so lessen the danger to her own precious skin. But she was a practical old wretch, and deep in her brain was the conviction that Plan One was weak. At last her mind reluctantly pumped out the word "Two!"

Jommy Cross tapped his feet. Simultaneously, he grew aware that Joanna Hillory was talking into her radio, giving his history and his proposal of co-operation, finally offering her own opinion that he must be destroyed.

The remote thought came to Jommy Cross that a few minutes before he would have been sitting almost with bated breath following the discourse, and the answers that began to come in one by one from the hidden loudspeaker. Deep-toned voices of men; the rich, vibrant tones of women! But now he scarcely more than followed the thread of their arguments. He was aware of some disagreement. One of the women wanted to know his name. For a long moment it didn't strike him that he was being directly addressed.

"Your name?" said the radio voice.

Joanna Hillory moved away from the radio toward the door. She said sharply, "Are you deaf? She wants to know your name."

"Name!" said Jommy Cross, and a portion of his mind registered surprise at the question. But nothing could really distract him at this supreme moment. It was now or never. As he tapped his feet, every extraneous thought was gone out of his brain. He was only aware of Granny standing behind the door, and of the vibrations that poured from her. The tensing of her body, the poising for action and, at the last moment, terror. He waited helplessly while she stood there, her ravaged body threatened with paralysis.

It was the thousand illegal forays she had made in her black career that rose up to give her strength. She launched into the room. Eyes glittering, teeth bared, she lunged against the back of Joanna Hillory. Her thin arms embraced the arms and shoulders of the slan woman.

Flame sparkled as the weapon in Joanna Hillory's fingers discharged in futile fury at the floor. Then, like an animal, the young woman spun with irresistible strength. For one desperate moment Granny clung to her shoulders. It was the one all-necessary moment. In that instant, Jommy Cross sprang.

In that instant, too, came a shrill squawk from Granny. Her clawlike hands were torn from their holds, and the gaunt, dark body skidded along the floor.

Jommy Cross wasted no time trying to match a strength he felt sure was beyond his present powers to equal. As Joanna Hillory whirled toward him like a tigress, he struck one hard, swift blow across her neck with the edge of his hand. It was a dangerous blow; and it required perfect coordination of muscles and nerves. It could easily have broken her neck; instead, it skillfully and efficiently knocked her unconscious. He caught her as she fell, and even as he lowered her to the floor, his brain was reaching into hers, past the broken shield, searching swiftly. But the pulse of her unconscious brain was too slow, the kaleidoscope of pictures too frozen.

He began to shake her gently, watching the shifting pattern of her thoughts, as the steady physical movement brought quick, subtle chemical changes in her body, which in turn changed the very shape of her thoughts. Still, there was no time for detail; and, as the outline of pictures grew more terrible in its menace, he abruptly deserted her and rushed to the radio.

In as normal a voice as he could manage, he called, "I'm still willing to discuss friendly terms. I could be a great help to the tendrilless slans." No answer. More urgently, he repeated his words, and added,

"I'm anxious to come to an arrangement with an organization as powerful as yours. I'll even return the ship if you can show me logically how I can escape without putting myself in a trap."

Silence! He clicked off the radio and, turning, stared grimly at Granny, who was half sitting, half lying on the floor.

"No dice," he said. "All this, this ship, this slan woman, is only part of a trap in which nothing has been left to chance. There are seven heavily armed hundred-thousand-ton cruisers trailing us at this very moment. Their finder instruments react to our antigravity plates, so even the darkness is no protection. We're finished."

The hours of night dragged, and with each passing moment the problem of what to do grew more desperate. Of the four living things up there in that blue-black sky, only Granny sprawled in one of the pneumatic chairs in uneasy sleep. The two slans, and that tireless, throbbing, hurtling ship, remained awake.

Fantastic night! On the one hand was the knowledge of the destroying power that might strike at any minute; and on the other hand—Fascinated, Jommy Cross stared into the visiplate at the wondrous picture that sped beneath him. It was a world of lights, shining in every direction as far as the eye could see—lights and more lights. Splashes, pools, ponds, lakes, oceans of light—farm communities, villages, towns and cities, and, every little while, mile on mile of megalopolitan colossus. At last his gaze lifted from the visiplate and he turned to where Joanna Hillory sat, her hands and feet tied. Her gray eyes met his brown ones questioningly. Before he could speak, she said, "Well, have you decided yet?"

"Decided what?"

"When you're going to kill me, of course."

Jommy Cross shook his head slowly, gravely. "To me," he said quietly, "the appalling thing about your words is the mental attitude that assumes that one must either deliver or receive death. I'm not going to kill you. I'm going to release you."

She was silent for a moment, then: "There's nothing surprising about my attitude. For a hundred years the true slans killed my people at sight; for hundreds of years now we have retaliated. What could be more natural?"

Jommy Cross shrugged impatiently. There was too much uncertainty in him about the true slans to permit him to discuss them now when his whole mind must be concentrated on escape.

He said, "My interest is not in this futile, miserable, three-cornered war among human beings and slans. The important thing is the seven warships that are trailing us at this minute."

"It's too bad you found out about them," the slan woman said quietly. "Now you will spend the time in useless worry and planning. It would have been so much less cruel for you to have considered yourself safe and, then, the very moment you discovered you were not, to die."

"I'm not dead yet!" Jommy Cross said, and impatience was suddenly sharp in his tone. "I have no doubt it is presumptuous of a half-grown slan to assume, as I am beginning to, that there must be a way out of this trap. I have the greatest respect for adult slan intelligence, but I do not forget that your people have now suffered several preliminary defeats. Why, for instance, if my destruction is so certain, are those ships waiting? Why wait?"

Joanna Hillory was smiling, her fine, strong face relaxed. "You don't really expect me to answer your questions, do you?"

"Yes." Jommy Cross smiled, but without humor. He went on in a tight, clipped voice. "You see, I've grown somewhat older during the past few hours. Until last night I was really very innocent, very idealistic. For instance, during those first few minutes when we were pointing our guns at each other, you could have destroyed me without resistance on my part. To me, you were a member of the slan race, and all slans must be united. I couldn't have pulled the trigger to save my soul. You delayed, of course, because you wanted to question me, but the opportunity was there. That situation exists no longer."

The woman's perfect lips pursed in sudden, frowning thought. "I think I'm beginning to see what you're getting at."

"It's really very simple." Jommy Cross nodded grimly. "You either answer my questions or I'll knock you over the head and obtain the information from your unconscious mind."

The woman began. "How do you know I'll tell the tru—" She stopped, her gray eyes widening with apprehension as she glared at Jommy. "Do *you* expect—"

"I do!" He stared ironically into her glowing, hostile eyes. "You will lower your mind shield. Of course, I don't expect absolutely free access to your brain. I have no objection to your controlling your thoughts on a narrow range all around the subject. But your shield must go down—now!"

She sat very still, body rigid, gray eyes agleam with repugnance. Jommy Cross's gaze was curious.

"I'm amazed," he said. "What strange complexes develop in minds that have no direct contact with other minds. Is it possible that tendrilless slans have built up little sacred, secret worlds within themselves and, like any sensitive human being, feel shame at letting outsiders see that world? There is material here for psychological study that may reveal the basic cause of the slan-versus-slan war. However, let that go."

He finished: "Remember that I have already been in your mind. Remember, also, that according to your own logic, in a few hours I will be blotted out forever in a blaze of electric projectors."

"Of course," she said quickly, "that is true. You will be dead, won't you? Very well, I'll answer your questions."

Joanna Hillory's mind was like a book whose thickness could not be measured, with almost an infinity of pages to examine, an incredibly rich, incredibly complex structure embroidered with a billion billion impressions garnered through the years by an acutely observant intellect. Jommy Cross caught swift, tantalizing glimpses of her recent experiences. There was, briefly, the picture of an unutterably bleak planet, low-mountained, sandy, frozen, everything frozen—Mars! There were pictures of a gorgeous, glass-enclosed city, of great machines digging under a blazing battery of lights. Somewhere it was snowing with a bitter, unearthly fury—and a black spaceship, glittering like a dark jewel in the sun, was briefly visible through a thick plateglass window.

The confusion of thoughts cleared as she began to talk. She spoke slowly, and he made no attempt to hurry her, in spite of his conviction that every second counted, that at any minute now death would blast from the sky at his defenseless ship. Her words and the thoughts that verified them were as bright-cut as so many gems, and as fascinating.

The tendrilless slans had known from the moment he started to climb the wall that an interloper was coming. Interested primarily in his purpose, they made no effort to stop him when he could have been destroyed without difficulty. They left several ways open for him to get to the ship, and he had used one of them, although—and here was an unknown, unexpected factor—the particular alarms of that way had not gone off.

The reason the warships were slow in destroying him was that they hesitated to use their searchlights over a continent so densely inhabited. If he should climb high enough or go out to sea, the ship would be quickly destroyed. On the other hand, if he chose to circle around on the continent, his fuel would waste away in a dozen hours or so, and before that, dawn would come and enable the electric projectors to be used with brief, deadly effect.

"Suppose," said Jommy Cross, "I should land in the downtown section of a great city. I could very possibly escape among so many houses, buildings, and people."

Joanna Hillory shook her head. "If this ship's speed falls below two hundred miles per hour, it will be destroyed, regardless of the risk involved, regardless of the fact that they hope to save my life by capturing the ship intact. You can see I'm being very frank with you."

Jommy Cross was silent. He was convinced, overwhelmed by the totality of the danger. There was nothing clever about the plan. Here was simply a crude reliance on big guns and plenty of them. "All this," he marveled at last, "for one poor slan, one ship. How mighty the fear must be that prompts so much effort, so much expense, for so little return!"

"We have put the snake outside our law," came the cool reply. Her gray eyes glowed with a quiet fire. Her mind concentrated on the single track of her words. "Human courts do not release prisoners because it will cost more to convict them than the amount of the theft. Besides, what you have stolen is so precious that it would be the greatest disaster in our history if you escaped."

He felt abruptly impatient. "You assume far too readily that the true slans are not already in possession of the antigravity secret. My purpose during the coming years is to analyze the true slans to their hiding-place; and I can tell you now that practically everything you have told me I shall not use as evidence. The very fact that they are so completely hidden is an indication of their immense resourcefulness."

Joanna Hillory said, "Our logic is very simple. We have not seen them in rocketships—so they have no rocketships. Even yesterday, in that ridiculous flight to the palace, their craft; while very pretty, was powered by multiple-pulse jet motors, a type of engine we discarded a hundred years ago. Logic, like science, is deduction on the basis of observation, so—"

Jommy Cross frowned unhappily. Everything about the slans was wrong. They were fools and murderers. They had started a stupid, ruthless, fratricidal war against the tendrilless slans. They sneaked around the country, using their diabolical mutation machines on human mothers—and the monstrosities that resulted were destroyed by medical authorities. Mad, purposeless destruction! And it simply didn't fit!

It didn't fit with the noble character of his father and his mother. It didn't fit with his father's genius, or with the fact that for six years he himself had lived under the influence of Granny's squalid mind and remained untouched, unsoiled. And, finally, it didn't fit with the fact that he, a half-grown true slan, had braved a trap he did not even suspect and because of one loophole in their net, one unknown factor, had so far escaped their vengeance.

His atomic gun! The one factor that they still didn't suspect. It would be useless, of course, against the battle cruisers coasting along in the blackness behind him. It would take a year or more to build a projector with a beam big enough to reach out and tear those ships to pieces. But one thing it could do. What it *could* touch, its shattering fire would disintegrate into component atoms. And, by God! he had the answer, given time and a little luck.

The glare of a searchlight splashed against his visiplates. Simultaneously, the ship jumped like some toy that had been struck an intolerable blow. Metal squeaked, walls shook, lights blinked, and then, as the sounds of violence died into little menacing whispers, he bounded from the depths of the chair into which he had been flung and snatched at the rocket activator.

The machine leaped forward in dizzy acceleration. Against the pressure of plunging fury, he reached forward and clicked on the radio.

The battle was on, and unless he could persuade them to desist, the chance to put his one lone plan into action would never come. The rich, vibrant voice of Joanna Hillory echoed the thought that beat in his mind.

"What are you going to do—talk them out of what they plan to do? Don't be so silly. If they finally decided to sacrifice me, you don't think they'd give *your* welfare any consideration, do you?"

ELEVEN

Outside, the night sky was dark. A sprinkling of stars glittered coldly in the moonless night. There was no sign of an enemy ship, not a shadow, not a movement against the immensity of turgid, deep, deep blue ceiling.

Inside, the tense silence was shattered by a hoarse choking cry from the next room. An angry barrage of vituperation followed. Granny was awake.

"What's the matter? What's happened?"

Brief silence, and then abrupt end of anger and mad beginning of fear. Instantly, her terrified thought poured out in frantic flood. Obscene curses, born of fear, assailed the air. Granny didn't want to die. Kill all slans, but not Granny. Granny had money to—

She was drunk. The sleep had allowed the liquor to take control of her again. Jommy Cross shut her thoughts and her voice out of his mind. Urgently he spoke into the radio.

"Calling the commander of the warships! Calling the commander! Joanna Hillory is alive. I am willing to release her at dawn, the only condition being that I be allowed to get up into the air again."

There was silence, then a woman's quiet voice entered the room. "Joanna, are you there?"

"Yes, Marian."

"Very well," the calm voice of the other went on. "We accept on the following conditions. You will inform us an hour before the actual landing where it will be. The point of landing must be at least thirty miles—that is, five minutes allowing for acceleration and deceleration—from the nearest large city. We assume, of course, that you believe you can escape. Very well. You will have two hours more of opportunity. We shall have Joanna Hillory. A fair exchange!"

"I accept," said Jommy Cross.

"Wait!" cried Joanna Hillory. But Jommy Cross was too quick for her. A second before the word jerked from her lips, his finger flicked off the radio switch.

He whirled on her. "You shouldn't have put up your mind shield. It was all the warning I needed. But, of course, I had you either way. If you hadn't put up the shield, I would have caught the thought in your brain." His eyes glinted at her suspiciously. "What is this sudden mad passion to sacrifice yourself simply to deny me two hours more of life?"

She was silent. Her gray eyes were more thoughtful than he had seen them all night.

He mocked gently, "Can it be that you actually grant me the possibility of escape?"

"I've been wondering," she said, "why the alarms back in the spaceship building didn't warn us of the exact way you approached this ship. There is a factor here that apparently we did not take into account. If you should really escape with this ship—"

"I shall escape," Jommy Cross said quietly, "and I shall live in spite of human beings, in spite of Kier Gray and John Petty and the ghoulish crew of murderers that live in the palace. I shall live in spite of the vastness of the tendrilless slan organization and their murderous intentions. And some day I shall find the true slans. Not now, for no youth can hope to succeed where the tendrilless slans in their thousands have failed. But I shall find them, and on that day—" He stopped, then gravely: "Miss Hillory, I want to assure you that neither this nor any other ship will ever be turned against your people."

"You speak very rashly," she replied with sudden bitterness. "How can you assure anything in the name of those ruthless creatures who dominate the councils of the snakes?"

Jommy Cross gazed down at the woman. There was truth in her words. And yet, something of the greatness that was to be his came to him in that moment as he sat there in that finely built control room, with its glittering instrument board, the shining visiplates, his body deep in the beautifully constructed chair. He was his father's son, heir to the products of his father's genius. Given time, he would be lord of irresistible power.

The soft flame of those thoughts was in his voice as he said, "Madam, in all modesty I can say that, of all the slans in the world today, there is none more important than the son of Peter Cross. Wherever I go my words and my will shall have influence. The day that I find the true slans, the war against your people will end forever. You have said that my escape would be disaster for the tendrilless slans; rather, it will be their greatest victory. Some day you and they will realize that."

"Meanwhile," the slan woman smiled grimly, "you have two hours to escape seven heavy cruisers owned by the real rulers of the Earth. What you do not seem to realize is that we actually fear neither human being nor snake, that our organization is vast beyond imagination. Every village, every town, every city has its quota of tendrilless slans. We know our power, and one of these days we shall come out into the open, take control and—"

"It would mean war!" Jommy Cross flared.

Her answer was cold. "We'll smash everything they've got within two months."

"And then what? What about human beings in that afterworld? Do you contemplate four billion slaves in perpetuity?"

"We are immeasurably their superiors. Shall *we* live in endless hiding, endure privation on the colder planets when we long for the green Earth and freedom from this eternal fight against nature—and against the men whom you defend so valiantly? We owe *them* nothing but pain. Circumstances force us to repay with interest!"

Jommy Cross said, "I foresee disaster for everyone."

The woman shrugged and went on. "The factor that worked in your favor back at the Air Center, when our attitude was the negative one of waiting for events, cannot possibly help you now, when our attitude is the utterly positive one of destroying you with our heaviest weapons. One minute of fire will burn this machine to ashes that will fall to earth in a fine sprinkling of dust."

"One minute!" Jommy Cross exclaimed.

He stopped short. He hadn't dreamed the time limit would be so short, and that now he had to depend on a flimsy psychological hope that the speed of his ship would lull their suspicions.

He said harshly, "Enough of this damn talk. And I'll have to carry you into the next room. I've got to rig up a vise at the inside of the nose of the ship, and I can't let you see what I put in that vise."

For a moment before Jommy Cross landed he saw the lights of the city to the west. Then the wall of a valley blotted the flashing sea of brilliance from his view. Soft as thistledown, the rocketship touched the ground and floated there with an unearthly buoyance as Jommy Cross set the antigravity plates at balancing power. He clicked open the door and then untied the slan woman.

Her electric gun in hand (his own weapon was fastened in the vise he had set up), he watched Joanna Hillory poised for a moment in the doorway. Dawn was breaking over the hills to the east, and the light, still a sickly gray, made a queer silhouette of her strong, shapely figure. Without a word, she jumped to the ground below. As he stepped forward to the threshold he could see her head on a level now with the bottom of the doorway, reflecting the flood of light from inside the ship.

Her head turned, and the face that looked up at him was marked by deep, thoughtful lines. She said, "How do you feel?"

He shrugged. "A little shaky, but death seems remote and not applicable to me."

"It's more than that," was the earnest reply. "The nervous system of a slan is an almost impregnable fortress. It cannot really be touched by insanity or 'nerves' or fear. When we kill, it is because of policy arrived at through logic. When death approaches our personal lives, we accept the situation, fight to the last in the hope of an unpredictable factor turning up to save us, and finally, reluctantly, give up the ghost, conscious that we have not lived in vain."

He stared at her curiously, his mind projecting against hers, feeling of the gentle pulsing of overtones, the strange half-friendliness that was in her voice and overflowed from her mind. His eyes narrowed. What purpose was forming in her alert, sensitive, unsentimental brain?

She went on. "Jommy Cross, it may surprise you to know that I have come to believe your story, and that you are not only what you say you are, but that you actually hold the ideals you have professed. You are the first true slan I have ever met and, for the first time in my life, I have a sense of tension eased, as if, after all these centuries, the deadly darkness is lifting. If you escape our guns, I beg you to keep your ideals as you grow older, and please don't betray us. Don't become a tool of creatures who have used only murder and destruction for so many, many years. You have been in my mind, and you know that I have not lied to you about them. Whatever the logic of their philosophy, it's wrong because it's inhuman. It must be wrong because its result has been unending misery."

If he escaped! So that was it! If he escaped, they would be dependent on his good will, and she was playing that angle now for all she was worth.

"But remember one thing," Joanna Hillory went on; "you can expect no help from us. We must, in the name of security, consider you as an enemy. Too much depends upon it, the fate of too many people is involved. So do not expect at some future date to obtain mercy, Jommy

Cross, because of what I have said or because you have released me. Do not come into our midst, because, I warn you, it means swift death.

"You see, we credit true slans with superior intelligence, or rather, superior development of intelligence, owing to their mind-reading ability. There is no cunning of which we would not believe them capable, no ruthlessness they have not already equaled. A plan requiring thirty or a hundred years to mature is not beyond them. Therefore, even though I believe what you have told me, the uncertainty of how you may develop as you grow older would make me kill you this instant were it in my power. Do not ever test our good will. It is suspicion, not tolerance, that rules us. But now, good-bye and, paradoxical as this may sound, good luck!"

He watched her as she walked lightly, swiftly, into the darkness that lay heavily on the valley to the west, the way that led to the city—his way, also. Her form became a shadow in the clinging mist of night. She was gone over a hill. Swiftly he closed the door, rushed into the storeroom, and snatched a couple of space suits from the wall. The old woman babbled in feeble protest as he stuffed her forcibly into one of them. He crowded into his own as he scrambled into the control room.

He closed the door on the sobering leer that twisted Granny's face behind the transparent headpiece, and in a second was sitting tensely staring into the "sky" visiplate. His fingers reached for the activator of the antigravity plates; and then came the hesitation, the doubt that had been growing in him each second that brought the inexorable moment of action nearer. Was it possible that his simple plan would actually work?

Jommy Cross could see the ships, little dark spots in the sky above him. The sun was shining up there, a spray of brilliance that picked out the tiny torpedo shapes like so many fly spots on an immense blue ceiling. The clouds and the haze of the valley were clearing with magical speed, and if the clarity with which he could see them through his visiplates was any criterion, then even the weather was against him. He was still in the shadows of this sweet, clean little valley, but in a few minutes now the very perfection of the day would begin to damage his chances of escape.

His brain was so tensely concentrated that for a moment the distorted thought that flowed into his mind seemed to come from himself.

". . . needn't worry. Old Granny'll get rid of the slan. Get some makeup and change her face. What's the good of having been an actress if you can't change your looks? Granny'll make a white, lovely body like she used to have, and change this old face. Ugh!"

She seemed to spit in convulsions at the thought of her face, and

Jommy Cross eased the picture out of his mind. But her words remained with him. His parents had used false hair, but the necessary mutilation of natural hair and the constant recutting had proved very unsatisfactory. Nevertheless, true slans must be doing it all the time, and now that he was old enough to be able to make a reasonably efficient job of it, with Granny's help and experience it might be the answer.

Strangely, now that a plan for the future had come, his hesitation vanished. Light as a dust mote, the ship fell away from Earth, and then jerked into enormous speed as the rockets kicked into life. Five minutes to accelerate and decelerate, the slan commander had said. Jommy Cross smiled grimly. He wasn't going to decelerate. At undiminished speed, he dived for the river that made a wide black swath at the outskirts of the city, the city he had picked because the river was there. At the very last moment he put on full deceleration.

And at that final moment, when it was already too late, the confidence of the slan commanders must have been shaken. They forgot their reluctance to use their guns and show their ships so near a human city. They swooped like great birds of prey; fire sparkled from all seven cruisers. Jommy Cross pulled gently on the wire that pressed the trigger on his own weapon, mounted in the vise at the nose of the ship.

From outside, a violent blow added speed to the three-hundred-miles-an-hour clip of his machine. But he scarcely noticed it, the only effect of the enemy fire. His attention was concentrated on his own weapon. As he pulled the wire there was a flare of white. Instantly a two-foot circle in the thick nose of the craft vanished. The white, malignant ray leaped forth fanwise, dissolving the water of the river in front of the torpedo-shaped craft, and into the tunnel thus created slid the spaceship, decelerating at full, frightful blast of the forward tubes.

The visiplates went black with the water above and the water below, then blacker as the water ended and the inconceivable ferocity of the atom smasher bored on irresistibly into the ground beyond, deeper, deeper.

It was like flying through air, only there was no resistance except the pressure of rocket blasts. The atoms of earth, broken into their component elements, instantly lost their mathematically unreal solidity and assumed their actuality of a space tenuously occupied by matter. Ten million million years of built-up cohesion collapsed into the lowest state of primeval matter.

With rigid gaze, Jommy Cross stared at the second hand of his watch. Ten, twenty, thirty—one minute. He began to ease the nose of the ship upward, but the enormous pressure of deceleration made no physical easing possible. It was thirty seconds before he cut the number of rocket blasts and the end was in sight.

After two minutes and twenty seconds of underground flight the ship stopped. He must be near the center of the city, and there was approximately eight miles of tunnel behind him, into which water would be pouring from the tortured river. The water would close up the hole, but the frustrated tendrilless slans would need no interpreter to tell them what had happened. Beside, their instruments would this very second be pointing directly at the location of his ship.

Jommy Cross laughed joyously. Let them know. What could they hope to do to him now? There was danger ahead, of course—immense danger, especially when he and Granny reached the surface. The entire tendrilless slan organization must be warned by this time. Nevertheless, that was of the future. For the moment, victory was his, and it was sweet, after so many desperate, tiring hours. Now there was Granny's plan, which involved his separating from her, and disguise.

The laughter faded from his lips. He sat thoughtful, then stalked into the adjoining compartment. The black moneybag he wanted lay on the old woman's lap under the protection of one clawlike hand. Before she could even realize his intention, he had snatched it up. Granny shrieked and jumped at him. Coolly he held her off.

"Don't get excited. I've decided to adopt your plan. I'll try to get by disguised as a human being, and we'll separate. I'm going to give you five thousand of this. The rest you'll get back about a year from now. Here's what you're to do.

"I need a place to live, and so you're going to go up into the mountains and buy a ranch or something. When you're located, put an ad in the local paper. I'll put an answering ad in, and we'll get together. I'll keep the money just in case you decide to double-cross me. Sorry, but you captured me in the first place, and so you'll just have to bear with me. But now I've got to go back and block that tunnel. Some day I'm going to fit this ship with atomic energy, and I don't want them coming here meanwhile."

He'd have to leave this city swiftly, of course, for the time being, the beginning of a continental tour. There must be other tendriled slans out there. Just as his mother and father had met accidentally, pure chance alone should enable him to meet at least one slan. And besides, there was the first investigation to be made on the still vague though great plan that was taking form in his brain. The plan to *think* his way to the true slans.

TWELVE

He searched—and he worked. In the quiet fastness of his laboratory on Granny's valley ranch, the plans and projects that his father had impressed upon him were slowly brought to reality. In a hundred ways he learned to control the limitless energy that he held in trust for slans and human beings alike.

He discovered that the effectiveness of his father's invention resulted from two basic facts. The source of power could be as tiny as a few grains of matter; and the output need not take the form of heat.

It could be converted to motion and to vibration, to radiation and—directly—to electricity.

He began to build himself an arsenal. He transformed a mountain near the ranch into a fortress, knowing that it would be inadequate against any concerted attack, but it was something. With an ever vaster protective science behind him, his search grew more determined.

Jommy Cross seemed always to be driving along roads that gleamed toward distant horizons, or in strange cities, each with its endless swarms of human beings. The sun rose and set, and rose and set, and there were dark days of drizzling rains, and there were countless nights. Although he was always alone, loneliness did not touch him, for his expanding soul fed with an always dissatisfied eagerness at the tremendous drama that was daily enacted before his eyes. Everywhere he turned, facets of the tendrilless slan organization met his gaze, and week by week he grew more puzzled. Where were the true slans?

The puzzle seemed a crazy, unanswerable thing that never left him. It followed him now as he walked slowly up a street of the hundredth—or was it the thousandth?—city.

Night lay upon the city, night spattered by countless glittering shop windows and a hundred million blazing lights. He walked to a newsstand and bought all the local papers, then back to his car, that very ordinary-looking, very special battleship on wheels which he never allowed out of his sight. He stood beside the long, low-built machine. A chilling night wind caught at the sheets of the paper as he turned page after page, briefly letting his gaze skim down the columns.

The wind grew colder as he stood there, bringing the damp-sweet smell of rain. A gust of cold air caught an edge of his paper, whipped it madly for a moment, abruptly tore it, then went screaming victoriously down the street, chasing the scrap of paper wildly. He folded the newspaper decisively against the rising clamor of wind and climbed into the car. An hour later he tossed the seven daily papers into a sidewalk wastepaper receptacle. Deep in thought, he reentered the car and sat behind the steering-wheel.

The same old story. Two of the papers were tendrilless slan. It was easy for his mind to note the subtle difference, the special coloration of the articles, the very way the words were used, the distinct difference between the human-owned papers and those operated by the tendrilless slans. Two papers out of seven. But those two had the highest circulation. It was a normal average.

And, once more, that was all there was. Human being and tendrilless slan. No third group, none of the difference that he knew would show him when a paper was operated by true slans, if his theory were right. It remained only to obtain all the weekly papers, and to spend the evening as he had spent the day, driving along the streets, searching each house, each passing mind; and then, as he drove toward the distant east, the gathering tempest charged like some wild beast through the night.

Behind him, the night and the storm swallowed up another city, another failure.

The water lay dark and still around the spaceship in that third year when Jommy Cross finally returned to the tunnel. He swirled around in the mud, turning the blazing force of his atomic-powered machines on the wounded metal thing.

Ten-point steel seared over the hole his disintegrator had carved on that day when he escaped the slan cruisers. And all through one almost endless week a snug-fitting, leech-shaped metal monstrosity hugged inch by inch over the surface of the ship, straining with its frightful power at the very structure of the atoms, till the foot-thick walls of the long, sleek machine were ten-point steel from end to end.

It took him some weeks to analyze the antigravity plates with their electrically built-up vibrations, and to fashion a counterpart which, with grim irony, he left there in the tunnel, for it was on them that the detectors of the tendrilless slans operated. Let them think their craft still there.

Three months he slaved and then, in the dead of one cold October night, the ship backed along six miles of tunnel on a cushion of resistless atomic drive, and plunged up through a mist of icy rain.

The rain became sleet, then snow; then abruptly he was beyond the clouds, beyond Earth's petty furies. Above him the vast canopy of the heavens glittered in a blazing array of stars that beckoned to his matchless ship. There was Sirius, the brightest jewel in that diadem, and there was Mars, the red. But it was not for Mars that he was heading today. This was only a short exploratory voyage, a cautious trip to the Moon, a test flight to provide that all-necessary experience which his logic would use as a basis for the long, dangerous journey that seemed to be becoming more inevitable with each passing month of his utterly futile search. Some day he would have to go to Mars.

Beneath him a blur of night-enveloped globe receded. At one edge of that mass, a blaze of light grew more brilliant as he watched and then, abruptly, his contemplation of the glory of the approaching sunrise was jarred by the clanging of an alarm bell. A pointer light flashed on and off discordantly far up on his forward visiplate. Decelerating at full speed, he watched the changing position of the light. Suddenly, the light clicked off and there, at the extreme range of his vision, was a ship.

The battleship was not coming directly toward him. It grew larger, became plainly visible just beyond the Earth's shadow, in the full glare of the sun. It passed by him, less than a hundred miles away, a thousand-foot structure of smooth, dark metal. It plunged into the shadows and instantly vanished. In half an hour the alarm stopped ringing.

And then, ten minutes later, it was clamoring again. The second ship was farther away, traveling at right angles to the path of the first. It was a smaller ship by far, destroyer size, and it did not follow a fixed path, but darted here and there.

When it was gone in the distance, Jommy Cross edged his ship forward, undecided now, almost awed. A battleship and a destroyer! Why? It seemed to indicate a patrol. But against whom? Not against human beings, surely. They didn't even know the tendrilless slans and their ships existed.

He slowed his ship, stopped. He was not prepared yet to risk running a gauntlet of well-equipped battleships. Watchfully, he swung his ship around—and in the middle of the turn he saw the small dark object, like a meteorite, rushing toward him.

In a flash he whipped aside. The object twisted after him like a living monster out of space. It loomed far up in his rear visiplate, a dark, round metal ball, about a yard in diameter. Frantically, Jommy Cross tried to maneuver his ship out of its path, but before he could make a turn there was a deafening, mind-shattering blast.

The explosion smashed him to the floor; the concussion kept him there, stunned, sick but still alive, and conscious that those sturdy walls had survived the almost intolerable blow. The ship was rocking in frightful acceleration. Dizzily, Jommy Cross picked himself up and climbed back into the control chair. He'd struck a mine. A floating mine! What terrifying precautions were here—and against what?

Thoughtfully he maneuvered his dented, almost disabled ship into a tunnel under the river that cut through Granny's ranch, a tunnel that curved up into the heart of a mountain peak, clear of the water that swirled after it. He could not even hazard a guess as to how long it must remain hidden there. Its outer walls were violently radioactive and therefore the ship was temporarily useless to him if only for that reason. And one other thing was certain. He was not ready yet either to oppose or to outwit the tendrilless slans.

Two days later, Jommy Cross stood in the doorway of the rambling ranch house and watched their nearest neighbor, Mrs. Lanahan, come tight-lipped along the pathway that led between the two orchards. She was a plump blonde whose round baby face concealed a prying, malicious mind. Her blue eyes glowed at Granny's tall, brown-eyed, brown-haired grandson with suspicion.

Jommy Cross eyed her with amusement as he opened the door for her and followed her into the house. In her mind was all the ignorance of those who had lived their lives in backward rural areas in a world where education had become a pale shadow, a weak, characterless reflection of official cynicism. She didn't know exactly what a slan was, but she thought he was one, and she was there to find out. She made an interesting experiment for his crystal method of hypnotism. It was fascinating to watch the way she kept glancing at the tiny crystal he had put on the table beside her chair—observing the way she talked on, completely in character, never realizing when she ceased to be a free agent and became his slave.

She walked out finally into the glare of the late fall sunshine, apparently unchanged. But the errand that had brought her to the farmhouse was forgotten, for her mind was conditioned to a new attitude toward slans. Not hatred—that was for a possible future that Jommy

Cross could envision; and not approval—that was for her own protection in a world of slan haters.

The following day he saw her husband, a black-bearded giant of a man in a distant field. A quiet talk, a differently attuned crystal, brought him, also, under control.

During the months that he relaxed with the hypnotically sweetened old woman that had been Granny, he gained mental control of every one of the hundreds of farm people who dwelled in the idyllic climate of the valley there in the ever green foothills. At first he needed the crystals, but as his knowledge of the human mind grew, he found that, although it was a slower process, he could entirely dispense with that atomically unbalanced glass.

He estimated. Even at the rate of two thousand hypnotized a year, and not allowing for new generations, he could hypnotize the four billion people in the world in two million years. Conversely, two million slans could do it in a year, provided they possessed the secret of his crystals.

Two million needed, and he couldn't even find one. Somewhere there *must* be a true slan. And during the years that still must pass before he could logically pit his intelligence against the intellectual task involved in finding the true slan organization, he must search and search for that one.

THIRTEEN

She was trapped. Briefly, Kathleen Layton grew tense. Her slim young body straightened there beside the open drawer of Kier Gray's desk, the contents of which she had been studying. Her mind reached out with startled alertness, through intervening doors, to where Kier Gray and another man were opening the door that led from her room through a corridor and another room to this, the dictator's own study.

She was conscious of chagrin. For weeks she had waited for the council meeting that would claim Kier Gray's attendance and give her safe access to his study—and now this wild accident. For the first time in her experience, Kier Gray had gone to her room instead of summoning her to him. With all the other exits guarded, her one avenue of escape had been cut off.

She was trapped! Yet she did not regret her action in coming. An imprisoned slan could have no purpose but escape. The seriousness of her position struck deeper instant by instant. To be caught here redhanded—Abruptly, she ceased putting the papers back into the drawer. No time. The men were just beyond the door now.

With sudden decision she closed the drawer, jerked the papers into a rough pile at one side of the desk and, like a fleeing fawn, rushed to an easy chair. Simultaneously, the door opened, and John Petty came in, followed by Kier Gray. The two men stopped as they saw her. The police chief's handsome face took on a darker color. His eyes narrowed to slits, then his gaze flicked questioningly to the dictator. The leader's eyebrows were lifted quizzically, and there was the faintest hint of irony in the smile that came into his face.

"Hullo," he said. "What brings you here?"

Kathleen had come to a decision about that, but before she could speak, John Petty cut in. The man had a beautiful voice when he wanted to use it, and he used it now.

He said gently, "She's obviously been spying on you, Kier."

There was something about this man with his incisive logic that brought chilling alarm to the girl. It seemed to be the dark destiny of the secret-police chief to be present at the critical moments of her life, and she knew with a stiffening of her courage that here was such a moment, and that of all the people in the world, John Petty would strive with the full passion of his hatred for her to make it deadly.

The police head went on calmly. "Really, Kier, we come dramatically back to what we were discussing. Next week this slan girl will be twenty-one years of age, for all legal purposes an adult. Is she to live on here until she eventually dies of old age a hundred and fifty or some such fantastic term of years from now? Or what?"

The smile on Kier Gray's face was grimmer. "Kathleen, didn't you know I was at the council meeting?"

"You bet she knew," John Petty interjected, "and its unexpected ending came as an unpleasant surprise."

Kathleen said coldly, "I refuse to make replies to any questioning in which that man participates. He's trying to keep his voice calm and logical but, in spite of the queer way in which he hides his thoughts, there is already a distinct glow of excitement streaming from him. And the thought has come to the surface of his mind that at last he will be able to convince you that I ought to be destroyed."

The leader's face was oddly hostile in the thoughtfulness that came into it. Her mind touched lightly at the surface of his brain, and there was a forming thought there, a developing decision, impossible to read. He said finally, "Historically speaking, her charge against you is true, John. Your desire for her death is—er—proved—a tribute, of course, to your antislan zeal, but a queer fanaticism in so enormously capable a man."

John Petty seemed to shake off the words in the impatient gesture he made. "The truth is, I want her dead, and I don't want her dead. To me she constitutes a grave menace to the State, located here in the palace and possessing mind-reading ability. I simply want her out of the way; and, being unsentimental about slans, I consider death the most effective method. However, I will not urge such a verdict in view of my reputation for bias in this case. But I seriously think that my suggestion at the meeting today is a good one. She should be moved to a different residence."

There was no thought near the surface of Kier Gray's mind to suggest that he intended to speak. His gaze was on her with unnecessary steadiness.

Kathleen said scathingly, "The moment I am removed from this palace, I will be murdered. As Mr. Gray said in effect ten years ago, after *your* hireling tried to murder me, once a slan is dead, inquiries into the affair are viewed with suspicion."

She saw that Kier Gray was shaking his head at her. He spoke in the mildest, most unconvincing tone she had ever heard him use. "You assume far too readily, Kathleen, that I cannot protect you. On the whole, I think it is the best plan."

She stared at him, stiff with dismay. He finished the virtual death sentence, his voice no longer mild, but even-toned, decisive.

"You will gather your clothes and possessions and prepare yourself for departure in twenty-four hours."

The shock passed. Her mind grew quite calm. The knowledge that Kier Gray had withdrawn his protection from her was too crystal clear a realization for her to require any anticlimax of emotional disbelief.

What astounded her was that there was as yet no evidence on which he could have based a criminal judgment. He hadn't even glanced at the papers she had arranged so hurriedly on the desk. Therefore, his decision was based on the mere fact of her presence here and on John Petty's accusations.

Which was surprising, because he had in the past defended her from Petty under far more sinister circumstances. And she had come unpunished, unchecked into this study on at least half a dozen other occasions.

It meant that his decision had been previously made, and therefore was beyond any argument she could hope to offer. She grew aware that there was amazement, too, in John Petty's brain. The man was frowning at his easy victory. The surface of his mind vibrated briefly a small stream of dissatisfaction, then abrupt decision to clinch the matter. His gaze flicked keenly over the room and came to rest on the desk.

"The point is, what did she find out while she was alone in your study? What are those papers?" He was not a shy man; and even while he asked the question he was stalking to the desk. As the leader came over behind him, Petty riffled through the sheets. "Hm-m-m, the list of all the old slan hideouts which we still use for trapping the unorganized slans. Fortunately, there are so many hundreds of them that she couldn't have had time to memorize their names, let alone descriptions of their locations."

The falseness of his conclusion was not what concerned Kathleen in that moment of discovery. Evidently neither man suspected that not only was the location of every one of the slan hideaways imprinted indelibly on her mind, but that she had an almost photographic record of the alarm systems which the secret police had installed in each unit to warn them when an unsuspecting slan was entering. According to the shrewd analysis of one report, there must be some kind of thought broadcaster which made it possible for strange slans to locate the hiding-places. But that was unimportant just now.

What counted was Kier Gray. The leader was staring curiously at the papers. "This is more serious than I thought," he said slowly, and Kathleen's heart sank. "She's been searching through my desk."

Kathleen thought tensely: It wasn't necessary for him to let John Petty know that. The old Kier Gray would never have provided her worst enemy with an ounce of ammunition to use against her.

Kier Gray's eyes were cold as he turned to her. Strangely, the surface of his brain showed as calm and cool as she had ever known it to be. He was, she realized, not angry but, with an icy finality, breaking with her.

"You will go to your room and pack—and await further instructions."

She was turning away as John Petty said, "You have said on various occasions, sir, that you were keeping her alive for observation purposes only. If you move her from your presence, that purpose is no longer applicable. Therefore, I hope I am safe in assuming that she will be placed under the protection of the secret police."

Kathleen shut her mind to their two minds as she closed the door behind her and raced along the corridor to her room. She felt not the vaguest interest in the details of any hypocritical murder plan which might be worked out between the leader and his henchman. Her course was clear. She opened the door leading from her room to one of the main corridors, nodded to the guard, who acknowledged her greeting stiffly—and then she walked calmly to the nearest elevator.

Theoretically, she was only allowed to go to the five-hundred-foot level, and not to the plane hangars, five hundred feet farther up. But the stocky young soldier who operated the elevator proved no match for the blow that struck him slantingly on the jaw. Like most of the other men, Kathleen saw in his mind, he had never accepted the idea that this tall, slender girl was dangerous to a two-hundred-pound male in the prime of strength. He was unconscious before he discovered his mistake. It was cruel, but she tied his hands and feet with wire and used wire to tie the gag she placed in his mouth.

Arrived at the roof, she made a brief, thorough mind exploration of the immediate vicinity of the elevator. Finally she opened the door, then swiftly shut it behind her. There was a plane less than thirty feet away. Beyond it was another plane on which three mechanics were working. A soldier was talking to them.

It took her only ten seconds to walk to the plane and climb in; and she had not picked the brains of air officers for nothing during the long years. The jets hissed, the great machine glided forward and became airborne.

"Huh," the thoughts of a mechanic came after her, "there goes the colonel again."

"Probably after another woman." That was the soldier.

"Yeah," said the second mechanic. "Trust that guy to—"

It took two hours of the swiftest southwest flying to reach the slan hideout she had selected. Then she set the plane on robot control and watched it fly off into the east. During the days that followed, she watched hungrily for a car. It was on the fifteenth day that a long, black machine purred out of a belt of trees along the ancient roadway and came toward her. Her body tensed. Somehow, she had to get that driver to stop, overpower him, and take his car. Any hour now the secret police would be swooping down—she must get away from here, and fast. Eyes fixed on the car, she waited.

FOURTEEN

The flat, wintry vastness of the prairie was behind him at last. Jommy Cross turned more directly east, then south. Far south. And ran into an apparently endless series of police barricades. No effort was made to stop him, and he finally saw in the minds of several men that there was a search on for—*a slan girl.*

That hit him with staggering impact. Just for a moment, the hope was too big for his mind to accept. And yet, it couldn't be a tendrilless slan woman. Men, who could not recognize slans except by their tendrils, would only be searching for a true slan. Which meant—here was his dream come true.

Deliberately, he headed for the area which they had orders to surround. He found himself presently off the main highway, following a side road that wound down among tree-filled valleys, and up over tall hills. The morning had been gray, but at noon the sun came out and shone gloriously from a sky of azure blue.

His clear-cut impression of being close to the heart of the danger zone was strengthened abruptly as an outside thought touched his mind. It was a gentle pulsation yet so tremendous in its import that his brain rocked.

"Attention, slans! This is a Porgrave thought-broadcasting machine. Please turn up the side road half a mile ahead. A further message will be given later."

Jommy stiffened. Soft and insistent, the flowing thought wave of the message beat at him again, gentle as a summer rain: "Attention, slans! . . . Please turn—"

He drove on, tense but excited. The miracle had happened. Slans, somewhere near, many of them. Such a thought machine might have been developed by an individual, but the message somehow suggested the presence of a community, and it could be true slans—or could it?

The swift, sweet flow of his hope became a trickle as he pondered the possibility of a trap. This could easily be a device left over from an old slan settlement. There was no real danger, of course, not with this car to deflect dangerous blows and his weapons to paralyze the striking power of an enemy. But it was just as well to take into account the possibility that human beings had left a thought-broadcasting machine here as a trap, and that they were now closing in upon it in the belief that someone was hiding there. After all, it was that possibility that had brought him.

Under his guidance, the beautiful, streamlined car rolled forward. In a minute, Jommy Cross saw the pathway; it was little more than that. The abnormally long car whipped into it and along it. The pathway wound through heavily wooded areas, through several small valleys. It was three miles farther on that the next message brought him to an abrupt stop.

"This is a Porgrave broadcaster. It directs you, a true slan, to the little farm ahead, which provides entrance to an underground city of factories, gardens, and residences. Welcome. This is a Porgrave—"

There was a great bouncing as the car struck a row of small ridges; and then the machine broke through a thick hedge of yielding willows and emerged into a shallow clearing. Jommy Cross found himself staring across a weed-grown yard to where a weather-beaten farmhouse drooped beside two other age-weary buildings, a barn and a garage.

Windowless, unpainted, the rickety old two-story house gaped sightlessly at him. The barn tottered like the ancient hulk that it was; its roller door hooked on one roller only, and the other end edged deep into the forsaken soil.

His gaze flashed briefly to the garage, then away, then back again thoughtfully. There was the same appearance of something long dead—and yet it was different. The subtle difference grew on him, bringing interest in its wake. The garage seemed to totter, but it was by design, not through decay. There were hard metals here, rigidly set against the elements.

The apparently broken doors leaned heavily against the ground, yet opened lightly before the pressing fingers of the tall, lithely built young woman in a gray dress who came out and gazed at him with a dazzling smile.

She had flashing eyes, this girl, and a finely molded, delicately textured face, and because his mind was always held on a tight band of thought, she came out thinking he was a human being.

And she was a slan!

And he was a slan!

For Jommy Cross, who had searched the world with caution for so many long years, his mind always alert, the shock and recovery from the shock were almost simultaneous. He had known that some day this would happen; that some day he would meet another slan. But for Kathleen, who had never had to conceal her thoughts, the surprise was devastating. She fought for control and found herself uncontrollable. The little-used shield was suddenly, briefly unusable.

There was a noble pride in the rich flow of thought matter that streamed from her mind in that instant when her brain was like an open, unprotected book. Pride, and a golden humility. Humility based on a deep sensitivity, an immense understanding that equaled his own, yet lacked the tempering of unending struggle and danger. There was a warm good-heartedness in her that had nevertheless known resentment and tears, and faced limitless hate.

And then her mind closed tight, and she stood wide-eyed, looking at him. After a long moment she unlocked her mind and let a thought reach out to him.

"We mustn't stay here. I've been here too long already. You probably saw in my mind about the police, so the best thing we can do is to drive away immediately."

He just stood there, gazing at her with shining eyes. Each passing second, his mind expanded more, his whole body felt warm with joy. It was like an intolerable weight lifting. All these years everything had depended on him. The great weapon he held in trust for that future world he sometimes dreamed of hung suspended like a monstrous sword of Damocles over the destiny of human being and slan alike by the single, fragile thread of his life. And now there would be two life threads to control it.

It was not a thought, but an emotion; all sad, sweet, glorious emotion. A man and a woman, alone in the world, meeting like this, just as his father and mother had met long ago. He smiled reminiscently and opened his mind wide to her. He shook his head.

"No, not right away. I caught a flash from your mind about the machines in the cave city, and I would like to have a look at them. Heavy machinery is my greatest lack." He smiled reassuringly. "Don't worry too much about the danger. I have some weapons that human beings cannot match, and this car is a very special means of escape. It can go practically anywhere. I hope there is room for it in the cave."

"Oh, yes. First you go down by a series of elevators. Then you can drive anywhere. But we mustn't delay. We—"

Jommy Cross laughed happily. "No buts!" he said.

Later, Kathleen repeated her doubts. "I really don't think we ought to stay. I can see in your mind about your marvelous weapons, and that your car is made of a metal you call ten-point steel. But you also have a tendency to discount human beings. You mustn't! In their fight against slans, men like John Petty have had their brains keyed to a pitch of abnormal power. And John Petty will stop at nothing to destroy me. Even now his net must be tightening systematically around the various slan hiding places where I might be."

Jommy Cross stared at her with troubled eyes. All around was the silence of the cave city—the once white walls that pushed bravely up to the cracking ceiling, the row on row of pillars, bent and worn more from the weight of years than from the heavy earth that pressed them down. To his left he could see the beginning of the great expanse of artificial garden and the gleaming underground stream that fed water to this little subworld. To his right stretched the long row of apartment doors, the plastic walls still gleaming dully.

A people had lived here and had been driven forth by their remorseless enemies, but the menacing atmosphere of the flight seemed to linger still. Looking around, Jommy guessed that the settlement had been evacuated not less than twenty-five years before; it all still seemed very near and deadly. His thought answer to Kathleen reflected the grim threat of that lowering danger.

"By all the laws of logic, we have only to be on the alert for outside thoughts and stay within a few hundred yards of my car to be absolutely safe. Yet I'm alarmed by your intuition of danger. Please search your brain and try to discover the basis for your fear. I can't do it for you as well as you can do it for yourself."

The girl was silent. Her eyes closed. Her shield went up. She sat there beside him in the car, looking strangely like a beautiful overgrown child fallen asleep. Finally her sensitive lips twitched. For the first time she spoke aloud.

"Tell me, what is ten-point steel?"

"Ah," said Jommy Cross in satisfaction, "I'm beginning to understand the psychological factors involved. Mental communication has many advantages, but it cannot convey the extent, for instance, of a weapon's power as well as a picture on a piece of paper, or not even as well as by word of mouth. Power, size, strength, and similar images do not transmit well."

"Go on."

"Everything I've done," Jommy Cross explained, "has been based on my father's great discovery of the first law of atomic energy—concentration as opposed to the old method of diffusion. So far as

I know, Father never suspected the metal-strengthening possibilities, but, like all research workers who come after the great man and his basic discovery, I concentrated on details of development, based partly on his ideas, partly on ideas that progressively suggested themselves.

"All metals are held together by atomic tensions, which comprise the theoretical strength of that metal. In the case of steel, I called this theoretical potential one-point. As a comparison, when steel was first invented its strength was about two-thousand-point. New processes rapidly increased this to around one-thousand, then, over a period of hundreds of years, to the present human level of seven-hundred-and-fifty.

"Tendrilless slans have made five-hundred-point steel, but even that incredibly hard stuff cannot compare with the product of my application of atomic strain, which changes the very structure of the atoms and produces the almost perfect ten-point steel. An eighth of an inch of ten-point can stop the most powerful explosive known to human beings and tendrilless slans!"

Briefly, he described his attempted trip to the Moon and the mine that sent him scurrying home, badly smashed. He concluded, "The important thing to remember there is that an atomic bomb obviously big enough to blow up a giant battleship did not penetrate a foot of ten-point, though the hull was badly dented and the engine room a shambles from transmitted shock."

Kathleen was gazing at him, her eyes shining. "What a silly fool I am," she breathed. "I've met the greatest living slan and I'm trying to fill him with the fears gathered from twenty-one years of living with human beings and their comparatively infinitesimal powers and forces."

Jommy Cross shook his head smilingly. "The great man is not me, but my father—though he had his faults, too, the biggest one being lack of adequate self-protection. But that's true genius." The smile faded. "I'm afraid, though, that we'll have to make frequent visits to this cave, and every one will be just as dangerous as this one. I have met John Petty very briefly, and what I've seen in your mind only adds to a picture of a ruthlessly thorough man. I know he's keeping a watch on this place, but really we cannot allow ourselves to be frightened by such a prospect. We'll stay only till dark this time—just long enough for me to examine the machinery. There's some food in the car that we can cook after I've had a little sleep. I'll sleep in the car, of course. But first, the machinery!"

Everywhere the big machines sprawled, like corpses, silent and moldering. Blast furnaces, great stamping machines, lathes, saws, countless engined tools, a half-mile row on tight row of machines, about 30 percent completely out of commission, 20 percent partially useless, and the rest usable up to a point.

The unwinking, glareless lights made a shadowed world as they wandered along that valley of broken floor in and out among the machine hills. Jommy Cross was thoughtful.

"There's more here than I imagined—everything I have always needed. I could build a great battleship with the scrap metal alone; and they probably use it only as a means of trapping slans." His thoughts narrowed on her mind. "Tell me, you're sure there are only two entrances to this city?"

"There are only two entrances given on the list in Kier Gray's desk—and I've located no others."

He was silent, but he did not conceal the tenor of his thoughts from her. "Foolish of me to think again of your intuition, but I don't like to let a possible menace out of my mind till I've examined every connective probability."

"If there's a secret entrance," Kathleen volunteered, "it would take us hours to find it, and if we found one, we couldn't be sure there wouldn't be others, and so we'd feel no more secure. I still believe we should leave immediately."

Jommy Cross shook his head decisively. "I didn't let you see this in my mind before, but the main reason I don't want to leave here is that, until your face is disguised and your tendrils are hidden by false hair—a really difficult job—this is the safest place for both of us. Every highway is being watched by the police. Most of them know they're looking for a slan, and they have your picture. I turned off the main road in the hope of being able to find you before they did."

"Your machine goes up, doesn't it?" Kathleen asked.

Jommy Cross smiled mirthlessly. "Seven hours yet till dark; and every other minute we'd run into a plane. Imagine what the pilots would radio to the nearest military airport when they saw an automobile flying through the air. And if we go higher, say fifty miles, we'll surely be seen by a tendrilless slan patrol ship.

"The first commander will realize instantly who it is, report our position, and attack. I've got the weapons to destroy him, but I won't be able to destroy the dozens of ships that follow—at least not before potent forces strike this car so hard that concussion alone will kill us. And besides, I cannot willfully put myself in a position where I may have to kill anybody. I've killed only three men in my life, and every day since then my reluctance to destroy human beings has grown until now it is one of the strongest forces in me—so strong that I have based my whole plan for finding the true slans on an analysis of that one dominant trait."

The girl's thought brushed his mind, light as a breath of air. "You have a plan for finding the true slans?" she questioned.

He nodded. "Yes. It's really very simple. All the true slans I have ever met—my father, my mother, myself, and now you—have been goodhearted, kindly people. This in spite of human hatred, human efforts to destroy us. I cannot believe that we four are exceptions; and therefore there must be some reasonable explanation of the monstrous acts true slans seem to be committing."

He smiled briefly. "It's probably presumptuous of me even to have a thought on the subject at my age and limited development. Anyway, I'm afraid it's been an utter failure so far. And I mustn't make a major move in the game until I've taken further defensive action against the tendrilless slans."

Kathleen's eyes were fixed on him. She nodded agreement. "I can see, too," she said, "why we must stay longer."

Queerly, he wished she hadn't brought up that subject again. For the barest moment (he hid the thought from her) he had a premonition of incredible danger. So incredible that logic brushed it aside. The vague backwash of it remained—made him say, "Just stay near the car and keep your mind alert. After all, we can spot a human being a quarter of a mile away even while we're sleeping."

Oddly enough, it didn't sound the slightest bit reassuring.

At first Jommy Cross only dozed. He must have been partly awake for some minutes, because though his eyes were closed he was aware of her mind near him, and that she was reading one of his books. Once, so light was his sleep, the question came into his mind, "The ceiling lights—do they stay on all the time?"

She must have reached softly into his brain with the answer, for suddenly he knew that the lights had been on ever since she came, and must have been like that for hundreds of years.

There was a question in her mind, and his brain answered, "No, I won't eat until I've had some sleep."

Or was that just a memory of something previously spoken?

Still he wasn't quite asleep, for a queer, glad thought welled up from deep inside him. It was wonderful to have found another slan at last, such a gorgeously beautiful girl.

And such a fine-looking young man.

Was that his thought, or hers, he wondered sleepily.

It was mine, Jommy.

What a rich joy it was to be able to entwine your mind with another sympathetic brain so intimately that the two streams of thought seemed one, and question and answer and all discussion included instantly all the subtle overtones that the cold medium of words could never transmit.

Were they in love? How could two people simply meet and be in love when, for all they knew, there were millions of slans in the world, among whom might be scores of other men and women they might have chosen under other conditions?

It's more than that, Jommy. All our lives we've been alone in a world of alien men. To find kindred at last is a special joy, and meeting all the slans in the world afterward will not be the same. We're going to share hopes and doubts, dangers and victories. Above all, we will create a child. You see, Jommy, I have already adjusted my whole being to a new way of living. Is not that true love?

He thought it was, and was conscious of great happiness. But when he slept, the happiness seemed no longer there—only a blackness that became an abyss down which he was peering into illimitable depths.

He awakened with a start. His narrowed, alert eyes flashed to where Kathleen had been sitting. The reclining chair was empty. His sharpened mind, still in the thrall of his dream, reached out.

"Kathleen!"

Kathleen came to the door of the machine. "I was looking at some of this metal, trying to imagine what would be most immediately useful to you." She stopped, smiling, and corrected herself. "To us."

Jommy Cross lay very still for a moment, reaching out with his mind, intently exploring, unhappy that she had left the car even for a moment. He divined that she came from a less tense atmosphere than himself. She had had freedom of movement and there had been, despite occasional threats, certainties that she could depend upon. In his own grim existence, an ever present reality was that death could result from the tiniest letdown in caution. Every move had to include a calculated risk.

It was a pattern to which Kathleen would have to accustom herself. Boldness in carrying out a purpose in the face of danger was one thing. Carelessness was quite another.

Kathleen said cheerfully, "I'll make something to eat while you quickly pick out a few things you want to take along. It must be dark outside by now."

Jommy Cross glanced at his chronometer, and nodded. In two hours it would be midnight. The darkness would conceal their flight. He said slowly, "Where's the nearest kitchen?"

"Just along there." She motioned with one arm, vaguely indicating a long line of doors.

"How far?"

"About a hundred feet." She frowned. "Now, look, Jommy, I can sense how anxious you are. But if we're going to be a team, one of us has to do one thing while the other does something else."

He watched her go uneasily, wondering if the acquisition of a partner would be good for his nerves. He who had hardened himself against any danger to himself must accustom himself to the idea that she also would have to take risks.

Not that there was any danger at the moment. The hideout was silent. Not a sound and, except for Kathleen, not a whisper of thought came from anywhere. The hunters, the searchers, and the erectors of barriers that he had seen all through the day must be home by now, asleep, or about to retire.

He watched Kathleen go through a doorway, and estimated that it was nearer a hundred and fifty feet. And he was climbing out of the car when a thought came from her on a strange, high, urgent vibration.

"Jommy—the wall's opening! Somebody—"

Abruptly, her own thought broke off and she was transmitting a man's words.

"Well, if it isn't Kathleen," John Petty was saying in cold satisfaction. "And only the fifty-seventh hideout I've visited. I've been to all of them personally, of course, because few other human beings could keep their minds from warning you of their approach. And besides, nobody could be safely trusted with such an important assignment. What do you think of the psychology of building these secret entrances to the kitchen? Apparently even slans travel on their stomachs."

Beneath Jommy Cross's swift fingers, the car leaped forward. He caught Kathleen's reply, cool and unhurried.

"So you've found me, Mr. Petty." Mockingly. "Am I, then, to beseech your mercy?"

The icy answer streamed through her mind to Jommy Cross. "Mercy is not my strong point. Nor do I delay when a long-awaited opportunity offers."

"Jommy, quick!"

The shot echoed from her mind to his. For a terrible moment of intolerable strain, her mind held off the death that the crashing bullet in her brain had brought.

"Oh, Jommy, and we could have been so happy. Good-bye, my dearest—"

In a desperate dismay, he followed the life force as it faded in a flash from her mind. The blackout wall of death suddenly barred his mind from that which had been Kathleen's.

FIFTEEN

There was no thought in Jommy Cross, no hate, no grief, no hope—only his mind receiving impressions, and his superlatively responsive body reacting like the perfect physical machine it was. His car braked to a stop; he saw the figure of John Petty standing just beyond Kathleen's crumpled body.

"By heaven!" snapped from the surface of the man's mind, "another of them!"

His gun flashed against the impregnable armor of the car. Startled by his failure, the chief of secret police drew back. His lips parted in a cry of rage. For a moment, the dark hatred of a man for the encroaching slan enemy seemed personified in his grim countenance, and in the tenseness with which his body seemed to await inevitable death.

One touch of one button, and he could have been blasted into nothingness. But Jommy Cross made no move, spoke no word. Colder, harder grew his mind as he sat there. His bleak gaze stared impersonally at the man, then at the dead body of Kathleen. And finally the measured thought came that as the sole possessor of the secret atomic energy he could permit himself no love, no normal life. In all that world of men and slans who hated so savagely, there was for him only the relentless urgency of his high destiny.

Other men began pouring from the secret entrance, men with machine guns that chatted futilely at his car. And among them he was abruptly aware of the shields that indicated the presence of two tendrilless slans. His searching eyes spotted one of them after a moment, as the man drew into a corner, and whispered a swift message into a wrist radio. The words ran plainly along the surface of his mind.

"7500 model, 200-inch base—general physique type 7, head 4,

chin 4, mouth 3, eyes brown, type 13, eyebrows 13, nose 1, cheeks 6—
Cut!"

He could have smashed them all, the whole venal, ghoulish crew.
But no thought of vengeance could penetrate the chilled, transcendental region that was his brain. In this mad universe, there was only the
safety of his weapon and the certainties that went with it.

His car backed, and raced off with a speed their legs could not
match. Ahead was the tunnel of the underground creek that fed the
gardens. He plunged into it, his disintegrators widening nature's crude
bed for half a mile. Then he turned down to let the water stream after
him and hide his tunnel, then up, so that the water wouldn't have too
much space to fill.

Finally, he leveled off, and plunged on through the darkness of the
underground. He couldn't head for the surface yet because the tendrilless
slans would have their cruisers waiting to meet just such a possibility.

Black clouds hid a night world when at last Jommy Cross emerged
from the side of a hill. He paused and, with meticulous care, undercut
his tunnel, buried it under tons of crashing earth, and soared into the
sky. For the second time, he clicked on his tendrilless-slan radio; and
this time a man's voice broke into the car.

"—Kier Gray has now arrived and taken possession of the body. It
appears that once again the snake organization has allowed one of its
own kind to be destroyed without a move to save her, without even the
sign of a move. It is time that we drew the proper conclusions from
their failures, and ceased to regard any opposition they might offer to
our plans as an important factor. However, there is still the incalculable
danger presented by the existence of this man Cross. It must be made
clear at once that our military operations against Earth will have to
be suspended until he is destroyed.

"His unexpected appearance on the scene today was, therefore,
one great advantage we gained from the affair. We have a description
of his car and an expert's description of his physique. No matter how
he disguises himself he cannot change the bony structure of his face;
and even immediate destruction of his car will not destroy the record
of the car itself. There were only a few hundred thousand 7500 models
sold. His will have been stolen, but it can be traced.

"Joanna Hillory, who has made a very detailed study of this snake,
has been placed in charge. Under her direction, searchers will penetrate
every district of every continent. There must be small areas on Earth
where we have not penetrated—little valleys, stretches of prairie, particularly farming districts. Such localities must be closed, police cells
set up in them.

"There is no way the snakes can contact him, for we control every avenue of communication. And from this day onward, our watchers will stop every person with his facial physique for examination.

"That will keep him off the road. That will prevent chance discovery of the snakes, and give us the time we need for our search. However long it may take, we must trace this dangerous slan to where he lives. We cannot fail. This is Great Headquarters signing off."

The rushing air whined and whistled against the hurtling car there beneath the swarming black clouds. So the war against the human world was now bound up with his own fate, an indefinite reprieve for both. They would find him, of course, these thoroughgoing slans. They had failed once before because of an unknown factor—his weapon—but that was known now; and besides, it was not a factor that would influence their remorseless search. For several minutes, he contemplated the prospective invasion of his valley, and finally emerged with one fact that remained in his favor, one question. Yes, they would find him, but how long would it take?

SIXTEEN

It took four years; and Jommy Cross had been twenty-three for two months on the day when the tendrilless slan organization struck with unexpected, unimaginable violence. He came slowly down the veranda steps on that sultry, oppressively hot day, and paused on the pathway that divided the garden. He was thinking with a quiet, gentle thought of Kathleen, and of his long-dead mother and father. It was not grief or even sadness that swayed him, but a deep, philosophical sense of the profound tragedy of life.

But no introspection could dull his senses. With abnormal, unhuman clarity he was aware of his surroundings. Of all the developments in himself during those four years, it was this perception of *anything* that marked his growth toward maturity. Nothing escaped him. Heat waves danced against the lower reaches of the mountain twenty miles away, where his spaceship was hidden. But no heat mist could bar a vision that saw so many more pictures per split second than the human eye could see. Details penetrated, a hard, bright pattern formed where a few years before there would have been, even for himself, a blur.

A squadron of midges swarmed past Granny, where she kneeled by a flower bed. The faint life wave of the tiny flies caressed the supersensitive receptors of his brain. As he stood there, sounds from remoteness whispered into his ears. Wisps of thought, shadowed by distance, touched his mind. And gradually, in spite of incredible complexity, a kaleidoscope of the life of his valley grew in his mind, a very symphony of impressions that rounded beautifully into a coherent whole.

Men and women at work, children at play, laughter; tractors moving, trucks, cars—a little farm community meeting another day in the old, old fashion. He stared again at Granny. Briefly, his mind dissolved into her defenseless brain, and in that instant, so utter was his power of receiving thoughts, it was as if she were another part of his body. A crystal-clear picture of the dark earth she was looking at flashed from her mind to his. A tall flower, directly under her gaze, loomed big in her mind, and in his. As he watched, her hand came into view, holding a small, black bug. Triumphantly she squashed the insect, then complacently wiped her stained fingers in the dirt.

"Granny!" Cross said. "Can't you suppress your murderous instincts?"

The old lady glanced up at him, and there was a belligerent thrust in her wrinkled, kindly face that was reminiscent of the old Granny.

"Nonsense!" she snapped. "For ninety years now, I've killed the little devils, and my mother before me had it in for 'em, too, heh, heh!"

Her giggle sounded senile. Cross frowned faintly. Granny had thrived physically in this West Coast climate, but he was not satisfied with his hypnotic reconstruction of her mind. She was very old, of course, but her constant use of certain phrases, such as the one about what she, and her mother before her, had done, was too mechanical. He had impressed the idea upon her in the first place to fill the enormous gap left by the uprooting of her own memories, but one of these days he'd have to try again. He started to turn away; and it was at that moment that the warning tingled into his brain, a sharp pulsing of faraway outside thoughts. "Airplanes!" people were thinking. "So many planes!"

It was years now since Jommy Cross had implanted the hypnotic suggestion that everybody who saw anything unusual in the valley was to signal through their subconscious, without themselves being aware of the act. The fruits of that precaution came now in the wave after wave of warning from dozens of minds.

And then he saw the planes, specks diving over the mountain heading in his general direction. Like a striking mongoose, his mind lashed out toward them, reaching for the minds of the pilots. Taut-held brain shields of tendrilless slans met that one, searching glance. In full racing stride he snatched Granny from the ground; and then he was in the house. The ten-point steel door of that ten-point steel house swung shut—even as a great, glistening, jet-propelled troop carrier plane settled like a gigantic bird among the flowers of Granny's garden.

Cross thought tensely: "A plane in every farmyard. That means they don't know exactly which one I'm in. But now the spaceships will arrive to finish the job. Thorough!"

Well, so had he been thorough, and it was obvious, now that his hand was forced, that he must push his own plan to the limit. He felt supremely confident, and there was still not a doubt in him.

Doubt and dismay came a minute later, as he stared into his underground visiplate. The battleships and cruisers were there, all right, but something else, too—another ship. A *ship!* The monster filled half the visiplate, and its wheel-shaped bulk sprawled across the lower quarter of the sky. A half-mile circle of ship, ten million tons of metal, floating down lighter than air, like a buoyant flattened balloon, gigantic, immeasurably malignant in its sheer threat of unlimited power.

It came alive! A hundred-yard beam of white fire flared from its massive wall—and the solid top of the mountain dissolved before that frightful thrust. His mountain, where his ship, his life, was hidden, destroyed by *controlled atomic energy.*

Cross stood quite still there on the rug that covered the steel floor of that steel laboratory. Wisps of human incoherency from every direction fumbled at his brain. He flung up his mind shield, and that distracting confusion of outside thought was cut off abruptly. Behind him, Granny moaned in gentle terror. In the distance above him, sledge-hammer blows were lashing at his almost impregnable cottage, but the dim bedlam of noise failed to touch him. He was alone in a world of personal silence, a world of swift, quiet, uninterrupted thought.

If they were prepared to use atomic energy, why hadn't they pulverized him with bombs? A thousand co-ordinating thoughts leaped up to form the simple answer. They wanted his perfect type of atomic energy. Their method was not a development of the rather superb, so-called hydrogen bomb of old times, with its heavy water and uranium base, and chain reaction. They had gone back to an even earlier stage, a crude expansion of the cyclotron principle. That alone could explain so much size. Here was a ten-million-ton cyclotron, capable of a wild and deadly spray of energy—and they undoubtedly hoped to use its mobility to force him to give them his priceless secret.

He whirled toward the instrument board that spread across the entire end of the laboratory. A switch clicked. Pointers set rigid. And dancing needles told the story of a spaceship out there under that dissolving mountain, a ship shuddering with mechanical life, now automatically burrowing deeper into the ground, and at the same time heading unerringly toward this laboratory.

A dial spun, and a whole bank of needles in their transparent cases danced from zero to the first fractional point, and wavered there. They, also, told a story—the story of atomic projectors rearing up from the ground where they had been hidden so long—and as he grasped the precision instrument that was his aiming device, twenty invincible guns out there swung in perfect synchronization.

The hairline sights edged along the unmissable spread of the ship's bulk. And paused. What was his purpose against these ruthless enemies? He didn't want to bring that monster machine to earth. He didn't want to create a situation where slans and human beings might launch into a furious struggle for the possession of the wreck. There was no doubt that the human beings would fight with a fearless ferocity. Their great mobile guns could still hurl shells capable of piercing any metal in the possession of the slans. And if any of those ships with their superior armaments ever fell into human hands, then it would be no time at all before they, also, had spaceships; and the devil's war would be on. No, he didn't want that.

And he didn't want to destroy the ship because he didn't want to kill the tendrilless slans who were in it. For, after all, tendrilless slans *did* represent a law and order which he respected. And because they were a great race, and definitely kin to him, they merited mercy.

Before that clarification, hesitation fled. Straight at the center of that immense cyclotron, Cross aimed his battery of synchronized weapons. His thumb pressed down the fire button. Above him, the half mile of spiral-shaped ship recoiled like an elephant struck an intolerable blow. It rocked madly, like a ship in stormy seas. And briefly, as it swung sickeningly, he saw blue sky through a gaping hole—and realized his victory.

He had cut that vast spiral from end to end. In every turn of it now was a hopelessly diffusing leak. No stream of atoms, however accelerated, could run that gauntlet unmutilated. The power of the cyclotron was smashed. But all the implications of that ship remained. Frowning, Cross watched the ship poise for a moment, shakily. Slowly it began to recede, its antigravity plates apparently full on. Up, up it mounted, growing smaller as it withdrew into the distance.

At fifty miles it was still bigger than the battleships that were nosing down toward that green, almost unharmed valley. And now the implications were clearer, colder, deadlier. The nature of their attack showed that they must have spotted his activities in this valley months ago.

Clearly, they had waited until they could approach in one titanic, organized battle, with the purpose of forcing him out where they could follow him night and day by means of their instruments and so, by sheer weight of numbers and guns, destroy him and capture his equipment.

Dispassionately, Cross turned to Granny. "I'm going to leave you here. Follow my instructions to the letter. Five minutes from now, you will go up the way we came down, closing all the metal doors behind you. You will then forget all about this laboratory. It is going to be destroyed, so you might as well forget. If men question you, you will act senile, but at other times you will be normal. I'm leaving you to face that danger because I'm no longer sure, in spite of my precautions, that I can come out of this alive."

He felt a chill, impersonal interest in the knowledge that the day of action had arrived. The tendrilless slans might intend this attack on him to be but part of a vaster design that included their long-delayed assault on Earth. Whatever happened, his plans were as complete as he could make them; and though it was years too soon, he must now force the issue to the limit of his power. He was on the run, and there could be no turning back—for behind him was swift death!

Cross's ship nosed out of the little river and launched toward space on a long, slanting climb. It was important that he should not become invisible until the slans actually saw that he was out of the valley, before they had razed it in futile search. But first, there was one thing he must do.

His hand plunged home a switch. His narrowed gaze fastened on the rear visiplate, which showed the valley falling away below. At a score of points on that green floor (he counted them in lightning calculation) white flame blazed up in a strange, splotchy-looking fire. Down there, every weapon, every atomic machine, was turning on itself. Fire chambers were burning out, metal running molten in that devouring violence of energy.

The white glow was still there as he turned away a few seconds later, grimly content. Now let them search through that ravaged, twisted metal. Let their scientists labor to bring to life a secret they craved so desperately, and to obtain which they had come out where human beings could see some of their powers. In every burned-out cache in that valley, they would find exactly nothing!

The destruction of all that was so precious to the attackers required a fraction of a minute, but in that time he was seen. Four dead-black battleships turned toward him simultaneously—and then hovered uncertainly as he actuated the mechanism that made his vessel invisible.

Abruptly, their possession of atom-energy detectors was shown. The ships fell in behind him unerringly. Alarm bells showed others ahead, closing toward him. It was only the unmatchable atomic drivers that saved him from that vast fleet. There were so many vessels that he could not even begin to count them, and all that could come near turned their deadly projectors where their instruments pointed. They missed, because during the very instant they spotted him, his machine flashed out of range of their most massive guns.

Completely invisible, traveling at many miles per second, his ship headed for Mars! He must have hurtled through mine fields, but that didn't matter now. The devouring disintegration rays that poured out from the walls of his great machine ate up mines before they could explode, and simultaneously destroyed every light wave that would have revealed his craft to alert eyes out there in the blaze of sun.

There was only one difference. The mines were smashed *before* they reached his ship. Light, being in a wave state as it flashed up, could be destroyed only during that fraction of instant when it touched his ship and started to bounce. At the very moment of bouncing, its speed reduced, the corpuscles that basically composed it lengthened according to the laws of the Lorentz-FitzGerald contraction theory—at that instant of almost quiescence, the fury of the sun's rays was blotted out by the disintegrators.

And, because light must touch the walls first, and so could be absorbed as readily as ever, his visiplates were unaffected. The full picture of everything came through even as he hurtled on, unseen, invisible. His ship seemed to stand still in the void, except that gradually Mars became larger. At a million miles, it was a great, glowing ball as big as the Moon seen from Earth; and it grew like an expanding balloon until its dark bulk filled half the sky, and lost its redness.

Continents took form, mountains, seas, incredible gorges, rock-strewn and barren stretches of flat land. Grimmer grew the picture, deadlier every forsaken aspect of that gnarled old planet. Mars, seen through an electric telescope at thirty thousand miles, was like a too-old human being, withered, bony, ugly, cold-looking, drooling with age, enormously repellent.

The dark area that was Mare Cimmerium showed as a fanged, terrible sea. Silent, almost tideless, the waters lay under the eternal blue-dark skies; but no ship could ever breast those placid waters. Endless miles of jagged rocks broke the surface. There were no patterns, no channels, simply the sea and the protruding rock. Finally, Cross saw the city, making a strange, shimmering picture under its vast roof of glass; then a second city showed, and a third.

Far, far past Mars he plunged, his motors dead, not the tiniest amount of atomic energy diffusing from any part of his ship. That was caution, pure and simple. There could be no fear of detector instruments in these vast distances. At last, the gravitational field of the planet began to check his flight. Slowly, the long machine yielded to the inexorable pull and began to fall toward the night side of the globe. It was a slow task. Earth days fled into Earth weeks. But finally he turned on, not his atomic energy, but the antigravity plates which he had not used since installing his atomic drives.

For days and days then, while centrifugal action of the planet cushioned his swift fall, he sat without sleep, staring into the visiplates. Five times the ugly balls of dark metal that were mines flashed toward him. Each time he actuated for brief seconds his all-devouring wall disintegrators—and waited for the ships that might have spotted his momentary use of force. A dozen times, his alarm bells clanged, and lights flashed on his visiplates, but no ships came within range. Below him, the planet grew vast, and filled every horizon with its dark immensity. There were not many landmarks on this night portion aside from the cities. Here and there, however, splashes of light showed some kind of habitation and activity, and at last he found what he wanted. A mere dot of flame, like a candle fluttering in remote darkness.

It turned out to be a small mine, and the light came from the little house where the four tendrilless slans who attended the mine's completely automatic machinery lived. It was almost dark before Cross returned to his ship, satisfied that this was what he wanted.

A mist of blackness lay like a black cloth over the planet the following night when, once again, Cross landed his ship in the ravine that led toward the mine head. Not a shadow stirred. Not a sound invaded the silence as he edged forward to the mouth of the mine. Gingerly, he took out one of the metal cases which protected his hypnotism crystals, inserted the atomically unstable, glasslike object into a crack of the rock entrance—jerked off the protective covering, and raced off before his own body could affect the sluggish thing. In the black of the ravine, he waited.

In twenty minutes, a door of the cottage opened. The flood of light from within revealed the outlines of a tall young man. Then the door closed; a torch blazed in the hand of the shadowed figure, glared along the path he was following, and brought a flash of reflected flame from the hypnotism crystal. The man walked toward it curiously, and stooped to examine it. His thoughts ran along the surface of his casually protected mind.

"Funny! That crystal wasn't there this morning." He shrugged. "Some rock probably jarred loose, and the crystal was behind it."

He stared at it, abruptly startled by its fascination. Suspicion leaped into his alert mind. He pondered the thing with a cold, tense logic. And dived for the shelter of the cavern as Cross's paralyzing ray flicked at him from the ravine. He fell unconscious just inside the cave.

Cross rushed forward, and in a few minutes had the man far down the ravine, out of all possible earshot of the mine. But even during those first minutes, his mind was reaching through the other's shattered mind shield, searching. It was slow work, because moving around in an unconscious mind was like walking under water, there was so much resistance. But suddenly, he found what he was seeking, the corridor made by the man's sharp awareness of the pattern of the crystal.

Swiftly Cross followed the mind path to its remote end in the complex root sources of the brain. A thousand paths streamed loosely before him, scattering in every direction. Grimly, with careful yet desperate speed, he followed them, ignoring the obviously impossible ones. And then, once more, like a burglar who opens safes by listening for the faint click that reveals he has reached another stage in the solution of the combination, once more a key corridor stretched before him.

Eight key paths, fifteen minutes, and the combination was his, the brain was his. Under his ministrations the man, whose name was Miller, revived with a gasp. Instantly, he closed the shield tight over his mind.

Cross said, "Don't be so illogical. Lower your shield."

The shield went down; and in the darkness the surprised tendrilless slan stared at him, astonishment flaming through his mind.

"Hypnotized, by heaven!" he said wonderingly. "How the devil did you do it?"

"The method can be used only by true slans," Cross replied coolly, "so explanations would be useless."

"A true slan!" the other said slowly. "Then you're Cross!"

"I'm Cross."

"I suppose you know what you're doing," Miller went on, "but I don't see how you expect to gain anything by your control of me."

Abruptly, Miller's mind realized the strangeness, the eeriness of the conversation there in that dark ravine, under the black, mist-hidden sky. Only one of the two moons of Mars was visible, a blurred white shape that gleamed remotely from the vast vault of heaven. He said quickly, "How is it that I can talk to you, reason with you? I thought hypnotism was a mind-dulling thing."

"Hypnotism," Cross cut in without pausing in his swift exploration of the other's brain, "is a science that involves many factors. Full control permits the subject apparently complete freedom, except that his will is under absolute outside domination. But there is no time to waste." His voice grew sharper, and his brain withdrew from the other. "Tomorrow is your day off. You will go to the Bureau of Statistics and ascertain the name and present location of every man with my physical structure."

He stopped, because Miller was laughing softly. His mind and voice said, "Good heavens, man, I can tell you that right now. They were all spotted after your description came through several years ago. They're always under observation; they're all married men and—" His voice trailed off.

Sardonically, Cross said, "Go on!"

Miller went on reluctantly. "There are twenty-seven men, all together, who resemble you in very great detail, a surprisingly high average."

"Go on!"

"One of them," said Miller disconsolately, "is married to a woman whose head was badly injured in a spaceship accident last week. They're building up her brain and bone again, but—"

"But that will take a few weeks," Cross finished for him. "The man's name is Barton Corliss. He's located at the Cimmerium spaceship factory and, like yourself, goes into the city Cimmerium every fourth day."

"There ought to be an enforceable law," Miller said glumly, "against people who can read minds. Fortunately, the Porgrave receivers will spot you," he finished more cheerfully.

"Eh?" Cross spoke sharply. He had already noticed about mindreading in Miller's mind, but it had not seemed applicable. And there had been other, more important things to follow up.

Coolly, Miller said, and his thoughts verified every word of it, "The Porgrave broadcaster broadcasts thoughts, and the Porgrave receiver receives them. In Cimmerium, there's one located every few feet; they're in all the buildings, houses, everywhere. They're our protection against snake spies. One indiscreet thought, and finish!"

Cross was silent. At last he said, "One more question, and I want your mind to give off a lot of thoughts on this. I want detail."

"Yes?"

"How imminent is the attack on Earth?"

"It has been decided," Miller replied precisely, "that in view of the failure to destroy you and obtain your secret, control of Earth has become essential, the purpose being to forestall any future danger from anybody. To this end vast reserves of spaceships are being turned out; the fleet is mobilizing at key points, but the date of attack, though probably decided on, has not yet been announced."

"What have they planned to do with human beings?"

"To hell with human beings!" Miller said coolly. "When our own existence is involved, we can't worry about them."

The darkness all around seemed deeper, the chill of the night beginning to penetrate even his heated clothes. Instant by instant, Cross's mind grew harder as he examined the implications of Miller's words. War! In a bleak voice, he said, "Only with the help of the true slans can that attack be stopped. I must find them—somewhere—and I've exhausted most of the possibilities. I am now going to the most likely remaining place."

The morning dragged. The sun gleamed like a festering sore in the blue-black vastness of the sky. And the sharp black shadows that it cast on the land grew narrow, and then began to lengthen again as Mars turned an unfriendly afternoon face to the insistent light.

From where Cross's ship crouched in the great chalk cliff, the horizon was a thing of blurred ridges against the shadowed sky. But even from his two-thousand-foot height, the nearness of the horizon was markedly noticeable. Twilight threatened, and then at last his patient vigil was rewarded. The small, red-striped, torpedo-shaped object drifted up from the horizon, fire pouring from its rear. The rays of the sinking sun glinted on its dull, metallic skin. It darted far to the left of where Cross waited in his machine that, like some beast of prey, lay entunneled in the swelling breast of the white cliff.

About three miles, Cross estimated carefully. The actual bulk of the intervening distance would make no difference to the motor that lay silent in the engine room in the back of the ship, ready to give forth its noiseless, stupendous power.

Three hundred miles, and that superb motor would vibrate on without strain, without missing a single beat—except that such titanic force could not be unleashed where its strength might touch ground, and tear a swath out of this already tortured land.

Three miles, four, five—he made swift adjustments. Then the force of the magnetors flashed across the miles and, simultaneously, the idea he had developed during his long trip from Earth took life from a special engine. Radio waves, so similar to the vibrations of energy he was using that only an extremely sensitive instrument could have detected the difference, sprayed forth from a robot motor that he had set up five hundred miles away. For those brief minutes, the whole planet sighed with energy waves.

Out there somewhere tendrilless slans must already be plotting the center of that interfering wave. Meantime, his small use of power should go unnoticed. Swiftly, yet gently, the magnetors did their work. The faraway, still receding ship slowed as if it had run into resistance. It slowed—and then was drawn inexorably back toward the chalk cliff.

Effortlessly, using the radio waves as a screen for further use of power, Cross withdrew his own ship deeper into the cliff's bulging belly, widening the natural tunnel with a spray of dissolving energy. Then, like a spider with a fly, he pulled the smaller machine into the lair after him.

In a moment a door opened, and a man appeared. He leaped lightly to the tunnel floor, and stood for a moment peering against the glare of the searchlight of the other ship. With easy confidence, he walked closer. His eyes caught the gleam of the crystal in the dank wall of the cave.

He glanced at it casually, then the very abnormality of a thing that could distract his attention at such a moment penetrated to his consciousness. As he plucked it out of the wall, Cross's paralyzing ray sent him sprawling.

Instantly, Cross clicked off all power. A switch closed; and the distant robot atomic-wave broadcaster dissolved in the fire of its own energy.

As for the man, all Cross wanted from him this time was a full-length photograph, a record of his voice, and hypnotic control. It took only twenty minutes before Corliss was flying off again toward Cimmerium, inwardly raging against his enslavement, outwardly unable to do anything about it.

There could be no hurrying of what Cross knew he must do before he could dare enter Cimmerium. Everything had to be anticipated, an almost unlimited amount of detail painstakingly worked out. Every fourth day—his holiday—Corliss called at the cave, coming and going, and as the urgent weeks passed, his mind was drained of memory, of detail. Finally, Cross was ready, and the next, the seventh holiday, his plans came to life. One Barton Corliss remained in the cave, deep in hypnotic sleep; the other one climbed into the small, red-striped craft and sped toward the city of Cimmerium.

It was twenty minutes later that the battleship flashed down from the sky and loomed up beside him, a vast mass of streamlined metal ship.

"Corliss," said a man's clipped voice in the ship's radio, "in the course of normal observation of all slans resembling the snake, Jommy Cross, we waited for you at this point, and find that you are approximately five minutes overdue.

"You will accordingly proceed to Cimmerium under escort, where you will be taken before the military commission for examination. That is all."

SEVENTEEN

Catastrophe came as simply as that. An accident not altogether unexpectable, but bitterly disappointing nonetheless. Six times before, Barton Corliss had been as much as twenty minutes overdue; and it had gone undetected. Now, five minutes of equally unavoidable delay—and the long arm of chance had struck at the hope of a world.

Gloomily, Cross stared into the visiplates. Below him was rock. Rock seamed and gnarled and unutterably deserted. No longer were the ravines like small arroyos. They slashed in all directions like a wild beast at bay. Vast valleys snarled into life; gorges sheered off into unplumbable depths, and then leaped up ferociously in ugly snags of mountain. This trackless waste was his way out, if ever he desired to escape, for no captured ship, however large and formidable, could hope to run the gauntlet that the tendrilless slans could throw up between himself and his own indestructible machine.

Some hope still remained, of course. He had an atomic revolver, which was built to resemble Corliss's gun and which actually fired an electric charge, until the secret mechanism for the atomic energy blast was activated. And the wedding ring on his finger was as near a copy as he could make of the one that Corliss wore, the great difference being that it contained the smallest atomic generator ever constructed, and was designed, like the gun, to dissolve if tampered with. Two weapons and a dozen crystals—to stop the war of wars!

The land that fled beneath his prison ship grew wilder now. Black, placid water began to show in oily, dirty streaks at the bottom of those primeval abysses, the beginning of the unclean, unbeautiful sea that was Mare Cimmerium.

Abruptly, there was unnatural life! On a tableland of mountain to his right a cruiser lay like a great, browsing black shark. A swarm of hundred-foot gunboats lay motionless on the rock around it, a wicked-looking school of deep-space fish that partly hid the even deadlier reality of the land on which their hard bellies rested. Before his penetrating vision, the mountain became a design of steel and stone fortress. Black steel, cleverly woven into black rock, gigantic guns peering into the sky.

And there, to the left this time, was another tableland of steel and time-tempered rock, another cruiser and its complement of pilot ships lying heavily in their almost invisible cradles. The guns grew thicker; and always they pointed skyward, as if waiting tensely for some momentarily expected and monstrously dangerous enemy. So much defense, so incredibly much *offense,* against what? Could these tendrilless slans be so uncertain about the true slans that even all these potent weapons could not quench their fear of those elusive beings?

A hundred miles of forts and guns and ships! A hundred miles of impassable gorge and water and frightful, upjutting cliffs. And then his ship and the great armored vessel that was his escort soared over a spreading peak; and there in the near distance glittered the glass city of Cimmerium. And the hour of his examination had come.

The city rode high on a plain that shrank back from the sheer-falling, ragged edge of a solid, dark tongue of sea. The glass flashed in the sun, a burning white fire that darted over the surface in vivid bursts of flame. It was not a big city. But it was as big as it could be in that forbidding area of land. It crowded with tight-fitting temerity to the very edge of the gorges that ringed its glass roof. Its widest diameter was three miles; at its narrowest point, it sprawled a generous two miles; and in its confines dwelled two hundred thousand slans, according to the figures he had obtained from Miller and Corliss.

The landing-field was where he had expected it would be. It was a flat expanse of metal at one projecting edge of the city, big enough to take a battleship, and it was streaked with shining threads of railway. Lightly his small machine settled toward one of the tracks onto metal cradle Number 9977. Simultaneously, the great bulk of warship above him surged off toward the sea, and was instantly lost to sight as it passed the towering cliff edge of glasslike roof.

Below him, the automatic machinery of the cradle rolled on its twin rails toward a great steel door. The door opened automatically, and shut behind him.

What his swift vision beheld in that first moment of entry was not unexpected, but the reality soared beyond the picture of it that he had seen in the minds of Miller and Corliss. There must have been a thousand ships in the section of the vast hangar that he could see. From roof to ceiling, they were packed in like sardines in a can, each in its cradle; and each, he knew, capable of being called forth if the proper numbers were punched on the section instrument board.

The machine stopped. Cross climbed casually down and nodded curtly to the three slans who waited there for him. The oldest of the three came forward, smiling faintly.

"Well, Barton, so you've earned another examination! You may be sure of a swift, thorough job—the usual, of course, fingerprinting, X ray, blood test, chemical reaction of the skin, microscope measurement of hair, and so on."

There was expectancy in the overtone of thought that leaked from the minds of the three men. But Cross did not need their thoughts. He had never been more alert, his brain had never been clearer, never more capable of distinguishing the subtlest exactness of details. He said mildly, "Since when has chemical reaction of the skin been a usual part of the examination?"

The men did not apologize for their little trap, nor did their thoughts show any disappointment at failure. And Cross felt no thrill at this first small victory. For no matter what happened at this early stage, he could not possibly stand a thorough examination. He must use to the limit the preparations he had made these last several weeks when he had analyzed the information from Miller's and Corliss's minds.

The youngest man said, "Bring him into the laboratory and we'll get the physical part of this examination over. Take his gun, Prentice."

Cross handed over the weapon without a word.

They waited then, the oldest man, Ingraham, smiling expectantly, Bradshaw, the youngest, staring at him with unwinking gray eyes. Prentice alone looked indifferent as he pocketed Cross's gun. But it was the silence, not their actions, that caught Cross's mind. There was not a physical sound, nowhere even a whisper of conversation. The whole community of the hangar was like a graveyard, and for the moment it seemed impossible that beyond those walls a city hummed with activity in preparation for war.

He actuated the combination, and watched his cradle and ship slide off soundlessly, first horizontally, then up toward the remote ceiling. There was abruptly the faintest squealing of metal, and then it settled into position. And silence grew again over the brief protrusion of sound.

Smiling inwardly at the way they were watching him for the slightest error of procedure, Cross led the way to the exit. It opened onto a shining corridor, the smooth walls of which were spaced at intervals with closed doors.

When they were within sight of the entrance to the laboratory, Cross said, "I suppose you called the hospital in time, telling them I would be delayed."

Ingraham stopped short, and the others followed suit. They stared at him. Ingraham said, "Good heavens, is your wife being revived this morning?"

Unsmiling, Cross nodded. "The doctors were to have her on the verge of consciousness twenty minutes after I was due to land. At that time they will have been working for approximately an hour. Your examination and that of the military commission will obviously have to be postponed."

There was no disagreement. Ingraham said, "The military will escort you, no doubt."

It was Bradshaw who spoke briefly into his wrist radio. The tiny, yet clear, answer reached to Cross.

"Under ordinary circumstances, the military patrol would escort him to the hospital. But it happens that we are confronted by the most dangerous individual the world has ever known. Cross is only twenty-three, but it is a proven fact that danger and adversity mature men and slans at an early age. We can assume, then, that we are dealing with a full-grown true slan, possessed of weapons and powers of unknown potentialities.

"If Corliss should actually be Cross, then the coincidence of Mrs. Corliss's return to consciousness at this important hour betokens preparation for all possible contingencies, particularly of suspicion at the moment of landing. He has already suffered a setback in that there is going to be an examination.

"Nevertheless, the very fact that postponement has been necessitated for the first time in our examination of men resembling Cross requires that experts trained in preliminary examination be with him every second of the time. You will, therefore, carry on until further orders. A surface car is waiting at the head of elevator Number One."

As they emerged into the street, Bradshaw said, "If he is not Corliss, then he will be absolutely useless at the hospital and Mrs. Corliss's mind will possibly be permanently injured."

Ingraham shook his head. "You're mistaken. True slans can read minds. He'll be able to do as good a job of sensing errors in the surgical room as Corliss with the aid of the Porgrave receivers."

Cross caught the grim smile on Bradshaw's face as the slan said softly, "Your voice trailed off there, Ingraham. Did it suddenly occur to you that the presence of the Porgraves will prevent Cross from using his mind, except in the most limited way?"

"Another thing"—it was Prentice who spoke—"the reason for Corliss's going to the hospital at all is that he will recognize when something is wrong because of the natural affinity between a husband and wife. But that also means that Mrs. Corliss will recognize instantly whether or not he is her husband."

Ingraham was smiling grimly. "We have, then, the final conclusion. If Corliss is Cross the revival of Mrs. Corliss in his presence may have tragic results for her. Those very results will go far to prove his identity, even if all other tests we make turn out negatively."

Cross said nothing. He had made a thorough examination of the problem presented by the Porgrave receivers. They constituted a danger, but they were only machines. His control over his mind should reduce that menace.

Recognition by Mrs. Corliss was another matter. Affinity between a sensitive husband and his sensitive wife was easily understandable, and it was unthinkable that he should contribute to the destruction of this slan woman's mind. Somehow he must save her sanity, but save himself, also.

The car sped smoothly along a boulevard that glowed with flowers. The road was dark, glassy in appearance, and not straight. It wound in and out among the tall, spreading trees that half hid the buildings that lined the far sides of the shaded walks to the left and right. The buildings were low-built structures, and their beauty, the flowing artistry of their design, surprised him. He had captured something of the picture they made from the minds of Miller and Corliss, but this triumph of architectural genius was beyond his anticipation. A fortress was not expected to be beautiful; gun turrets ordinarily were built for usefulness rather than to serve as poems of architecture.

As it was, they served their purpose admirably. They looked like actual buildings, part of an actual city, instead of being merely a thick armored screen for the true city below. Once again the vastness of the defense forces showed with what respect the true slans were viewed. A world of men was going to be attacked because of the tendrilless slan fear, and that was the ultimate in tragic irony.

"If I'm right," Cross thought, "and the true slans are living in with the tendrilless slans, as the tendrilless slans in their turn live with the human beings, then all this preparation is against an enemy that has already slipped inside the defenses."

The car stopped in an alcove that led to an elevator. The elevator dropped as swiftly into the depths as the first elevator had come up out of the hangar. Casually Cross took one of the metal "crystal" cubes out of his pocket and tossed it into the wastepaper receptacle that fitted snugly into one corner of the cage. He saw that the slans had followed his action. He explained.

"Got a dozen of those things, but apparently eleven is all I can comfortably carry. The weight of the others kept pressing that one against my side."

It was Ingraham who stooped and picked up the little thing. "What is it?"

"The reason for my delay. I'll explain to the commission later. The twelve are all exactly the same, so that one won't matter."

Ingraham stared at it thoughtfully, and was just about to open it when the elevator stopped. He put it decisively into his pocket. "I'll keep this," he said. "You go out first, Corliss."

Without hesitation, Cross stepped into the broad marble corridor. A woman in a white cloak came forward. "You'll be called in a few minutes, Barton. Wait here."

She vanished into a doorway, and Cross grew aware of a surface thought from Ingraham. He turned as the older slan spoke.

"This business of Mrs. Corliss worries me so much that I feel that before we allow you in there, Corliss, we ought to make a simple test that we haven't used for years because of its lack of dignity, and because of other equally effective tests."

"What's the test?" Cross asked curtly.

"Well, if you're Cross, you'll be wearing false hair to cover your slan tendrils. If you're Corliss, the natural strength of your hair would enable us to lift you right off the ground, and you'll scarcely feel it. False hair, artificially fastened on, could not possibly stand pressure. So, for the sake of your wife, I'm going to ask you to bend your head. We'll be gentle, and apply the pressure gradually."

Cross smiled. "Go ahead! I think you'll find that it's genuine hair."

It was, of course. Long since, he had discovered a kind of answer to that problem—a thick fluid that, worked over the roots of his hair, gradually hardened into a thin layer of rubbery, flesh-looking stuff, sufficient to cover his betraying tendrils. By carefully twisting the hair just before the hardening process was completed, tiny air holes were formed through to the hair roots.

Frequent removal of the material, and long periods of leaving his hair and head in the natural state, had in the past proved sufficient to keep the health of his head unimpaired. Something similar, it seemed to him, was what the true slans must have been doing these many years. The danger lay in the periods of "rest."

Ingraham said finally, grudgingly, "It doesn't really prove anything. If Cross ever comes here, he won't be caught on anything as simple as that. Here's the doctor, and I guess it's all right."

The bedroom was large and gray and full of softly pulsing machines. The patient was not visible, but there was a long metal case, like a streamlined coffin, one end of which pointed toward the door; the other end Cross couldn't see, but he knew the woman's head was projecting from that far side.

Attached to the top of the case was a bulging, transparent test tube affair. Pipes ran from it down into the "coffin," and through these pipes, through that bulbous bottle, flowed a rich, steady stream of red blood. A solid bank of instruments sat just beyond the woman's protruding head. Lights were there, glowing with the faintest unsteadiness, as if now one, now another was yielding obstinately to some hidden pressure. Each time, the one affected fought stubbornly to regain the infinitesimal loss of brightness.

From where the doctor made him stop, Cross could see the woman's head against the background of those whispering machines. No, not her head. Only the bandages that completely swathed her head were visible; and it was into the white pulp of bandage that the host of wires from the instrument board disappeared.

Her mind was unshielded, a still broken thing, and it was into the region of semithoughts that flowed along in dead-slow time that Cross probed cautiously.

He knew the theory of what the tendrilless slan surgeons had done. The body was entirely disconnected from nervous contact with the brain by a simple system of short circuit. The brain itself, kept alive by rapid tissue-building rays, had been divided into twenty-seven sections; and, thus simplified, the enormous amount of repair work had been swiftly performed.

His thought wave sped past those operation "breaks" and "mends." There were faults in plenty, he saw, but all of a distinctly minor character, so superbly had the surgical work been done. Every section of that powerful brain would yield to the healing force of the tissue-building rays. Beyond doubt, Mrs. Corliss would open her eyes a sane, capable young woman, and recognize him for the imposter he was.

In spite of urgency, Cross thought, "I was able to hypnotize human beings without the aid of crystals years ago, though it took a great deal longer. Why not slans?"

She was unconscious, and her shield down. At first, he was too aware of the Porgrave receivers, and the danger they offered. And then he grooved his mind to the anxiety vibration that would be normal for Corliss regardless of the circumstances. All fear drained from his brain. He strained forward with frantic speed.

It was the method of the operation that saved him. A properly knit slan brain would have required hours. So many millions of paths to explore, without a clue to the proper beginning. But now, in this mind, split by master surgeons into its twenty-seven natural compartments, the mass of cells comprising the will power was easily recognizable. In one minute he was at the control center, and the palpable force of his thought waves had gained him control.

He had time then to place the earphones of the Porgrave receivers over his head, noting at the same time that Bradshaw already had on a pair—for him, he thought grimly. But there was no suspicion at the surface of the young slan's mind. Evidently, thought in the form of an almost pure physical force, completely pictureless, could not be translated by the Porgraves. His own tests were confirmed.

The woman stirred mentally and physically, and the incoherent thought in her mind clattered as a sound in his earphones.

"Fight—occupation—"

The words fitted only because she had been a military commander, but there was not enough to make sense. Silence, then: "June—definitely June . . . be able to clear up before winter then, and have no unnecessary deaths from cold and dislocation . . . that's settled, then . . . June tenth—"

He could have repaired the faults in her brain in ten minutes by hypnotic suggestion. But it took an hour and a quarter of cautious cooperation with the surgeons and their vibration-pressure machine, and almost every minute of the time he was thinking about her words.

So June tenth was the day of the attack on Earth. This was April fourth, Earth reckoning. Two months! A month for the journey to Earth and a month—for what?

As Mrs. Corliss slipped quietly into a dreamless sleep, Cross had the answer. He dared not waste another day searching for the true slans. Later, perhaps, that trail could be picked up again, but now, if he could get out of this—

He frowned mentally. Within minutes he would be under physical examination by members of the most ruthless, most thoroughgoing and efficient race in the solar system. In spite of his successful attempt at delay, in spite of his preliminary success in getting a crystal into the hands of one of his escort, luck had been against him. Ingraham was not curious enough to take the crystal out of his pocket and open it.

He'd have to make another attempt, of course, but that was desperate. No slan would be anything but suspicious at such a second try, no matter how the approach was made.

His thought stopped. His mind stilled to a state of reception as an almost inaudible voice spoke from Ingraham's radio, and the words flowed across the surface of Ingraham's mind.

"Physical examination completed or not, you will bring Barton Corliss immediately before me. That supersedes any previous order."

"Okay, Joanna!" Ingraham replied quite audibly. He turned. "You're to be taken at once before Joanna Hillory, the military commissioner."

It was Prentice who echoed the thought in Cross's mind. The tall slan said, "Joanna is the only one of us who spent hours with Cross. She was appointed commissioner with that experience and her subsequent studies of him in mind. She supervised the world-wide successful search for his hideout and she also predicted the failure of the attack that was made with the cyclotron. In addition, she's written a lengthy report outlining in minutest detail the hours she spent in his company. If you're Cross, she'll recognize you in one minute flat."

Cross was silent. He had no way of evaluating the tall slan's statement, but he suspected that it might be true.

As Cross emerged from the case room, he had his first glimpse of the city of Cimmerium, the true, the underground city. From the doorway he could see along two corridors. One led back to the elevator down which he had come, the other to a broad expanse of tall, transparent doors. Beyond the doors lay a city of dreams.

It had been said on Earth that the secret of the materials that made up the walls of the grand palace had been lost. But here in this hidden city of the tendrilless slans was all the glory of it, and more. There was a street of soft, changing colors, and the magnificent realization of that age-old dream of architects, form-perfect buildings that were *alive* as music was alive. Here was—and no other word could apply, because no word in his knowledge was suitable—here was the gorgeous equivalent in architecture of the highest form of music.

Out in the street, he cut the beauty of it from his mind. Only the people mattered. And there were thousands in the buildings, in bustling cars and on foot. Thousands of minds within reach of a mind that missed nothing and searched now for one, just one, true slan.

And there was none; not a trace of betraying mind whisper; not a brain that did not *know* its owner was a tendrilless slan. Definitely, finally, the leaky brain shields gave of their knowledge. His conviction that they must be here was shattered, as his life would now be. Wherever the true slans were, their protection was slan-proof, beyond logic. But then, of course, logic had said that monster babies were not created by decent folk. The facts, it happened, were otherwise. What facts? Hearsay? But what other explanation was there?

"Here we are!" Ingraham said quietly.

Bradshaw said, "Come along, Corliss, Miss Hillory will see you now—alone!"

The floor felt strangely hard beneath his feet as he walked the hundred feet to the open door. Her inner sanctum was large and cozy, and it looked like a private den rather than a business office. There were books on shelves. Against one wall was a small electric filing-cabinet. There was a soft-toned sofa and multipneumatic chairs and a deep-piled rug. And finally there was a great gleaming desk behind which sat a proud, smiling, youthful woman.

Cross had not expected Joanna Hillory to look older, and she didn't. Another fifty years might put lines into those velvet-smooth cheeks, but now there was only one difference, and that was in himself. Years before, a boy slan had gazed at this glorious woman; now his eyes held the cool appraisal of maturity.

He noted curiously that her gaze was eager-bright, and that seemed out of place. His mind concentrated. The coordinated power of his sense abruptly dissolved her facial expression into triumph and a genuine joy. Alertly, his brain pressed against her mind shield, probing at the tiny gap, absorbing every leak of thought, analyzing every overtone, and second by second his puzzlement grew. Her smile flashed into soft laughter; and then her shield went down. Her mind lay before him, exposed to his free, untrammeled gaze. Simultaneously, a thought formed in her brain.

"Look deep, John Thomas Cross, and know first that all Porgrave receivers in this room and vicinity have been disconnected. Know, too, that I am your only living friend, and that I ordered you brought before me to forestall a physical examination which you could not possibly survive. I watched you through the Porgraves and, finally, I knew it was you. But hurry, search my mind, verify my good will, and then we must act swiftly to save your life!"

There was no credulity, no trustfulness, in his brain. The moments fled, and still he probed the dark corridors of her brain searching for those basic reasons that alone could explain this wondrous thing. At last he said quietly, "So you believed in the ideals of a fifteen-year-old, caught fire from a young egotist who offered only—"

"Hope!" she finished. "You brought hope just before I reached the point where most slans become as hard and ruthless as life can make them. 'Human beings,' you said, 'what about human beings?' And the shock of that and other things affected me beyond recovery. I deliberately gave a false description of you. You may have wondered about that. I passed it off because I was not supposed to have an expert's knowledge of human physiology. I didn't, of course, but I could have drawn you from memory perfectly, and the picture grew clearer every day. It was considered natural that I become a student of the Cross affair. And natural, also, that I was appointed to most of the supervisory positions that had any connection with you. I suppose that it was equally natural that—"

She stopped almost expectantly, and Cross said gravely, "I'm sorry about that!"

Her gray eyes met his brown ones steadily. "Whom else will you marry?" she asked. "A normal life must include marriage. Of course, I know nothing of your relationship to the slan girl, Kathleen Layton, except that you were with her at her death. But marriage to several women, frequently at the same time, is not unusual in slan history. Then, of course, there is my age."

"I recognize," Cross said simply, "that fifteen or twenty years is not the slightest obstacle to marriage among long-lived slans. It happens, however, that I have a mission."

"Whether as wife or not," said Joanna Hillory, "from this hour you have a companion on that mission provided we get you through this physical examination alive."

"Oh, that!" Cross waved a hand. "All I needed was time and a method of getting certain crystals into the hands of Ingraham and the others. You have provided both. We'll also need the paralyzer gun in the drawer of your desk. And then call them in one at a time."

With one sweeping movement of her hand, she drew the gun from the drawer. "I'll do the shooting!" she said. "Now what?"

Cross laughed softly at Joanna Hillory's vehemence and felt a strange wonder at the turn of events, even now that he was sure. For years he had lived on nerve and cold determination. Abruptly, something of her fire touched him. His eyes gleamed.

"And you won't regret what you have done, though your faith may be tried to the utmost before we are finished. This attack on Earth must not take place. Not now, not until we know what to do with those poor devils aside from holding them down by force. Tell me, is there any way I can get to Earth? I read in Corliss's mind something about a plan to transfer to Earth all slans resembling me. Can that be done?"

"It can. The decision rests entirely with me."

"Then," said Cross grimly, "the time has come for quick action. I must get to Earth. I must go to the palace. I must see Kier Gray."

The perfect mouth parted in a smile, but there was no humor in her fine eyes. "And how," she asked softly, "are you going to get near the palace, with its fortifications?"

"My mother spoke often of the secret passages under the palace," Cross answered. "Perhaps your statistics machine will know the exact location of the various entrances."

"The machine!" said Joanna Hillory, and was momentarily silent. Finally: "Yes, the 'Stics knows. It knows many things. Come along."

In the outer room, he followed her as she led the way in and out among row on row of great, thick, shiny, metallic plates. This, Cross knew, was the Bureau of Statistics, and these plates were the electric filing-cabinets that yielded their information at the touch of a button, the spelling out of a name, a number, a key word. No one knew (so Corliss's mind had informed him) how much information was in those cabinets. They had been brought from Earth, and dated back to the earliest slan days. A quadrillion facts were there for the asking. Included, no doubt, was the entire story of the seven-year search for one John Thomas Cross—the search that Joanna Hillory had directed from the inner sanctum of this very building.

Joanna Hillory said, "I want to show you something."

He stood watching her as she pushed the name plates *Samuel Lann* and then *Natural Mutation*. Swiftly, then, her fingers touched the activating button, and they read on the glowing plate:

Excerpts from Samuel Lann's diary, June 1, 2071:

> *Today, I had another look at the three babies, and there is no doubt that there is an extraordinary mutation. I have seen human beings with tails. I have examined cretins and idiots, and the monsters that have turned up in such numbers recently. And I have observed those curious, dreadful, organic developments that human beings are subject to. But this is the opposite of such horrors. This is perfection.*

> *Two girls and a boy. What a grand and tremendous accident. If I were not a cold-blooded rationalist, the exact rightness of what has happened would make me a blubbering worshipper at the shrine of metaphysics. Two girls to reproduce their kind, and one boy to mate with them. I'll have to train them to the idea.*

June 2, 2071, began the machine. But Joanna pressed urgently at the dissolver, manipulated the number key, and produced *June 7, 2073*.

A damn fool journalist wrote an article about the children today. The ignoramus stated that I had used a machine on their mother, whereas I didn't even know the woman till after the children were born. I'll have to persuade the parents to retreat to some remote part of the world. Anything could happen where there are human beings—superstitious, emotional asses.

Joanna Hillory made another selection—*May 31, 2088.*

Their seventeenth birthday. The girls thoroughly accept the idea of mating with their brother. Morality, after all, is a matter of training. I want this mating to take place, even though I found those other youngsters last year. I think it unwise to wait till these latter grow up. We can start crossbreeding later.

It was August 18, 2090, that produced:

Each of the girls had triplets. Wonderful. At this rate of reproduction, the period when chance can destroy them will soon be reduced to an actuarial minimum. Despite the fact that others of their kind are turning up here and there, I am continually impressing on the children that their descendants will be the future rulers of the world.

Back in her office, Joanna Hillory faced him and said, "You see, there is not, there never has been, a slan-making machine. All slans are natural mutations."

She broke off abruptly. "The best entrance to the palace for your purpose is located in the statuary section, two miles inside the grounds, constantly under brilliant lights, and directly under the guns of the first line of heavy fortifications. Also, machine-gun emplacements and tank patrols control the first two miles."

"What about my gun? Would I be allowed to have it on Earth?"

"No. The plan of transferring the men resembling you includes their disarmament."

He was aware of her questioning gaze on him, and his lean face twisted into a frown. "What kind of a man is Kier Gray, according to your records?"

"Enormously capable, for a human being. Our secret X rays definitely show him as human, if that's what you're thinking."

"At that time I did think about that, but your words verify Kathleen Layton's experience."

"We've got off the track," Joanna Hillory said. "What about the fortifications?"

He shook his head, smiling humorlessly. "When the stakes are great, risks must match them. Naturally, I shall go alone. You"—he gazed at her somberly—"will have the great trust of locating the cave where my ship is, and getting the machine through to Earth before June tenth. Corliss, also, will have to be released. And now, please call Ingraham in."

EIGHTEEN

The river seemed wider than when Cross had last seen it. Uneasily he stared across the quarter mile of swirling waters. In the swift current were patches of darkness and light, reflections from the ever changing wonder-fire of the palace. There was late spring snow in the concealing brush where he removed his clothing, and it tingled coldly against his bare feet when he stood at last stripped for his task.

He held his mind almost blank. Then came the ironic realization that one naked man against the world was a sorry symbol of the atomic energy he controlled. He'd had so many weapons and not used them when he could. And now this ring on his finger, with its tiny atomic generator, and its pitiful two-foot effective range—this was the only product of his years of effort that he dared to take with him into the fortress.

Trees on the opposite bank made shadows half across the river. The darkness streaked the ugly swell of racing water, which carried him half a mile downstream before his long backstrokes finally brought him to the shelter of the shallows.

He lay there, his mind reconnoitering the thoughts that came from the two machine-gunners hidden in the trees. Cautiously, he edged into a patch of concealing brush and donned his clothes. He lay then, patient as an old tiger stalking its prey. There was a clearing to be crossed, and it was too far for hypnotic control. The moment of their carelessness came abruptly. He covered the fifty yards in a fraction over three seconds.

One man never knew what struck him. The other jerked around, his long thin face strained and ghastly in the flicker of light that peered through the foliage. But there was no stopping, no evading the blow that caught his jaw and smashed him to the ground. In fifteen minutes of crystalless hypnotism, they were under control. Fifteen minutes! Eight an hour! He smiled ironically. That certainly precluded any possibility of hypnotically overpowering the palace with its ten thousand or so men. He must have key men.

He brought the two prisoners back to consciousness and gave them his orders. Silently they took their portable machine guns and fell in behind him. They knew every inch of the ground. They knew when the tank patrols rolled by in their night rounds. There were no better soldiers in the human army than these palace guards. In two hours there were a dozen trained fighters slipping along like shadows, working in a silent, swift co-ordination that needed only an occasional soft-spoken command.

In three more hours, he had altogether seventeen men, a colonel, a captain, and three lieutenants. And ahead was the long cordon of exquisite statuary, sparkling fountains, and blazing lights that marked at once his goal and the end of the first simple operation.

The first hint of the coming dawn misted the eastern sky as Cross lay with his little army in the shadows of shrubbery and stared across the quarter mile of brilliantly lighted area. He could see the dark line of woods on the other side, where the fortifications were hidden.

"Unfortunately," the colonel whispered, "there is no chance of tricking them. The jurisdiction of this unit ends right here. It is forbidden to cross to any one of the dozen fortified rings without a pass, and even a pass can be used only in the daytime."

Cross frowned. There were precautions here beyond his expectations, and he saw that their strictness was of recent enactment. The slan attack on his valley, though no one believed the wild peasant tales about the size of the ships involved or suspected they were spaceships, had produced tension and alertness that might defeat him now.

"Captain!"

"Yes?" The tall officer slid up beside him.

"Captain, you look the most like me. You will, therefore, exchange your uniform for my clothes and then you, all of you, will return to your regular stations."

He watched them slip off and vanish into the darkness. Then he stood up with the stiff carriage of the captain, and stalked into the light. Ten feet, twenty, thirty. He could see the fountain he wanted, a glittering shape with its sparkling streams of water. But there was too much artificial light, there were too many minds around, a confusion of vibrations that must be interfering with the one thought wave his mind was reaching for, if the damned thing was still there after all these hundreds of years. If it weren't there, God help him!

Forty feet, fifty, sixty—and then to his tense brain came a whisper, the tiniest of tiny mind vibrations.

"To any slan who penetrates this far—there is a secret passage into the palace. The five-flower design on the white fountain due north is a combination knob that operates on a secret door by radio. The combination is—"

He had known—the 'Stics machine had known—that the secret was in the fountain, but no more than that. Now—

A harsh magnified voice smashed out from the far trees. "Who the devil are you? What do you want? Get back to your commanding officer, obtain a pass, and return in the morning. Quick!"

He was at the fountain, his swift fingers on the flower design, his body and action half hidden from the host of staring, suspicious eyes. And there was not an ounce of energy to spare from his intense concentration. Before that singleness of purpose, the combination yielded, and a second thought came from a second Porgrave broadcaster.

"The door is now open. It is an extremely narrow tunnel leading down through dense darkness. The mouth is in the center of the equestrian group of statuary a hundred feet due north. Have courage."

It was not courage that was lacking. It was time. A hundred feet north, toward the palace, *toward* those menacing forts. Cross laughed curtly. The ancient builder of the secret entrance had certainly picked a hell of a spot to practice his ingenuity. He walked on, even as the harsh voice lashed out again.

"You out there—you will stop at once, or we fire. Return to your district, and consider yourself under arrest. At once!"

"I've got a very important message!" Cross called out in a clear voice that was as similar to the captain's as he could make it without practice. "Emergency!"

And still they didn't consider one man dangerous. Still he walked on.

The answer blared back, "No possible emergency justifies such a flagrant breach of regulations. Return immediately to your district. I warn you for the last time!"

He stared down at the little black hole, and dismay struck into him, a piercing claustrophobia, the first he had ever known, black and terrible as the tunnel itself. Entrust himself to the rabbit's burrow with its potentialities of suffocation, possibly to be buried alive in some cunningly contrived human trap! There could be no certainty that they had not discovered this, as they had already discovered so many other slan hideaways.

Abruptly it was urgent. A torrent of sibilant pulsations reached out of the trees ahead, little whispers that breathed against his brain like soft physical things. Somebody saying, "Sergeant, train your gun on him!"

"What about the horse statuary, sir? Be a shame to nick them!"

"Aim at his legs and then at his head!"

And that was that. With clenched teeth, body stiff and straight, and arms flung over his head, he leaped like a diver going feet first, and came down so perfectly in the tunnel that it was several seconds before his clothes scraped the vertical walls.

The passage was smooth as glass, and it was only after Cross had fallen an immense distance that it started to tilt away from the vertical. Pressure of friction grew stronger; and after more swift seconds, he was sliding at a distinct angle that grew flatter by the instant. His breathless speed slowed measurably. He saw a glimmer of light ahead. Abruptly he emerged into a low-roofed, dimly lighted corridor. His line of motion was still slightly downward, but it straightened rapidly. His journey ended, he lay dizzily on his back, his vision spinning.

A dozen revolving lights above him gradually tightened their circle and became a single, dim bulb shedding a dull refulgence around it: a wan, almost futile, light that hugged the ceiling and melted into darkness before it reached the floor. Cross climbed to his feet, and found himself staring at a sign that was just high enough up on the wall for the ceiling light to touch it. He strained and read.

YOU ARE NOW TWO MILES BELOW THE SURFACE. THE TUNNEL BE-
HIND YOU IS BLOCKED BY STEEL AND CONCRETE SHAFTS, WHICH WERE
ACTUATED, EACH IN ITS TURN, BY YOUR PASSAGE. IT WILL TAKE AN
HOUR TO GET FROM HERE TO THE PALACE. SLANS ARE FORBIDDEN UN-
DER SEVERE PENALTIES TO ENTER THE PALACE PROPER. TAKE HEED.

There was a tickling in his throat. He fought back the sneeze but it came, followed by a half dozen more. The tears ran down his cheeks. It was dimmer where he stood than when he had first come into the corridor. The long row of ceiling lights, which faded into the remote distance ahead, were not as bright as they had been. Dust obscured them.

Cross bent in the half-darkness and ran his fingers lightly over the floor. A soft, thick carpet of dust lay there. He peered ahead, searching for footprints that would show that this corridor had been recently used. But there was only dust, an inch at least, years of it.

Countless years had passed since that order with its vague threat had been placed there. Meanwhile, there was more real danger. Human beings would now know where to look for the secret entrance. Before they discovered it, he must, in defiance of the slan law, penetrate the palace and get at Kier Gray!

It was a world of shadows and silence, and insidious choking fingers of dust that kept reaching for Cross's throat, and then—ludicrous paradox—tickled instead of strangled. He went through many doors and corridors, and great stately rooms.

Suddenly, there was a soft metal click behind him. Whirling, he saw a solid sheet of metal door flow softly into the floor over which he had just passed, creating a smooth, hard wall. He stood very still, and for a moment he was a sensitive machine receiving impressions. There was the long, narrow corridor, ending just ahead, the dim lights above, and the floor beneath him, the latter cushioned by a thick, yeilding dust. Into the silence a second click projected harshly. The walls creaked metallically and began to move, coming at a deliberate pace toward him, and toward each other.

Automatic, he decided, for there was not the faintest tendril of thought anywhere. Coolly, he examined the potentialities of the trap, and presently discovered at the extreme end of each wall a nook. Each nook was six feet four inches in height. A shallow place large enough to hold half a human body sideways. The contours of the body were grooved into those nooks.

Cross smiled grimly. In a few minutes, the walls would come together, and the only available space for him would be where the two nooks would then be joined. A neat trap!

True, the atomic energy of the ring on his finger could probably disintegrate a pathway for him through the walls or the door, but his purpose demanded that this trap be successful up to a point. He examined the nooks more carefully. This time his ring flashed twice in brief fury, dissolving the handcuffs that waited in the handholds for the helpless, carving also enough space to give himself freedom of movement.

When the walls were a foot apart, a four-inch-wide crack opened the full length of the floor, and the small mountain of dust poured into it. A few minutes later the two walls met with a metallic band.

A moment of silence! Then machinery whirred faintly, and there was a swift flow of upward movement. The movement continued for minutes on end before it slowed and finally stopped. But the machinery still whispered beneath him. Another minute, and then the cubicle in which he stood began to revolve slowly. A crack appeared before his face, a crack that widened into a rectangular hole through which he could see into a room.

The machinery stopped whirring. There was silence again while Cross examined the room. There was a desk in the center of a highly polished floor, with walnut-paneled walls beyond. Some chairs and filing-cabinets and the edge of a floor-to-ceiling bookcase completed what he could see of the spare, businesslike room.

Footsteps sounded. The man who came in and shut the door behind him was magnificently built, grayed at the temples now, lines of age showing. But there was no one in all the world who would not have recognized that lean face, those piercing eyes, the ruthlessness that was written indelibly in those thin nostrils and line of jaw. It was a face too hard, too determined, to be pleasant. But withal it was a noble countenance. Here was a born leader of men. Cross felt himself dissected, his face explored by those keen eyes. Finally, the proud mouth twisted into the faintest sneer.

Kier Gray said, "So you got caught. That wasn't very clever."

It was the words that did it. For with them came surface thoughts, and those surface thoughts were a deliberate screen held over a mind shield as tight as his own. No leaky tendrilless slan shield this, but an enormous fact. Kier Gray, leader of men, was a man who believed himself to be—

"A true slan!"

That one explosive sentence Cross uttered, and then the fluidity of his mind chilled into an ice of quiet thought. All those years that Kathleen Layton had lived with Kier Gray, and not suspected the truth. Of course she had lacked experience with mind shields, and there had been John Petty with a similar type of shield to confuse the issue, because John Petty *was* human. How cleverly the dictator had imitated the human way of thought protection! Cross shook himself mentally and, determined to get reaction this time, repeated, "So—you *are* a slan!"

The other's face twisted sardonically. "That's hardly the right description for a man without tendrils who cannot read minds, but yes, I am a slan."

He paused, then continued earnestly. "For hundreds of years we who knew the truth have existed for the purpose of preventing the tendrilless slans from taking over the world of men. What more natural than that we should insinuate our way into control of the human government? Are we not the most intelligent beings on the face of the Earth?"

Cross nodded. It fitted, of course. His own deductions had told him that. Once he knew that the true slans were not, actually, the hidden government of the tendrilless slans, it was inevitable they would be governing the human world, for all Kathleen's belief and the tendrilless slan X-ray pictures showing Kier Gray to be possessed of a human heart and other nonslan organs. Somewhere here there was still a tremendous mystery. He shook his head finally.

"I still don't get it all. I expected to find the true slans ruling the tendrilless—secretly. Everything fits, of course, in a distorted fashion. But why antislan propaganda? What about that slan ship which came to the palace years ago? Why are true slans hunted and killed like rats? Why not an arrangement with the tendrilless slans?"

The leader stared at him thoughtfully. "We have tried on occasion to tamper with antislan propaganda, one such attempt being that very ship to which you have referred. For special reasons I was forced to order it down in the marshes. But in spite of that apparent failure, it succeeded in its main purpose, which was to convince the tendrilless slans, who were definitely contemplating their attack, that we were still a force to be reckoned with.

"It was the palpable weakness of the silver ship that convinced the tendrilless slans. They knew we could not be that impotent and so once more they hesitated and were lost. It has always been unfortunate, the number of true slans being killed in various parts of the world. They are the descendants of slans who, scattered after the War of Disaster, never made connection with the slan organization. After the tendrilless slans came on the scene it was, of course, too late to do anything. Our enemies were in a position to interfere with every communication device that we possessed.

"We tried our best, naturally, to contact such wanderers. But the only ones who really got through were those who came to the palace to kill me. For them we provided a number of easy passageways into the palace. My instruments tell me that you came the hard way, through one of the ancient entrances. Very daring. We can use another bold young man in our small organization."

Cross stared at the other coolly. Kier Gray obviously did not suspect his identity nor did he know how near was the hour of tendrilless slan attack. It made the moment a great one as he said, "I'm amazed that you allowed me to catch you by surprise like this."

Kier Gray's smile faded abruptly. He said in a tight voice, "Your remark is very pointed. You assume that you have caught me. Either you are a fool, a possibility refuted by your obvious intelligence, or else, in spite of your apparent imprisonment, that imprisonment is not actual. And there's only one man in the world who could nullify the hard steel of the handcuffs in that cubicle."

Amazingly, the strong face had gone slack, the hard lines were faded, but it was the eyes that showed strength now. A glad, eager, wide-eyed joy. He half whispered, "Man, man, *you've done it!* in spite of my being unable to give you the slightest help—atomic energy in its great form at last." His voice rang out then, clear and triumphant. "John Thomas Cross, I welcome you and your father's discovery. Come in here and sit down. Wait a minute while I get you out of that damn place! We can talk here in this private den of mine. No human being is ever allowed here."

The wonder of it grew with each passing moment. The tremendousness of what it meant, this world-wide balancing of immense forces. True slans with the human beings, who knew not of their masters, against the tendrilless slans who, in spite of their brilliant, far-flung organization, had never guessed the truth behind the mystery.

"Naturally," said Kier Gray, "your discovery that slans are naturals and not machine-made is nothing new to us. We are the mutation-after-man. The forces of that mutation were at work many years before that great day when Samuel Lann realized the pattern of perfection in some of the mutations. It is only too obvious now in retrospect that nature was building for a tremendous attempt. Cretins increased alarmingly; insanity advanced by enormous percentages. The amazing thing about it was the speed with which the web of biological forces struck everywhere across the Earth.

"We have already assumed far too readily that no cohesion exists between individuals, that the race of men is not a unit with an immensely tenuous equivalent of a blood-and-nerve stream flowing from man to man. There are, of course, other ways of explaining why billions of people can be made to act alike, think alike, feel alike, given a single dominating stimulus, but slan philosophers have, through the ages, been toying with the possibility that such mental affinity is the product of an extraordinary unity, physical as well as mental.

"For hundreds, perhaps thousands, of years, the tensions had been building up. And then in a single stupendous quarter of a millennium more than a billion abnormal births occurred. It was like a cataclysm that paralyzed the human will. The truth was lost in a wave of terror that swept the world into war. All attempts to revive the truth have been swamped by an incredible mass hysteria—even now, after a thousand years. Yes, I said a *thousand* years. Only we true slans know that the nameless period actually lasted five hundred hellish years. And that the slan children discovered by Samuel Lann were born nearly fifteen hundred years ago.

"So far as we know, very few of those ultra-normal births were alike. Most were horrible failures, and there was only an occasional perfection. Even these would have been lost if Lann had failed to recognize them for what they were. Nature relied on the law of averages. No preconceived plan existed. What happened seemed simply to have been a reaction to the countless intolerable pressures that were driving men mad, because neither their minds nor their bodies were capable of withstanding modern civilization. These pressures being more or less similar, it is understandable that many of nature's botches should bear a resemblance to each other, without being similar in detail.

"An example of the enormous strength of that biological tide, and also of the fundamental unity of man," Kier Gray continued, "is shown in that nearly all slans born in the first few hundred years were triplets or, at lowest, twins. There are few such multiple births now. The single child is the rule. The wave has spent itself. Nature's part of the work ended, it remained for intelligence to carry on. And that was where the difficulty came.

"During the nameless period, slans were hunted like wild beasts. There is no modern parallel for the ferocity of human beings against the people they considered responsible for the disaster. It was impossible to organize effectively. Our forefathers tried everything—underground hideouts, surgical removal of tendrils, replacement of human hearts for their own double hearts, use of skinlike stuff over tendrils. But it proved useless.

"Suspicion was swift beyond all resistance. Men denounced their neighbors, and had them medically examined. The police made their raids on the vaguest of clues. The greatest difficulty of all was the birth of babies. Even where a successful disguise had been achieved by the parents, the arrival of a child was always a period of immense danger, and all too frequently brought death to mother, father, and child. It was gradually realized that the race could not survive. The scattered remnants of the slans finally concentrated on efforts to control the mutation force. At last they found how to shape the large molecules that made up the genes themselves. It proved to be the ultimate life stuff that controlled the genes as the genes in their turn controlled the shape of the organs and the body.

"It remained then to experiment. That took two hundred precarious years. No risks could be taken with the race, though individuals risked their lives and their health. They found at last how complex groups of molecules could control the form of each organ for one generation or many. Alter the pattern of that group, and the organ affected was transformed, only to turn up again in a later generation. And so they changed the basic slan structure, keeping what was good and had survival value, eliminating what had proved dangerous. The genes controlling the tendrils were altered, transferring the mind-reading ability inside the brain, but insuring that the ability did not turn up for many generations—"

Cross interrupted with a gasp. "Wait a minute! When I first started to search for the true slans, logic said they were infiltrated into the tendrilless slan organization. Are you trying to tell me that the tendrilless slans will eventually *be* the true slans?"

Kier Gray nodded matter-of-factly. "In less than fifty years they'll have the ability to read minds, although the faculty will for a time be located inside their minds. Eventually, of course, the tendrils will come back. We haven't discovered yet whether we can make any change permanent."

Cross said, "But why were they ever stopped from having the mind-reading ability—particularly during these decisive years?"

The reply was earnestly spoken. "I can see that you still do not recognize the inescapable realities of the lives of our ancestors. The capacity and knowledge of mind reading were withheld because it was necessary to observe psychological reactions—because as people acted not knowing they were true slans, so they would have acted knowing it. What happened?

"We—the slan leaders—had altered so many of their distinguishing organs to protect them from predatory human beings that they acted as if they had no interest in being anything but quiet-living folk in the remote corners of the world. The truth might have roused them, but not in time. We have discovered that slans are by nature antiwar, antimurder, antiviolence. We used every argument, but no logic would produce anything more than the general feeling that in a hundred years or so they would start thinking in terms of action.

"It was impossible to permit them to stay that way. Human existence has been like a bomb fuse. Life burned slowly for millions of years, then the fire reached the bomb—which exploded. The explosion managed to set another fuse alight, but, though we only suspected it then, the old bomb and fuse were finished. Now, it is certain that human beings will sputter out, vanish from the Earth as a result of the sterility that has already started on a vast scale, though it is not yet noticeable. Man will go into history along with the Java ape man, the Neanderthal beast man, and the Cro-Magnon primitive. Undoubtedly, the sterility which will cause this will be blamed on the slans, and when human beings discover it there will begin the second great wave of ferocity and terrorism. Nothing but the most powerful organization, expanded at top acceleration, under constant and dangerous pressure, could have been properly prepared."

"And so," Cross said softly, "you drove out the tendrilless—the protected—slans with violence that bewildered them, then brought an equally ruthless reaction. Ever since you've been a spur on their expansion and a check on that artificially engendered, ruthless spirit of theirs. But why haven't you told them the truth?"

The leader smiled grimly. "We tried that, but those we selected as confidants thought it was a trick, and their logic led them instantly to our hiding-place. We had to murder them all. We've got to wait till the mindreading ability comes back.

"And now, from what you've told me, I can see that we must act swiftly. Your hypnotism crystals, of course, could be the final solution to the problem of human antagonism. As soon as there are enough slans with the know-how, that difficulty at least may be overcome. As for the imminent attack—"

He reached toward a buzzer button on his desk, and pressed it.

He went on, "That will bring a few colleagues of mine. We must have an immediate conference."

Cross said slowly, "Slans can safely hold conferences in the grand palace?"

Kier Gray smiled. "My friend, we base our operations upon the limitations of individual human beings."

"I'm not sure I understand."

"It's quite simple. Years ago, many human beings knew a lot about many of the secret passageways of the palace. One of my first acts, as soon as I was able, was to classify this knowledge. Then, one by one, I transferred to other parts of the world the men who had the information. There, isolated in various obscure government departments, they were skillfully assassinated."

He shook his head grimly. "It doesn't take long. And, once the secret has been established, the very vastness of this place—and the strict military control of every avenue—prevents rediscovery. There are seldom less than a hundred slans around the palace. Most of them are tendriled, although a few tendrilless ones—descendants, like myself, of the earliest successful volunteers for the survival experiments in gene transformation—have always known the truth and been part of our organization. We could operate on the tendriled ones, of course, and make it safe for them to go outside, but we've reached the stage where we want a few tendriled slans around, so that the others can see what their descendants will be like in a few generations. After all, we don't want *them* suddenly becoming panicky."

"What about Kathleen?" asked Cross slowly.

The older man gave him a long, measured look, and said finally,

"Kathleen was an experiment. I wanted to see if human beings who grew up with a slan might not come to realize that kinship was possible. When it was finally evident that this could not be achieved, I decided to transfer her here, to these secret chambers, where she could begin to benefit from association with other slans, and help in all the things that had to be done. She proved to be bolder and more ingenious than I had anticipated—but you know about that escapade."

The word *escapade* was about as mild a description of a major tragedy as Cross had ever heard. Evidently, this man was even more inured to death than he was.

Before he could comment, Kier Gray said, "My own wife, who was a true slan, fell victim to the secret police in a somewhat different, though equally grim, manner, except that in her case I was not present until long after—" He stopped. For a long moment he sat with narrowed eyes, and there was nothing casual about his manner now. He said abruptly, "And now that I've told you so much—what *is* your father's secret?"

Cross said simply, "I can go into it in greater detail later. Briefly, my father rejected the notion of critical mass, on which the first bombs were based. Atomic energy is available that way—in torrents, in explosive form, in the form of heat, and for certain medical and industrial purposes. But it is almost impossible to control for direct use. My father rejected it partly because it was useless to slans in that form, partly because he had a theory.

"He also rejected the massive cyclotron principle, but it was the cyclotron that gave him at least a part of his great idea. He evolved a central core of positive electrons spun out like a fine wire. At this core, but not directly at it—a comparison would be the way a comet comes at the sun in an elongated orbit—at this 'sun' he discharged his negative-electron 'comets' at the speed of light.

"The 'sun' whipped the comets around and flung them out into 'space,' where—and here the comparison is very real—a second positive core which might be called 'Jupiter' pulls at the 'comets' already traveling at the speed of light, and catapults them *faster than light* completely out of their orbits. At that speed, each electron becomes matter in a minus state, with a destructive power utterly out of proportion to its 'size.' Normal matter loses its coherence in the presence of this minus stuff and reverts instantly to a primeval state. It—"

He paused, and looked up as the door opened. Three men with golden slan tendrils in their hair came in. Their mind shields went down as they saw him; Cross lowered his a moment later. There was a lightning interchange among the four of them—names, back history, purposes—data of every kind necessary to a fuller comprehension of the meeting. The process was dazzling to Cross, who, except for his brief contact with the inexperienced Kathleen, and his undeveloped childhood relationship with his parents, had previously only imagined how effective such an interchange might be.

He was so intent that he was caught by surprise when the door opened again.

A tall young woman came in. She had flashing eyes, and a strong, mature, finely molded, delicately textured face. Looking at her, his muscles stiffened, his nerves grew taut, and a chill enveloped his body. Yet, even as his amazement grew, he thought with a sharp logic that he should have realized after the way the smashed head of Mrs. Corliss had been repaired on far-off Mars. He should have known the moment he discovered that Kier Gray was a true slan. Should have guessed, knowing the hates and envies of the palace, that only death, and a return from death in secret, could ultimately and effectively keep Kathleen safe from John Petty.

It was at that point in his thought that Kier Gray's voice cut across the silence with the rich tones of one who had secretly relished this instant for years.

"Jommy Cross, I want you to meet Kathleen Layton Gray—my daughter."

SLAN HUNTER

FOREWORD
—by Lydia van Vogt

It is wonderful to be asked to tell the story of the evolution of *Slan Hunter*—or *Slan II* as our family knew it for years.

Since its original publication in 1940, *Slan* has continued to be Van's most popular novel. There have been fan clubs, discussion groups, countless articles and dissertations, and even a commune inspired by *Slan*. The novel remains in print to this day, half a century after its original publication.

Van and others discussed the possibility of a sequel over the years, but nothing was ever seriously considered until my son, Greg, began pursuing the idea with Van in late 1988. Moved by his enthusiasm and his view that *Slan* and its fans deserved a conclusion to the story, Van told Greg to put together his ideas, and they would go from there. By mid-1989 a working outline had been completed, and Van began writing the actual novel.

Prior to this, neither Greg nor I had actually been involved in the creation of one of Van's works. Though we knew, to an extent, how he wrote notes of ideas and dialogue, we did not know how he put it all together. Van usually took a year to get to the final draft of a novel, so we gave him his space to create.

As he continued to add pages to the working files of *Slan II*, the project seemed to be moving along quite well. At the beginning of 1990, however, an unexpected conversation regarding the choice of endings for the novel raised concerns with us that things were not as they seemed. We had offered different possible endings in the outline, depending on whether Van and the publishers wanted to do a third *Slan* novel and/or a prequel. In this conversation, though, Van seemed completely unaware of the issue that had already been discussed many times, and further conversations revealed a very troubling picture. His work on the new novel had progressed, but not nearly as far as we had been led to believe.

We had known for a few years that Van's memory was diminishing, and while we consulted doctors, they attributed the problems to "just getting older" and did not express a great deal of concern. This was now, however, much more serious than a touch of old-age senility.

Van was a remarkably intelligent man. None of us realized how effectively he had used that intelligence to mask the grip Alzheimer's was beginning to have on his mind. It is so painful to think back now, knowing how frightened, confused, and frustrated he must have been. He would have realized something terrible was happening to his brain's ability to remember and cohesively tie thoughts together; try as he might, he could not stop it from progressing. All Van could do was use his brilliance and wit to conceal those months of total bewilderment.

With the sad reality now exposed, we began in earnest to find out all we could about what was actually happening to him and what we could do about it. At that time, information on the disease was sketchy, and doctors actually seemed reluctant to commit to a specific diagnosis. It wasn't until late 1990 that doctors stopped referring to Van's condition as senility or dementia, and recognized that he was suffering from Alzheimer's disease.

What had begun as an exciting new project for Van, and the beginning of a new era of family involvement, was now tragically a realization of what the family's focus would be from that point forward. Van endured and struggled with this progressively debilitating disease until it took his life and last brilliant thought on January 26, 2000.

As you can imagine, the completion of this novel means a great deal to me and our family. Not only does *Slan Hunter* complete Van's last great project, incorporating his ideas, characters, and dialogue; but it is also a fun, grand adventure reminding us of the inventiveness and forward thinking of one of the grand masters of the Golden Age of science fiction.

I must express my deepest and most sincere thanks to Kevin J. Anderson. Without his interest, dedication, and tremendous talent, the dream of a sequel to *Slan* would not have come true, and this book would not be in your hands today. Seldom is an author given the opportunity to be reborn in the public eye. Kevin's inspiration and determination have brought that opportunity to my beloved husband, A. E. van Vogt. From the bottom of my heart and Van's, "Thank you, Kevin."

Throughout his life, almost everything A. E. van Vogt studied had to do with people: how they thought, felt, loved, or pursued their dreams. A review of his works, fiction or nonfiction, shows us how devoted he was to the idea of helping us see ourselves more clearly, helping us find better ways to achieve our goals, helping us become better than we already were—helping us, if you will, become like slans.

Ultimately, I believe, this is what people saw in him and his work, and why to this day he has so many wonderful fans. The outpouring of letters and Internet discussions from all of you after his death was so overwhelming to me that, to this day, I am overcome with emotion thinking about it. Thank you all so very much for all of your kind and heartwarming thoughts about my wonderful husband, A. E. van Vogt.

ONE

The world was already falling apart when her first contractions hit.

"Perfect timing—" Anthea Stewart clenched her teeth to stop a hiss of pain, holding her rounded abdomen.

Beside her, driving recklessly, her husband Davis said, "Don't worry, Anth. I'll get you there in time." He took a hard right so that the wide whitewalled tires squealed on the asphalt. "Plenty of time. Don't you worry about a thing." The hospital was just ahead. He accelerated.

"Why are you telling *me* not to worry? Because you're doing all the work?"

"I'm doing every bit as much as I can." He flashed her a grin so full of love that she forgot the pain. Then Anthea gripped the handrest as she concentrated on the spasms, the clenching of her muscles, and the restless baby inside her.

She felt a strange, bittersweet anticipation. Soon, the healthy infant she had carried for nine months would emerge into the world. He would no longer be an integral part of her, and their lives would be permanently changed. But Anthea looked forward to it with anticipation as well as trepidation. She would stop being a "pregnant woman" and become a "mother"; they would stop being a "married couple" and become a "family." The thought brought a smile to her lips. So many changes ahead!

The AM radio blared, laced with occasional threads of static, as the edgy-sounding announcer talked about the current crisis. Davis had turned on the car radio as he drove, hoping for some soothing music for his wife, but the emergency broadcasts were not comforting. "Slan attack imminent. Radar images show the possibility of numerous enemy ships approaching."

Anthea wiped sweat from her forehead and turned to look at him. Davis was alarmingly pale, disturbed by the tense news as well as having the jitters of an expectant father. He turned the knob again, trying a different station.

"—President Kier Gray arrested. The world has been rocked to learn that their leader was secretly a slan in disguise. The noted slan hunter John Petty, chief of the secret police, has assumed provisional control of the government after making the arrest himself. Several of the President's cabinet members, also shown to be slans, were killed in the altercation. Gray's arrest raises the uncomfortable question of how many more of the telepathic mutants might be living among us, completely unnoticed."

Davis snapped off the radio in disgust. "I guess we'll just have to hum if we want music." A slow-moving car driven by an old man hunched over the steering wheel swerved out of the way as Davis rushed past.

"How could Kier Gray be a slan?" Anthea said, trying to distract herself. "I thought they all had tendrils coming out the back of their heads. He couldn't possibly have hidden what he was."

"Don't underestimate how devious they can be. They use makeup, prosthetics, hairpieces to cover up their tendrils. It really is a conspiracy." He stared intently ahead as he drove. "I wish we'd just wiped them all out during the Slan Wars."

She squeezed her eyes shut, trying to sound conversational despite the spasms, but she failed miserably. "It's not . . . as if . . . we didn't try."

The telepathic humans were physically superior, with great strength and improved healing abilities; they considered themselves a master race. Long ago, the mutant slans had tried to dominate and enslave the rest of humanity. Centuries of warfare ensued as brave humans fought slans, defeated them, and drove the few survivors into hiding.

Though the media was rife with rumors about an expansive underground slan organization and numerous concealed bases, only a few loners were ever caught. Sinister slan ships occasionally flew over the great cities on Earth, sometimes dropping off messages, other times just gathering reconnaissance. Obviously, the slans were building their numbers, gearing up for some sort of concerted attack. No wonder humanity was terrified.

Somehow, though, being with Davis made her feel safe, no matter what the radio news said. Her husband had brown eyes in contrast with her blue ones, dark curly hair as opposed to her straight, strawberry-blond. But Anthea and Davis Stewart were not opposites:

They had been soul mates since their first meeting. Some romantics called it "love at first sight"; others talked about chemistry and matching personalities. From the moment she had met Davis, it seemed their very heartbeats had synchronized. They had known they were meant for each other. Now with the coming baby, their love, their family, would be stronger than ever before.

Unbearable affection seeped through the concern on his face like fresh rain washing away a stain. "It won't be long now, Anth. Just hang on."

After riding through another contraction, she gave him a strange smile. "No, Davis . . . no, it won't. But I don't think I can concentrate on politics anymore . . . okay?"

Davis raced toward the tall, brown-brick Centropolis General Hospital, turning into the marked driveway for the emergency-room entrance. He wasn't going to let even a planet-sized war get in the way of the medical attention his wife needed. He pulled up to the curb in front of the double doors, then jammed the shift lever into park and opened his door all in one gesture. "Just wait here. I'll get somebody."

Anthea was tempted to walk by herself into the emergency room, but then another contraction hit, harder than the previous ones. "All right," she gasped. "I'll just wait here."

Running into the hospital with his hair mussed, awkwardly waving his arms, Davis looked utterly adorable. She knew she would never forget that sight.

Anthea closed her eyes and counted, trying to time the contractions, though it was merely a trick to occupy her mind. She had always been able to shunt aside pain, to concentrate on her body. Did all mothers feel so connected to their babies? It wanted to come out—*he* wanted to be born, and she experienced an inexplicable confidence that the delivery would be smooth. She had nothing to worry about.

Davis returned in less than a minute, pushing a wheelchair. A gangly orderly jogged along beside her husband, scolding him and trying to wrest the wheelchair from him, but Davis wanted to do this himself. The two men quickly helped Anthea out of the car and into the emergency-room waiting area. The orderly shouted for a nurse, who in turn shouted for a doctor, and they all rushed toward the delivery room.

Anthea looked up just long enough to see several policemen milling about in the emergency room. A grim-looking, dark-suited man wore an armband with the insignia of the secret police, a scarlet hammer across a web. A slan hunter here in the hospital? Her thoughts were fuzzy, but she realized that if the slans were going to attack Centropolis, many casualties would be pouring into this medical center. Slan terrorists probably thought the hospital would be a good place to sabotage. What if one of them took her baby? She had heard of the terrible things slans did to babies. . . .

The man with the armband was scolding a plump woman behind the reception desk. "I must insist, ma'am. The secret police have the legal authority to inspect all of your admissions records. I want your carbon copies."

While halfheartedly clacking away on her manual typewriter, she popped her pink gum with a sound like the shot from a toy gun. "Sir, don't you think that if we found a slan in our treatment rooms we would report it?"

"I need to look at blood tests and any X-rays. Their internal organs are different from ours, you know. President Gray was a slan in disguise—we can't trust anyone. We have evidence that there may be a new breed of slans, ones that don't have tendrils."

The receptionist continued typing as she talked. "Surgically removed so that they can infiltrate our society better? I assure you, we would notice such scars."

The man from the secret police scowled. "That is not for you to decide, ma'am. These new mutations may even be born without the tendrils. In fact, some of them might not even know they're slans."

The receptionist chuckled nervously. "Oh, come now! How can they not know?"

With a grim expression, the man simply held out his hand. The plump receptionist heaved a put-upon sigh and turned in her swivel chair. She opened a gray metal filing cabinet and pulled out the curling carbon-copy records of all recent admissions. Her expression made it perfectly clear that she thought the secret policeman was wasting her precious time.

The gangly orderly ran back out into the waiting area. "Delivery Room Four is ready." In a rush, he and Davis wheeled Anthea down the hall. A nurse opened the swinging door, but then she put out a stern hand. "Mr. Stewart, I'm afraid you'll have to wait out here."

"I want to be with my wife." Davis craned his neck to look after her.

"Sorry, sir. Men aren't allowed inside the delivery room. Go wait with the other nervous fathers. Hand out cigars to each other."

Anthea saw his deeply disappointed frown. "Don't worry, Davis. I'll be fine. I'll be here."

He gave her hand a squeeze. "I love you."

"You can prove it by changing more than your share of diapers," she joked. Then the contractions hit again, and she knew the baby was close.

The rest happened in a blur. She was on the delivery table, her feet up in stirrups. The doctor, an older man with owlish eyes behind round spectacles, muttered reassuringly, but the words sounded as if he had memorized them from a script, praises and encouragement that he used many times a week.

The nurses seemed concerned. Even the doctor was tense, no doubt because of the news on the radio. One of the nurses said in a quiet voice as if expecting that Anthea couldn't hear her, "I don't know what kind of world that poor baby's going to be born into. If the slans take over and enslave us all—"

"Enough of that, Nurse! We have our jobs to do. There are no slans here, only this woman and her baby, and I'm determined to see that it's born healthy—healthy enough to fight for the human race, if it comes to that." He patted Anthea on the shoulder. "Now don't you worry, young lady. Just push. I'm going to coach you through this."

She closed her eyes. She and Davis were both fit and strong. She couldn't remember the last time either of them had even been sick. Yes, the baby would be just fine.

"Now, push again," the doctor said.

The nurse leaned closer, encouraging. "Push, honey—as hard as you can."

Anthea did as she was told. It was what her body wanted to do.

The doctor leaned over. "That's perfect. Easy, now. I can see the top of the head. You're almost there."

Anthea felt a compulsion to press harder, not to let up. The rush of increased pain didn't matter. She wished Davis could be there holding her hand, but she reassured herself with the knowledge that he was just outside the delivery-room door. She pushed and pushed again, and then she knew the baby was coming. Tears streamed through her shut eyes. With a rush of release, she felt it flow out—her son, a new life, a child emerging into the open air.

"That's it. Here it comes. I have him." The doctor held up a slick, red infant. She heard the baby start to cry as it gasped its first breath.

"Mrs. Stewart, you have a fine little boy—" The doctor halted in midsentence. "Good Lord!"

The nurse began to scream.

"How can this be?" The doctor still held up the baby, but now his face bore a look of disgust. "How can this happen?"

Anthea struggled to sit upright. She felt utterly exhausted and drained; her strawberry-blond hair was plastered with sweat to her head. "What is it? I want my baby."

The doctor looked at her with an expression of horror, his mouth open. Anthea glanced up to see the newborn baby.

He had tiny twisting tendrils coming out the back of his head.

The President of Earth, leader of billions, commanded a certain amount of respect. For decades Kier Gray had been a strong and charismatic ruler. He led with a mixture of sternness and compassion, guiding the citizenry along a dangerously narrow path between paranoid terror and complacency.

Now, though, as the secret police dragged him down the stone-walled hall, Gray was no longer treated with much respect. Until now, no one had ever suspected the President's true heritage as a hidden slan, his actual alliances, the covert work he had done among the surviving slans on Earth. The secret police grabbed him roughly by the arms and pulled him along. Gray knew exactly where they were taking him.

John Petty, the chief of the secret police and notorious slan hunter, waited for his deposed leader inside the primary command-and-control center deep beneath the grand palace. Around him, technicians studied cathode-ray tubes, receiving reports from all their operatives.

"Hail to the President," Petty said with feigned applause. He had short, dark hair, brows that looked like smudges of soot, and glittering eyes like the buttons on his dark uniform. The chief slan hunter seemed satisfied to see the great Kier Gray so helpless.

The guards shoved the President forward, tripping him by his ankles and knocking him to his knees. Petty looked down at him as if he were no more than a discarded cigarette butt in the rain gutter. "We've already rooted out and killed dozens of slans working in the palace. Others have fled like rats in the night. Whatever you were planning, it's over—and I'm in charge now."

Gray didn't curse, didn't protest his innocence, but simply looked up at the bloodthirsty man who had long been his rival. During his long administration, he had weathered numerous conspiracies, assassination attempts, and backstabbings. Only hours ago he had watched the guards shoot down three of his trusted advisers—true slans—in a shielded cabinet room. All of his quiet plans had crumbled in less than a day; he'd gone from great hope and optimism to this disaster.

Gray recovered his dignity. "I don't suppose you have any basis for these treasonous actions, Mr. Petty? Or is the rule of law simply an inconvenience you'd rather not bother with right now?"

"Law? Allow me to cite the Emergency Powers Act: 'In these times of perpetual crisis, any person suspected of being a slan or in league with slans is to be held for immediate questioning. The due process of law is suspended in such cases for the benefit of national security.' "

Gray's anger flared. His secret organization had worked so hard, been so careful . . . but not careful enough. Over the years, the President had even authorized quiet assassinations of people who posed a threat, advisers who accidentally discovered too much about the slans. He'd had no choice but to replace them with a small band of loyal comrades dedicated to changing the world and ending centuries of unnecessary witch hunts. He had *thought* his plans were secure. . . .

Petty crossed his arms over his chest. "We caught you meeting with the infamous slan rebel Jommy Cross in your private quarters. We have recordings in your own voice revealing that the slan specimen you kept in your palace, Kathleen Layton, is your own daughter."

"Where are Kathleen and Cross? Did you just shoot them, like you executed my cabinet members?"

The slan hunter paced inside the command-and-control center. "Oh, we didn't execute those two—not yet. They're too valuable. They have been taken to the detention cells in the lower levels of the palace. You need not worry about their welfare."

If you aren't careful, John Petty, Gray thought, *you may need to worry more about your own welfare.* Despite Petty's obsessive fear, he would probably underestimate Jommy and Kathleen. Gray hoped that some of the unobtrusive slans working around the government center had managed to escape and disappear.

When he'd surreptitiously met with young Jommy Cross, Gray had explained the situation among slans and humans. Very few knew that the true danger came from a different group of mutants, slans born *without tendrils,* who had infiltrated society while preparing to launch their takeover. The tendrilless passionately hated both humans and slans and meant to exterminate both rival races, leaving themselves the sole inheritors of the Earth.

Jommy had slipped into the main tendrilless base on Mars, where he had found startling information about an imminent invasion. Returning to Earth, he had slipped through the palace's defenses to warn the President. After they had begun to make plans, Jommy returned with his own highly advanced car and a deadly disintegrator weapon invented by his father. For only one day, President Gray had believed that he and his shadow government—including Jommy and Kathleen—could change the world.

Then the secret police had arrested them all.

"I myself confiscated Cross's unusual weapons—something he called a disintegrator tube and a ring with an embedded atomic generator. Amazing little things." Petty's lips quirked in a smile. He seemed in control of himself, in charge of the situation, but Gray could sense just a hint of uneasiness in his demeanor. "I gave the items to one of my isolated research teams, but as soon as they tampered with the ring, it dissolved. Now my people have strict orders to exercise extreme caution in their investigations of the disintegrator tube. Once we disassemble it, we'll add it to our own arsenal. *My* arsenal. Hmm, we might even use it to execute you. That would be quite an irony!"

The deposed President rose to his feet, squared his shoulders, and faced the slan hunter. "I'm surprised that I wasn't 'accidentally killed' resisting arrest. It would save you a great deal of time in your coup d'etat."

"A coup? I prefer to call it my transition to a new slan-free government." Petty scratched his blunt chin as he pretended to consider options. "Killing you would waste too much propaganda value. I look forward to hauling you before the world courts, exposing you as a slan, and discrediting all your works, all your supposed peace conferences with the enemy. Somehow, you have had your tendrils removed, or you were born without them—a mutant among mutants!—but I'm positive that genetics tests will reveal slan genes in your DNA."

Despite their vastly diminished numbers, slans were still feared as bogeymen. During his presidency, Gray himself had been forced to play upon that fear because it was the only way to survive politically, but he had managed to remove the teeth from the most vicious proposals.

Petty had stalked around behind the President, but Gray didn't turn to follow him. "You have had your theatrics, but you'll have a far more difficult time proving that any of my actions in office harmed the human race."

"Prove? Simply *existing* as a slan is a treasonous act. You knowingly deceived the people of Earth. I, on the other hand, will be held up as a hero of mankind for removing yet another terrible threat. Slans in our own government, in the presidency itself!" He gave another one of his smiles. "Your scheme is over, Gray. From now on, it's simply a mop-up operation. It will save me a lot of difficulty, and you a lot of pain, if you just confess and reveal how many members of your cabinet are secretly slans."

"There aren't any," Gray insisted.

The slan hunter rolled his eyes. "Your advisers and cabinet members were sound asleep with their wives or mistresses. We rounded them up and found out that several of them had slan tendrils in the backs of their heads, hidden by prosthetics. We've already killed them. Next, we'll dig through the records to find out who cooperated with your most destructive policies. It won't be difficult to prove collusion and thereby treason against humanity. You see, I have all the angles!"

When more men came into the command center and delivered their reports, Petty seemed upset, ready to strike the messengers. He turned back to the President. "We've just uncovered the identity of one of your main coconspirators. I never would have suspected it." He scratched his head. "Then again, it makes a certain amount of sense."

"I don't know what you're talking about," Gray said.

"Your chief adviser, Jem Lorry, has vanished. He disappeared like a puff of smoke, as if he knew what we were planning." Petty balled his fists. "Could he read it in our minds? Did you send him a telepathic message?"

Gray did not need to pretend his confusion. He had appointed Jem Lorry years ago, after a particularly close assassination attempt. Lorry had served extremely well ever since, taking a hardline stance against slans. He had even proposed an innovative if preposterous scheme to marry lovely young Kathleen. Lorry wanted to breed with her in (according to him) an attempt to water down the slan genes, to gradually erase them over a few generations. Lorry had been very angry when Kathleen rebuffed his advances, but Gray was personally pleased that the girl managed to get out of the trap.

"Honestly, I had nothing to do with his disappearance." The President was far more concerned about his own survival and even above that, the survival of his daughter Kathleen and Jommy Cross, the hope of humanity. "You should know that Jommy Cross came to warn me—to warn all of us—of an impending attack on Earth. Another group of slans, tendrilless slans, have built a large base on Mars and recently launched their battle fleet against us. The tendrilless mean to destroy us all."

"Yes, yes, and you and Jommy Cross are our only hope." Petty yawned extravagantly. "I'm not buying it."

THREE

Lying on the table in the hospital delivery room, Anthea struggled to comprehend what she had seen. Her baby had tendrils! *Slan tendrils!*

Impossible. Completely impossible.

The doctor, seemingly in shock, quickly cut the umbilical cord and tied it off. "Pay attention!" he snapped at the nurse, who stood staring. "Save the mother first. Then we'll take care of . . . of that abomination."

"No!" Anthea was weak, but she found the strength to prop herself up on her elbows. "What happened to my baby? Why is—" She tried to make sense of it, but all she could remember was the conversation between the plump receptionist and the man from the secret police. *How can they not know that they're slans?*

Two normal people wouldn't have a slan baby, would they? Anthea couldn't accept that she herself might have been one of those slans without tendrils, and probably Davis as well. Ridiculous! She had never imagined such a thing. They were both healthy, they both healed swiftly, and the two of them had felt a mutual bond that went beyond anything they shared with other humans. *Normal* humans. She felt sick.

"Doctor," she gasped. "What's going to happen?"

He ignored her question as he set the baby down. When he turned to the nurse, his voice was cold and brittle. "Get me a full syringe of hydroxylex-black."

"Yes, Doctor." The nurse looked hardened now, no longer hysterical. "It's what we have to do."

Anthea felt a surge of uneasiness within her. "Davis!" she called, but her voice was alarmingly thin.

The gangly orderly assisting with the delivery finally shook himself out of his surprise. "Doctor, the procedure is clear. We have to report this to the secret police."

"Yes, they're already here in the building," the doctor said, his voice shaky. "Alert security. John Petty himself might want to talk with these two. Make sure the father doesn't leave." He shot a sidelong glance at Anthea on the operating table, as if she were a particularly nauseating specimen. The doctor no longer seemed to consider her human at all. The nurse handed him a long syringe filled with a dark, oily substance.

"What are you going to do with that?" Anthea demanded, struggling to turn. "Answer me!" She heard a commotion outside the doors to the delivery room.

"Don't worry," the doctor said to her with cool reassurance. "This will be quick and painless. Your baby won't feel a thing." He bent over where her newborn baby lay helpless on the adjacent operating table, extending the ominous hypodermic needle.

A surge of panic shot through her heart and mind like a fire siren. It wasn't just her own fear, but something tangible, a wave of panic transmitted by the tendrils of her baby—her slan baby.

The shouts grew louder outside the delivery room, then the swinging doors crashed open. Davis stood there, looking both angry and terrified, his fists clenched. The gangly orderly tried to block him, but Davis knocked him aside with a roundhouse punch. She had never seen him hit anybody before in her life.

"Davis! They're trying to kill our baby." Another blast of emotions seemed to be directed at Anthea and at Davis. The newborn infant somehow understood that these two were his parents!

When Davis saw the doctor bending over the baby with the long, wicked syringe, he charged forward. "What do you think you're doing?"

Screaming again, the nurse tried to throw herself in the way, but Davis knocked her aside as if she were an empty cardboard box. The stunned orderly had gotten to his feet and staggered out of the delivery room, bawling for guards.

Davis fought with the owl-eyed doctor, grabbed the hand that held the poison-filled hypodermic needle, and slowly twisted it away. "You're a *doctor*. You're not supposed to kill people! You're trying to murder a baby!"

"It's not human."

When Davis spotted the tendrils on the baby, *his baby*, he froze. His face became stony and then hardened into a determination that Anthea recognized. When Davis looked like that, no one was ever going to change his mind. "He's my son."

Then, with remarkable strength, he bent the doctor's hand backward, turned the syringe around. The other man gasped and struggled, but Davis easily directed the needle toward him.

Anthea fought to swing her legs over the table, wondering if her husband was using some vestige of . . . slan strength that had just now been unlocked within him. Though she was weak from giving birth, this emergency was making her recover faster. Was something awakening inside her, too? Her heart pounded.

The frantic nurse threw herself upon Davis again, but with a backhand he sent her sprawling into the tray of medical instruments. She and all of the tools fell to the floor with a loud clatter.

"I will not let you kill my son." With a flood of strength, he pushed the hypodermic needle into the doctor's throat and depressed the plunger. The doctor's eyes bulged behind his round spectacles. Judging from his gagging sounds and writhing spasms as he fell to the operating-room floor, the poison was not quite as quick and painless as the doctor had promised.

Davis looked in horror and disbelief at what he had done. The nurse scuttled back to the wall, hiding next to a respirator machine. "Don't kill me! Don't kill me."

Davis helped his wife off the table. "Can you stand? We've got to get out of here."

She clung to his neck for just a second. She wished she could hold him forever, but knew they didn't have the time. "Our baby's a slan, Davis! They're going to kill him."

"He's still our baby." Davis's grim voice was totally inflexible. "I know they want to kill him, and they'll kill us as well. We have no choice." He snatched one of the hospital blankets and quickly wrapped the baby.

Anthea swayed on her feet, found strength miraculously returning to her. She could stand because she *had* to stand. Her body knew what was required of her. All of her preconceptions and prejudices had changed. She and Davis had never intended to harm anyone. They weren't a threat to human society! And how could their innocent child deserve to die, just because he happened to be born with tendrils?

Anthea had always hated slans because she'd been told to hate them. She'd heard a distorted version of history, and now she wondered how many stories about slan atrocities were merely propaganda spread by people like John Petty.

With each step she seemed to grow stronger. "Let me hold him." She took the blanketed baby in her arms. Just touching the infant seemed to give her more strength. She couldn't tell if it was her imagination or genuine mental feedback from the little child.

Davis quickly led her out through the swinging doors of the delivery room, and they stumbled down the hall. Alarms had begun to sound. A harsh voice over the intercom shouted for security.

A flash of realization went through Davis's head. Anthea saw his expression go from stunned confusion to determination and then resigned anger. "You have to go, Anth." He pushed her sideways to another hall that went in the opposite direction. "Take our baby and run. Hide. *Live.*"

"Davis, come with us!"

"If you don't get away, they'll kill both of you, and I'm sure they'll kill me. I murdered the doctor. I won't get a trial. With all the news about the slans preparing to attack us, they'll just gun me down and mount my head on the wall of secret police headquarters."

Suddenly, led by the flustered-looking orderly, three uniformed guards came charging toward them with their weapons drawn.

Davis took one glance at her hospital gown, at her weary features and bedraggled hair. He gave her a quick kiss, the most passionate kiss she had ever received. "Go! I'll buy you enough time to find a hiding place. Don't waste it."

"No, there's got to be another way!" In her arms, the baby began to cry.

Without listening to her, Davis ran into the main corridor, shouting at the guards. Anthea moaned, wanting to go to him, wanting to stand beside him, but the baby in her arms was her priority.

She allowed herself only a moment to look at Davis's back as he charged toward the guards, shouting wildly. Though they were armed, the guards were afraid of Davis, as if they expected him to sprout horns from his forehead and call down evil curses upon them. The man from the secret police had joined them. His face was red with anger.

With a hitch in her throat, Anthea ran barefoot away from the delivery room. Steadying herself against the heavily painted cinderblock walls, holding the baby, she worked her way down the side hall, no longer feeling weak—she couldn't afford to feel weak. The infant was calm in her arms, not sapping her strength, not distracting her.

She tried several locked doors and finally found a dark office. Inside, on a coat tree, a doctor had hung a long trench coat, wet from that day's misty rain. At least it would cover her hospital gown.

She pulled on the trench coat and found that it was baggy enough to cover the swell of the baby that she held close. Under his desk, the doctor had a pair of slip-on shoes, comfortable loafers that were too large for her, but she made do. Anthea hoped her disguise would be good enough to get her out of the hospital. Hurrying—but trying not to look like she was hurrying—she rushed down the hall, averting her gaze when nurses ran past her. Everyone looked terrified and confused.

Alarms continued to blare, and the intercoms were filled with overlapping voices that shouted contradictory orders. Security guards scrambled from room to room, as if expecting to find a slan hidden under every bed. Anthea took advantage of the momentary chaos, praying that Davis would delay the guards and the secret police long enough. Somehow, she still fooled herself into believing that he would get away as well.

From behind, she heard shouts, cries of fear, and then the rapid sharp staccato of gunshots. Four shots, a pause, three more . . . then complete silence.

Anthea nearly collapsed. The sounds themselves were like cold, leaden bullets striking her in the back. Part of her heart seemed to die, and she felt an emptiness in her mind. She hadn't realized until now how much Davis had filled her emptiness. Now that feeling was gone. *He* was gone. The guards and the secret police hadn't questioned him, hadn't sent him to trial; they had simply gunned him down because he'd dared to defend his baby and his wife.

She felt as if her soul were torn in half. She wanted to run back, to throw herself upon his attackers, to pick up her husband's body and cradle him. But the warm baby in her arms kept her running toward safety. She had to get away. Davis had sacrificed himself so that she and the child could escape. She wouldn't lose that, for his sake.

Despite the alarms, no one knew where to find her. Police would be converging on the hospital from all quarters of the city. Teams would be scouring block after block, hunting for her. They'd assume Anthea would run as fast and as far from the hospital as she could go.

Biting back tears, she followed the exit signs, picked her way down a flight of stairs, and found a door that opened to a large parking garage, the hospital's motor pool. Several cars filled reserved spaces, expensive new models with large tailfins, extravagant hood ornaments, and white-walled tires. Two ambulance vehicles sat parked and waiting.

She had a sudden idea. If they expected Anthea to panic and run, then the safest thing she could do, the best place to hide, would be to remain here close to the hospital. While the slan hunters ranged far and wide, she crept over to one of the two ambulances and opened the back door.

The dim interior contained a soft pad, a stretcher, emergency medications, first-aid equipment—and plenty of shadows. It was a quiet and undisturbed place for her to hide, and recover, and grieve.

Holding her baby close, Anthea crawled inside, quietly closed the door behind her, and held her newborn baby as she wept silently for her lost husband.

FOUR

The barred door rolled on its tracks and slammed shut, sealing Jommy Cross in an isolated cell deep beneath the grand palace. Trapped, imprisoned—and unable to warn the rest of humanity of the impending attack. He was completely cut off from any hope of escape. Nobody trusted a slan.

With his tendrils, Jommy could sense that the guards' fear of him was greater than their confidence in their weapons. He considered himself lucky that they hadn't just killed him on sight, as the secret police usually did with slans . . . as they had done with President Gray's slan cabinet members.

When he was only nine, slan hunters had murdered Jommy's mother in the streets; she'd sacrificed herself so that her boy could get away and live to reach the potential that his parents knew he had inside him. After his mother's death, young Jommy had lived as a fugitive, first falling in with warped old Granny, who forced him to steal for her. When he'd come of age and discovered the treasures left hidden for him by his dead father, the great slan scientist Peter Cross, Jommy had vowed to discover where the rest of his race had gone into hiding. . . .

From across the hall, just one cell down, he heard Kathleen struggling with the guards. "You have no right to do this! We have the protection of the President himself. We—"

They showed her no kindness. "The President's been arrested. Shut your mouth."

"Better not let her talk at all," said a second guard. "These slans can hypnotize you with a word."

If only that were so . . . If slans were as powerful as people imagined them to be, neither he nor Kathleen would ever have been captured. Jommy was still reeling from the whole swirl of events.

The young girl had been raised in Kier Gray's palace, a slan specimen to be poked and prodded and analyzed so that the secret police could find ways to fight against a slan insurgency. Though she'd been scheduled for execution when she turned the age of eleven, the President had managed to keep her alive under various pretexts.

No one had guessed that Kathleen was actually Gray's own daughter. After discovering records of a hidden slan settlement, Kathleen had escaped from the palace, running for her life. Though the base was abandoned and empty, Kathleen had taken refuge there while Petty and his secret police launched a large manhunt.

Jommy had found her there in the protected redoubt. With the telepathic bonding of true slans, both he and Kathleen had instantly known each other, loved each other. That short time together in the underground hideaway had been the most perfect time of Jommy's life. Everything had seemed possible.

But Petty's slan hunters had attacked the hidden base, and Kathleen was shot in the head. Jommy barely escaped with his own life. Hardened by grief, sure she was dead, he had gone on a determined quest to find other slans, to understand the strange and ruthless "tendrilless" ones who hated both slans and humans, as well as to bring down the hated Petty. When he finally broke into Kier Gray's palace to warn of the imminent tendrilless attack, Jommy was astonished to find that Kathleen had been healed by ultra-advanced slan medical equipment. Alive again!

She and Jommy had spent a tense but glorious day with Gray and his advisers, working out ways to face the coming crisis. When Jommy had first slipped into the palace, he had parked his high-tech armored vehicle in the forest on the other side of the river, and he had also left his father's disintegrator weapon there.

Once he knew the President accepted his help, Jommy and Kathleen had returned together to his car to retrieve the disintegrator, which would be invaluable during the fight against the tendrilless. He had hardly believed that she was back, that she was with him again. Even with the brooding danger all around them, they had been swept up in each other's presence. Jommy and Kathleen barely had a moment to experience the joy of their reunion before everything crashed around them. . . .

All the while, John Petty had been eavesdropping on Gray, setting up a trap. When Jommy and Kathleen returned, his secret police had charged in, arresting all of them, dragging them away. Petty had confiscated the disintegrator, killed the other slan advisers, and then taken over the government. No one would listen to them about the real imminent threat. . . .

As she struggled against the guards trying to push her into the cell, Jommy could tell the thugs were on the verge of violence. "Don't fight them, Kathleen. I don't want you to get hurt again." His voice was quiet and gentle, but it carried clearly in the enclosed corridors of the prison level, wanting the guards to hear as well. "These men don't matter. We have greater enemies."

After she let them shove her inside, her own cell door rolled shut with a crash. She went to the bars, but their cells were on the same side of the hall, and he couldn't see her. "We will get out of here," Kathleen said. It was a promise.

"That's up to Mr. Petty and the law, miss," a guard said. "And right now neither one appears to be on your side."

Jommy longed to stretch his arm through the bars to touch her fingers, but the separation was too great. That was a crueler punishment than the imprisonment itself.

The guard captain stood in front of the bars, glaring in at Jommy. "Don't try anything. We'll have two men stationed here on this level, and these cells were designed to hold the worst political criminals."

Jommy sat down on his cot, looking defeated. The secret police probably had hidden cameras somewhere. "Then obviously it's useless for us to try to escape."

"Glad you figured that out, Cross." The guard walked briskly away, eager to break eye contact.

Jommy had not given up, though. He wished he knew where his disintegrator weapon had been taken. That invention had saved Jommy's life more than once; no doubt the secret police would disassemble it, analyze it, try to figure out how the weapon worked . . . but even Jommy had never been able to decipher his father's intricate invention.

Jommy suspected President Gray was in dire straits of his own right now, facing John Petty. But the arrest of the President wasn't the worst crisis—the attack from the tendrilless slans was imminent. Jommy had risked everything to come to Gray's palace in the first place, to deliver a warning. While humans wasted time and energy hunting down true slans, fearing the wrong enemy, the tendrilless ones moved freely in society, preparing for a complete and violent takeover. The attack would occur very soon. Pleased with his little victory, Petty would not be watching for another danger coming from the skies. Earth would be completely unprepared.

Therefore, he and Kathleen would have to do something about it.

He closed his eyes and felt his golden tendrils move at the back of his head, rising into the air. He concentrated, broadcasting his thoughts like radio signals. *Kathleen, can you hear me?* He waited, felt a tingle, then a familiar presence.

Yes, Jommy. I'm here. I'm close.

Jommy felt the urgency build within him. *We've got to get out of here. We have to find President Gray, and we have to alert the Earth defenses about the tendrilless attack.*

Kathleen's mind was also in turmoil. *We can't do anything trapped in these cells.*

Kathleen's presence in his mind strengthened him. He looked around his cell, saw nothing he could use as a weapon. He had only a cot, a sink, and a hygiene station; no mirror, no table, nothing else. Though his body was stronger than an average human's, Jommy could not break his way out. The cell was impregnable. Therefore, the weakest point was the human factor. Jommy would have to "encourage" the two guards to open the door.

He sent a thought message, summarizing what he wanted to do. *Kathleen, follow my lead and transmit the same image. It's got to be convincing.*

Together, separated by thick block walls, Jommy and Kathleen sent the same thunderous idea. It struck the two already frightened and suspicious guards. It took Jommy a moment to find their muddled centers of thought. The brains of the two guards were so closed off by walls of paranoia that he could barely get inside. But finally he played upon that irrational fear, sending an image of Jommy Cross using slan strength to tear a hole in the cell wall, ready to escape.

The guards came running. "Open the door! We have to stop him."

"I told you slans were dangerous!"

The lock clicked from the control panel on the wall. The two men pulled the rattling bars aside, completely convinced they saw a gaping hole and the prisoner escaping. Before the deceptive image could fade, Jommy launched himself forward like a boulder from a medieval catapult. He was not a brutal fighter, but he did have great physical strength and the element of surprise. He knocked the guards aside. As they squawked and tried to reconcile what they saw with what they'd been *sure* was happening, Jommy punched them both.

He grabbed one man's arm and yanked him inside the cell. He punched the other guard in the ear and then swung him into a heap atop his partner inside the small cell. Shouting, the two guards tried to disentangle themselves, but Jommy pulled the rattling cell door shut on them, and the lock dutifully clicked home.

He sprinted partway down the corridor. The guards had pulled out their large-caliber pistols and fired at him from between the bars, but they could not aim well because of the extreme angle. Out of view, Jommy pressed himself against the bars of Kathleen's cell, and the bullets simply struck the walls, whining and ricocheting. She rushed forward, and he put his hands through the bars to clasp hers.

Using the outside controls, he worked the simple cell lock, and in moments, Kathleen was free beside him. "Come on. We've got to figure out a way through these levels."

The two began to run, still hugging the walls, out of range of the guards. The locked-up men continued to shout after them, firing their guns several more times, but the bullets hit nothing.

At the end of the hall Jommy and Kathleen found a door that led to a steep set of concrete stairs. Before they could open it, loud alarm klaxons rang out inside the palace, sounding a Level One emergency.

"How could they have discovered we've escaped?" Kathleen said, waiting for another surge of guards to come charging after them. "It's only been a few minutes."

Jommy froze. "The emergency's not because of us. Not us at all." Next, the alarms were accompanied by the bone-grating sound of an air-raid siren. "It's the tendrilless slans. Their attack has begun."

FIVE

Jem Lorry had lived among humans for most of his life, pretending to be one of them. His mind shields were perfect. Strategically placed in the Earth government, working his way up through his own intelligence (and the occasional necessary assassination), he became the closest, most influential adviser to Kier Gray. In the sure progress of the tendrilless plans, he should soon have been the President himself.

Now, from Mars, Jem was engineering the downfall of Earth.

Here on the red planet, the tendrilless had created more than just a strategic base and a hideout. The third breed of humanity had forged an entire civilization with outposts, settlements, and industrial complexes ringing the central canyon city of Cimmerium. From where Jem stood inside the large vaulted chamber, the distant sun streamed through the glass ceiling that covered the whole, expansive canyon. A large armored city crowded the habitable flatlands on the edge of the deep gorge, but the highest-ranked and richest tendrilless had built a warren of structures into the stark cliff wall, beneath the transparent canopy.

His people had superior mental capacity to humans, though greatly limited telepathic abilities compared with true slans. No one—not Jem Lorry, not the Tendrilless Authority, probably not even the slans themselves—knew where or how the tendrilless ones had originated. The true slans had turned against them, launching what amounted to a genocide to eradicate their genetic stepbrothers. Jem didn't know why true slans hated them so much, but the feeling was certainly mutual. He didn't need explanations.

Pleased that the full-fledged attack on Earth was finally about to commence, Jem stood before the seven members of the Tendrilless

Authority, expecting to receive well-deserved applause. This entire attack had been his brainchild. He had sacrificed much to reach this point, and he intended to get what he had earned. The council members peered down at him with stony faces.

The Authority chamber was like an ancient Roman arena. When all the tendrilless citizens gathered for primary meetings, thousands would sit on ringed seats staring down at the main podium, listening to petitions and plans, watching the Authority issue its judgment.

Today, though, Jem was by himself in the vast room, staring up at the seven men. He would have preferred a cheering audience; after his guaranteed victory, the tendrilless would certainly applaud his dreams and ambitions. They had waited, lurked, and planned for far too long. Only a few, like the stodgy Authority members, bled away that enthusiasm with "caution" and "patience"—thinly disguised words for "cowardice."

"The initial attack has commenced," Jem announced. "Our heavily armed vanguard ships have arrived at Earth in the past hour. At this very moment, our warriors should be bombarding their cities. It is time for us to launch the much larger occupation fleet. All those ships and personnel will require a week to get to Earth. The victory is all but assured."

"Nothing is ever assured, my son, until it has happened," answered Altus Lorry, Jem's father. The old Authority Chief had a head that seemed too large to balance on the wattled stalk of his neck. His hair was shaggy, giving him a leonine appearance. Altus Lorry was a grandiose leader who had spent his lifetime playing politics among the most influential tendrilless in Cimmerium. But he had no real understanding of the human enemy.

Jem struggled to keep his expression neutral. "I urge you to hear my recommendations, Father. Have I not earned it? I lived for years among humans. I know all the systems we have put in place." He could not entirely hide his impatience. "It's no surprise that after years of living comfortably on Mars, you and the other Authority members have grown complacent. You are afraid of things you need not fear and suspicious of that which poses no threat. You give the humans far too much credit."

Altus laughed without humor. "Better safe than sorry, my son, as you well know."

"Actually, I don't! You have always been safe here, but I have never been sorry for what I did or accomplished." Jem sensed an uneasiness among the Authority members, and it made him angry. If they didn't act soon, their swift advantage would begin to trickle away. "While the first stage of the attack shatters the government and breaks their ability to resist, we must launch the main occupation fleet. We need the big ships and our overwhelming ground forces in place to consolidate our hold on Earth."

Not long ago, Jem had watched as hundreds upon hundreds of sleek vanguard warships launched from Mars, kicking up crumbled red dust, spewing clouds of steam and fuel exhaust. They had risen to the sky and out into orbit, streaking across space like sharks scenting blood in the water. The blood of normal humans.

And that was only the first wave of the attack.

The initial volley of devastating bombs would be dropping upon the main cities of Earth right now. At last, Jem would feel vengeance for his people, who had been forced to run here centuries ago and hide. The tendrilless would finally get what they were owed. So why delay the occupation fleet?

"Patience, my son." The old man was unintentionally condescending. "We intend to do so. The occupation fleet will be on its way by tomorrow. Or the day after."

Jem took a deep breath. The Tendrilless Authority had always been a roadblock to his ambitions. Eventually, before he could accomplish anything worthwhile, he would need to replace the old members with a more proactive group. Or, he mused, he might have to do away with the Authority entirely. Who needed a seven-member council when one visionary leader—a king, for lack of a better term—could do the job much more efficiently?

"Another factor makes our timing impeccable." Jem had stopped thinking of himself as a petitioner seeking permission. He fancied himself a great general, and the tendrilless armies were under his control; he was simply delivering a report to the Authority. "Earth itself is in turmoil. President Kier Gray has just been arrested and exposed as a true slan. Even I never suspected it! The power vacuum weakens them even more. They will barely be able to mount a defense, I guarantee it. But only if we move *now*."

Jem's resentment toward Kier Gray was personal rather than political. He had been in love with Kathleen (or perhaps *lust* was a better term, though he used the words interchangeably). He had made persuasive arguments to the President, claiming (falsely, as he well knew) that interbreeding with slans would dilute their mutant traits and make their descendants into "real people" again. Instead, Jem knew that slan genetics were dominant, and he intended to bring Kathleen's superior powers directly into the tendrilless breed.

"What about this man named John Petty, the leader of the secret police?" said Altus. "You have described him as a powerful administrator. Perhaps he will rally the survivors."

"He's a thug with a tendency for brutality and excess. The people will never accept him as their leader. After seeing what Petty does, the humans will welcome us with open arms. Ha! I bet they'd prefer to be our slaves rather than live under his boot heel. Launch the occupation fleet, Father, and I will take care of the rest."

Without waiting to be dismissed by the ostensible leaders, Jem turned his back and marched out of the vast, echoing chamber. The Martian sun streaming through the ceiling of glass seemed very bright, very bright indeed.

SIX

Huddled in the rear of the ambulance, Anthea held the baby close and pulled a reflective emergency blanket over herself. Poor, brave Davis! The infant stirred restlessly, as if he knew he shouldn't cry even though he felt his mother's powerful emotions with his delicate tendrils.

Anthea propped him up and for the first time looked closely at the newborn's face. His bright hazel eyes were wide open, as if the child could see her clearly and recognize her as his mother. Newborns weren't supposed to be capable of that . . . but a normal husband and wife shouldn't have had a baby with slan tendrils, either.

With a curious sense of wonder, Anthea reached out to touch the tiny strands like long threads of nerve fibers, antennae extending from the baby's superior brain. When she stroked the tendrils, they twitched and curled, making both her fingers and her mind tingle. How could she and Davis have had such a potential within them without knowing it? Had her own parents known they were different genetically? Had Davis's?

Anthea couldn't help but feel herself bonding with the infant. He was a blank slate, full of potential but without any experiences, knowledge, or personality. Given the right guidance and inspiration, her son could become a great man. She made a promise to herself, and to the memory of Davis, that she would do everything possible—give up her very life if necessary—to protect this baby so he could grow up and meet his destiny.

She and her husband had never even decided on a name for their son. Anthea remembered a candlelight dinner only a week ago, when they had both proposed names for the baby boy. Davis preferred Raymond or maybe William.

"How about Geoffrey with a 'G'?" Anthea had suggested. "Or Elliott? Or Sam?"

"Could you live with Stefan?" Davis asked. "Or how about Leroy? It means 'the king.' "

"No, definitely not Leroy."

The more suggestions they made, the more impossible it seemed to find a name they could both agree to. Finally, at the end of that dinner, Anthea and Davis had set aside the discussion, deciding to wait until she had the baby. When they could actually hold it, look at it, and see its face, they were sure they could choose the perfect name.

Now they would never have that chance. Anthea didn't know how she could bear to choose a name all by herself.

Suddenly she was startled out of her reverie by shouts and running footsteps in the hospital's garage. "Have you checked everywhere? We can't let the slans escape."

"The one we killed didn't even have tendrils."

"Without tendrils, his head won't make much of a trophy for John Petty's wall. But if he wasn't a slan, then he was a traitor helping them."

Anthea felt the burn of tears, but she drove them back, sitting up just enough so that she could see the round side mirror on the door of the ambulance. In the reflection she could view part of the underground parking garage.

Several uniformed security men spread out, searching, their revolvers drawn. The ominous man with the secret police armband stood at the doorway, looking into the shadows, scanning for any sign of her or the baby. "I will be very disappointed if you allow them to escape."

The methodical security men began to look in the cars. Anthea huddled down, pulling the blanket over her, sending out a desperate thought. *We're not here. We're not here.* The baby seemed to pick up and amplify the message.

She heard footsteps moving along, reports shouted from one man to another. They were going toward other cars nearer the exit ramp, away from her, without even checking the ambulance. She wondered if her son had actually influenced the guards, or if it was just a fortunate coincidence. Anthea held her breath.

Then the terrifying shrieks of air-raid sirens ratcheted up and down the streets, amplified by broadcast systems in the hospital, drowning out even the normal security alarms. The sounds of chaos outside greatly increased; she heard racing automobiles, squealing tires, then a series of distant explosions.

The searchers in the hospital's motor pool parking lot shouted to each other, then dashed back inside the building. Air-raid sirens continued to wail, but now they were blurred by the drone of heavy jet engines. Unfamiliar flying craft cruised overhead approaching the heart of Centropolis. The slan attack! Then came the percussive flurry of anti-aircraft fire, large defensive guns that President Gray had installed on skyscraper roofs.

As the gunfire continued, she heard a thin whistle that grew louder and culminated in an ear-shattering eruption. More bombs dropped from above, smashing into the streets, setting buildings afire. Centuries ago, Earth's greatest cities had been leveled in the Slan Wars. Anthea hoped that the rebuilt skyscrapers had been reinforced to withstand an attack. Or had humanity grown too complacent?

Yet another explosion echoed down the block from the hospital. She heard brisk footsteps and more shouts as two men ran for the ambulance. Anthea cowered back down as two rescue squad techs jumped inside and slammed the doors. The driver started the engine with a roar, and the ambulance began to roll forward as soon as his partner threw himself into the seat.

Huddling in the back, she hoped they wouldn't look behind them to see the emergency blanket she had pulled down to cover herself.

Its siren bawling, the medical vehicle shot out of the hospital's parking bay and into the chaos of the war-torn streets. The driver turned right and accelerated down the avenue into the city. Explosions peppered the buildings around them; bricks and shattered glass rained down onto the street. Traffic ground to a halt. Swerving cars smashed into each other, and the ambulance zigzagged past the wrecks without slowing.

A falling bomb struck a car limping along on a flat tire, and the fuel tank detonated so close to the rushing ambulance that the side panels in the back rattled. Screaming pedestrians were running everywhere, trying to flag down the medical vehicle. The driver just drove past the flaming debris. Anthea wondered exactly which injured people the rescue squad intended to save.

The driver slammed the brakes hard just as half of a building slid down into the street, blocking their way. The violent lurch caused loose supplies to clatter forward from storage bins in the back of the ambulance.

Anthea nearly tumbled to the floor of the vehicle, and the infant began to cry as the blankets slid off of them. Before she could shush him, before she could grab the blankets to hide them again, both the driver and his fellow rescue squad tech turned around, staring with saucerlike eyes.

"She's the one the secret police were looking for! She killed Dr. Elton."

With the ambulance blocked in the street, both men scrambled out of their seats and lunged toward the back of the ambulance.

Anthea held the baby defensively against her. She should have been weak and exhausted, barely able to move after giving birth only an hour ago. But her body had healed remarkably, and energy sang through her muscles. The unexpected strength had always been there, but it lay fallow. Now that Anthea knew what she was, now that she had a baby to protect, she could feel it awakening.

"Don't worry, she's trapped in here," said the driver. "There's two of us. We can easily grab her."

"Careful. Slans can wipe your brain."

The driver paused to open a first-aid kit, withdrew a long syringe. "This should knock her out."

His partner blinked. "That's three times the standard dose! It could kill her."

The other man shrugged. "The reward's the same either way, and she'll be a lot less trouble for us."

Anthea understood how animal mothers in the wild fought to protect their young. As the driver came close, looking for an opportunity to jab her with the syringe, Anthea reacted. She didn't think, didn't even understand what her body was capable of doing. She kicked him hard in the chest—and it was as if he'd tried to catch a cannonball. The man flew backward, struck the windshield with so much force that he crashed directly through and onto the hood of the ambulance. He sprawled there, bloody and motionless, most likely dead. Anthea didn't care. He had meant to murder her and the baby.

The other emergency tech recoiled, astonished at what he had seen. He grabbed a bright red fireman's axe mounted on the side panel of the ambulance. "All right. No more playing nice with the slans."

Anthea turned around, and using the same unknowable adrenaline force, she smashed open the back doors. Carrying the baby in one arm, she bounded out into the streets.

The emergency tech shouted curses after her, scrambled to the swinging door of the ambulance. "She's a slan! Stop her! Stop her!"

But the streets were full of blood-streaked people running for shelter, while overhead, strange angular spacecraft swooped low, dropping more bombs. Anthea ran out, disappearing into the frenzied battle zone.

SEVEN

Inside Kier Gray's palace (technically, *John Petty's* palace at the moment) everything was in chaos. Even before the first bombs started dropping, perimeter alert systems and distant early warnings detected the enemies converging in Earth orbit.

"Mr. Petty, sir!" said a wide-eyed officer named Clarke. "There's a full fleet coming in—from space! Unidentified ship designs, definitely military." In the past hour, the chief of secret police had put Clarke in charge of monitoring the defensive systems and scanners in the command-and-control center. With so many dirty slans hidden among the government, Petty didn't trust anyone who wasn't already his own.

The young man bent over his curved screens, flicked toggle switches, and turned knobs to adjust the focus on the cathode-ray tube. Under the sweeping arc of a radar beam, blips showed up. "They're spacecraft, sir. Battleships. Backtracking their trajectory . . . it looks as if they've come from Mars."

"Invaders from Mars?" All his career, the great slan hunter had been trying to track down their secret bases. He had uncovered and documented numerous slan redoubts, but knew he could not account for the entire vanished race of mutants. Now it all became clear: They must have fled Earth entirely and gone to Mars, leaving only a few stragglers—or spies—behind.

Since the devastating Slan Wars, human society—*pure* human society—had developed television and radar, jet aircraft, but only a fragmented space program, a few satellites and pie-in-the-sky plans for rocket ships. A long time ago, human civilization had been much more ambitious, stretching their boundaries and approaching the stars. The

Slan Wars had wrecked all that, knocking human civilization back by many centuries.

But the insidious slans must have maintained their superior technology. All these years they had been hiding on Mars, building up their invasion force.

Just like Gray warned us! Before the first slan air strikes, guards had taken the deposed President to a secure holding cell in the interrogation sector. Not wanting to let Gray anywhere close to Jommy Cross, he had kept the President far removed from the other two slans, in a completely different detention level. But Petty hadn't decided what to do next with the prisoners. He had to take care of it himself.

"Mount all of our defenses. Now that we've exposed what Gray really is, the slans must be trying to free him."

"But we only just arrested President Gray," Clarke said. "If these ships came from Mars, they launched days ago—"

"Don't argue fine points with me. Just call out the military."

The technician fiddled with his switches and displayed the incredible oncoming force on the big screen. It took his breath away. "Um, sir—since we've arrested President Gray, and Jem Lorry has disappeared, who has the executive authority necessary? Who's in charge?"

"*I'm* in charge!" He lifted his chin. "It's about time that someone with common sense, a proven track record, and a hard fist started taking care of things." He sounded as if he were delivering a campaign speech.

Petty paced around the bustling stations in the command-and-control center, ignoring the racket of alarms. "Summon all our troops. Get our aircraft in the skies, put soldiers on the rooftops to man our anti-aircraft guns. Tell them to shoot down anything that moves." He ground his teeth together, then glanced again at the blips on the display. The enemy ships kept coming, as if Mars had an infinite supply.

As the bombs started dropping from the skies, detonating in the streets of Centropolis—possibly all across the world—Petty quickly saw that Earth didn't have a chance against this sort of attack. He would have to take unorthodox action, much as he hated to do so.

His face flushed with frustration, Petty chose the three largest and most muscular guards. "Follow me back to the President's cell. I'm going to make him see reason. And if I can't manage that, then you three are going to help change his mind." Perhaps they weren't the brightest men, little more than thugs, but Petty would do all the thinking. He just needed someone who could break a few bones, if necessary.

The sheer racket of the alarms probably caused as much confusion and fear as the actual attack. Outside, the distant muffled rumble of explosions continued, barely heard over the obnoxious, incessant alarms. The enemy intended a full-fledged invasion, and no doubt they wouldn't stop until most of the city was destroyed.

In the upper levels of the palace, functionaries, staff, and even a few political visitors ran about in a panic. The streets were a stew of chaos. The surveillance cameras and periscope viewers showed much of Centropolis already in flames.

He hurried along brightly lit tunnels and narrow passageways, accompanied by the guards. If John Petty was going to rule the world, he wanted it to last longer than an hour or two.

His guards were armed with blunt-muzzled, large-caliber pistols. One slug fired from such a weapon would tear a hole the size of a grapefruit in a victim; the secret police rarely worried about simply wounding a slan prisoner. Right now, the guards would have to content themselves with using stiff clubs, perhaps even sharp-pointed electrical prods. He needed the "slan President" alive.

The burly guards stopped as Petty faced the other man's holding chamber. Inside, Gray paced and sweated, desperate to get out. Seeing the chief of secret police, he rushed to the bars. "Why didn't you listen to me? You have to let me out."

"I don't have to do anything, but *you* do. Remember who's holding the cards here."

"You'll just be holding a handful of rubble if we don't solve this."

Grudgingly, he gestured for the guards to activate the cell's unlocking mechanism. The barred door rattled aside, and the slan hunter stepped into the chamber with his three guards close behind him. "The slans are bombarding our city. Tell me how we fight against them."

"They aren't true slans. They are our stepbrothers, tendrilless slans bred centuries ago to move undetected among humanity. Now they mean to destroy both races." When Petty gave him a skeptical frown, the deposed President insisted, "It is the tendrilless ones you should fear, not us. They have infiltrated your news media, your utility companies, your transportation systems."

"You're trying to make me paranoid."

"You had a head start on that all by yourself."

"Why should slans hate other slans, whether or not they've got tendrils?"

"Many shameful acts have been committed by both sides, and all the while humans were blind to it. Samuel Lann, the father of all slans, would disown every one of us if he were here."

A small-statured mousy man dashed down the hall, panting. He wore the crisp gray uniform and blue armband of the palace service personnel, a courier. He clutched a scrap of paper in his hand. "Mr. Petty, President Gray . . . uh, whoever's in charge. I have an urgent message! News." He skidded to a stop and heaved great breaths. His face was red from the effort of running.

The three guards glared at the mousy courier. Petty said, "Well, out with it, man!"

"Jommy Cross and Kathleen Layton have escaped. Those two slans are on the loose!"

The President saw his chance. While the others were startled by the announcement, he lunged from the cot and wrapped his hands around Petty's thick neck. The momentum knocked the burly slan hunter back. "You fool, you've brought us all to ruin!" Gray cried. "We could have set up defenses in time. Now how many thousands, maybe millions, are going to die?"

Two of Petty's thugs grabbed the President's arms, fighting so hard they ripped his shirt, but finally they tore his hands free from the chief's throat. Petty coughed and choked. Thick red marks stood out on his neck. "How . . . dare you!"

"In order to achieve true victory, one must dare a great deal." It was the voice of one of the three brutish guards. He sounded unexpectedly erudite.

Rubbing away his blurred vision, Petty turned to look at the man who now stood in a broad-shouldered fighting stance, his heavy-caliber pistol drawn from its holster. The wide, blunt muzzle pointed directly at John Petty.

"What's going on?" His damaged voice box allowed no more than a rasp.

The guard continued to act strangely. "Once I kill you and Kier Gray, the humans won't have even a thread of hope. No one can lead them." The pistol never wavered.

"You—you're one of them!" Petty squawked.

"A tendrilless victory is assured."

With an explosive sound, the gunshot echoed in the cell, but the burly guard merely staggered, then stared in astonishment at the wet red hole the size of a grapefruit that had been blown through his chest.

Outside, trembling at the door of the cell, the meek courier held his own gun in shaking hands. The blast seemed to have deafened him, while the recoil had nearly knocked him backward off his feet. "They . . . they said I was supposed to come armed before I delivered my message." The man blinked, not sure who he was supposed to explain himself to.

Petty dropped to his knees, weak and disoriented. "A slan—among my own secret police!"

"Not a slan," Gray insisted. "Don't be an even bigger fool than you already are. He wanted to kill me as well as you. Look at the back of his head. It's one of the tendrilless."

The other two shaken guards grabbed the traitor's head, probed among his bristly dark hair, but could find no prosthetics, no makeup, nothing that covered the telltale signs of a hidden slan.

As the guard lay choking in his own blood, he exhibited great strength, slan healing powers. "You don't have a chance against *my people*." Then he died.

Petty glared at the remaining two guards, as if afraid they might pull their weapons and open fire, too. He brushed at the droplets of blood that had sprayed on his clean uniform, then whirled toward Gray. "You were telling the truth." It sounded like an accusation. "You were telling the truth! There *are* tendrilless slans."

"They are the ones you've always needed to fear," Gray said.

Petty backed out of the cell and gestured to his guards. "Get the body out of there, and lock *him* in again." He turned to the surprised and meek courier. "All three of you, stay here and guard Gray." This information changed everything. "I have to get back to the command-and-control center. We're going to need new battle plans."

EIGHT

Jommy and Kathleen ran. Outside, the attack seemed to be growing worse.

The underground levels of the grand palace were a labyrinth of corridors, subterranean chambers, shielded self-contained rooms like small bank vaults. Ages ago, slan conquerors had designed and constructed the immense structure during their brief reign over humanity. After so many subsequent administrations, Jommy doubted that anyone—even President Gray—knew the extent of all the passageways and secret underground rooms.

He wondered if there were also interrogation rooms and torture chambers down here. How often had Gray himself used these detention cells?

Each of the innumerable underground sectors was accessed by a different security protocol. Even veteran workers could easily get lost in the confusing monumental structure that was as large as a small city. The two escapees used that to their advantage now.

After breaking out of their cells, they ran along, peering around corners, dashing down open stretches, trying doors that were either locked or led to empty rooms or simple offices. Klaxons blared and magenta warning lights flashed in the halls, sounding an evacuation, summoning security, unnecessarily warning of the invasion.

"We have to find President Gray." Kathleen hesitated, then added, "We have to find my *father*."

"We'll find him." Jommy squeezed her hand. "It may seem an impossible task, but people have always feared slans for our abilities. We may as well give them something to fear."

One large room had windows for walls. Inside, fifteen chairs surrounded a long boardroom table; black-and-white computer screens
were embedded in the flat wood surface. "This must be a secondary
command-and-control center." Jommy looked around, perplexed.
"But it's empty, not even a backup team. What about the emergency?"

Kathleen studied the room. "The palace probably has at least
twenty rooms like this. The government is compartmentalized, everyone with their separate areas of responsibility. The President and his
various advisers don't trust each other during the best of times, and
now that we're being attacked . . ." She let her voice trail off. "I'll bet
there's plenty that even John Petty doesn't know about the palace."

He was about to continue the search for Kier Gray's location, but
Kathleen called him back. She pulled up a rolling chair in front of one
of the black-and-white screens. "Wait, Jommy—help me. The two of
us can figure out these systems. We'll search for where they've taken
my father."

He joined her at the head of the table, looking down at the largest
cathode-ray tube. Text scrolled down the screens, reports of damage,
estimated enemy strengths, suggested numbers of casualties. Paper tape
rattled through a reader, and a status report in block letters appeared
on the curved screen.

Kathleen flicked toggle switches, then typed long strings of com-
mands into the keyboard. A bird's nest of lines appeared on the screen,
and Kathleen turned a knob, adjusting the focus. "There! A blueprint." Diagrams of floor after floor of the huge building complex appeared, all superimposed on top of each other.

She spread them out until she had found hundreds of images, each
one filling a full computer screen, each one showing one floor of one
wing. She flicked from screen to screen, searching so rapidly that the
blueprints became a blur. Thanks to the eidetic memory possessed by
all slans, he and Kathleen were able to take a mental snapshot of each
image.

Jommy stared in amazement. "I never realized the extent of this
place. The grand palace covers the whole skyline of Centropolis. After
my mother was killed and I went to live with old Granny, I used to
look across the rooftops and see the beautiful palace. It was like something out of a fairy tale with its beautiful lights and towers. It made me
think of what great things people could accomplish if they worked together . . . how much more wonderful it was to build something than
to destroy."

He leaned closer to the screen. "But this is unbelievable. What I
could see above ground is barely the tip of an iceberg. It spreads down,

deep underground. There are tunnels and access shafts, like the ones I used to get in here." He glanced sideways at Kathleen. "My vehicle is waiting for us in the forest across the river. If we can only get to it . . ."

Kathleen toggled to another screen image, then another, still searching for the secret police lockdown zones. "Not without my father. We've got to save the President. Who else could lead us through this time of crisis?"

Jommy reached over and gave her a hug. "I'm proud of you for saying that." Then he glanced down, disheartened at the hundreds of screens of blueprints. "But how are we going to find him in all this? His cell was nowhere close to ours."

Kathleen rattled her fingers across the keyboard. Metal pins chattered through paper tape. When a tongue of paper spat out from the printer slot, she tore it off, looked at the numbers, then nodded. "At least Petty's men are efficient—they've logged in my father's incarceration. This is the blueprint we need. I'll find the exact sector."

As Jommy zeroed in on the appropriate diagram, Kathleen determined the floor number, the corridor, and even the cell number where President Gray had been taken. Collating through the information in his head, he settled on the best route to get there. "We can take the internal transport cars."

He and Kathleen dashed down the hall, found an exit door that led to a set of steep metal stairs. He counted the floors, looked at the painted numbers on the fire doors, and emerged four levels below. They cautiously poked their heads through the doorway and saw no one, only a single flickering light that marked the internal transport station. Jommy pushed the call button to summon the rapid oval car used for shuttling people throughout the vast palace. Within minutes they heard a rattling hum, and a white egg-shaped vessel swept toward them along magnetic rails.

After the door hissed open, Jommy and Kathleen climbed inside, punched their destination request, and sat back as the bullet car shot along. The two sat close to each other in a brief moment of privacy where they could feel safe, where they could just be together. Jommy knew they should use the time to make plans, to discuss what they would do once they found and freed the President. On the other hand, he just wanted to be with Kathleen, now that they had found each other again. Alas, the swift car reached the destination station much too soon, barely giving the two of them time to catch their breath.

The transport car came to a stop, and the door slid open. "Not far now," Kathleen said.

"Let's hope our luck holds. We'll get him free, soon." Jommy still had no idea how they were going to manage it.

He grabbed her hand, and they dashed out. Jommy half expected to see a group of secret police waiting for them with weapons drawn. One man did rush across the corridor, startling them, but he hurled himself into a room, then slammed the door shut, locking it with a loud click. They saw no one else.

Up another two flights of stairs, they emerged into a complex of cubical offices. People hunched over heavy black telephones, clacked on manual typewriters, and rushed reports and documents to each other. None of the workers paid attention to Jommy and Kathleen. The two hurried past the cubicles, opened another double door, and saw a long, straight hallway before them.

Kathleen paused. "That leads to the high-security detention area. My father is there." The hammer-and-web symbol of the secret police marked the wall.

Bright overhead lights gave the long passage a sterile appearance, and six metal doors set into the painted cinder-block walls were closed tight. Isolation cells? Torture chambers? They would be incredibly exposed running down that long hall. Jommy reviewed the memorized blueprints in his mind, but he could see no other way to where they had to go. "It looks like a gauntlet we have to traverse."

As they sprinted down the endless empty corridor, he was sure camera eyes must be watching them. By now John Petty must have learned of their escape and would be searching the whole palace for them. Jommy doubted even the tendrilless attack would distract the slan hunter from that.

When they were halfway down the long corridor, far from any hiding place, the double doors at the far end of the hall began to swing open. Jommy and Kathleen threw themselves against one of the recessed metal doors. He tried to turn the knob so they could duck inside and hide, but it was locked. Even using slan strength, he could not break it open.

At the far end of the corridor, three men wearing secret police uniforms pushed through the double doors and began to march down the hall. All of the men were armed with heavy pistols. Jommy and Kathleen pressed themselves into the small indentation of the doorwell, knowing they couldn't possibly remain out of sight. They were trapped, right out in the open. The guards would see them at any moment.

"We have to make them not see us," Kathleen said in a quick whisper that was little more than a hiss. Then she squeezed her eyes shut and concentrated. *Don't see us. You don't see us.*

With his tendrils, Jommy immediately picked up on what she was trying to do. Jommy would have preferred to use one of his hypnotism crystals to enhance the output from his tendrils, but he had lost the last of them on Mars. Instead, he and Kathleen would have to use their powers jointly to send out a camouflaging suggestion. He joined her thoughts. *You don't see us. Don't see us.*

The secret police hurried along the corridor at a brisk pace, intent on their own mission, enthusiastically discussing the crisis among themselves. *You don't see us.*

The three men strode directly past them, looking straight ahead, not bothering to glance from side to side. They passed within two feet of Kathleen, but her concentration was fixed. The slan tendrils at the back of Jommy's head waved gently as he continued to send out his thoughts. The armed men reached the far end of the corridor without looking back, and they exited into another part of the palace.

Kathleen let out a long sigh of relief, and Jommy realized he was trembling from the tension. He shook his head in amazement, then grabbed her hand again. "All right, the easy part's over now." The two of them ran to the far end of the long hall, reaching the doors into the high-security sector where Kier Gray was being held.

"We don't have any disguise or any weapons," she said. "We're just going to walk into the secret police zone?"

"I was planning to move faster than a walk." Jommy knew their chances were slim, and he was sure it would only get worse from this point forward. "That last little trick worked very well, and they're awfully preoccupied right now. I can't even imagine what's going on out in the streets."

"All right, I'll think calming thoughts. Don't let them be suspicious. We need to get close enough to my father that we can fight them. Once we open the door of his cell, he can help us fight."

"I'm counting on it," Jommy said.

Steeling themselves, they ran forward. Most of the holding chambers were empty; no prisoners extended beseeching hands through the bars, clamoring to be set free during the tendrilless attack. Ahead on the left, two guards and a mousy-looking courier waited in front of a sealed cell. All three of them were armed with blunt-nosed pistols.

"That's got to be the right place," Kathleen said.

She and Jommy marched determinedly forward. He focused on his thoughts. *We belong here. Don't be suspicious. Don't raise the alarm. We're no threat to you. Nothing to worry about.*

The guards glanced at them, then looked away, seemingly dismissing the two. The meek courier appeared perplexed and confused at his whole situation.

Nothing to worry about. We belong here.

As Jommy and Kathleen approached, the guards looked at each other again with questions starting to form on their lips, and troubled expressions slowly began to dawn on their faces. It wasn't working anymore!

Knowing their control was slipping, he and Kathleen threw themselves forward in unison with all the speed they could muster. Jommy seized the first guard's pistol and shot the second man, while Kathleen knocked away the skinny courier's arm. Because the man's hands were already slick with nervous sweat, the pistol slipped out of his grip and clattered to the floor.

Gray reached through the bars of his cell. "Kathleen! Jommy! You shouldn't be here. You're going to get caught."

"No, sir—we're going to free you," Jommy said.

Kathleen snatched the courier's pistol from the floor and pointed it at the remaining two men. "Step away from the bars."

Jommy found the controls and opened the cell door. Breathless with relief and grim-faced with urgency, Gray stumbled out into the corridor. He said, "Petty has seized control of the government, but he has no clue what he's up against. We've got no time to lose."

Before they could get away, though, four uniformed guards threw open the double doors through which Jommy and Kathleen had entered. At the opposite end of the security wing, another group of secret police barged in, led by John Petty himself. A trap! Kathleen, holding the pistol in her hands, pointed from the two men they had disarmed, then toward the oncoming guards.

"Don't shoot, Kathleen," Jommy warned. From both sides, the secret police closed in.

Gray's shoulders slumped, and the slan hunter came forward. "Well, well, look at the two fish I caught in my net!" He looked down at the dead guard whom Jommy had shot. "I seem to be losing a lot of guards today."

Petty disarmed Kathleen himself. The meek courier looked woefully embarrassed, and the other thug at the cell looked sheepish for having been duped.

The slan hunter shook his head. "We've been watching this pathetic little escape attempt unfold. After one of my own guards almost shot me, you didn't honestly think I would leave your cell unmonitored, Gray? You could have spies everywhere."

"Then what took you so long?" Jommy asked.

"I found it amusing, but time pressure forced me to act. I require your access codes and your command knowledge back in the control center, Mr. President."

Gray straightened. "Then you finally believe me about the extent of our current crisis? How deeply the tendrilless infiltration goes?"

Petty looked as if he had just swallowed a lemon whole. "I don't trust you, Gray, any more than I trust these other two dirty slans. But I have no choice at the moment." He gestured to the guards. "Bring the three of them to the command-and-control center. Even with all the resources of the secret police, I can only destroy one enemy at a time."

NINE

Even though the enemy spacecraft continued to drop their bombs all across the city, the looters were already out. Such people wouldn't miss an opportunity like this.

Ducking instinctively against the concussions of explosions and showers of dust and debris, Anthea ran alongside the trembling buildings in search of a place where she could protect herself and her infant son. She still wore only her hospital gown, the loose overcoat, and too-large shoes stolen from the doctor's office.

In an upscale shopping district she found several department stores with smashed display windows, brick and stone fallen onto the sidewalk. Before this, Anthea had never stolen anything in her life, but many things had changed. She clung to the baby and picked her way over the rubble, venturing into one of the stores.

A young man loomed in front of her. He had bad teeth, frizzy black hair, and dust all over his face. "This is my store! Don't you even think about coming in here to steal." His clothes hung awkwardly on him—a new and expensive leather jacket, suit pants, a formal shirt. She noticed tags still dangling from the garments. He squared his shoulders and leaned closer, as if to frighten her away with his bad breath. "The police have orders to shoot looters, you know."

"I just need some clothes. That's all."

"Steal clothes from somewhere else. Don't take mine. These are all mine!"

Remembering how she had sent the ambulance driver crashing through the windshield with a single kick, Anthea knew that she could easily subdue this overblown creep. But she did not want to draw attention to herself, and she was afraid of what she might do to him. "I'll go somewhere else, then."

"That's for sure." The young man puffed out his chest and pretended to threaten her again.

She continued along the street, dodging debris as a nearby building exploded. Four of the angular attack craft swooped toward one of the Centropolis defense planes as soon as it took off, blasting it out of the sky. A fireball erupted in a skyscraper directly across the street, sending down a shower of broken windows and shattered concrete. Anthea ducked under the green-and-white awning of a deserted coffee shop as shards of glass rained down, stabbing into the stretched canvas.

Farther down the street, Anthea found another clothing store, as yet unclaimed by scrawny looters. She kicked open the door. Inside the dim shadows, she ransacked the hangers and racks until she found a serviceable dress and comfortable shoes. She also tried on a beige overcoat and rounded up a soft powder-blue blanket for the baby. She wrapped him carefully to hide his fine tendrils.

Now they appeared normal, even if the rest of the world had gone crazy. She felt a faint hope that she and her baby might actually have a fighting chance. "I won't let you down, Davis," she whispered.

Anthea longed to go back to the brownstone apartment she had called home, but after the alarms in the hospital, the secret police would have tracked down Davis's address. They had his body, his wallet. Even during the ongoing attack, the ruthless slan hunters might have sent operatives to her home.

Neither she nor her husband had ever done anything that might threaten the security of Earth, but the secret police weren't going to ask for explanations or alibis. If they found her and the slan baby, they would simply open fire and chalk up the victims as another victory.

She kept looking for a place where she and the baby could hole up and wait. The city itself was on fire. Curls of black smoke rose like chimneys to the sky. Attacking spacecraft and Centropolis defense planes engaged in dogfights overhead.

Then she came upon a building made of thick, reinforced stone. So far it had withstood the air attacks. Chiseled in crisp letters above the entrance were comforting words: MAIN PUBLIC LIBRARY.

Anthea dashed inside the large building. Due to the attack, all the patrons had fled, and the library was like a hollow mausoleum. The homey, familiar scent of books surrounded them. "Hello?" Her voice echoed among the stacks.

Hearing her voice, a potbellied man with a blue-striped necktie strutted out of an office and came to greet them with open hands and a broad smile. "Hello, hello! Welcome to the library."

"Are you open? Can we come in here?"

"Oh, ma'am, we're certainly open for business. Didn't you see the library hours posted on the door?"

"I was afraid with the air-raid sirens and everything—"

The man made a dismissive gesture. "Tut, tut! The library hours are set in stone and have been followed for many years. We can't change things just because of an external distraction. Is there something in particular you were looking for? A reference book, perhaps? A good novel?"

Relief rushed through her. "Sanctuary. My baby and I need a place to . . . to wait out the attack. We can't go home."

"Ah, of course. I was hoping you might want to browse the shelves, but you're certainly welcome here. All are welcome."

The librarian had large, expressive eyes and heavy jowls that looked like hanging suitcases of extra skin. His straight hair was chestnut-brown, but an inch or so near the roots was grayish white, as if he had once regularly dyed his hair but had given up because it was too much effort. Round spectacles made his eyes seem larger.

"I'm Mr. Reynolds, the head librarian—apparently the *only* librarian who puts his responsibilities above personal fear." Reynolds scratched the jowl on his right cheek. "As soon as the bombs began to fall, my fellow workers became ill and had to go home. Apparently, something called an 'air-raid flu.' I intend to research it when I have a spare moment." He pushed his glasses up on his face. "Come into the central stacks and my administrative office. It's safest there."

They reached a room filled with shelves of bound reference books, neatly organized volumes of records and transcripts. "I keep our history section here. Fiction is on floor one, periodicals and study carrels located on floor two. Is there anything in particular I can assist you with right now? Since all of my coworkers have disappeared, I have gotten behind on my shelving work. But the patron always comes first."

Anthea felt intolerably weary. "I'd just like a chair to sit in and maybe a glass of water." Soon she would have to breast-feed the infant. She had no supplies, no diapers or bottles. *I'm not a very prepared new mother,* she realized. Then again, she hadn't expected to be hunted down like an animal, or for enemy ships to bombard the city.

Reynolds showed her a comfortable chair and dutifully brought her a cone-shaped paper cup from the gurgling watercooler. She took a grateful sip. Outside they could hear the rumbles of continued bomb strikes.

The librarian looked toward the window with indignation. "The enemy can destroy our buildings and kill our people, but so long as they do not eliminate our books, they cannot destroy our civilization." He smiled at her. "Without our historical and scientific knowledge, without our great tales and brave heroes, we would be giving up our very humanity."

Humanity, she thought, suppressing a shudder.

He saw the desperation on her face, the helpless baby wrapped in a powder-blue blanket. "Of course I will help you. Stay here, and I'll do whatever I can."

Then, as if to spite him, all the power went out. The racks of fluorescent lights died, plunging the stacks into darkness relieved only by the faint light from outside windows. The baby fussed and cried, picking up on Anthea's own anxiety.

Untroubled, Mr. Reynolds moved chairs and a metal cart like a blind man perfectly familiar with the layout of the room. Before long, he returned, struck a long wooden match, and lit several candles, which he placed in holders on the table. "Always be prepared, that's what I say. I would never want to be without the ability to read."

Carrying a candle in one hand, he rolled a book-laden cart through the stacks and, squinting in the dimness, continued to shelve volumes where they belonged. He piled reference tomes in the middle of a table so that all could peruse them.

Within moments, surrounded by unread books in the glow of candlelight, Anthea felt warm and cozy and safe for the first time in hours. She held the baby on her lap, kissed his forehead. He began to coo and make noises, not crying but simply experimenting with his vocal cords, his lungs.

"I hate to be a bother, but I must remind you that this is a library, ma'am." Mr. Reynolds pushed a battered old book back into place. "I will allow you to stay, but only if your baby remains quiet. We abide by strict rules here."

As soon as Reynolds had half jokingly stated his conditions, the baby in her arms instantly fell silent.

TEN

Guards and emergency response personnel ran through the halls of the grand palace. Panicked civil servants scrambled for bomb shelters or tried to evacuate from the huge building, streaming to designated rendezvous points. Others frantically grabbed telephones to call their families and loved ones.

Despite the evacuation signal, many administrative functionaries, protocol officers, and bureaucrats remained at their desks, deluded into believing that their jobs were important to the survival of Earth. There was nothing they could do, but they remained at their posts, transmitting orders, forwarding reports, filing forms, and monitoring the destruction outside.

In the midst of this, Jommy, Kathleen, and President Kier Gray were escorted under heavy guard to the main command-and-control center.

On the main display screens radar blips showed the swarm of invading ships. The size of the battle group was breathtaking. The enemy had been planning this assault for years, decades, even generations while they quietly assumed positions of power on Earth. The tendrilless had long held an impossible grudge against both true slans and humans, and they meant to wipe out their rivals.

"Give me a status report!" Petty called. His people inside the control room snapped to attention.

"Sir!" said technician Clarke. "We've tried to rally our forces, but it's mass confusion out there. We can't establish contact with our main power centers. The landing zones are hopelessly muddled, and we can't even launch most of our ships. The Air Center control towers are off-line. News stations are making their own announcements without even waiting for official word from us, so the public is completely confused."

The slan hunter regarded the President as if this were somehow all his fault. For years, staged air raids had sent the citizens of Centropolis into frenzied evacuations. Anti-aircraft guns mounted on skyscraper rooftops had prepared to open fire against imaginary slan spaceships. "I thought you had defensive armaments and response squadrons in place."

"That doesn't help if the tendrilless have infiltrated our radio towers, the Air Center, and the news media. One or two disloyal commanding officers can easily sabotage the entire plan."

Clarke looked harried and dismayed as he stared at the readouts. He pressed a bulky padded headphone against his ear, listening to reports as they came in from the field. "Half of our rooftop anti-aircraft guns are nonoperational. Several squads assigned to fire at the attacking ships have deserted their posts. Sixteen of the main batteries have failed disastrously—the big-bore guns exploded the first time they were used. Outright sabotage."

"That is the taste of betrayal," Gray said to Petty with a bitter smile. "I'm very familiar with it myself of late." He looked pointedly at the shackles on his wrists.

"We have to fight fire with fire." Petty stalked back and forth in the command-and-control center. "Launch Earth's best military forces—now."

"They still don't respond, sir."

"Then shout yourself hoarse. *Make* them hear. Make them respond. Find a way to get us out of this trap."

Gray stepped up next to Petty as if he could simply resume his role as President. "What about our ground forces? Have the tendrilless landed yet? We need to keep them from getting a foothold."

"A foothold?" Petty blinked at him. "They're blowing up every defense we have. We don't have any way—"

"Contact our space division. As President I set up a full-fledged military force with orbital and even interplanetary combat abilities. I planned ahead."

The slan hunter raised his dark eyebrows. "A space division? But we don't have the technology for—"

Gray looked at him mildly. "I'm the *President*. I have access to technologies that the public doesn't necessarily know about. Even your secret police couldn't keep watch over everything. Use this command authorization." He spouted a string of code phrases and numbers. Seeing nothing else he could do, Petty told the technicians to do as Gray suggested.

Across the continent, special sharp-winged ships rose up on lifting platforms from hidden underground bunkers. Heavy circular doors slid aside from unmarked paved areas to expose unmarked launchpads. The new ships carried the best weapons that humans had developed over the past fifty years.

During his administration, President Gray had secretly used black money in the budget to build defenses against the threat that he knew was out there, the threat he could never admit publicly. He trusted very few people, but he did use a handful of slan advisers and he did control the strings of many classified programs. While he staged enemy air raids, while he pretended to receive communiqués from the mysterious leaders of underground slan forces, Gray had built his own space fleet. Just in case.

Wide-eyed, John Petty watched the live images piped into the command center's screens. He was both astonished and delighted to see hundreds of well-armed spaceships ready to launch. *Earth* spaceships.

Gray was pleased to note the man's surprise. "I knew you were spying on my every move, whether I was protecting Kathleen or maintaining the constant state of emergency. But I also knew how you were prone to the abuses of power, Mr. Petty. I wasn't going to let you in on all of the emergency preparations."

"Abuses? I did what was necessary."

"If you and I are supposed to cooperate for the time being, then let's not mince words. I had no choice but to take precautions without your knowledge. I needed some assistance from my small circle of slan advisers, and they designed these ships. It's decent technology, but probably not good enough. Our knowledge is out-of-date, compared to what all the tendrilless scientists have developed over the years."

As they watched, the heroic human spacecraft leaped into the sky like a school of angry fish, weapons primed and ready to take out the tendrilless vanguard. On the radar screen, the new set of blips rose toward the myriad targets still in orbit.

Jommy was thrilled to see this unexpected fleet of defenders. "For so long, we've been stuck on the ground with our space program decimated. That was why I built my own ship and used it to spy on the tendrilless preparations. I thought I was the only one who could figure it out."

The slan hunter shook his head, seeking a target for his anxiety. "Listen to the boy genius."

Jommy's eyes flashed. "This boy genius has flown away from Earth,

infiltrated the enemy headquarters on Mars, and dealt with their representatives. I knew more about this threat than you ever imagined, Mr.
Petty. That's why I came back here with a warning."

"And you arrested him," Kathleen said accusingly.

Jommy nodded. "You spent far too much time chasing pebbles
while I was trying to stop a whole avalanche."

Petty seemed embarrassed. "I'd watch what you're saying, slan
boy. You're still my prisoner."

"Only until the palace blows up around us," Kathleen muttered.

Jommy emphasized his point. "The tendrilless have taken over
interplanetary space, and I know they've placed traps there. I ran into
a deadly minefield myself during my explorations." He spun to the
President. "Mr. President, you should warn your forces about the
mines. The tendrilless won't allow you to simply—"

With a cry of shock, Kathleen pointed to the screen. The blips
showing Earth's defensive spaceships began to flicker and flare. Over a
quarter of them winked out in only a few seconds.

"Looks like they found the minefield," Petty said.

Jommy groaned. "Even I didn't think the tendrilless had distributed so many. They knew we had no real space program. What could
they have been so afraid of?"

"Slans," Gray said. "They're worried about how much the hidden
slans will fight back. They're not concerned about humans."

Jommy stared at the afterimages, knowing that each set of glowing
phosphors represented a fully armed ship, now destroyed. Over a thousand human vessels had just been wiped out in a single blow!

But then the Earth forces fought back, blasting away with weapons
built into their fleet. Even the human pilots did not know that some of
their defenses were secret slan innovations; at the moment, they probably didn't care. Once the pilots learned how to detect and avoid the
space mines, they launched into an incredible dogfight, plowing into
the vanguard forces. It looked like a snowstorm of symbols swirling in
incomprehensible patterns. Ships clashed with ships, and many of the
tendrilless vessels were damaged or wrecked.

But not enough of them.

Knocking Clarke aside, Petty seated himself in the technician's
swivel chair, as if he didn't believe his knees would continue to support
his weight. To their continued horror, the blips showing the tendrilless
fleet looped around and went after the remaining human defenses.

Many of the Earth ships' weapons failed, inexplicably. Their pilots
shouted that navigation systems had just shorted out. They flew blind,

but still pursued the numerous enemy vessels. Engines gave out, armaments failed to fire, guidance systems died, leaving the Earth space navy helpless.

"Do the tendrilless have some kind of jamming system?" Kathleen asked. "Can we get them on line again?"

As he listened to the cries of surprise and frustration—then the static of destruction—Jommy could only conclude that the answer had to do with sabotage. "If you kept this fleet secret from Petty, who was in charge of it?"

"Jem Lorry. My chief adviser." Gray looked deeply troubled. "Who has now vanished. Could he have been a tendrilless spy? Could his mental shields have been so powerful that even I didn't suspect him?" He could not tear his eyes from the screens.

The fleet from Mars still outnumbered Gray's surprise space force more than three-to-one, and the battle swiftly turned into a rout. The Earth ships fought to the last, knowing that they could not surrender. On the screens, blip after blip vanished.

The sweep of the radar arc showed little detail, but Jommy didn't need any explanation as the pinpoints of human spacecraft brightened like stars going nova, then faded into darkness. Dozens more of the tendrilless attack ships were destroyed, and then the Earth defenders were gone. Completely gone.

Gray looked astonished. "It's a massacre. I didn't think . . . I never knew the enemy was so powerful. Our best defenses are no more effective than leaves blown in the wind. The tendrilless have undermined us, disconnected our weapons, sabotaged our plans."

Kathleen put her arms around her father. Gray's shoulders drooped. He found a seat by one of the empty diagnostic stations and slumped into it, brushing aside the torn rolls of printouts, ignoring the chattering computers that still attempted to analyze the situation. "I have failed us all."

With the ground forces neutralized and the last vestiges of the Earth space navy annihilated, the tendrilless ships were ready to complete their destruction. The inbound ships came down, unhindered now, and streaked across the skies of the capital city. Earth was completely at the mercy of the tendrilless.

Jommy barked his words so loudly that even the stunned technicians and disoriented leaders took heed. "The grand palace is sure to be a target. Now that our defenses are gone, they're going to turn this entire place into rubble."

"The palace is the most secure structure in all of Centropolis.

We're ten levels underground, and these rooms are reinforced against any aerial attack," said Petty, though he didn't sound convinced.

"Not reinforced enough. The tendrilless can level this whole structure. Once they've decapitated the government, they won't even need to bother with negotiating peace terms. They'll want to stand victorious on the rubble of the great government center."

Kathleen stepped close. "Jommy's right. We've got to get out of here, all of us."

Despite his handcuffs and his disheveled appearance, Gray still looked presidential. "There is no defeat while we still live. We must escape from the palace—now. We can become a government in exile."

"A government of what?" asked Petty.

"That is for us to define." Looking at his frantic rival, Gray extended a hand, letting it hang there in the air. "I suggest an alliance, Mr. Petty. I know of your plan to overthrow me. I know of your power plays with the secret police. But right now we face an enemy greater than either of us."

Kathleen chimed in. "It'll be the humans and the true slans against the tendrilless."

Jommy boldly pushed his way toward the door of the command-and-control center. "I have a means of escape—my advanced car is hidden in the forest on the other side of the river. Trust me."

"A car?" Petty looked at him in disbelief. "But Centropolis is under attack."

"The *whole planet's* under attack, and the tendrilless won't stop until they've crushed our cities. But my car is armored with ten-point steel and full of new inventions. If anything can withstand the bombardment, that vehicle can. But if we don't act soon, we'll all just be bloodstains in the rubble."

When another terrific explosion shook the reinforced walls of the palace, it was enough to help make up Petty's mind. Gray thrust his hands forward. "Uncuff me, and let's get out of here." The slan hunter grudgingly did so.

As they left the command-and-control center, Petty yelled for his guards to get to safety. He wanted to be sure that his supporters—the men who would do whatever brutal action he required—were not all killed in a single attack. The slan hunter was sure to need them later on, and he could summon any remnants that remained from around the country.

Overhead, the attacking tendrilless forces began their full-scale bombardment to destroy the palace.

ELEVEN

Though she was herself a tendrilless, Joanna Hillory was not part of the vanguard fleet during the attack. An operative trained to live and work among human beings, she excelled in being a spy, not a soldier. Her people had used her well, and she had helped them set up their plans for this conquest.

But that was before Jommy Cross had changed her mind. Now, remaining behind on Mars, Joanna had other plans of her own.

She was an attractive woman with a full figure, as tall as most men. Her brown hair was kept short and curled, close to her head. She wore clothes that gave her freedom of movement, with few concessions to human standards of beauty. As a spy, it had been important for her to keep a low profile, though her appearance was enough to turn heads and even earn her an occasional wolf whistle from men on the streets of Earth.

While the bombardment continued on Earth's primary cities, Joanna received a summons to stand before the seven-member council in the glass-ceilinged Martian city. Cimmerium seemed practically empty as she walked along the wide balcony roads along the edges of the cliffs. Towers extended out into the sheer gulf of the canyon, rising up toward the flat crystalline ceiling.

Joanna touched a pearlescent ID scanner mounted outside the vaulted doorway to the Authority chamber. Recognizing and approving her, the door controls unlocked with a hiss, then silently swung inward, beckoning her inside. She had always been a favorite of Altus Lorry, the head of the Tendrilless Authority.

Inside the rainbow-filled chamber, dim sunlight was intensified by prismatic angles, flooding the chamber with warmth and reminders of paradise, the way Earth would be once they conquered it.

Centuries ago, during the first Golden Age of Mankind and before the devastating Slan Wars, true pioneers had begun terraforming Mars. Humans had bombarded the red planet with comets, thickened the atmosphere, added liquid water in the low-lying canyons, filling Mare Cimmerium with enough liquid to turn it into a small, shallow sea. They had released algaes and bacteria, which worked on the once-sterile environment for more than a thousand years as the breeds of humanity fought and tried to destroy each other.

By the time the tendrilless slans came seeking refuge, Mars was a much more hospitable place. The air was thick enough to capture the sun's distant heat. Water vapor long locked in frozen underground layers began to percolate upward. The bacteria and algae continued to convert water molecules hydrated in the rocks and break down minerals to release oxygen.

Cimmerium became a complex settlement. Buildings were made from reinforced glass produced by melting the inexhaustible supplies of Martian sand, and before long a shining metropolis clung to the walls of the deep canyon.

While it was comfortable here, the half-terraformed Martian environment was still less hospitable than Earth. In a half-facetious comment, Jem Lorry had once growled a suggestion that President Gray and some of the more intractable humans should be sent back *here* in exile, so they would know what had made the tendrilless strong for so many generations.

The biggest mystery concerning the tendrilless civilization, Joanna knew, lay in finding their hated stepbrothers, the hidden slans, who had persecuted and tried to eradicate the tendrilless. All that had changed, however, when she'd met Jommy Cross.

Back when she'd been on assignment on Earth, Jommy had broken into the secret tendrilless headquarters at the Air Center. On the run from the law, Jommy and an old crone he called Granny had the sheer unexpected bravado to steal a tendrilless spacecraft, but Joanna had intercepted them.

Jommy was a clever young man, certainly her equal in strength and mental abilities. She had interrogated him, sure that Jommy worked for a large enclave of true slans, though he insisted he was acting alone, that his mother had been shot dead by slan hunters when he was only nine years old; his father, a great slan scientist, had been killed when he was six.

When Jommy told her that there didn't need to be war between the races, she had thought him incredibly naive. But his earnestness was infectious, and *he* was fervently convinced. Afterward, the more Joanna thought about what he'd said, the more she considered his plans and his determination to follow them, the more she actually started to believe that he might have a chance to achieve his utopian dreams.

Maybe the tendrilless were wrong, after all. When Jommy was nearly caught again after sneaking inside Cimmerium, Joanna herself arranged for him to get away, to race back to Earth and warn President Gray of the imminent attack. She had remained behind, hoping to convert a few more allies among the tendrilless.

That had been Joanna's desperate secret, which she'd kept close to her heart for days now. The Tendrilless Authority would command her immediate execution if they suspected her involvement. Jem Lorry had launched his major attack before she could make any headway against his stubborn beliefs.

Joanna had learned not to underestimate Jommy, however. She hadn't yet admitted even to herself that she was in love with him.

As she walked forward to face the council members behind their high bench, she drove back her fear and anxiety. They couldn't possibly know what she had done.

Ahead of her, she heard a shrill, petulant voice challenging the more ponderous, deeper tones of Altus Lorry. "You miss the primary question, Father. The occupation fleet has just launched, but by the time they get to Earth, the vanguard ships and our tendrilless ground troops will have completed much of the work. Think about the next step. We must decide whether to leave a handful of humans alive as our slaves and perhaps even experimental subjects—or should we just save ourselves the trouble and exterminate them all?"

"Those are not the only two options," Altus said with maddening calm. "Your hatred blinds you. If we mean to take over Earth, it makes no sense to destroy everything. What is the purpose in that? Why should we rebuild from scratch, pick up every broken piece?"

Another Authority member added, "The humans must be resoundingly defeated, we agree, but mass extermination is not logical."

"It would sound more logical if you'd bothered to live among them," Jem grumbled. "Try watching them every day, smelling them, observing their habits, knowing that you must keep your true identity a secret or else they would lynch you! They are like animals living in a primitive society."

Hearing her approach, Jem turned, and his eyes lit up with a fervor he had kept carefully hidden while playing his political role in the President's palace. "Joanna, you can speak on my behalf! You've lived among them as much as I have. Explain to my"—he struggled with his words—"my esteemed father and his fellow Authority members that we can assure our future only by ensuring that humans are not part of it."

She gave him a calm smile. "How can I speak on your behalf, when you are fundamentally wrong? Such a wholesale slaughter would accomplish nothing but give you a brief rush of personal vengeance." Amused by the shocked expression on his face, she turned her gray-eyed gaze up at the seven council members. "Authority Chief Lorry, you are wise to advocate caution and forethought."

Old Altus gave her a kindly and satisfied nod, while Jem fumed, as if she had just betrayed him.

Joanna continued. "Would you rather spend our efforts consolidating a new government for tendrilless slans—or engage in an endless pursuit to eradicate all of the humans in hiding? You would force them into creating resistance cells, possibly even drive them into an alliance with the true slans. Imagine the debacle."

"They would still never be strong enough against us!" Jem insisted.

"Irrelevant. Either way, it would waste a great deal of our time."

Realizing he would never convince them, Jem stalked out of the Authority chambers with a disappointed glare at Joanna.

When she saw how the council reacted to her, Joanna convinced herself that they did not suspect her collusion with Jommy Cross. Her secret was safe.

"Please forgive my son," Altus said. "He has obsessed on humans for too long. I still hold out hope for him, and I give him chance after chance, but sadly we may have to remove him before he causes irreparable damage."

She gave a noncommittal nod. The Authority Chief had always been kind toward her, even to the point of expressing his desire for political matchmaking between Joanna and his son, though she had recoiled at the notion. "You summoned me here, sirs?"

"We need you to take care of a very specific threat," Altus said. "An important threat."

"What threat is that?"

"His name is Jommy Cross."

Her heart skipped a beat, and she was sure she paled, but Joanna fought not to show any reaction. "He is just one slan, a young man presumably working alone."

"Cross has quite remarkable talents. He was here in our city, as you well know, but he escaped. He escaped *you,* he escaped us, he escaped the greatest security measures in all of Cimmerium."

Another Authority member interrupted, "That in itself proves he is a danger. Cross returned to Earth in time to warn them of our attack, and it was only sheer luck that political turmoil there kept the humans from preparing themselves. We do not wish to trust to such luck again. Cross must be stopped."

Realizing she hadn't been breathing, Joanna inhaled, waited a long second to calm herself, then exhaled. They weren't accusing her of anything. "And what is it you would like me to do?"

"Take one of our fastest scout ships and go to Earth. In the midst of our assault, we order you to hunt down and seize Jommy Cross."

TWELVE

By the warm candlelight in the shelter of the library, Anthea held her baby, quietly breast-feeding him as she listened to the buzzing roar of attacking aircraft outside. But she was more afraid of *people* than falling bombs. She closed her eyes and tried to figure out what to do next. She had no one in whom she could confide. The candles flickered, casting a warm but somehow medieval glow throughout the stacks of thick tomes.

Today she had been confronted with the unexpected and unreasoning hatred of total strangers. All her life she had heard news broadcasts about the insidious schemes of "evil slans." The secret police had spread hatred and fear.

Before, it had all meant little to her. She and Davis were just a normal married couple with good jobs—Anthea in a bank, her husband in a sporting goods store. They'd been happy with each other, and they anticipated a long and fruitful life, looking forward to starting a family.

After the birth of the baby, though, she had stepped on a land mine of prejudice and murderous anger.

When a bomb shattered the stone lion statues in front of the library, the pudgy Mr. Reynolds grabbed two of the flickering candles and gestured for Anthea to do the same. "Come with me. We have to go to the inner vault. There's better shelter inside, and an emergency generator."

Before leaving, he diligently and conscientiously blew out the remaining candles and led Anthea through a maze of bookshelves to an office at the heart of the building. Their flickering lights were like bobbing will-o'-the-wisps.

The walls here were thick and entirely without windows. The baby stirred in her arms, and she bent down to shush him, holding the candle in her other hand. "Is this the rare book section?"

"I have the distinct privilege and honor of being the chief librarian at one of the few designated True Archives commissioned by the government. President Gray himself came for the ribbon-cutting ceremony fifteen years ago."

"What's a True Archive?"

The librarian beamed, delighted to find a willing listener. "During the Slan Wars and centuries of guerrilla warfare and wanton destruction, much history has been lost. Most people don't even know what the truth is anymore."

Anthea looked hard at him. "Do you know the truth? About the slans?"

Mr. Reynolds fumbled a little and turned his back, marching farther down the hall into a larger, open lobby. "This library is one of the repositories of genuine information about the Slan Wars and Dr. Samuel Lann. Many of the reports are contradictory, of course. A few are written by eyewitnesses, while some are rather clumsy government propaganda. But that's the way it usually is. With so much information, you have to separate opinion from fact, exaggeration from documentation."

He stopped in front of a great metal door and set his candles down on a small table. The thick hatch was steel-gray, polished to a dull luster, reinforced with riveted panels and a locking mechanism of gears and dials. The combination wheels themselves were secured with a steel padlock. The thick door seemed as impregnable as a bank vault.

"Inside this vault are original papers, some of the notebooks of Dr. Lann, and actual correspondence from previous presidents who fought in the Slan Wars."

Since the birth of her unexpected slan baby, she felt a desperate need to know. All of the background material in that vault would reveal the answers. "I'd like to see them. I'm sure it's fascinating."

The librarian seemed befuddled. "Oh, I'm afraid that's not possible, ma'am. Those records are classified."

"But if this is a True Archive, why can't people see the truth?"

"Most people are not ready for it," Reynolds said sadly. "*Possessing* information and *distributing* it are two different things. Even President Gray wanted to control how much the public knew." He shook his head, his jowls sagging like a hound dog's. "From what I heard on the wireless this morning, it seems the President has been secretly in league with the slans all along. What has he brought us to?"

The distant thunderous rumble of more explosions rattled the ceiling.

"I think there's a great deal we don't understand," Anthea said. "But those records might help us unravel it. Besides, didn't you say there was a backup generator inside? We'd have electricity again, and we'd be safe."

The baby squirmed in his mother's arms and she saw just a hint of the fine golden tendrils rising out like long strands of hair from the powder-blue blanket. She quickly tucked them back.

Reynolds was more agitated now, loosening his necktie. "Only I know the combination to unseal this door, ma'am. I have strict instructions not to open it for anyone who doesn't have presidential authorization."

"You're the only one with the combination? How can you be sure you remember it?"

"Oh, the numbers are very clear in my mind." Reynolds tapped his forehead.

The baby remained very still as if he had fallen asleep, but suddenly Anthea saw numerals sharply in her brain, as if someone had painted them in bold ink behind her eyelids: 4 . . . 26 . . . 19 . . . 12. She caught her breath as she realized what must have happened. The slan baby had easily read those numbers as Mr. Reynolds had recalled them, and the infant had shared them with his mother's mind as well. Anthea knew exactly how to open the vault.

Making an excuse, the librarian scuttled back to a long wooden table just outside the armored vault door. "However, these particular volumes are available to the general public, though not often requested, I'm afraid. Many people instinctively hate the slans, but don't want to understand anything about the reasons for doing so. The slans did terrible things to human society, oh, yes. The Slan Wars were the greatest holocaust in our civilization's history, like the burning of a thousand libraries of Alexandria."

He heaved a great, grieving breath. "The endless centuries of destruction leveled our cities, brought us down to the level of barbarism. It took the human race a long time to rebuild, and even now our society has returned only to the equivalent of the United States of America back in the 1940s, as calculated in the old-style calendar." He gestured for Anthea to take a seat and began arranging books on the table. "Some of the cultural similarities to that time period are quite striking. It's as if we've been set on a well-worn path. We're following technology, styles, and habits that were forgotten long ago, but are now coincidentally commonplace."

Anthea arranged some of the books to make a support, like a cradle, in which she could tuck the blanket-wrapped baby. Then she pulled other volumes toward her. "But these books are not classified? I can read them?"

"They're the official records of the Slan Wars. I hope they hold your interest. When all this messy business outside is over, maybe we can submit a request to whichever government is in charge next? I would so enjoy having a real scholar look over the True Archives with me."

"So, you've read them yourself?"

He seemed embarrassed. "Not . . . entirely. Just enough to make a cursory inventory. There's always so much to do in the library itself, you know."

"Thank you very much. These will do fine for now." Anthea found newspaper clippings, reprinted letters, and many books describing the "slan peril" and the "terrible threat of the evil superhumans." She brought one of the candles closer.

Reynolds made disapproving sounds as he stood in front of a cart full of books. "Some of these are in sections 820.951 through 825.664, right down here in the sheltered area. Will you be all right for a little while?" After she reassured him, Reynolds rattled off with his heavy cart, balancing one of the thick candles to light his way.

Alone now, Anthea opened the books and began to skim them. She had always enjoyed reading, but now—after having the baby, after realizing who and what she was—a key had opened in her mind. She was astonished to discover that in only a few minutes she had completely skimmed—and absorbed, and *remembered*—a full five-hundred-page volume!

The reports carried some surprises, but generally they were the same inflammatory stories she'd been told all her life. She skimmed the spines of other books, selected a second one, and raced through the pages as well, flipping them so swiftly she nearly tore the paper. Then she read a third book, and a fourth. She felt like a dry sponge plunged into a bucket of water.

Anthea learned how the first slan mutations had appeared, babies born with tendrils that amplified their telepathic abilities. They could read minds, influence people; their bodies were stronger.

The most prominent figure in all of the records was Dr. Lann. Some portrayed him as a genius, others as a victim of his own hubris, still others called him an evil mastermind who had caused an evolutionary avalanche that resulted in the deaths of billions. The records were unclear as to whether the slan mutations had occurred naturally, or if Samuel Lann had created a machine or special ray that invoked the changes in his own three children, turning them into the first slans.

Contradictory reports hinted that tendrilled babies had been born spontaneously all around the planet, from civilized countries to rough wastelands. Before long, slans began to appear everywhere. They found each other and bore children. Within a few generations, their numbers had grown great enough that their leaders quietly made plans. Slans infiltrated important positions in government and industry, and then they took over the world, insisting that they were meant to be the masters of "mere humans."

Anthea shuddered as she continued to read. Nearby, warm and comfortable, wrapped in blankets, the baby seemed capable of absorbing everything his mother knew, assimilating all the new knowledge she learned.

Mr. Reynolds, whistling happily to be doing something productive, trundled an empty cart back into the protected room outside the thick vault door. He took another loaded book cart and went about his business. Anthea barely noticed him as she eagerly devoured the records in front of her. . . .

From the point after which the slans had made their first move against humanity, the news reports became much less objective. She doubted any of them was entirely true. Previously, a handful of conspiracy theorists denounced the slans as freaks and monsters. Then, when one hundred thousand slans took over the world, they proved to everyone that the paranoid fears had been correct. The slans *did* mean to enslave humanity.

But the angered humans formed a powerful resistance. The slans might have been supermen, but one hundred thousand could not stand against a vengeful population of billions.

The devastation on both sides was horrendous. As the wars flared up, died down, then burst into flames again, Earth itself was rocked. Eventually, after centuries of bloodshed, the slans were defeated. The survivors went into hiding, built secret enclaves, protected bases from which they could continue their insidious scheming (or so the reports claimed). Some said the slans went out into space, perhaps to Mars, where they bided their time, rebuilt their numbers, and prepared for a further attack. Earth's technology had been set back so far, the survivors could not even dream of launching a concerted space program.

Every once in a while, a slan was caught and killed in Centropolis, lending credence to the fears that hundreds or thousands more remained in hiding. The secret police crowed about each such victory, proud to be rooting out the evil infiltrators.

It seemed indisputable that those first megalomaniacal slans had indeed meant to dominate humanity, had tried to take over the world and enslave others. But that was so many centuries ago. Did the few wild survivors still mean such harm? What about the "accidents," like her own baby? Could every innocent child born with tendrils be sentenced to death for the sins of long-forgotten fathers? She shook her head and looked up, startled to realize that she had finished reading fourteen of the books on the table.

Mr. Reynolds had come back, having emptied his carts. He now stood smiling, bent over her baby. He whispered and cooed, stroking the boy's nose, his forehead. Before Anthea could react, he pushed the blanket back, revealing the baby's head. "Look at you. Such a cute little—"

Then he gasped in horror.

The baby's tendrils rose like tiny antennae in the air, wafting as if in a gentle breeze. Reynolds stumbled backward, gaping at the slan tendrils. "Oh, my!"

THIRTEEN

The tendrilless bombers were already on their final approach.

"Deep underground will be the safest," Kathleen said. "Jommy, can we get to your vehicle from there?"

"Yes, there are transverse tunnels." With his perfect recall, he could envision all the tangled passageways and routes from the blueprints he had seen. "I know of an old slan passageway that goes all the way beneath the river."

After the guards and secret police had scattered following their chief's orders, Petty easily kept pace with the other three. Jommy wished the slan hunter had abandoned them, but apparently he trusted the slans to know a better escape than his own people. Petty directed them to a high-speed lift, but the doors were sealed and the controls refused to operate. The secret police chief pounded the wall in frustration. "We've got to get down to shelter!"

Gray nudged him aside. "This is one of the palace's private elevators, high security, limited access." He slid aside a hidden metal covering to expose a translucent plate and several code buttons. He pressed his open left eye against the scanner and keyed in a code. A bright beam played across his retina, mapped the patterns there, and confirmed his identity. The lift hummed, then whisked open. "I *am* the President, after all—no matter what Mr. Petty says."

The slan hunter glowered at him.

Jommy urged them all inside, then turned to the control plate. "Thirty-eighth level would be our best starting point." He punched the number. The doors closed, and the private car shot downward.

Only seconds later, the palace was engulfed in a roar of light and fire.

Shock waves slammed into the descending elevator car, making a sound as if they were trapped within a bronze church bell. The bright ceiling light went out, and the car shuddered to a stop, dislodged from its tracks. More explosions thundered overhead. The walls trembled.

"Brilliant idea, Cross," Petty said in the darkness. "Now we're stuck here."

"We would have all been happier if you'd stayed in the command-and-control center," Kathleen retorted. "Why did you bother coming along with us?"

"I couldn't let three slans get away. That would be shirking my duty."

Trying to solve the problem he faced, ignoring the heated conversation, Jommy felt with his fingertips along the metal wall of the chamber. He found the crack in the sealed lift door. "We have to pry it open, get out of this elevator car, then climb to an access hatch." Gripping with his fingers and palms, he pressed with all his enhanced strength, straining until the doors began to peel apart. "There . . . making progress!"

Then, with a squeal and a groan, the stalled elevator dropped farther down the shaft, grinding along its tracks with a spray of sparks. They were in free fall for a moment, plunging out of control. Through the crack he'd been able to open in the door, Jommy watched one floor, then another and another, streak past as the detached elevator picked up speed. Then it slammed to a clamorous halt, caught again in precarious balance.

"Have we hit the bottom?" Kathleen asked after a moment of stunned silence. "Why didn't we crash?"

"We're jammed in the shaft again," Jommy said. "But I don't know how long it'll hold."

"We could figure that out for ourselves," Petty added sarcastically. "Maybe we're almost to the bottom."

"There's at least sixty more levels down," Gray said. "I suggest we get out of here before we drop the rest of the way."

Applying all his strength, Jommy wrenched the door open farther. The tracks in the elevator shaft had been knocked severely out of alignment from the bombardment high above. One of the broken rails had twisted to one side, and the falling car had wedged to an unstable balance. Two feet above them, Jommy saw another hatch that opened to a floor—their way out. "Kathleen, I'll boost you up. You can open the door from within the elevator shaft."

She didn't hesitate, and Jommy was surprised at how easily he could support her weight. As she reached out through the open door, though, the elevator groaned uncertainly. If the car fell now, Kathleen would be sheared in half.

Kier Gray moved to the other side of the elevator to compensate for the weight shift. They all knew the car could drop out at any time and plunge screeching and sparking for sixty floors until it struck the bottom like an asteroid impact.

Kathleen stretched out her hand, and with the barest tip of her finger she managed to hit the emergency hatch control in the main wall. Lights blinked, and with a sedate hum, the emergency hatch slid aside to reveal a corridor well lit by flickering ceiling lights.

Jommy gave Kathleen another boost, and she scrambled out of the elevator and through the hatch. Once safely inside, she called for her father to come up. As Gray moved to the open door and the emergency hatch, the readjusting weight made the elevator groan ominously again.

Showing no sign of fear, Gray accepted Jommy's assistance to climb out, leaving the young man trapped in the elevator with the slan hunter. Anxious not to be last, Petty lurched toward the door. He was sure they meant to abandon him—and with good reason. Petty could shield his thoughts well enough, but even so Jommy sensed the building panic in the secret police chief.

As Petty stepped across the floor, the elevator gave a sickening lurch and dropped eighteen inches. The man froze, refusing to take another step.

Jommy stared at him. "Are we going to just look at each other until the elevator falls to the bottom, or do you intend to move and get out of here?"

Petty didn't need to be encouraged again. When Jommy offered him a hand, the other man refused. "I don't need help from one of your kind." He reached up for the bottom of the emergency hatch in the shaft wall, which was now more difficult to reach. From the safety of the hall, Kier Gray looked down at the man who had overthrown him. A simple slip, a nudge at just the right moment, and the slan hunter would fall to his death.

Nevertheless, Gray grabbed his rival's arm and hauled him up.

Now mostly empty, the elevator creaked, began to work itself loose from the tracks. "Jommy, hurry!" Kathleen reached down beside her father, both of them trying to grab him, stretching out their hands.

The binding metal began to slip, grinding away the twisted track. With only a second left, Jommy tensed and sprang upward. His leap carried him at least two feet higher than a normal man could have jumped, and he hooked his elbows inside the emergency hatch. Gray and Kathleen seized his shoulders, his shirt, and pulled him into the hall. Jommy squirmed out of the shaft and pulled himself into the corridor just as the elevator jarred loose. When the last obstruction broke away, the elevator plummeted in a wail of sparks and grinding gears, falling down into the depths.

Panting, Jommy recovered and got to his feet. He glanced up. Petty was just standing there, arms crossed, watching, then the slan hunter turned around and began marching down the hall, as if nothing unusual had happened. "Well, now where do we go?"

Jommy studied a numbered plate on the wall to determine where they were. "We still have to go down seven levels." The President again used his ID to provide access to a restricted stairwell, and they hurried down the metal steps, one flight after another.

Petty continued to find reasons to question. "If you're an outsider, Cross, how is it that you found a secure passage to get into the palace? Even my secret police weren't aware of hidden tunnels down here."

"The slans built them long ago. I received information, partly from old records, partly from certain telepathic broadcasts in the palace specifically attuned for someone able to hear them. Someone with tendrils, I mean."

He opened the door at the appropriate level. The hall looked like any other, but inside his head he could detect the thin, dull tone, a guiding beacon for his slan senses. Kathleen looked at him, amazed. "I can hear it."

Gray nodded. "I was aware of these, but I didn't investigate because I feared being observed. I couldn't let anyone—especially Petty—know what was down here."

"Just like you kept a full space navy secret from me?" Petty snorted. "I still should have kept a better eye on you, and on Jem Lorry."

"Lorry isn't one of us," Gray insisted.

"Seems like he did a good job sabotaging the Earth spaceships, from what we saw on the battle screens."

Not knowing what trials they might face once they worked their way into the besieged city itself, Jommy wished he still had his father's disintegrator weapon. That invention would provide options they wouldn't otherwise have, but Petty had locked the confiscated device in a secure vault for secret police analysis. It was probably still intact, even with the collapse of the palace, but it could be buried anywhere. Long ago, he had added a tiny tracer to the disintegrator but had no time to construct a detector to pick up the signal. Right now, they had to get safely away from the ruins of the palace. And for that, they needed his special vehicle.

Jommy moved down the hall, trailing his fingers along the painted cement blocks. He found a spot that looked no different from the rest, but when he depressed the blocks in a certain sequence, a hidden door slid inward and then aside to reveal a well-lit tunnel that extended a great distance.

"Inside there, not far down, is the old maintenance tunnel that goes all the way under the river. The slans commandeered it for their own purposes a long time ago, and it's been completely forgotten. We can follow it outside and get to the forest where I left my armored vehicle. I'm sure it's still there and safe."

The embedded detectors recognized him as a slan, and Jommy felt a rush of relief. Once Jommy had opened the secret door to the tunnel, Petty did not wait for the others. He pushed forward, taking the lead. No one but slans had entered this tunnel for many years.

Jommy's tendrils suddenly picked up a shrill vibration, a distinct sensation of uneasiness that built to panic. A Porgrave transmitter, one of the special broadcasters that only slans could hear. The signal focused, and he could understand the words: an automated warning installed by long-forgotten slan inventors. The Porgrave signal shouted in his head: *Non-slan detected. Unauthorized presence.*

Jommy felt a thrumming in the air as retaliation devices swung into action. Also recognizing the signal, Kathleen backed abruptly into her father. Petty, though, was unaware of anything unusual. He strode forward.

Defense systems activating. Targeting . . . now.

"Petty, look out!" Jommy lunged forward, grabbed the slan hunter by the back of his shirt, and yanked him off his feet.

The burly man stumbled and cried out angrily just as a spiderweb of searing yellow-white beams crisscrossed the air where he had been. A smell of ozone accompanied the whip-crack sound of deadly defenses.

The slan hunter got back to his feet and brushed himself off, shocked and then nonplussed. "You saved my life." He seemed more upset than relieved that Jommy had saved him. He lowered his voice. "Don't think you bought yourself any mercy from me because of that, Cross."

Kathleen let out a quick, bitter laugh. "If you think mercy is something that can be bought, Mr. Petty, then you don't understand mercy at all."

The slan hunter gave her a dismissive wave. "Oh, you're just angry because I shot you in the head."

They followed the dim passage for at least a mile, trending always upward. Jommy remained alert for other booby traps and defensive measures, deactivating several, though part of him longed to just let the evil slan hunter get himself fried by the systems. It would have been what he deserved, a poetic justice.

"Explain again why we should bring you along, Petty?" Jommy asked, pausing before he deactivated another security system. "As far as I'm concerned, you don't have any redeeming qualities."

Buried far underground, and now lost inside a labyrinth of booby-trapped tunnels, the slan hunter looked alarmed. "You need me. I can be useful."

"Exactly how?" Gray said. "You overthrew my presidency."

"And killed my mother," Jommy said.

"And shot me," Kathleen added. "You haven't done much to endear yourself to us. I say we should just leave him here." She looked to her father for support. "There's a slight chance he could make his way out and deactivate the security systems himself."

Turning pale, Petty quickly said, "Wait! My network of secret police is distributed all across the country. We have emergency procedures, too—and you can bet those men were better prepared than most other people. We always expected something terrible to happen."

"The advantages of being paranoid," Jommy said.

"We have contact protocols. I can help you bring them together, maybe mount a resistance. Who else is going to be organized enough to fight for Earth? You couldn't have a better starting point, once the dust settles here."

"If he does have that network," Kathleen realized, "then it's better to have him with us, where we can keep an eye on him, rather than off by himself where he can turn the secret police against us."

"If nothing else, he might make a good hostage," Jommy said. The slan hunter didn't seem to know whether to be pleased or annoyed with their assessment of his value.

"For the time being, you have your uses, Mr. Petty," Gray said. "Now let's get out of here before the whole thing comes down on our heads."

Finally, they emerged into the shadowy forest, swinging open a vine-covered grate that would have been all but invisible to anyone wandering among the trees. Getting his bearings, Jommy cast around for where he had left the car, then he led them on an hour-long search until they at last discovered the dark machine hidden in the underbrush.

Jommy had never seen anything so beautiful in his life (with the exception of Kathleen). He had designed and built the vehicle using all the best technologies and materials he had been able to put together.

Petty had encountered the car once before, just after his secret police had shot Kathleen in the slan hideout. Even so, he had a difficult time pretending that he wasn't impressed.

Gray went immediately to the vehicle's door. "We've got to get out of here, and it's best if the tendrilless think we're all dead."

They all climbed inside, and Jommy sat behind the driving controls, which were keyed to him alone. The engine powered up, and the guidance responded to his touch. "I can drive us out of here, and fast."

"But where will we go?" Kathleen called from the backseat. "If Centropolis is under attack and the tendrilless are looking for us—"

"I know the perfect secluded place, a distant valley where we can all be safe." As he accelerated out of the shielded tunnel and burst into the open smoke-filled sky, Jommy quirked his lips in a wry smile. "I just hope Granny will take us in."

FOURTEEN

From his headquarters office in the Martian city of Cimmerium, Jem Lorry received the vivid images from his vanguard forces at Earth. This was one of the most satisfying moments in his life.

Jem played the footage twice more just to savor it, then he picked up the display plate and hurried to show his father and the Authority members. Seeing this, they would have to admit that he had been right all along.

He marched into the cavernous crystal-ceilinged room, where the council members were packing up for the day. With a shout, he made the seven old men turn around. "I have news from Earth, glorious news! I must show it to you."

Altus looked impatient, as if he had tolerated enough from his son, but Jem stepped directly up to the podium where supplicants addressed the Tendrilless Authority in open session. He plugged in his display plate and transferred the images to the tandem screens in front of all seven members. "Behold the fall of the human government! We have won. It was even smoother and more absolute than I had dreamed possible."

The transmitted images showed the devastation of Centropolis in impeccable detail. At first the cameras tracked across the city streets: collapsing skyscrapers, flaming vehicles, panicked pedestrians. Then the view centered in on the towering palace. Like a flock of hungry raptors, the tendrilless attack ships zeroed in, exchanged orders, then swooped down in perfect formation. Their bomb-bay doors opened to drop load after load of weapons on the grand structure.

The detonations occurred simultaneously, shock waves crashing against each other, reinforcing and amplifying the destruction.

Flames roared to the skies. Ornate and spectacular towers that had stood as landmarks for centuries now toppled into rubble.

A hundred stories tall, highlighted with crystalline spires, parapets, and remarkable architecture, the ancient slan-designed palace collapsed under the bombardment. The presidential quarters, the administrative chambers, staff rooms and records vaults, formal dining halls and galleries lined with state portraits. After the palace collapsed, secondary detonations spat out bright orange flowers, columns of black smoke, and plumes of debris. The images zoomed in on the burning rubble and smoking pit.

Jem stood tall, supremely confident. "Right now, every surviving human in the city is staring in despair, weeping for what they've lost. Even I didn't expect their defenses to crumble so easily, though I did take care to make their small space navy ineffective. I'll bet President Gray was quite surprised."

Altus scratched his chin as he watched the replaying images. "We expected more resistance from Earth because we thought the true slans would come out of hiding at last. Are you sure there has been no sign of them?"

"None at all. If anything could flush out the snakes, this should have done it. It is time for the Authority to face the only possible conclusion: *There are no more true slans.* We've heard rumors for so long, but they're just that: rumors."

"Rumors? And what about Jommy Cross or Kathleen Layton?"

Jem covered his pained expression at the thought of Kathleen. With her true slan genetics and Jem's tendrilless bloodline, their offspring would certainly have been superior. But she had rebuffed his advances. What a fool the girl had been! No doubt Kathleen had been inside the palace when it was destroyed. His lips pulled down in a bitter frown. She could have been with him.

"The only slans left are insignificant throwbacks, one or two genetic mistakes. They belong in a museum with other extinct species."

Altus said, "You draw sweeping conclusions from a relatively small amount of evidence."

One of the other Authority members added, "We can't be too careful." The other old men nodded, mumbling to each other.

A flush of anger came to Jem's cheeks. The Authority—and his own father—seemed intent on stalling every bit of progress he made. "Our irrational fear of the slans has set us back by centuries! We were so sure they were hiding, building great weapons, preparing invincible defenses against us. We wasted generations establishing our fortified city here on Mars, building an invincible fleet. We laid down an extensive space minefield around Earth orbit to guard it—and from what? We've squandered a fortune and years of effort building bastions against an enemy that doesn't even exist."

"Thank you for your interesting summary, my son. We will draw our conclusions once we've received a report from our operative on the scene." Altus switched off the display plate, and his fellow Authority members did the same. "She should arrive soon."

Jem blinked, feeling left out. "What other operative? I am in charge of this strike."

"Joanna Hillory. We have already dispatched her to Earth."

"On what mission? How dare you go around me?"

"We are the Tendrilless Authority. We decide what is best," Altus said in a patient voice. "We sent her to find Jommy Cross, whom we consider to be our largest threat. After we have interrogated that outlaw slan—by whatever extreme means necessary—we will discover all we need to know."

FIFTEEN

The sleek armored car raced toward the outskirts of the city, escaping from the holocaust. Behind them, the palace was completely destroyed. Overhead, enemy spacecraft continued to crisscross the sky in search of targets. Once they had leveled Centropolis, the tendrilless attackers would spread out to the fringe areas, the smaller cities and towns. The invaders would not leave the job half finished.

Jommy drove through the late afternoon, dodging rubble, and continued to accelerate. The thick tires hummed across the cracked and blistered pavement. His reflexes were sufficient to dodge stalled cars, an overturned wagon, even a wide crater made by a stray bomb.

"Jommy, are you sure we'll be safe where we're going?"

"I can't guarantee we'll be safe anywhere, Kathleen, but we've got a good chance." His fingers danced across controls on the dashboard, illuminating a map. "It should take us about five hours to get there."

"That's assuming the roads and bridges along the way aren't blown up," said John Petty from the back.

"If there are obstacles, we will deal with them," Gray said.

"Obstacles?" Petty said. "I'd say the end of the world as we know it is a pretty substantial obstacle!" Then the slan hunter slumped back into silence.

Jommy's special car hugged the ground, moving almost as fast as an aircraft. After they left the outskirts of the city and headed toward the farmland and forested hills, he began to feel safer.

The car roared along isolated roads, making steady progress on the map projected on his dashboard. The ranchers and farmers who lived in the rolling countryside had holed up in storm shelters and root cellars, hiding from the interplanetary attack. No one else moved about. The sun would set soon, and then they would be safer.

His unusual vehicle, moving alone, inadvertently called attention to itself.

Red lights flashed on his sensitive detection systems, and from outside he heard a whining tone. He gripped the steering mechanism and looked around wildly. "Proximity alert. Something coming closer." Flipping a toggle switch, he shifted the ten-point steel of the car's roof into its transparent phase so that he could look overhead. "There!"

Three dark craft swooped down, the stubby-nosed tendrilless cruisers. For many years in his youth, he had seen similar fast vehicles launched regularly from the rooftop of the Air Center. "They've spotted us."

"Worse—they've *targeted* us." Kathleen craned her neck.

Plunging like hungry hawks, the tendrilless cruisers dropped focused explosives. The bombs blasted craters on either side of the country road, coughing up thick plumes of dirt and smoke. Jommy swerved, squeezing more power from the engine, but even with all his technological improvements, he could not make the car go faster.

The tendrilless bombers curved upward in a graceful loop, as if to show off their aerial maneuvers, then they came back down like a trio of executioners' axes. They would never let the car get away.

Jommy narrowed his eyes, his senses alert. He had to time this very carefully. Once the tendrilless ships dropped their next array of focused bombs, he needed to react perfectly and unexpectedly. The invaders cracked through the air, and the cluster of bombs dropped down exactly where the car should have been.

Jommy swerved, spun the rear tires, and hoped he had built sufficient clearance into the armored vehicle. The car bucked off the paved road, kicked up gravel as it went over the shoulder and through the shallow ditch. He didn't slow for an instant, but careened across the fallow countryside into the roadless rolling fields and grassy hills. Dirt and cornstalks flew up in a roostertail behind him. Ahead, past a small marker fence, he saw a thick line of dark trees, a patch of forest that had regrown after the old Slan Wars.

As he hit boulders and ruts, soft dirt and gravel, Jommy had a hard time maintaining his grip on the steering controls. At full speed, he dove through a small pond, hoping it wasn't too deep. Muddy water gushed in all directions, and then he was clear, arrowing straight toward the line of trees and, he hoped, shelter.

The tendrilless bombers had turned about again and raced after him, launching another volley. Coughing explosions left fresh craters in the field, but the tendrilless were overreacting. Jommy continued to dodge, spinning the wheels right and then left.

Petty, who had not properly strapped himself in, was thrown sideways into Kier Gray. The deposed President shoved him away in a tangle of arms and legs.

As the woods loomed in front of them and the tendrilless ships closed in, Jommy knew he would have to crash and dodge his way through the trunks, grind underbrush with his wheels, and hope the armor could withstand any impacts.

One of the dropped bombs exploded right behind the vehicle, and the concussion threw the car several feet into the air. After they crashed to the ground, Jommy spun and swerved, still accelerating toward the forest.

Flying low, the first enemy bomber streaked past the car, its pilot furious at having missed. He skimmed just above the speeding vehicle, as if he meant to smash the car's roof with his landing wheels.

Tall trees loomed up like a wall directly in front of the attacking craft. The tendrilless pilot pulled up frantically, but too late. Unable to clear the treetops, the attack craft scraped the high branches, which ripped out the underbelly. Hurtling out of control, the tendrilless fighter reeled, arced around, and plunged like a missile into the ground.

While the others in the car cheered, Jommy couldn't let his attention waver for a second. He drove headlong through the small marker fence and into the line of trees. Once in the forest, he was forced to slow, threading his way through the randomly spaced trunks. Branches crashed and crunched beneath him. He caromed off a thick spruce, ripping away a great chunk of bark, then he lumbered through a gully, spraying dry leaves. Ahead, the forest was even thicker.

The two remaining tendrilless bombers soared over the treetops, still searching. Now that their comrade was dead, Jommy knew they would never give up. The canopy was dense enough that they could not easily see the car, but they must have some kind of technological scanners that could pick up the heat of his engine or the ten-point steel of the vehicle's armor.

He knocked down a small tree, which did not even damage the reinforced bumper. The gauges showed the engines overheating. He crunched along, plowing a path through the woods, all the while knowing he couldn't hide.

The two invader ships came back over the treetops in a methodical search pattern. When they spotted the car and homed in on it, they dropped another volley of aerial bombs. They meant to destroy the whole forest if they needed to.

Jommy saw them coming. "Hold on! We can't get away from this." Despite himself, he closed his eyes, hoping the armor would be sufficient against the destruction.

Like fireworks, a dozen explosions erupted through the woods. Fireballs knocked down trees; blast waves snapped trunks like toothpicks. All around the car, tall pines and oaks toppled. Boughs smashed across the car's roof and hood. A towering pine crashed immediately to their left, scraping and scratching with its needle-filled branches. A thick, shattered trunk fell on top of them like a sledge hammer, burying them.

But the car's armor held.

As the fire continued to swell and trees fell all around, the car was trapped under the avalanche of broken wood. Even when the trees stopped falling, the blaze increased in intensity, rapidly becoming an inferno that spread through the forest. The car was immobilized, caught in the heart of a furnace.

Jommy shut down the systems, hoping the filters would provide enough fresh oxygen to keep them alive. "There. We're completely safe."

SIXTEEN

As the librarian stared at her baby's exposed tendrils, Anthea's own thrill of fear was echoed and doubled in her mind. The newborn somehow knew that he had been discovered—and instinctively understood the danger to both of them.

"Oh, my!" Mr. Reynolds took a half step backward. He raised his hands in a warding gesture, as if afraid he had touched something that might contaminate him.

Anthea tried to come closer. "Please, Mr. Reynolds! It's not what you think."

His eyes wide and round, the librarian jumped, as if he wanted to bolt out into the streets, regardless of the danger. "Not what I *think*? I think it's a slan baby!" He blinked several times, gaping at the child. "Yes, indeed, I'm sure it's a slan baby."

"Believe me, we're no threat to you—"

Outside, thunderous explosions made the walls shudder. The candles threw uncertain light and strange shadows.

The librarian made a quick move and dashed around the table. "Help!"

Anthea bounded in front of him, drawing strength from what she had been through, from what she knew might happen. She picked up one of the heavy tomes on the table. Without thinking, she swung it hard and bashed him on the back of the head. The hardcover hit his skull with a loud thump. Reynolds let out a heavy "Oof," then sprawled face first on the polished floor. His round glasses bounced off his face and clattered to one side.

Anthea knelt beside him, her heart pounding. "I didn't mean that! I'm so sorry, but you didn't give me any choice."

The librarian groaned, though he remained unconscious. Anthea touched his head, then the pulse at his neck. "I think you'll be all right." She looked at the book with which she had hit him, noted the irony. The title was *The Hidden Slan Threat*.

On the table, the baby had turned his head so he could see her. She felt the continued strange connection with him. Her infant son seemed very aware of what was happening, and she felt a wash of secondhand relief coming from him, confident that his mother had taken care of the danger.

Anthea hated herself for hurting Mr. Reynolds. She had never been a violent person. She worked in a bank! Before today, she had never struck another person. But she had seen the doctor try to kill her newborn baby, and her own husband had been gunned down trying to protect them. When she'd fled, more people had tried to kill her. The city had been bombed, and now Earth itself was in the middle of a war. Anthea was fighting not only for her life, but for their child's as well. A slan child—a slan born from two apparently normal people! How many other "normal" people had the same potential?

She had been driven to do many extraordinary things this day, and she feared she would be forced to do many more.

In order to stay safe, she had to keep the librarian out of her way. Finding strength, she rolled Mr. Reynolds over, picked up his hands, and began to drag him down the slippery hall. Either through adrenaline or newfound physical strength, Anthea pulled the heavyset man along without difficulty. Conscientiously, she picked up his eyeglasses, folded down the bows, and tucked them into his pocket. She didn't want to inconvenience the man any more than she had to. Knocking him unconscious was bad enough.

The librarian's office was just outside of the archives wing. She could tie him up there, she needed him safely out of the way before he regained consciousness. She hated to leave her baby alone even if the room was not far away, but she could sense that the child was in no immediate danger.

Inside the librarian's office, stacks of books and periodicals were on Reynolds's desk, on the floor, on top of filing cabinets. Neatly lettered labels on colored index cards identified each stack. Plastic wrappers and open cardboard boxes indicated that the man did much cataloguing of his new acquisitions here. For managing a large city library, Reynolds didn't seem to have a very large staff. At the moment, she was glad that no one else was in the building.

On a special table were five old books, dog-eared, their spines cracked and dust jackets torn. But they had been lovingly taped and bandaged, the bindings reglued. She could picture Reynolds spending hours under his bright desk lamp, like a surgeon performing an operation on these beloved and well-read tomes.

She wrestled Mr. Reynolds into the chair behind his desk, then looked around for something to tie him with. When nothing obvious presented itself other than cellophane tape on the desk dispenser, she removed the librarian's blue striped necktie and quickly lashed his wrists to the chair arms. Then she unthreaded the laces from his black Oxford shoes and used those to tie his ankles in place. When that didn't seem terribly secure, she also used the full roll of tape.

When he groaned, she felt sorry again for what she'd been forced to do. It seemed so unfair. Reynolds had been kind to her. She didn't want to hurt him. She had never wanted to hurt anybody—but the slan hunters had certainly changed that. With herself and her baby at stake, she couldn't trust anyone. But Anthea loved her baby far more than Reynolds could ever love his books. The man would be safe enough here until someone else rescued him.

Anthea took a sheet of paper from the desk and quickly scrawled a note. "I'm very sorry. We didn't mean to hurt you. I did not ask for this, but I had to protect my child. I hope someday you'll forgive us."

Rummaging in his desk drawer, she found a set of keys in a red envelope with a handwritten word. *Archives.* For the padlock that secured the combination wheels? She took the keys. Even without thinking, she knew she would have to open the vault and discover what secret information the government had hidden from the public. Why didn't they want anybody to know the truth about the slans?

She ran back to the thick vault door and its heavy combination wheels. The padlock itself couldn't have been more than a minor deterrent for anyone determined to break in, but it was one extra time-consuming step. She removed the key from the red envelope, inserted then twisted it. When the padlock popped open, she removed it with one hand and set it aside.

The large combination wheels that locked the heavy vault were ready for her. In her mind she remembered the combination Mr. Reynolds had so vividly recalled, the numbers that her baby had detected with his slan tendrils. 4 . . . 26 . . . 19 . . . 12.

The baby's bright eyes watched as Anthea turned the first wheel, felt it clicking through numbers. She stopped at the mark for 4, ratcheted the next wheel into its appropriate position, then the third, and finally the fourth. She heard a humming inside. It wasn't just a simple gear lock: She had activated an entire mechanism. Pistons and dead bolts rose up and down, pulling aside, clicking into place, and with a hiss like a tired sigh, the vault door moved out of its frame.

She bunched the soft blanket to prop the infant's small head as she picked him up from the table. Holding the baby, Anthea stepped back as the thick barrier groaned open. The hinges and heavy hydraulics seemed well lubricated and maintained.

She wondered how often anyone ever studied these archives. Considering the security Mr. Reynolds had mentioned and how few curiosity seekers the government allowed, she doubted very many had read the information contained within.

But now she intended to.

SEVENTEEN

With Jommy's car buried under the inferno of collapsed trees, he had sealed off the vehicle's environment systems, opaqued the windows, and switched on the air scrubbers and recyclers. Then he sat back to wait.

He reassured his companions. "This may look like a normal car, but it's practically a battleship on wheels. The armor is sufficient against any temperatures a mere forest fire can generate. The self-contained air systems can last for a day underwater, so they'll easily filter out a little smoke. It might get a little warm in here, but I prefer to call it cozy."

"Have you ever tested it under those conditions?" Petty asked, clearly uneasy.

"Not exactly, but you can trust my calculations."

While the forest fire burned for the next three hours, the car was buried in a furnace of coals. Though the interior temperature became uncomfortably warm, the four occupants were never in real danger. By the time night fell, the blaze had begun to die down. The barricade of fallen trees and branches that had buried them was now little more than a rubble of charred logs and ashes. Even if the two enemy bombers had circled the spreading inferno, keeping watch, they would have departed by now, confident they had destroyed their quarry.

With the last vestiges of the blaze still shimmering against the purple night, Jommy activated his engines again, cleared the front screens, and slowly crunched their way through the live coals, emerging with a spray of sparks like an orange blizzard. As they drove out of the now devastated woods, the car smoked, covered with soot and ash, but the vehicle made it out to the fields, across the bumpy ground, and back to the paved road.

Jommy raced forward again, back on their way, this time under the cover of a starry night. The car's sharp headlights sent lances ahead of them. The interior was much cooler now, and the fresh air smelled wonderful and exhilarating.

"I told you Jommy could do it," Kathleen said.

From the back of the vehicle, John Petty began to laugh with relief and delight.

By morning, they had reached open country far from Centropolis, passing over a line of hills and into a broad and beautiful river valley. The landscape was green and peaceful, with a smattering of widely separated ranch houses and farms.

"It's lovely." Kathleen rubbed weariness from her red eyes as she watched the buttery-yellow sunrise come over the hills. One of the larger mountains was distorted, half collapsed, as if a great force had smashed it down.

This valley had always been a sheltered place where he and a hypnotically modified Granny had built a sanctuary for themselves. Jommy explained to his companions that he had spent four years building underground laboratories, an arsenal, even turning the interior of a nearby mountain into a fortress. But the tendrilless had already struck here, using a gigantic attack vessel to melt part of his mountain fortress in search of his underground laboratories and industries.

"I don't recall hearing about any tendrilless attack," Petty said, looking at Gray. "How could something like this be kept quiet, especially from my secret police?"

"The tendrilless controlled the news media, and they *wanted* to keep it a secret," the President said.

"I first bumped into one of the tendrilless when I was just a boy, not long after my mother was murdered." Jommy pointedly looked behind him at the slan hunter. "At the time I was thrilled, since I'd been looking for other slans. I knew I couldn't be the only one. I naively assumed the tendrilless would be happy to see me. Instead, they tried to kill me."

Petty said, "So, even the great Jommy Cross can make a mistake."

Kathleen glared at him. "The more I'm around you, Mr. Petty, the more I wonder why exactly we've taken you with us."

"You need me. I still control a sizable force of the secret police, if I ever get in touch with them."

"We need a lot of things, but I've learned to live without them," Gray said. Petty became quiet.

Jommy continued. "When the tendrilless tracked me to this valley, I booby-trapped my extensive laboratories so the enemy couldn't get their hands on my technology. It was the only way. I left everything behind . . . everything and everyone." He had sent Granny to safety in their armored ranch house while he fled in his ship, luring the tendrilless after him.

He hoped that at least some of his notes and equipment were intact at whatever remained of the old ranch. He'd already begun to imagine how he might rebuild what he needed. Once he got a transmitting station up, President Gray could make wide broadcasts, rally the surviving humans, even establish a government in exile. And Jommy could create the arsenal they needed to fight back in an outright war.

As he drove down the narrow country lanes past other houses, farmers and ranchers looked up and waved congenially. He felt warm inside as he remembered how much he had loved this valley.

"It certainly seems a friendly place," Kathleen said. "Isolated, peaceful."

"I helped that along a little bit. In the years I lived here, I used my mental skills and hypnosis crystals to gently guide my neighbors in their thinking."

Petty seemed indignant. "So you used your mind powers to brainwash them."

Jommy frowned back at him. "On the contrary, after generations of propaganda and lies, I used my powers to *un*-brainwash them."

Driving smoothly along a lane and then up a gravel drive lined by maple trees, they arrived at a ranch house. It was a small affair, painted red with white trimming, but Jommy knew that the walls, roof, and floors were made of reinforced steel. The decorative shingles on the roof had been patched. The familiarity of the place made Jommy grin.

He parked the car on the gravel pad in front of the house's big garage. The potted geraniums by the front porch were overflowing with bright coral-red flowers. Tulips planted along the front of the house blossomed in bright colors, and a small vegetable garden sported rows of beans, corn, potatoes, onions, and carrots—just enough for one person. Several feral-looking chickens squawked and ran along the front of the house, pecking at insects.

Jommy climbed out of the car with Kathleen beside him and saw how the vehicle had been battered and scraped. Considering what it had been through, though, it seemed in good shape. Petty and Gray stretched their legs, taking deep breaths of the fresh, clean valley air. The slan hunter rubbed his finger along the hood, smearing a long track in the soot. He wiped his blackened finger on his dark jacket.

Jommy took one step toward the front door of the house when someone yanked it open. A rail-thin old woman stepped onto the porch. Her skin was wrinkled and leathery, her gray hair pulled back. She wore an apron and a drab work dress. Her eyes were like a crow's, black but bright, flickering from side to side.

He grinned, raising a hand. "Granny!"

Without acknowledging, the old woman reached inside the door and came back out with a loaded shotgun. She raised the barrel, glaring at Jommy, glaring at them all, and aimed directly at him.

EIGHTEEN

Joanna Hillory's ultra-fast ship soared across interplanetary space from Mars to Earth. She would cover the distance in a fraction of the time that the lumbering occupation fleet required. She had only a few days to complete her mission—to find Jommy and make an emergency plan—before the main tendrilless forces reached their target.

As she streaked past them in space, Joanna gazed at the impressive armada of tendrilless battleships: giant wheel-shaped vessels powered by internal cyclotrons, bristling with atomic-powered weapons. Each gigantic craft was loaded with ground assault vehicles and the bulky equipment needed to crush any remaining resistance and establish an invincible presence. The heavy vessels carried most of the population of Cimmerium in a great exodus to occupy conquered Earth.

As she sped past the occupation fleet, Joanna transmitted the special signal that verified her business for the Tendrilless Authority. In a flurry of messages, the captains of the giant vessels wished her luck while making brave claims about how much damage they intended to wreak upon human civilization. She sent a gruff acknowledgment, feeling a knot in her chest, and flew onward.

When she made her final approach to Earth, she encountered a treacherous debris zone in the orbital lanes. A great battle had taken place here. Had the humans found some way to mount a space defense?

She saw blackened ships hanging dead in space, their hulls ripped open, cockpits and propulsion engines torn away by explosions—either from the tense dogfights or from detonation of the space mines. Hazardous shrapnel consisted of drifting hull plates, globules of molten metal that had solidified in the frozen vacuum.

Using the sensitive detectors aboard her scout ship, Joanna scanned and then projected a three-dimensional map of all the obstacles, including the remaining tendrilless space mines in orbit. Carefully avoiding collisions, she studied patterns among the wreckage, trying to piece together what had happened. When she studied the ruined hulks more closely, she could not identify the ship design. One hull fragment, though, had colors painted on it and she recognized the insignia. A secret human fleet. Astonishing!

For the past century, humans had made only minimal attempts at resurrecting their space program, which had once flourished during the First Golden Age of mankind. The very idea of President Gray building enough ships to pose a threat to the tendrilless was absurd. And yet the humans had indeed managed to launch their own space defensive fleet. The brashness and bravado amazed her.

For a long time now, tendrilless had controlled the airways, industries, and communications centers on Earth. Somehow Kier Gray had managed to create a significant space force without anyone—not even her—knowing about it. Did the humans have unexpected help? Slan collaborators, perhaps?

Joanna knew that the Tendrilless Authority was far more worried about the true slans. Jommy Cross had proved how frightfully talented others like him could be. Now that she had thrown her lot in with Jommy, she needed to reconcile her loyalties—and in the middle of a war.

Looking at the wreckage all around her, thousands of shards glinting in slow revolutions as they caught the light from the sun, she admitted that the human space fleet had failed, but they had caused great damage to the tendrilless ships.

Finalizing her approach, Joanna spotted a few spaceships from the vanguard fleet still cruising around the battle zone. While bombers and small fighters continued to pound the cities below, vanguard scouts patrolled the orbital zone, waiting for the main occupation force to arrive, hunting down any last human spaceships, alert for any last-ditch tricks.

Unexpectedly, her communications apparatus picked up the steady, rhythmic beacon of an S.O.S. signal. As she maneuvered her ship toward the source of the beacon, Joanna realized that it was a distress call from a lifepod.

One of the human defenders had somehow managed to eject an escape pod! As the lifepod drifted along, the lone survivor aboard begged for assistance, but all of his comrades were eradicated. He had no chance for rescue, with Earth completely under fire.

Uncertain what to do, Joanna followed the signal, homing in on a small ellipsoidal container. The automated beacon droned on, calling attention, pleading for someone to come and help.

Joanna imagined the bravery of this soldier. She had seen enough of human society to know that the man would have been terrified of the inhuman slans, but he would not have known any difference between the tendrilless ones and the "snakes." Even so, when his planet was in danger, this man had climbed aboard one of the Earth spaceships—far inferior to the advanced tendrilless vanguard fleet—and launched into orbit to fight against the enemy. What folly! The soldier was either a hero, she decided, or a fool.

"Is anyone still alive there?" she transmitted, closing in on the drifting lifepod.

"Yes, I'm here!" came a shrill voice, a young man's. "Captain Byron Campbell, sole survivor of my ship. Gunner and navigator both killed in the explosion. Please, I need help."

"How is your oxygen?"

"My recyclers are still operating. I can last for another day or two. Please bring me back to Centropolis. The fight must still be going on down there." Joanna couldn't believe his naiveté. "My squadron flew up to engage the enemy, but the dirty slans had planted mines throughout orbit. Booby-trapped our whole planet! Most of my fellow ships were destroyed. Filthy cowards."

Around her in space the drifting debris could not convey the scope of the massacre. "Captain Campbell, Earth has already fallen. No one will rescue you."

"But there's you."

A lump formed in her throat. Before Joanna could respond, another ship streaked in, one of the sharklike vanguard scouts. "Commander Hillory, I apologize for not intercepting you sooner! Welcome to Earth. You'll find that everything is in order. We have taken care of most of the distractions. I'm sorry for this one. Just a loose end to tie up."

Campbell's voice cracked, full of betrayal. He shouted at Joanna. "You! You're one of *them!*"

The vanguard ship swooped in and opened fire with a blaze of energy bolts, disintegrating Captain Byron Campbell and his lifepod. Joanna caught her breath, but did not speak out. The damage was done. The man was dead, the lifepod destroyed.

"I need to get down to the surface," she said, cold and businesslike. "I have orders from the Authority." She watched the burning debris of the lifepod, chunks of glowing metal slowly drifting apart. "I don't require an escort, so long as you guarantee me clear passage to Centropolis."

The vanguard pilot transmitted a verification, and she plunged down toward the main cities of Earth. In the turbulence of war she wasn't sure how she could ever find Jommy Cross, but she had an idea where to start looking. She and Jommy had already begun to make plans during his last hours in Cimmerium, but now all those had fallen apart, thanks to the impatient and brash violence of Jem Lorry.

She *had* to find him if she had any chance of stopping this disaster. She was sure Jommy was the only one who could pull a solution out of the air.

With a sinking heart, Joanna cruised over the smoldering ruins. He was down there somewhere, and she knew he must still be alive. Tendrilless ships crisscrossed the air, hunting down any remaining resistance, though Centropolis looked sorely beaten. Rooftops had been blown apart, anti-aircraft guns and defensive measures entirely removed from the equation.

Zooming in closer, she was dismayed—yet not completely surprised—to discover that the grand palace had been utterly leveled. Now, nothing remained of it.

Joanna set down her ship in the vicinity. This was where she would concentrate her search. Amid the continuing explosions and the chaos in the streets, no one gave a second glance to her small craft. Angular invader ships still scattered occasional bombs to maintain the heightened state of fear.

Joanna stepped out of her craft, brushing curly brown hair from her forehead. It had been some time since she'd breathed the fresh air of Earth. Curls of smoke from burning buildings rose into the sky, adding a sour, raw smell. She stood in the rubble and looked toward the collapsed fragments and the burned-out zone.

Nothing could have survived that devastation.

In her heart she wanted to believe that Jommy had found a way out. But even if he had, how could she link up with him? He wouldn't know that she was searching for him, or that she had come to Earth at all. How could she find out for sure?

As she stared around the obliterated palace, she had no idea where she should start to look.

NINETEEN

Not one step closer," the old woman said. The barrel of the shotgun in her hands did not waver. "You have a lot of nerve to come back here. Granny intends to protect her home."

Jommy smiled at her, unintimidated by the weapon. "I believe it's *my* home, Granny. I paid for it."

"My home!" She swung the shotgun around, pointing at all of them. Petty dove for cover behind the car, while Gray stood next to his daughter, placing a protective hand on her shoulder.

Through his tendrils Jommy sent questing thoughts, soothing emotions. During the four years he had lived here with the old woman, he had done much work to alter her personality, to smooth over the corruption in her twisted mind. He had changed her into some semblance of a normal human being, but she had been through much recently—and he hadn't been around to reinforce his work. The old woman certainly didn't know how to show compassion—at least not naturally.

"Granny, is this any way to say hello?"

"I would prefer to say goodbye. Or better yet, rest in peace."

Still smiling, Jommy was sure he could do this. No one in the world knew Granny and her weaknesses better than he did. The greedy woman had manipulated him when he was just a boy, coerced him into committing many crimes. But she had also saved him from killers like Petty. He had owed her a debt of gratitude, though by any reasonable measure, he had already paid her back a thousand times over.

"Well, for my part I'm glad to see you alive and healthy. After the tendrilless almost destroyed this valley, I wasn't sure just how you had recovered."

The old woman cackled, still gripping the shotgun. "Oh, Granny's good at surviving. Do you have any idea how much misery you put her through? How much work it was to rebuild this house?"

In all the time he had known the old woman, Granny was allergic to physical labor. He stepped closer until the shotgun barrel was only a few feet away, still pointed directly at his chest. "And it looks like you did a fine job."

"Damn right I did." Four of her chickens strutted around the yard in front of them. One scuttled under the big car. "I went through a lot of hard times because of you, Jommy Cross." Maintaining her huffy act, she glared at Kier Gray and Kathleen. "And if one slan wasn't enough to cause me misery, who are all these people? Are they slans, too?"

Petty barely poked his head up from behind the car. One of the chickens pecked at his ankle, and he cried out in pain, kicking at the bird. Feathers flew as it ran squawking toward Granny.

Jommy extended a hand behind him; Kathleen came forward and took it. "This is Kathleen Layton. She's the love of my life." The young woman blushed.

Granny grew misty-eyed for just a moment, then forced her wrinkled face into a scowl. "How sweet. And what about the other two? And you better impress me. Otherwise, why should I keep you here on my property? Granny's got enough shotgun shells for all of you."

"That man cowering behind the car is the great slan hunter, John Petty, chief of the secret police."

Granny grinned with her papery lips. "Oh, Mr. Petty! I've admired your work."

The slan hunter blinked at her, then stood to his full height. Ashes and soot from the car smeared his chest, cheeks, and jacket.

"And this is Kier Gray, the President of Earth," Jommy said. "Is that impressive enough for you?"

Cradling the gun in the crook of one arm, Granny fumbled in a pocket of her apron and withdrew a ten-credit note, flapping it to unfold the paper. She held it up with her bony fingers, stared at the portrait on the money, comparing it with Gray. "Yes, that's him all right. You haven't aged a bit, Mr. Gray."

The President couldn't shake Granny's hand because she was gripping the shotgun too tightly. Jommy could tell the old woman was starting to relax, but she wanted to maintain her semblance of power for as long as possible. It was Granny's way.

"From what the wireless says, he's not President of much anymore. I wasn't surprised to hear about those evil slans attacking. I always knew there were thousands of them just waiting to come after decent, law-abiding humans."

"They aren't slans, Granny. They're a different breed—"

"They're all slans to Granny! And I wouldn't be surprised for a second to find out that you and all your ilk were behind this."

Kathleen looked indignant. "We most certainly aren't! We've been hunted down. The grand palace is destroyed."

"Don't excite yourself, missy. This is a peaceful valley, and I intend to keep it that way—through force of arms if necessary." She looked down at the shotgun, then finally rested the stock on the porch beside her. "And having you folk here increases Granny's danger. Who knows how many people are after you? Could be angry mobs, could be assassins . . . maybe more slans, maybe even secret police."

Then her eyes got that familiar greedy gleam. "Hmm, on the other hand, there'll be a big reward for you. Could be enough money to put a nice addition onto the ranch house."

Gray's rich familiar voice was very regal. "I'll make you a proposal, ma'am. As the President of Earth, I could dredge up a ransom a lot larger than any reward offered by those hunting for us. Consider it your reward for services rendered."

"It would be more money than one woman could imagine," Petty said.

She turned her steely glare at him. "Granny has a very good imagination, Mr. Petty." The wheels were turning in her head. "But if the world is overrun by slan traitors, how can even *President Gray* pay me anything? Sounds like your wallet could very soon be empty."

The President turned on his charm. "Think of it this way: If the world is destroyed by our enemies, how could you spend a reward even if you have it? It makes much more sense to help us out, and then send us a bill."

Granny considered for a long moment and then, in a fluid motion as fast as a snake striking, she reached down and snatched up the chicken pecking around the flowers at the porch. She lifted it into the air and wrung its neck. The bird barely had time to squawk.

"All right, you can stay for supper." The old woman grinned. "Then I'll show you how I welcome my guests."

TWENTY

Once she entered the library's archive vault, the lights came on automatically, powered by the emergency generator. The stale air had a metallic flatness of recyclers, filters, and dehumidifiers.

Anthea saw a maze of wonders, historical treasures beyond her wildest imagining. Even with her new speed-reading ability, she had a lot to study. Standing inside, she just stared for a moment; her baby's small hazel eyes were hungry, looking around him.

Metal shelves were stacked high with bulging and yellowed boxes of documents. Books bore red-and-white CLASSIFIED and RESTRICTED USE stickers; many of the volumes seemed incredibly old. One small table held a stack of polymer-coated papers, preserved newspaper clippings from when slans had first appeared. Some clippings quoted outspoken supporters, while others declared that these new "terrible mutants" posed a severe danger to humanity. The dates on the newspapers came from a different calendar entirely; she couldn't tell how old they really were.

After finding a safe and comfortable place for the infant to rest, Anthea turned her attention to the old records. When tendrilled children first began to be born—unexpectedly, it seemed—they were treated as freaks, oddities, and misfits. By the time the public began to suspect the powers of the new race, a flood of slans had been born all around the world. Was the emergence of mutations an accident or part of a carefully coordinated plan? The records were unclear on that point.

As the first generation of slans grew to adulthood, the reports became darker and more disturbing. New radical groups formed, in particular a masked and black-robed society calling itself the Human Purity League. Bloodthirsty vigilantes, they hunted down and lynched slans.

Some brave first-generation slans acted as spokesmen on television and radio talk shows, begging for understanding and acceptance. The spokesmen claimed that slans did not choose to be what they were, but that they could not give up their birthright. They simply wanted to live in peace like any other human, to go about their business.

Their detractors, however, insisted that "slan business" was to destroy "inferior" humanity much the same way that modern man would have hunted down and eradicated Neanderthals. "How can a slan not feel this way?" claimed the leader of the Human Purity League. "They must believe themselves to be superior—and if they believe themselves superior, then all humans need to be concerned."

This attitude sparked protests from militant slans, who retaliated against the prejudice and persecution by standing up for themselves. "We *are* superior. We are the next step in human evolution. Why should we be ashamed of our skills and abilities? We should use them, not hide them."

Absorbing information as swiftly as she could sift through the records, Anthea read with growing horror. In four separate incidents, black-robed vigilantes dragged outspoken slan advocates out of their homes in the middle of the night, then drugged them into a stupor to dull their mind powers. The Human Purity League hacked off the tendrils of the advocates, then hung the victims from lampposts or trees as an example "for all good humans to follow."

These terrifying acts drove many slans into hiding. Slans went to back-alley clinics to have their tendrils surgically removed so they could live quietly among human society. Entire networks and underground railroads sprang up to give these "neutered" slans new identities in safe places.

Saddest of all, Anthea thought, was one small article reporting (with no particular significance) that a large percentage of those shamed slans who had chosen the illicit tendril-amputation surgery exhibited an extremely high incidence of suicide afterward. Approximately eighty percent of those desperate enough to take such measures chose not to survive with dulled senses and mental blindness; they killed themselves within months.

The Human Purity League began to sport clean-shaven heads as proof of their tendril-free scalps. Flagrantly bragging about their actions, the Purity League insisted that anyone with long hair—male or female—had to be hiding something. Their thugs knocked down people in the streets and forcibly shaved their heads. Very few of their targets turned out to have tendrils, but this did not stop their antics.

Anthea felt a tightening in her gut as she continued reading. She already knew how history would turn out, and now she could see the events escalating toward a full-scale war between slans and normal humans.

Pushed into a corner, slan activists began to fight back more aggressively. They formed support groups and protective societies. They met openly where they thought their large numbers would guarantee them safety. But in a particularly appalling incident, the Human Purity League surrounded one such hall where they claimed the evil slans were plotting the overthrow of Earth. They barricaded the doors, barred the windows, then set the whole building on fire, burning to death over three hundred slans.

That had been the tipping point that turned slans entirely against their human persecutors. From there, it had only grown worse and worse.

Trembling with all she had learned, Anthea realized that very few people alive knew this truth. Humans still exhibited an undiminished hatred toward the mutant race. No wonder the true slans (if any of them still remained) lived in desperate hiding.

Weary of the sickening reports, Anthea stretched her legs and moved along the shelves, pulling down boxes and poking among the other paraphernalia. She found dusty devices, strange laboratory equipment that looked antique while at the same time futuristic. The sealed items were labeled merely "unknown slan weapon" or "dangerous slan mind-control device."

In one cabinet she found an old-fashioned video viewer and canisters of tapes. "S. Lann recordings: Original statements. Highest Security Access." Dr. Samuel Lann, the first investigator—some said the *creator*—of the slans! She knew she had to watch the tapes.

She lifted the viewer and brought it back to the table where the baby still lay, wide awake. She spent several minutes deciphering the player and loading the old and brittle tapes. She feared the tape might snap as it rattled through the viewing mechanism, but she had to learn what Samuel Lann had said in his own words.

Once she activated the power switch and heard the wheels clattering, jumpy images began to flicker on the screen. She saw a handsome man with dark brown hair, wide-set eyes, high cheekbones, and a square jaw that denoted confidence and trustworthiness. He seemed defiant yet patient as he faced his questioners. She realized that this was Lann and that these were interrogation tapes. Even back before the Slan Wars, there must have been an organization equivalent to the secret police and the slan hunters.

"Why do you fear my children?" Lann said. "I love them. Two fine daughters and a son—triplets—who happen to have been born with an unusual birth defect. They're no threat to you."

The interrogator said in a gruff voice, "Anyone with powers such as theirs is a threat to us. Anyone who has the ability to control minds must themselves be controlled before they harm our government or our population."

"But they're just children, barely fifteen," Lann said mildly. Even Anthea could tell he was hiding something.

"They are *weapons,* living weapons that could be turned against us if we do not control them."

Another voice, a woman's, spoke up from outside the field of view, "And how many others like this are there, Dr. Lann? How many children have tendrils? We've heard reports from other countries—countries that *you* visited. Wouldn't you like us to bring together these other mutants, just so we can give them proper medical care?"

Lann wasn't falling for it. "Ask the other parents. How can I judge how many have been born?"

"Born? Or *created,* Dr. Lann?" said the male voice.

"What are you suggesting?"

"In your laboratory we found and confiscated many devices, strange machines that had the ability to alter human brains."

The woman continued in a soothing voice. "Your research is well known, Doctor. You are quite prominent in the field of mental enhancement."

"Yes, I have made a career of studying the nature of the human mind, of memories and knowledge. My dream is to record and share those components that make up a person's history and personality."

The male interrogator seized on the comment. "And did those diabolical machines also expand the brains of your children, mutate them into these powerful creatures who can manipulate thoughts? You could be manufacturing enhanced humans, putting your own fingerprints on the evolution of the race."

"Don't be absurd." Lann laughed at first, then saw that the others were serious.

"We know you have the capability," the woman added.

"No one has that capability. I may be a genius in my field, but not even my children—who are far smarter and more imaginative than I am—could concoct such a bizarre conspiracy of using mind machines to produce a whole new race of human beings. Surely you can see that's ridiculous?"

"What we see, Dr. Lann, is that your three children have powers we do not understand. We've already received reports from our counterpart agencies that an alarming number of others just like them have begun popping up in the most unlikely places. Children born with tendrils—"

The woman interjected, harsher now, "Or perhaps innocent babies were exposed to unusual rays produced by your machines, which caused the tendrils to grow. Are you seeding them around the world, Dr. Lann, trying to create a quiet revolution?"

"Of course not."

There was a long silence, and finally the interrogators decided to let him go. "You watch yourself, Dr. Lann—because we'll certainly be watching you."

With a shudder, Anthea removed the tape and put in the next one. Beside her, the baby was fully alert. When she looked at her little boy, she experienced a poignant understanding of how Dr. Lann must have felt upon seeing his own three children born with strange tendrils. Was he surprised, or intrigued?

There was no record of the woman who had been mother to those first three slan children. Had the mother been normal, or a secret slan all along? Maybe the race had existed far longer than anyone suspected. Had that long-forgotten woman—or Dr. Lann himself—been exposed to some strange chemical or mutagen? She doubted she would ever know.

In the next interrogation tape, Dr. Lann looked haggard. Purple bruises surrounded one eye, and a bandage covered his forehead. His clothes were rumpled, even torn, but his face held a murderously defiant spark that hadn't been there before.

"By being so outspoken, you call attention to yourself, Doctor," said the interrogator, a different one than before. "If you don't want to be singled out for our special attention, then you shouldn't speak on the behalf of these dangerous mutants."

"Someone has to," Lann snapped back. "Someone needs to be the voice of reason. Obviously, it won't come from your new secret police organization." A stiff gloved hand struck him across the face. Lann spat a mouthful of blood and saliva at his interrogator. "You have no right to hold me here. I have committed no crime."

"You have attempted to destroy the human race. That's a significant crime in our book. Mutants are cropping up everywhere—it's a veritable plague! I doubt we could possibly stop the spread now, even if we exterminated all of them before they have a chance to breed. They keep appearing even from seemingly normal parents."

"I have nothing to do with that," Lann said. "It's the next step in evolution. Why fight it? Embrace it, for the betterment of the human race."

"There's nothing natural about it. Everyone knows of your machine for transforming babies into telepathic monsters. You use your rays on pregnant mothers and newborn infants, causing them to develop tendrils."

"That is absurd propaganda. Everyone 'knows' about it only because of the lies you and your organization have spread." Another slap across his face. Dr. Lann didn't even seem rattled.

"We know your son and daughters have barricaded themselves inside your fortress lab. One can only guess what they're doing in there. Is it true both daughters are pregnant? Who is the father?"

"None of your business. We have done nothing wrong."

Then why won't they let us come in and inspect?"

Lann sneered at the interrogators. "Because you've already proved yourselves to be prejudiced oafs. You wouldn't understand what you find. You could easily plant evidence."

"If you cooperate, Dr. Lann, perhaps we'll be merciful."

"I think this interview is over." Lann struggled to stand up, but the gloved hands shoved him back down into the chair.

"It's over when we finish asking you questions."

But Lann clenched his jaws, crossed his arms over his chest, and refused to say another word. The tape ran for several long minutes. The interrogator prodded and provoked him, but he would not answer. Finally the recording ended.

Anthea could only stare. This information had been kept from the public! How could the government have sealed away such details from everyone? It was as if someone—someone in control—*wanted* the slans to remain hated.

TWENTY-ONE

While the chicken was roasting in the oven, sending savory smells throughout the house, Granny showed the fugitives their separate rooms and allowed them to clean up and rest. But she had other business with Jommy.

As he followed the old woman, he suspected that she had a scheme up her sleeve. Even though he had worked to adjust her corrupt attitudes over the years, she could easily have reverted to her villainous old self. At the moment, however, he had few other choices.

Spry with eagerness, Granny walked around to the back of the house, where she lifted up the wooden door to the root cellar. Instead of the traditional smells of dirt, cobwebs, and old vegetables, Jommy saw bright lights, tiled walls, and metal stairs leading to one of his underground chambers. "I thought you might like to see this—I salvaged a few scraps. Important scraps." Her eyes glittered. "I'm sure it's worth something to you."

Jommy looked around in amazement and confusion. "But I triggered the self-destruct myself, just before I led the tendrilless away from here on a wild-goose chase! I gave you a hypnotic instruction."

"Yes, you did, but Granny's mind found a way around it." She propped her hands on her bony hips. "And I had a devil of a time saving some of your papers and blueprints and designs. I had burns and blisters on my face and hands for weeks!"

"But why would you do that? It was dangerous, and foolish." He stepped ahead, amazed to see so many intact boxes and shelves. He had expected it all to be destroyed, and he couldn't keep the appreciation and admiration out of his voice. "You saved so much of my work."

She snorted. "It could have been valuable. I always intended to sell it, but I wasn't sure how much it was worth. I didn't want to be cheated. Everybody wants to cheat Granny." She narrowed her eyes. "And what's it worth to you now, Jommy? Take a look around."

She led him into a chamber where she had stacked a pile of singed lab notebooks along with some of his personal inventions, instruments he used for testing circuits and improvising power sources. With a flourish, she opened a metal cabinet full of small components, valuable micro-generators, and a host of other devices the world had never seen before.

Jommy was grinning. "It's a starting point for me to rebuild everything, Granny. But I'm still missing a great many of my records and notes. Most of those were burned, I'm sure."

"Oh, they burned all right. But Granny has more. Not everything was lost." Her expression was very devious. "During our four peaceful years here, when everybody liked each other in the whole valley, I used to sneak into your laboratories at night. I copied many of your notebooks—and you didn't suspect a thing!" She cackled. "It was just a precaution. Common sense, actually. You would have done it yourself. Maybe old Granny's figured out how to block your slan mind probing, eh?"

"That was very risky, Granny. If the tendrilless got their hands on this information—"

She pointed a scolding finger at him. "Don't you get all high and mighty, Jommy Cross. It was a bit of insurance, and if you were to leave me—which you *did*—then I had something I could sell. I was sure there'd be many buyers for these notes and blueprints."

"So why didn't you sell them?"

Now the old woman looked away. "I was afraid to. What would I say? 'A slan criminal left me these designs because I sheltered him for so long'? I would have been arrested by people like that John Petty you brought into this house."

Jommy knew the old woman was right.

"So now you owe it to Granny. I'm an old woman with modest needs. I don't have to be filthy rich." She smiled at him, and he wondered how much, if any, of the changes he had tweaked in her mind and personality had stuck with her. "But, of course, I wouldn't mind a little wealth here and there."

She took him through several of his old laboratory rooms, which were cluttered and dark. The walls bore serious burn and smoke marks, and half of the lights didn't work. She'd used his precision testing room to store canned vegetables and sacks of sugar, flour, and beans. It would take him quite a while to clean and set up his lab again, but it was quite a head start.

Granny led him with her stiff-legged gait down the tunnel that went under the ranch house to one of the outbuildings. "This way. One last thing. Extremely impressive. And valuable—very valuable." Her chuckle turned into a dry cough.

They climbed a set of metal stairs. Granny flicked a switch to activate the lights, then raised a hatch to the small hangar shed Jommy had built. He climbed out onto the sealed concrete floor and just stared. "It's still intact!" His fast rocket-plane, which he had built for his special explorations.

"Not just intact, young man—it's fully fueled and ready to launch, just the way you left it."

He startled the old woman by throwing his arms around her in a hug. She felt like a sack of sharp elbows and ribs and shoulder blades. "Granny, you may well have helped save the world. That must be worth a very large reward. I am very impressed."

The next day, with Kathleen sitting beside him in the well-lit laboratory chamber, Jommy carefully cracked open the first of his father's notebooks in the stack on the table. He didn't want Petty close to him while he looked at the papers, and President Gray had left the two of them alone, preoccupied with possible plans to defend what remained of civilization on Earth.

Jommy had slept for only a few hours the night before, too excited to lie around in bed. Kathleen also got up at dawn, looking refreshed and beautiful. Granny brought them a pot of strong coffee, and the bitter roasted scent drifted into the air. She had also cooked a big breakfast of fried eggs and potatoes, which Gray and Petty gladly devoured, but Jommy was anxious to get to work in the laboratories.

"This is very interesting stuff," Kathleen said, scanning the records as she sat beside him. Granny had copied many of the documents onto fresh paper, but they devoted their initial efforts to the original records. "Your father's conclusions are . . . remarkable."

"He was killed when I was only six, but he placed these volumes in storage for me, to help me reach my potential. But they weren't just gifts—they were clues, his way of showing me what I could become. I wish I'd known him better." He heaved a sigh.

Kathleen picked up the bottom journal on the stack, the one most severely singed around the edges. Granny must have pulled it directly from the flames. She turned the brittle, brown pages, looking at Peter Cross's tight, neat handwriting. As she flipped from one page to the other, she frowned, then held one page up to the light. "Jommy, look! There's something more here. I thought it was just a stain, but . . ."

Leaning close, he saw faint lines and scrawls, diagrams and symbols that might have been shadows of letters etched into the paper. "Thermal-response ink. The heat from the fire must have activated it."

"It's all just gibberish. Can you decipher it?"

"If my father created the code, then I can translate it. It just might take a little while."

"And help," Kathleen added, "which I'm glad to provide."

Jommy picked up the other notebooks, carefully warmed some of the pages over a small flame, and saw that many of the pages did bear secondary messages. Messages for *him*. Peter Cross's notebooks were already so full of unexpected details and incredible revelations that he would never have thought to look for additional information.

But the information he found between the lines was even more amazing.

Jommy and Kathleen worked intensely for hours, transcribing the symbols onto clean sheets of paper. Jommy set up graphs to decode the messages, while Kathleen scrutinized them, remembering all the intensive schooling Kier Gray had given her at the grand palace. Back then, many detractors had complained about the waste of time and energy in educating a slan girl who was due to be executed on her eleventh birthday. But the President had insisted. She knew a great deal about encryption and secret messages, more than the palace workers ever suspected.

Jommy finally discovered a connection, figuring out that one of the symbols indicated a letter in his mother's name and another in Jommy's own name. From that point, they possessed a key to part of the alphabet, and by translating bit by bit, unfolding incomplete words and filling in blanks, they picked up speed. Jommy and Kathleen vigorously cracked the code, both of them grinning, their slan tendrils waving as they shared telepathic excitement. They laid out the real message Peter Cross had hidden in his journals.

Jommy read the lines of text, barely daring to breathe. "It's directions to my father's main laboratory. A major slan base containing technology far beyond anything I've ever invented. It was there that he did his greatest work."

"The diagrams are a map, and these numbers are geographical coordinates." Kathleen eagerly leaned over his shoulder, reading. Jommy felt her nearness, smelled the faint perfume of soap on her skin, and a great warmth filled him. She picked up on his thoughts and let her fingers trail down his shoulder as she kept reading. "It sounds like the greatest repository of slan knowledge in the world. Look here." She pointed. "He says it includes machinery and stored energy sources dating all the way back to the time of Samuel Lann himself."

"Maybe that's where the other slans are hiding. We could sure use their help. That place could be the key!" He looked up at her, suddenly frowning. "But now I've lost my father's disintegrator weapon, thanks to Petty. My father left it for me. He considered it his greatest, most dangerous weapon. With the tendrilless taking over the Earth, we have a huge fight ahead of us. We'll need every advantage we can get."

"Can you build another one? I'll help—"

"The technology is beyond even me, and my father didn't leave the designs. He considered the weapon to be too deadly for anyone but his own son. It could have been our greatest advantage." He squeezed her hand.

"No, Jommy. *We ourselves* are the greatest advantage. The disintegrator was destroyed along with the palace. You'll have to learn to do without it."

He caught his breath as an idea occurred to him. "Not necessarily. I placed a locator tag on the weapon." He gestured to the metal cabinet against the wall. "I can modify some of this equipment to pick up the signal. I could easily trace it, even if it's buried in the rubble of the palace. If I find the disintegrator, then we can hold our own—and take back the world."

She looked at him puzzled, not sure what he meant. Her tendrils waved in the air.

"I'm going back to the city. I intend to retrieve it, no matter what it takes."

TWENTY-TWO

The remaining Samuel Lann records were a hodgepodge of media reports and news items. Wanting to know more, to know *everything*, Anthea viewed them all, drinking in the horrifying details.

One clip blared that the dangerous Dr. Lann had escaped from custody and interrogation. A squat, angry-looking man spoke to the reporter, "Our security is tight, but his mutants possess abilities against which we have no defenses. It's clear to me that Dr. Lann's own corrupted children were involved in the breakout. They twisted our minds, hypnotized us so they could free their father." He sounded quite indignant.

"This proves two things. First, this implies that Dr. Lann is indeed guilty of everything we suspect him of doing. If he had nothing to hide, as he insists, why would he escape? Second"—the man pointed now at the camera—"it proves that these slans are a genuine threat. Look what happened here! With such mind powers, they could walk into any home, rob our families, assault our wives, kidnap—or even *mutate*—our children! Be afraid of them. We should all be very afraid."

The next clip showed a large building completely engulfed in flames. Fire vehicles and army troops had surrounded the structure, but did nothing to quench the blaze. The emergency personnel stood back and watched, waited, like predators. They didn't seem to be there to help.

Finally, a lone man broke out of the doors and ran away from the blazing laboratory. His clothes were on fire. He waved his hands, screaming. Anthea recognized Dr. Lann himself. Instead of helping him, though, the soldiers raised their rifles and shot him in full view of everyone. Lann's body jittered as a dozen bullets struck him full in the chest. Then he collapsed to the pavement.

"Do not approach!" a military commander shouted through a bull-horn. "There could still be some danger." The cordon remained in place as the uncontrolled fire raged through the laboratory. No one came within twenty feet of Dr. Lann's still-smoldering body.

Watching the records, Anthea felt sick.

"His three children are in there," bellowed the incident commander. "They're a bigger threat than the doctor is. If they come out, your orders are to shoot to kill. Don't give them a chance to twist your minds. Remember, these are *slans* we're talking about. They could hypnotize you into opening fire on a comrade. We can't risk that. Slans are a danger to all humanity, and they must be wiped out."

But the laboratory building continued to be consumed by flames; the roof collapsed, timbers fell, but no one else emerged. Having seen what had happened to their father, Anthea couldn't blame them. The son and daughters of Dr. Lann were doomed, either way.

The brittle tape footage jumped. Anthea could feel her baby's agitation as he drank in the knowledge. She sensed an undertone in the air of the archives vault, a humming that grew louder. Before she could wonder about the strange background sensation, though, the next footage showed the same laboratory complex in daylight. The building had burned to the ground; only skeletal beams and blackened construction blocks remained.

Grim-faced workers sifted through the wreckage. Their cheeks were covered with soot, their eyes irritated from smoke as they reported to the commander. "There are no further bodies, sir. We've sifted the ashes. Dr. Lann must have been the only person inside the building."

"How could that be? We *know* the children were all in there. That's why they made this place into a fortress. They barricaded themselves so we couldn't get in."

"Commander! Over here!" one of the workers called.

The incident commander ran over to where three men wearing gloves and insulated jackets shoved a smoldering wooden cross-beam aside to reveal a previously hidden metal hatch. "Is it a safe room? Are they holed up in there?"

One of the firemen laughed scornfully. "It would have been a pressure cooker in there. We might have a few well-done slans inside."

They undogged the hatch, opened it—and the commander cursed to see a tunnel leading down into a catacomb of passageways. "You two men—go down there. Follow it! See where it leads."

The excavators looked at each other in nervous concern. "But what if the slans blast our brains?"

"Then shoot them before they have a chance." The incident commander shook his head, letting out a heavy sigh. "I doubt you'll find them, though. The slans went to a lot of trouble to build this barricade. They wouldn't leave themselves with no escape."

A few moments later, the men came back up looking defeated but oddly relieved. "Sorry, Commander. The tunnel leads to several escape hatches that open directly into the city streets. Those three slans are long gone by now."

The commander chewed on his lip. "Then why didn't Dr. Lann escape with them?" He scratched his head. "He must have sacrificed himself so that we'd keep thinking the others were inside. He bought time for his children to get away. Now those dangerous slans are loose." His eyes took on a far-off, frightened look. "Who can tell what they'll do now?"

The tape ended, and Anthea was left with a strange sense of foreboding. Though those events had occurred many centuries ago, they felt real to her.

Her baby was restless, perhaps reading her own mood. She realized that the bone-jarring hum had grown louder and louder. The signal seemed to come from the back of her head, in her ears, rattling her teeth. However, when she concentrated on it and tried to listen more closely, she could hear nothing.

Anthea understood with a jolt that it wasn't a tone any human could hear. A secret signal? She turned, eyes widened, and looked at the baby. His fine tendrils were waving like antennae, picking up a transmission meant only for slans—and passing it on to her.

Her son couldn't move, but he transmitted his need. She had to follow that sound, find out what was making it. She looked on the equipment shelves, found the strange and indecipherable devices that had been confiscated and sealed so long ago. She was sure the secret police had no idea what it was they had taken.

One of the stored devices turned out to be the source of the piercing hum. It was labeled as "Unknown Slan Mind-Control Device—never tested." The humans must have been too afraid to toy with it.

Instinctively, Anthea understood which buttons she was supposed to push on the long-quiescent device. The humming gadget began to vibrate in her fingers. Status lights illuminated, and the needles on gauges swung over to their maximum markings. She saw a fuzzy image form, but not with her own eyes. It was the face of a man, but it seemed distant, coming to her in thoughts instead of visions. *Her baby* was doing it!

The man talking looked like Dr. Lann, but subtly different. His son, probably, one of the first slans. "If you are receiving this, then I know you are a slan. For our own protection, we have attuned this Porgrave recording so that only those with tendrils can receive it. Those foolish humans who have caused us so much harm and pain will never know how much vital information we transmit right under their noses. All slans, hear me—you must understand who you are, know your destiny, and help gain revenge for the heinous crimes that have been committed against our new race. It will be war.

"We do not know how our fight will proceed, whether or not we'll be victorious, but we must lay plans so that the battle can continue for as long as necessary. Our father was the first to see the potential in the race of slans, and he was murdered for his support of our cause. Blind and prejudiced normals harassed him, interrogated him, and then they set his lab on fire. They shot him down while we watched."

The blurry face smiled. "But we all knew his conspicuous laboratory was primarily a sham. A diversion. We did very little real work there, but all the humans were afraid of it. Our real laboratory was a completely different complex, well hidden. There, our father did his groundbreaking work with mental enhancement, brain recordings, and studies of thought processes. All of his real equipment remains there, a true fortress, a place where we slans can build our defenses. In this recording we will implant the location of that secure hideout. The machinery, records, and primary mind imprints of our great father are there. Use what you find, if you can. Help us win this unjust war."

Anthea suddenly knew where to go. The picture was clear in her mind. She couldn't explain any coordinates or directions, but she *knew*.

Even though this strange telepathic beacon had been made centuries before she was born, she felt confident. She went over to her baby, smiling. "Thanks to you, we know of a place now—a place where we can be safe."

TWENTY-THREE

Kier Gray watched as Jommy packed up the armored vehicle and said his farewells. The President admired the young man's dedication and drive, though he was concerned about the dangers he might encounter in the war-torn city.

"This is a great risk you're taking, Jommy. We're safe here for now, and we can start to rebuild the government in exile with anything and anybody we can find. Are you sure it's wise to go back to Centropolis?"

"Mr. President, once I recover the disintegrator weapon, we can stand against this invasion. We can't just hide here."

"Isn't that what slans are good at? Hiding?" Petty said rudely and Granny smacked him across the back of his head. The slan hunter spluttered in surprise.

While Jommy prepared to depart, Petty had grudgingly admitted that his men had taken the disintegrator weapon to a protected sealed vault for his researchers to study in safety.

"Why are you being so cooperative?" Jommy had asked suspiciously.

"I was always cooperative—just not too happy about it." The slan hunter's brows furrowed. "With a weapon like that, we could withstand the tendrilless even if they track us down here on the ranch. It just might save my skin."

With the mind block he had learned over the years, Petty made it impossible for Jommy to read his true thoughts. The secret police chief almost certainly meant to seize the disintegrator for himself as soon as he had the chance, but Jommy would never let that happen.

Kathleen hugged him before he got into the car. "Be careful. I should be going with you—"

He was sorely tempted. "I can't risk losing you again. Even if the immediate attack has ended, it'll be dangerous back in the city."

"Then let me help!"

"I'll do my work better and faster this way—but I'm not alone. We have a connection through our tendrils. Your mind and my mind. You'll know that I'm safe, and I'll sense you thinking about me." Jommy climbed into his car and sealed the doors. When the engine roared to life, he drove off, leaving his friends behind.

Gray watched him go, sent his hopes with the young man, then rounded up the others to get to work putting together the shreds of a government.

They monitored news reports using battery-powered radios and a short-wave transmitter in Granny's sitting room. Eyewitness accounts claimed that slans were behind the continued bombings of Earth's largest cities, even though the attacking armies had no tendrils that anyone could see. No one challenged the claims, thanks to propaganda distributed for years by tendrilless rebels. One account claimed that *John Petty* was himself a disguised slan and had seized the presidency so that he could launch this attack upon all humanity. The timing couldn't possibly be a coincidence, the commentator observed.

Petty couldn't believe what he was hearing. "That's absurd!"

"The public has been trained to believe absurd things," Gray said. "You did it yourself."

"Yes, my secret police were actually quite good at that," Petty admitted. "Disinformation is a simple and commonly used tactic. If you give people enough crazy stories, they won't believe the truth more than any other lie."

"And now you've been beaten at your own game," Kathleen said. "How are we going to convince the population of the truth, that the *tendrilless* slans are their enemies and they should rise up against them?"

"That would trigger another whole round of Slan Wars," Granny said. "Do you want more centuries of endless bloodshed? We'd never see the end of it." She shook her head scoldingly.

"*Or,*" Gray continued, "we can suggest a meeting with the tendrilless leaders. They have a vendetta against slans, and there's cause for grief on both sides, but maybe they'll listen if we tell them the true story. I doubt they even know their own origins. The only way we all win is if we can work out a peace, a way for us to live together in prosperity."

"Sounds like you're dreaming," Petty said.

"Jommy managed to make it work here in this valley," Granny interrupted. "I've never seen so many good neighbors."

Kathleen sat next to her father. "But what *is* the true story of the tendrilless? Why do they hate the slans so much? Where did they come from?"

Gray sighed and leaned back in his chair. "It's a long story."

"Oh, then I'll make coffee." The old woman came back in a few minutes with a reheated pot of bitter old brew.

Petty slurped his coffee, then winced at the taste. "And what about yourself, Gray? You don't have tendrils, yet you seem to be on the side of the slans, not the tendrilless. You're obviously a spy, an infiltrator— but which side are you on?"

The President accepted a cup, thanked Granny, and searched in his mind for the proper spot to begin. "During the long dark ages of the Slan Wars, slan geneticists decided that for the survival of our race they had to breed a new offshoot that couldn't be detected by outsiders, slans that had no tendrils. But consequently, the tendrilless had none of the superior telepathic abilities of true slans. They were sleepers, like dormant seeds planted in the recovering society."

"What happened to all the other true slans?"

"They went into hiding somewhere. I don't know the details, since it was so long ago. But many more of them survived than was apparent."

"Not after my men rooted out the ones you kept in the grand palace." Petty chuckled. "That diminished your numbers quite a bit! And my secret police are probably still hunting them down."

Granny poured more hot coffee into Petty's cup . . . and onto his hand, and onto his lap. He yelped. The old woman walked away with an innocent expression, which broke into a smile.

Gray continued. "As vigilante groups killed anyone with tendrils, my forefathers began to create slans that still had the same mutant genes, the same physical strength, but genetically designed to manifest no tendrils, not for several generations. Their telepathic abilities were dormant. Originally, when we infiltrated them into human society, the tendrilless were supposed to know what they were and what their mission was."

"Spies among us," Petty muttered.

Granny waved a stern finger in front of his face. "Let the man talk. He's the President."

"He's been deposed."

The old woman said with a smirk, "Until you have *your* picture on a ten-credit bill, Mr. Petty, you'd better listen to him."

Gray continued. "The tendrilless offshoots could live as humans, among humans, and act as humans. Because of their superior intelligence and physical strength, the tendrilless wouldn't take long to work their way into important positions, running governments and industries. Before the normal humans knew it, slans would have a tight hold on society. By the time the tendrilless began to have true slan babies again, once the genetic clock brought the chromosomes back to the forefront and they bred true, our disguised sleeper agents would have made another slan war impossible. They would have created an environment where slans and humans really could live together."

"Sounds like that whole idea backfired." Granny slurped her own coffee.

"The tendrilless convinced themselves that we had betrayed them, that we had robbed them of their telepathic abilities. By depriving them of tendrils, they felt as if we had"—he searched for a word—"*castrated* them in a way. They claimed that we had stolen their birthright. And so, when true slans came to teach them what they needed to know, the tendrilless turned on them. They declared open war and killed any true slan they could find. That erupted in a terrible slaughter—and it's never stopped."

Kathleen gave him a puzzled frown. "But if the tendrilless were indistinguishable from normal humans, how could they know each other?"

"Oh, they could still sense the differences," Gray answered. "Jommy found that out when he tried to approach them as a young boy, thinking they were allies. And because the tendrilless were as intelligent as any other slan, they developed devices to detect us. They could track us down, ambush true slans. Many were murdered before we knew they had this ability. In turn, some radical slans declared open war on the tendrilless. And it got worse from there."

"People never seem to get tired of killing. It's one of the things we do best." The old woman gulped more coffee. "This is good. Maybe I should go burn another pot."

Gray, Petty, and Kathleen all spoke out in a quick chorus. "No, no thank you. We've had enough."

The President leaned back in his chair. "Numerous tendrilless lost contact with each other over the centuries. Plenty of their descendants don't even know what they truly are. And right now, all across the race, the dominant genes are beginning to manifest themselves. Once embedded in their chromosomes, the modifications can't be changed. Even the militant tendrilless who want to destroy all true slans are beginning to give birth to babies with tendrils. In another generation or two, they'll all be true slans."

"Then they would have killed us all for nothing," Kathleen cried. "By killing us, they'll be killing themselves. If we could just explain to the tendrilless leaders what happened, they'll stop trying to exterminate slans and humans."

"If they'll listen to us," Gray said.

The secret police chief made a rude noise, then cringed as if expecting Granny to smack him again.

"I'm still the President. I'll try to contact the leaders of the tendrilless." He turned to the old woman. "I can use the equipment in Jommy's laboratory to boost the signal and build a powerful transmitter. I'll hold out an olive branch to the tendrilless. Then it'll be in their hands."

Gray, Kathleen, Granny, and even Petty worked together to erect a tall signaling tower on the roof of the back shed. Announcing himself as the President of Earth, Commander in Chief and head of the legitimate government in exile, Kier Gray transmitted a bold message to Mars, where they knew the tendrilless had established their base. He hoped his words would fall upon receptive ears.

Gray requested a peace conference, a summit to discuss the current war on Earth. He was careful not to phrase it in terms of a proposed surrender, though he was sure the tendrilless would view it as such.

Then they waited. Because of the sheer distance between Earth and Mars, a signal would take hours to cross space and come back. Even so, someone monitored the shortwave constantly, waiting for an answer. The Tendrilless Authority would be surprised, even horrified, by Gray's revelations. They would argue and disagree, but the tendrilless scientists were intelligent enough to discover their own proof. With the invaders bombarding cities and setting up occupation headquarters, Gray hoped the enemy council would at least give him the benefit of the doubt.

Petty took his own shift waiting by the shortwave. He was grudgingly cooperative, even helpful. Gray found it suspicious, and he wondered about the slan hunter's true motives. The secret police chief had been trying to gather his scattered operatives into a full-fledged defense, but so far claimed no success. The President would have to rely on diplomacy, because he had no military strength to fall back on.

Finally, at three o'clock in the morning, the crackling answer came when a sleepy Kathleen was waiting at the radio, missing Jommy. "This is Authority Chief Altus Lorry representing the tendrilless slans on Mars. We have received and considered your message. Your claims are as unexpected as they are unbelievable. However, it is the feeling of this council that we should give it due consideration. Therefore, we will send a representative to meet with you and hear your case. After so many centuries of betrayal and distrust, you should expect no more than that."

Kathleen frantically answered, "Of course. We accept! I will have President Gray transmit his suggestions to you." She switched off the unit and ran through the house to wake everyone up.

TWENTY-FOUR

Under the great glass sky-ceiling of Cimmerium, the woman sat by herself on a red-rock balcony. Peaceful, she looked out over the deep dry canyon, then turned her face upward and closed her eyes, basking in the distant sunshine. Her light brown hair had grown back in bristly patches, not long enough to be attractive but sufficient to cover the large scars on her scalp.

Ingrid Corliss had been dead, or at least brain-dead, after a terrible spaceship accident on Mars. Tendrilless medical knowledge had restored her, regrown the damaged parts of her brain, and returned her to some semblance of life. With conditioning, mental priming, and careful therapy, she had reached the limits of what her people could do for her. The doctors had said that Ingrid would never be normal, that nothing could be done.

Until Jommy Cross came.

While previously infiltrating the city on Mars, Cross had found the injured woman. He had disguised himself as Ingrid's husband and used that deception to gather vital information about the tendrilless plans for taking over the Earth. And, though he didn't have to, he had helped to put her brain back together. . . .

Now, in the quiet and near-empty city, Jem Lorry stepped up behind the too-peaceful woman, frowning. He could see what she must be thinking. Cross had a way of manipulating people, brainwashing them into forgetting how evil he was.

Ingrid opened her eyes. She stiffened when she saw him. "I'm aware of what you want, Mr. Lorry, but I can't help you. I don't know where Jommy Cross is."

"You don't know—or you refuse to tell us?"

She languidly reached up to scratch the scars on her scalp. "I won't lie to you—I have no desire to see him caught and punished."

"Sympathizing with slans is treason, Mrs. Corliss."

Her eyes lit up with anger. "You don't understand, do you, Mr. Lorry? Jommy Cross gave me my life back. He restored my mind. I would still be a vegetable were it not for him. He had no obligation to help me, and no reason to. The tendrilless mean to destroy him and all true slans. Why should he care about me? And yet he did."

Jem wondered what it would feel like to strangle her. "Friendship and bleeding-heart dreams have no place in politics. That young man doesn't even know his own powers. He must be stopped."

"I owe him an obligation I can never repay. Given what he did for me, can you truly believe that every slan is bad? The evidence does not lead to that conclusion."

"The evidence I have is centuries of true slans killing the tendrilless, preventing us from achieving a rightful place among the superior races of humanity. You know they bred us without tendrils to prevent us from having powers like theirs. And then they began to kill us off, one by one."

"I believe there was killing on both sides, Mr. Lorry. So we should condemn Jommy Cross and all other surviving slans for the sins of the fathers? Why not trace the crime all the way back to Samuel Lann?"

Jem looked over the sheer drop to the bottom of the dry red gorge. Though the filtered sunshine was warm enough, he continued to feel a chill in his bones. His father was a doddering fool, the Authority members were passive and ineffective, and now this woman, a tendrilless, seemed to be siding with the enemy.

"If you think we have nothing to fear from the true slans, then you haven't realized the insidious ways they continue to strike at us. In the past two months, sixteen babies have been born with tendrils in Cimmerium—*here*, on our very doorstep! Somehow the slans have been transmitting their mutation rays to Mars. That's the only explanation." He pointed a stern finger at her. "Of course we couldn't allow those babies to live. They would have grown up to be spies among us, so we quickly destroyed them. Their parents have been arrested and are currently undergoing detailed genetic profiling. I suspect they were true slans all along, surgically modified to fit in among us."

"You're paranoid, Mr. Lorry."

"I'm a realist." He stormed away.

Unbothered, Ingrid Corliss lay back in the sun and closed her eyes, continuing to heal.

The Tendrilless Authority had called an emergency session to talk about the news they had just received, the unexpected proposal from the President-in-hiding on Earth. When Jem barged in, uninvited, his father looked down his nose at him. "You are not a member of this council, my son."

But I certainly should be. And one day after Earth is conquered, no one will deny me my right. He forced a respectful expression on his face. "But I'm sure I could help, given my background. What is the basis for this session?"

His father scratched his neat white beard. "We've received a direct communication from President Gray requesting a summit. He's provided some rather disturbing historical information that explains a great deal about our background. It even explains the babies recently born with tendrils."

"We already have an explanation for that. Anything Gray says is bound to be a trick."

"Nevertheless, we should consider this carefully. Gray has requested that we send a delegation to hear what he has to say."

Jem leaned against a stone column, casual in front of his leaders. "It's bound to be a trap. You do not know Kier Gray the way I do, Father. None of you Authority members do. I worked with him for years. If he truly is a slan, then he was working against us all along. As President he pretended to be human, while plotting against his own kind. If he'd known I was a tendrilless among them, he probably would have hurled me from the highest tower of the palace." Jem smiled. "Fortunately, there aren't any towers left."

One of the old men said in a creaky voice, "Nevertheless, President Gray has revealed historical explanations that make us question many of our preconceptions."

"Take it with a grain of salt," Jem said. "Gray is trying to save his skin. He's working with Jommy Cross, as far as we know."

Altus seemed intrigued, and expected his son to be as well. "Ah, but hear him out, Jem. It makes a great deal of sense."

He listened with horror, disbelief, then anger as the council members repeated the story of the origin of the tendrilless. Gray suggested that the entire tendrilless race was a mere temporary offshoot, never intended to survive for more than a few centuries. The very idea appalled him. Worse, his own father and the Tendrilless Authority seemed to believe the ridiculous notion. Gullible fools! It was obviously a trick of some kind, an excuse to lull the tendrilless into doubts.

He saw only one way out. Covering his true mood, Jem bowed formally. "Father, this summit meeting will be very important, and it must be done with exquisite care. Perhaps I have been overly hard and aggressive in order to protect our race, but I can be cautious as well. I know Gray's mannerisms and schemes, and I can spot a trap. Please allow me to go to Earth as your representative."

Bleary-eyed, Altus perked up. He seemed pleased with his son's apparent change of heart. "A mutually beneficial solution will be best for all of us. Listen to what Gray has to say."

Smiling carefully, Jem bowed. "If it is not a trap, then I am willing to consider alternatives. No one knows Earth better than I do. I can handle this."

"We never wanted the option of complete annihilation, as you're well aware," Altus said. "Make us proud."

Inwardly furious with the soft passivity of the Authority, he went to the transmitting center and opened a channel. "This is Jem Lorry. By now, President Gray, you will have realized that I was a tendrilless slan working in your own government. My father is the leader of the Tendrilless Authority here in Cimmerium. He has delegated me to work out the details of the summit." He paused, considered his words carefully. "I am skeptical about what you have said, but I will listen with an open mind. Tell me how to meet you, and we'll proceed from there."

When enough time had passed for a return signal to be received, he paced the floor, waiting and annoyed. The responding voice that came over the transmitting system, though, was a complete surprise to him. "Lorry, you're a bastard! You worked with me, and you worked with the President, and you fooled us all. You were a snake in our midst." It was John Petty.

Jem wished he could have seen the great slan hunter's face when he'd learned the President's chief adviser was a tendrilless turncoat.

Then Petty surprised him even more. "We are two of a kind, Lorry. It galls me to be here with the President, who has revealed himself as my greatest enemy. You and I have something in common—we each want to get rid of Kier Gray, so listen to me well. We'll set up this summit, but I propose a double-cross. I'll deliver Gray's head on a platter."

Jem's eyebrows shot up. At first he didn't trust the suggestion, but he and Petty had known each other for years, both of them ruthless and ambitious. He had to admit that a double-cross sounded like Petty—a way to turn the tables on the government in exile, to kill off

Gray, his slan daughter Kathleen, possibly even Jommy Cross. It was an opportunity he simply couldn't pass up.

Hoping that his signal would not be intercepted by the wrong person, Jem answered immediately. The slan hunter should still be there at the communications console awaiting his answer. "I like your proposal, Petty. What I really want is to destroy President Gray and eliminate the government. Despite what my foolish father says, I have no interest in suing for peace with slans or with humans. Why should I? We've already won. You're a realist. Maybe I could find some way to make accommodations for you and a few other human beings. I'm willing to compromise."

Jem smiled to himself as he signed off, knowing Petty would accept the terms. It was all coming together. And once they had everything set up, Jem thought, why stop at just a *double*-cross? This meeting would be the convenient answer to everything.

TWENTY-FIVE

When Jommy arrived back in Centropolis, cautiously dodging debris and trying to avoid detection, he saw that the grand palace wasn't the only thing utterly destroyed.

He had driven through the night, keeping his vehicle out of sight whenever possible. Hidden in the darkness, Jommy had seen bright signal lights overhead indicating the flybys of bold enemy spacecraft. Parked under a dense stand of trees, he sat waiting in his dark and silent car until the tendrilless patrols passed out of sight.

Though the airships were a threat, he knew these were just scouts, not outright attack squadrons. With Earth's defenses already crushed, the bombardment of cities had stopped. The invaders' vanguard forces expected no further resistance from the vanquished people of Earth.

But Jommy and his friends still stood against them. He had his father's notebooks; he had superior slan technology; he had President Kier Gray. Unfortunately, Kathleen's father had not been able to contact any of his slan operatives from the old government, and Petty could not reach his secret police, who—he claimed—could form an organized resistance. One of Jommy's other hopes for this mission was to find the hidden enclave of slans in ruined Centropolis, the ancient highly secure hideout his father had marked in his logs. He was convinced that some of his people must still be alive, and they had to be willing to fight.

The remaining slans had certainly been driven into hiding, but what had once been a superior race couldn't have been so utterly exterminated. And yet, where were they? Why hadn't they fought against the invasion? Could it be that the true slans were even more afraid of the tendrilless? Jommy knew he could not be the only one willing to fight for his planet.

He'd been striving to find the lost slans all his life. If a large population did survive, he doubted they were anywhere on Earth—and if they *were* still here and had chosen to do nothing, then perhaps he didn't want to know them after all. . . .

When the night sky was clear again, Jommy drove his car along the deserted roads. At last he arrived at the outskirts of the main city as the first light of sunrise painted the east with colors of blood and fire.

The streets of Centropolis were a mad turmoil of collapsed buildings and hollow-eyed survivors. Fires had gone unchecked, and entire blocks had burned down. For all their military superiority, the tendrilless had not attempted to mitigate the wanton destruction. They could have assured their victory with far less carnage. Did they really want to take over Earth if they left nothing but a charred ball? It made no sense.

As he drove along, always wary, Jommy understood that the desperate survivors might not be rational. They had gone through two days of hell, and at the very least would try to take his vehicle from him. Though the controls were keyed to operate only to his touch, the mob wouldn't know that. He would have to shed a great deal of unnecessary blood in order to defend himself—and they weren't his real enemies.

Hoping to prevent that, Jommy found a quiet alleyway full of long shadows cast by the intact buildings. With the extra awareness from his tendrils, he listened to the static of frantic thoughts and fear, but sensed no one watching him. He drove the already-scuffed car into a partially collapsed shed structure, then quietly piled debris around the hood and roof. The camouflage wouldn't bear careful inspection, but most people glancing at it would assume the car had been buried during an explosion.

Taking careful note of the car's location, Jommy trudged out into the dangerous streets. He wore nondescript clothes and carried only the small tracking device that would help him locate his disintegrator tube, wherever it might be buried in the palace rubble.

As the morning brightened, he passed people going about the business of survival. They pushed wheelbarrows, carried rucksacks full of canned food or jewelry. Looters ran in and out of stores, breaking open display cases and ransacking cash registers. Pale and frightened faces stared out of darkened windows.

He heard sporadic gunfire, screams, and laughter. One man ran past him with long chickenlike strides, carrying three overstuffed bags filled entirely with colorful hats. Jommy couldn't understand what the man was doing, but a second red-faced man chased after him, yelling, "Give those back! They're mine. Bring them back!"

Moments later, somebody shot at Jommy. He dove out of the way as ricochets peppered the pavement and the building walls next to him. He couldn't see where the shots were coming from or whom he had offended. He got to his feet and ran out of range.

Across one main thoroughfare, someone had strung barbed wire and built a rough barricade of old furniture, a refrigerator, and automobile parts. A huge sign bore dripping red letters that said MY TERRITORY. Three mangled bodies were strung on the barbed wire like gruesome trophies. Jommy chose an alternate route.

When he finally reached what had once been the grand palace, he saw only a wide rubble-filled crater. Somewhere buried inside that wreckage, hopefully close to the surface, was his powerful, one-of-a-kind weapon.

"Like finding a needle in a thousand haystacks," Jommy said aloud. "But at least this particular needle has a locator beacon." He held out his tracking device, and tiny flashing lights indicated the scan of the area, the search for a signal.

Smoke still rose from the pile of rubble, curling out from hundreds of fires still smoldering in vaults and smashed office levels below. He climbed over the debris like an explorer in a dangerous new mountain range. He found thick reinforced walls broken in half, leaving jagged edges like the teeth in a skull.

He balanced on fallen blocks, then climbed on top of a battered metal desk half buried in the rubble. From there, he pointed the tracking device into the wreckage, turning in a slow circle. Nothing but gray static filled the screen. Leftover thermal signatures from cooling girders and simmering fires masked the signal.

Jommy ventured deeper into the rubble, walking precariously on fallen blocks. He poked into dark and dead-end passageways that looked like dangerous mine shafts, hoping to catch just a flicker of the signal on the detector. Once he determined the weapon's location, though, then he would be faced with the even more difficult task of digging it out, perhaps under a mountain of debris. That would put his slan physical strength and his engineering ingenuity to the test.

By noon, painted with sweat and dust and soot, he sat down to rest, trying not to be too disheartened. As he propped his elbows on his knees, he suddenly caught a faint signal on the device's screen. Startled, he pointed the nose of his locator device downward, increased the gain, and picked up a louder ping. When he made his best guess of the location, he pocketed the device and used his bare hands to shove the fallen rock plates aside. Uprooting a broken metal pipe, he used it as a lever to pry away more heavy debris.

With no one around in the bombed zone, he dug down with renewed energy and enthusiasm, scraping rubble, gravel, and broken plaster away. Then he found an armored hatch. Confirming that the locator signal came from the chamber behind the hatch, he continued to dig until he uncovered a massive door, sealed and locked. He couldn't believe the detector had picked up any signal at all through such an obstruction.

After another hour of tireless excavation, Jommy realized that he had found an entire isolated chamber, like a self-contained bank vault—just like Petty had said. The armored chamber had remained intact even as the rest of the palace collapsed around it. Now the cubical vault rested in the rubble, tilted at an angle, like a treasure chest buried in debris.

Activating the detector again, Jommy saw that the static was thinner, the signal stronger. Yes, the vault's thick metal walls had blocked much of the beacon, but the disintegrator tube was definitely inside the chamber. He had to find a way to open the heavy door! Now that he had a chance, he had hope, and that was enough to keep him going long past the point where he was normally exhausted.

At last, when he had cleared all obstructions from the door, Jommy considered his options. The vault door weighed several tons and was held secure with thick pistons. However, despite its bulk, the motors and the lock were controlled by a simple spring-loaded hydraulic mechanism.

Completely focused on his task, Jommy tinkered with the dead controls. He needed only a power source to activate them, and then he could short-circuit and bypass the vault's standard combination. For him, this was child's play.

Now that he no longer had any need for the handheld locator device, he removed the back plate and exposed its circuits. Pulling out the tiny power source, he inserted and adapted it for the vault door's security controls. He was rewarded to see the lights on the locking panel glow green and amber. Jommy pulled more wires from his tracker, cross-connected them, then hooked the detector to the motor controls for the large locking wheel.

Powered again, the locking bolts slid aside, making the sealed chamber vibrate. The motion caused the whole self-contained vault to shift and settle where it rested precariously in the unstable rubble. Jommy knew that if the rubble pile collapsed beneath him, he—and the vault—could be buried in a giant cave-in. He fought for his balance, ready to leap free at the last moment.

Then the thick locking bolts finally thumped into place, and the door unsealed itself with a hiss. Thick, lubricated cylinders heaved the

massive barrier on gigantic hinges. Because the vault box lay tilted backward, the door lifted against gravity, then groaned to a grudging halt,
leaving a door gap barely two feet wide.

The shifting rubble stabilized, and the ground beneath Jommy's feet
stopped trembling. He approached the laboratory chamber cautiously.
Wafting from the thick darkness of the interior, he could smell stale
air, spilled chemicals, burned circuitry. The disintegrator tube would
be in there.

Moving anxiously, Jommy squirmed through the gap and
climbed partway inside, fearing that the uncertain pistons would release their hold at any moment. Even though the jury-rigged power
source kept the controls active, the several-ton door could easily slam
back down. He slipped inside quickly, dropped to the tilted floor, and
squatted, catching his breath. Still not safe, though: If the door
crashed shut now, he would be trapped in a tomb.

Jommy fumbled his way forward, straining to see details in the
darkness. Even with his excellent eyesight, there simply wasn't enough
illumination. He wished he'd bought a small handlight. Then he
tripped on something and crashed to his knees. Catching himself with
palms flat against the metal floor, he found himself staring face-to-
face with a pallid corpse.

The man had been smashed, his face bruised, his eyes open. Jommy
scrambled backward and bumped into a second dead man. As his eyes
adjusted, he noted that both men were wearing the armbands of the secret police. Both looked like broken dolls, tossed about in the tantrum
of a hyperactive child.

Jommy realized what had happened. Though the vault walls were
impregnable, this whole room had crashed down during the intense
bombardment of the palace. To the men sealed inside, it would have
been like being in a barrel going over a waterfall. They had been
smashed to a pulp.

The slice of daylight shining through the open door provided just
enough illumination for him to make his inspection. Forcing himself to
ignore the corpses, Jommy searched the debris. His tendrils gave him no
advantage; in the thick-walled vault, he could sense nothing around
him, nothing outside. A table lay overturned among smashed bottles;
papers were strewn like the feathers of a startled chicken. Wall brackets
had snapped, tumbling and twisting metal shelves into piles. Jommy
flung the shelves aside with a loud clatter, searching for his disintegrator.

With a distant rumble, the shaking vault continued to settle, and
the floor tilted at a more substantial angle. Jommy scrambled to keep

his balance. Three unbroken canisters and a metal pipe rolled down to the low point of a back corner. Then, as the room came to rest at a new unstable point, he spotted the slender, polished tube that had saved his life so many times. His father's weapon!

With a wash of relief and a sudden flood of urgency—something from his slan senses, even here in the thick-walled vault?—he knew he had to get out of there. He grabbed the weapon and worked his way up the steep and slippery floor, past the scarecrowish corpses. Victorious, with the disintegrator in one hand, he worked his head and shoulder through the door gap, then balanced on his elbows. He had done it!

As he blinked in the low light of sunset, cradling the weapon, he heard voices outside, other people moving through the rubble. Nearby. Scavengers must be looking for valuable artifacts and antique treasures in the palace ruins. He hadn't sensed them from inside the thick-walled chamber.

He oriented himself and turned in the cramped gap, then felt a tingling, sensed someone very close—and then hands grabbed his shoulders from behind. A man was standing right on top of the partially open vault door above him. "Here he is! I told you I saw someone up here."

Caught halfway in and halfway out of the door gap, Jommy struggled, but the metal floor and walls were slippery and he couldn't get a solid grip. People rushed forward to grab him. To his dismay, he dropped the disintegrator weapon as he tried to wrench himself free. He heard the tube clatter back down among the debris.

More scavengers clutched at him, wrenching his arm. Someone wrapped fingers in his hair and yanked it with a painful tug. "Hey, look at this. He's got tendrils!"

"Tendrils! He's a bloody slan!"

"Looks like we caught ourselves one of the enemy."

TWENTY-SIX

Now that Anthea's head was filled with wonderful, horrible knowledge from the library's "true archives," she knew what she had to do. Long ago, the children of Samuel Lann had built a large subterranean hideout right under the noses of the humans. The Porgrave message said that it had been designed to last for centuries.

That was where she would go.

The baby rested comfortably against her chest as she hurried down the corridor from the vault room. Before she could leave the great stone building, however, Anthea heard a ruckus coming from Mr. Reynolds's office. "Help me, somebody! Is anybody out there?"

As she heard his plaintive tone, a lump formed in her throat. So many people had been awful to her since the birth of the baby, but not Reynolds. What sort of person was she turning into? Did she have to leave the poor man there, helpless? With all the turmoil in the city, there would be looters, marauders—and no police or rescue workers. What if Mr. Reynolds starved to death because she had tied him up, left him with no chance of escape.

She swallowed hard, hesitated, then made up her mind. When she stepped into his office, he flinched when he saw her. "Don't hit me again! I won't hurt you."

"Right now you'd say anything to get yourself free."

He hung his head. "Yes, in fact, I probably would. I don't understand who you are, or what you want—"

"I just want to live in peace, to get from day to day without strangers trying to kill me!"

"But you have a *slan baby*, madam. Even if I wanted to, how could

I harm you? Can't you just . . . manipulate my thoughts? Why not brainwash me so that I won't even remember you were here?"

Anthea marched toward where he was tied up in his chair. "Now you listen to me, Mr. Reynolds." She showed him the back of her head, and though he squinted without his glasses, he could definitely see that she had no tendrils. "I'm not a slan. Neither was my husband. But somehow I gave birth to a baby with tendrils. Don't ask me how." She turned back around, let him take a good look at the infant's innocent face. "I never expected this to happen, but I am not going to give up my baby. I will not let him be harmed by lynch mobs of ignorant and prejudiced people. We're getting out of here, to safety."

"But . . . but, madam—I didn't threaten him in any way."

She crossed her arms. "I saw the look of horror on your face."

"Probably more a look of surprise. I've never seen a slan baby. In fact, we don't get many babies in the library." A look of alarm crossed his face. "Wait! If you're going away, please don't leave me tied up like this!"

Though she tried to be stern, Anthea simply wasn't very good at looking tough. "It's your lucky day, Mr. Reynolds. I've decided not to."

"My lucky day . . ." he groaned.

She took the eyeglasses from his pocket and set them on a filing cabinet in the far corner of the room. "I just want a head start." She unbound both of his arms. "You can free your own feet. By the time you get out of this chair and find your glasses, we'll have vanished into the streets. It won't do you any good to chase after us."

"I have no interest in chasing after you, madam! You'd just beat me up again. I wish you'd asked for my help instead . . ."

She felt a twinge in her heart. "I feel the same, Mr. Reynolds. But the sad fact is, if you helped me, you'd be putting yourself in danger, too." She winced at the memory of poor Davis, how he'd been killed so that she and the baby could get away. As she turned to leave, Anthea hesitated at the door of his office. "You're a man of books and of learning. Don't let prejudice and ignorance get the best of you. In fact, why don't you go into that archives vault and take a good look at those reports from the Slan Wars? Learn the truth. There's plenty of blame to go around, for humans and slans alike. Protect those records. Someday, they might help us all understand each other."

She left the room, not even feeling the need to hurry. She could see something trustworthy in the librarian's round eyes.

From the mysterious Porgrave transmission, Anthea had an instinctive grasp of how to get to the safe underground base—if it still existed. Slans had apparently hidden there for many generations, and the old redoubt had been built to last for centuries, maybe even millennia, as a stronghold. However, Centropolis itself had changed a great deal after such a long passage of time and the long rebuilding from the devastating Slan Wars.

Anthea had faith it would still be there.

Leaving the shelter of the library, she discovered it was a new morning, though the city was a chaos of still-burning fires, collapsed skyscrapers, smashed cars, and crushed bodies. Anthea spent most of the day picking her way through the streets, hiding from anyone who might see her. In normal, civilized times, no one would have refused to help a mother and her baby; now, though, she looked like a victim, an easy target. And if anyone should notice the baby's tendrils . . .

When she finally stood at the supposed entrance to the hidden underground base, she fought back her disappointment and surprise. Maybe it had been a wild-goose chase after all.

The small, old building was nondescript, intentionally designed so that no one would give it a second glance. A small sign in the window said that it was a "Museum of Sewing Machines"—a legitimate-sounding place, but one that would not entice great crowds of visitors. Even with the blast marks and rubble in the streets, this structure remained intact and untouched. Anthea realized that the building was incredibly old, deceptively ancient, and reinforced to the point that it must be virtually indestructible. The small, quiet museum had probably existed in this spot since the days of the Slan Wars.

Looking around furtively, Anthea scurried over to the Museum of Sewing Machines and found the door unlocked. That seemed strange to her, but then she realized that the mobs had many more tempting places to ransack.

The current owners of the small building probably didn't even know its connection to the ancient slan hideout . . . or maybe hidden slans watched over the building. She clung to that hope. If there were others, she could find safety among them. They would help protect her and the baby.

"Hello?" she called into the shadowy lobby. No one answered.

On tables and in transparent cases, strange contraptions were on display, spindles and pulleys, specialized industrial stitching devices and models used by homemakers from days past. One battery-powered demonstration unit slowly bobbed up and down, pumping its needle endlessly through a patch of cloth like a mechanical mosquito.

"Hello?" She crept around behind a desk where an attendant would have waited fruitlessly for paying visitors who never came. She found a small file room, a broom closet, a cold coffeepot, and a packet of stale crackers, which she wolfed down, but no hidden passage that led to the underground vault. Of course, if this secret had endured undetected for centuries, the door or hatch would be well hidden. She wandered back out to the display room, at a loss for what to do next.

The baby was restless in her arms, and she felt a thrumming inside her skull. Another Porgrave signal was coming from here, a pinpointing beacon like the one transmitted from inside the archives vault. The infant could not speak, could not direct her, but she could sense things through him. Anthea was not entirely on her own.

The vibrations seemed strongest in the main museum room, surreptitious scanners or detectors that no human would notice. She continued to search, tapping on walls, looking for hidden doors. She walked from one old sewing machine to the next, from the bulky and old-fashioned to the sleek and modern.

Anthea felt drawn again to the battery-powered demonstration model that continued pumping its needle up and down. When she touched it with her outstretched hand, she felt a thrill of *rightness* about this machine. The baby's tendrils waved in the air, and the beckoning signal grew stronger. She heard a click, as sensors detected the baby, accepted him.

The sewing machine stopped, and Anthea froze as well. Then she heard a whirring release, and the display stand moved slightly. She stepped back, fumbled around, and realized that the whole podium rested on a clever pivot. When she pushed it, the stand slid easily on lubricated tracks to expose a hatch in the floor—the entrance!

As she bent down with the baby, a metal covering whisked back to reveal a ladder leading down into a narrow chamber. Weak-kneed with relief, Anthea wrapped one arm around the baby and painstakingly made her way down seven rungs until she found herself in a small metal-walled room. She could make out no doors or hatches. A dead end.

Overhead, the covering slid back into place, sealing her inside. With a whirring noise, the sewing machine display case pivoted back into its normal position. She held the baby against her; this felt like a trap.

Anthea could find no controls, no windows, no posted instructions. "Well, now what?" she asked, a rhetorical question.

Then the whole room fell into a stomach-lurching plunge. Cables hummed and the walls vibrated as the elevator shot downward. In her arms the baby cooed and gurgled happily, sensing no danger.

Because the machinery still worked, because of the well-maintained sewing machine museum overhead, she was sure they'd find another population of slans inside the underground base. She would ask them for help. She could be at home among the other refugees, who would protect her.

When the elevator finally stopped, one wall whisked aside to reveal a huge, warm, and well-lit cavern. Anthea formed her most welcoming smile and stepped out, carrying the infant and expecting to be greeted by a group of slans, people who would help her, protect her baby, and explain everything to her.

Instead, she found only skeletons.

TWENTY-SEVEN

As the angry mob grabbed for him in the wreckage of the palace, Jommy was precariously caught in the vault door gap. He had dropped the disintegrator, and now hands clutched at him, seizing his arms, his hair. He tried to let himself drop back down into the chamber, but somebody grabbed his collar, dragging him back up.

If he struggled too much, Jommy feared he might jar loose the tracking device wired up to the door mechanism, and then the thick pistons would release the heavy door. Or, the whole armored chamber might collapse into the unstable rubble. As a trick, he went limp, forcing the scavengers to drag him out; they would underestimate him, believe he was weak. As soon as he was free, though, he flew into a frenzy.

Jommy punched the nearest man with strength that surprised his attackers, knocking him back head over heels. Then he flung two more far away as they threw themselves on him. Like a pair of rag dolls, they tumbled into the rubble, smashing into the jagged stones. One slipped and fell into a wide gap, dropping deep into the unseen lower levels; a rumble of a cave-in accompanied his fall, cutting off his screams.

The murderous scavengers circled, wary now. "Dirty slan!"

"Careful, he might fry your brain."

"You didn't have a brain to start with, Jerome."

One scrawny man who wore several layers of mismatched clothing was much more interested in the vault Jommy had been investigating. Ducking away from the fight, the scrawny man shouted, "Looks like a treasure room! I bet he was hiding something in there. Slan treasure." He started to crawl headfirst into the vault.

Jommy fought each attacker that came at him, but more and more people swarmed over the rubble, at least a hundred, all of them carrying makeshift clubs and pipes; a few had firearms, but they did not shoot. Jommy could tell they wanted to tear him apart with their bare hands.

When a man jumped on his shoulders, Jommy clawed to get the attacker away. A red-haired man sprang at him as well, but Jommy spun, knocking him with the other attacker's thrashing feet. Pinwheeling his arms, the redhead stumbled against the door controls and knocked loose the device that powered the unlocking mechanism.

The scrawny treasure hunter had crawled halfway through the gap, peering into the darkness of the chamber. When several tons of vault door dropped shut on him like a mammoth guillotine blade, he made a sound more like a cough than a scream. On the outside, separated from the rest of his body, his legs kept twitching.

Several of the scavengers stepped back with expressions of queasy disgust. Two men began to laugh like hyenas at their comrade's misfortune.

Jommy slugged an oncoming attacker in the chin with enough force that he heard both the man's jaw and his neck snap. Then he snatched up chunks of rock at his feet and began to throw them like cannonballs, smashing several more scavengers in the face. But still they kept coming, swinging their clubs, closing in.

Jommy couldn't possibly fight them all. A heavy pipe smashed down on his left arm, numbing it from the elbow down, and another caught him a glancing blow on the temple. He reeled, but kept fighting.

A square-shouldered man with a scabbed cut on his left cheek drew a long knife and came at the stunned slan. Jommy threw another sharp-edged chunk of rubble at the knife-wielder, but his aim was off and the burly man ducked to one side. Jommy held up both fists, ready to fight, barely keeping his feet on the shifting ground.

The knife-wielder was apparently the leader of the mob, judging from the way he barked orders and how the others deferred to him. The rest of the mob backed away to let the leader have his chance. He slashed designs in the air with his dagger, taunting Jommy. The scavengers hooted and chuckled roughly, enjoying the show, while more vermin streamed over the ruins of the palace, coming from side streets. While Jommy defended himself from the dancing blade, more attackers seized his arms—far too many for him to throw off. The leader with the knife just smiled, letting the others do the work for him.

One of the scavengers swung a wooden club that struck Jommy squarely in the forehead. The blow would have killed a normal human, and even Jommy's slan strength was not enough. His legs went limp, and he fought to remain conscious. The men surrounding him laughed, grabbing his arms and holding him.

"What shall we do with him, Deacon?"

"Hey! I've got an idea! Let's break him into little pieces, just like he chopped Thompkins in half." The scavengers glared at the partial body severed by the falling vault door. The detached legs continued to jitter, as if impatient to be on their way. The redheaded man squatted beside the lower half of the bloody torso, clearly wondering what treasures might be inside the vault, but unable to open the door.

Deacon, the knife-wielder, was unimpressed. "If he'd been busy fighting alongside us, he wouldn't be in two pieces now. Thompkins got what he deserved." He tapped the dagger tip against his cheek as he considered possibilities. Jommy then noticed the leader wore a gruesome necklace from which hung several discolored and shriveled strips of flesh. They were unmistakable. *Slan tendrils*—as trophies!

Still struggling weakly, Jommy cursed his stupidity. He should have been watching more closely, aware of other dangers. He'd been so excited to find the disintegrator at last, and the thick vault walls had shielded him from outside thoughts and senses. He'd forgotten about the human mob mentality.

"Shall we take turns killing him?" said one heavy-browed young man. His voice was eager and high-pitched.

"We can only kill him once, Jerome. Don't be stupid."

"Oh. I meant kill him partway, lots of times."

Deacon fingered the blade. "As long as I get to keep the tendrils." He stroked the disgusting strands at his neck. "I hate slans as much as the next man, but I do like my collection." Jommy could barely focus on the man who paced around him, toying with his knife, drawing out the moment. "As much as I'd enjoy torturing this snake for the next week or so, there's too much loot to be had. So let's get on with it."

Jommy found a surge of energy, fought furiously, and threw off two of his captors. Then someone pummeled him again with the thick, wooden pole. He staggered, barely able to think straight. The pain rang in his ears.

"Knock him down and turn him over, then hold him real still." He stroked the discolored tendrils on his necklace. "I don't want to get ragged ends."

The men did as they were instructed. Jommy barely remained conscious. "I'm not your enemy," he croaked. "You don't need to hurt me."

The scavengers snickered and guffawed. "Oh, sure, slans aren't our enemies. The whole city's blown up around us, but that was a slan gesture of friendship, wasn't it?"

Deacon bent over with his long knife, whispering in his ear. "You slans think you're superior to us because of your tendrils. They give you some kind of super mind powers. Doesn't seem fair to me. I think you should feel like one of us mere mortals for a few minutes before you die." Deacon yanked Jommy's thin golden tendrils, pulling them straight.

A sudden icy fear plunged down Jommy's back. "No, don't!" With heroic strength he nearly knocked aside the four men holding his shoulders.

Deacon made a quick slash. The knife blade cut swiftly, severing the tendrils in a single sweep.

Jommy felt an indescribable blaze as if a lightning strike had gone off in his mind. The pain was incredible. He felt suddenly blind. Deafness roared in his ears and in his thoughts, but he could still hear laughter echoing in the background. He heard a low moaning sound that warbled higher, then lower, and he realized that it was his own voice expressing his agony. He couldn't move, couldn't fight any longer. He felt utterly helpless.

Deacon stood up with an evil grin, holding his hand high. In a clenched fist, he held twitching fleshy tendrils. Tiny droplets of blood oozed out of the amputated ends. He waggled them in front of Jommy's glazed eyes.

Jommy groaned, seeing only red confusion. Deacon and his gang could easily kill him now. He couldn't find the will inside of himself to resist.

"Pathetic." The square-shouldered man stepped away, satisfied with what he had done. The rest of the mob came forward to finish up. Awash in agony, Jommy tried to face them, to fight one last time.

Then they looked up into the sky, shouted, and scattered in all directions. A shadow like a giant hawk swept over the debris of the palace, then explosions rocked the rubble nearby. Jommy squinted, saw one of the tendrilless ships cruising very low. The pilot took potshots at Deacon and his mob, like shooting fish in a barrel.

As the unexpected attack continued, Jommy crawled into the uncertain shelter of a fallen wall. The tendrilless pilot could easily have targeted him, but instead seemed interested in blasting away at the frantic scavengers as they clattered through the shifting rubble of the collapsed palace. Some of Deacon's men shot their firearms at the ship, but its hull was far too tough.

Groaning, feeling little more than his pain and his absolute loss, Jommy crawled and staggered, trying to get away from all the various enemies who wanted him dead. He ducked into a black crevice, out of sight, as the tendrilless ship came back around, searching for him.

TWENTY-EIGHT

Back at Granny's ranch, Kathleen waited anxiously for the summit meeting, now that Altus Lorry and the Tendrilless Authority had agreed to the terms. She had done everything possible to be of assistance to her father, but until the emissary ship arrived from Mars, she and Gray had little to do but wait. If the President could talk sense into the tendrilless leadership, convince them of what had really happened in their history, her father just might cement a peace between humans, slans, and tendrilless. It was their best chance.

Despite all the turmoil and uncertainty, Kathleen knew she could count on Jommy to get through, to find his disintegrator if it was at all possible—and to investigate the slan hideout from the maps in Peter Cross's logbooks.

She had felt a pure love for Jommy as soon as they'd been reunited; their thoughts, their hearts, were linked through their tendrils. Slans could know each other's minds, could look inside each individual soul. She knew Jommy was a good person, and she knew she loved him. From the moment they had encountered each other in that first slan redoubt, years ago, it seemed as if she and Jommy had lived a lifetime together.

But then the slan hunter's bullet to her head had crashed everything into silence. Some long time later, after a slan medical miracle had helped her recover, Kathleen was amazed to find herself alive but dismayed to be without Jommy. Completely separated, cut off. She knew he had to believe she was dead. For a long time she had been so miserable, but when they were reunited in the grand palace, all her agony had passed away like smoke in a rain shower.

Missing him, she busied herself in Granny's kitchen, helping the old woman bake apple pies to welcome the representatives for the important meeting. "You mark my words, girl, once they taste Granny's apple pie, they won't have any further thoughts of war and killing in their minds. I might even sell them the recipe—if the price is right."

Kathleen was better versed in politics and scientific studies than she was in cooking, but she enjoyed working beside Granny, rolling out the dough, peeling and slicing apples, sneaking a few bites whenever the old woman wasn't looking. When Granny thought Kathleen was paying no attention, she snitched a few bites as well.

When the pies were in the oven, filling the house with a delicious cinnamon-sugar aroma, Kathleen went out to the hangar shed and studied the rocket-plane Jommy had built. She instinctively understood the controls, the design. Jommy's genius never ceased to amaze her.

Also waiting for the tendrilless emissary to come, her father wandered around the ranch house and found her in the hangar. "A splendid machine, isn't it? If only we could find the lost slans, we could have a whole race of people building advanced vessels and weapons like that. With such geniuses at our disposal, no tendrilless would dare threaten Earth. They might just as well hide in their Martian city and never show their faces again."

"Given the chance, Jommy could probably do all those things by himself," Kathleen said, forcing a smile.

Gray detected something in her voice. "You're concerned about him, aren't you?"

"Of course I am. I know how dangerous the city is and . . . and Father, I love him."

"I didn't need slan tendrils to figure that out, Kathleen."

She blushed. "I suppose it's obvious." She turned from the silver rocket-plane, noting the red fins and the personal symbol Jommy had painted on its side. "I'm going back to study his father's notebooks. Maybe I'll learn something there."

While the President went off to plan his negotiations and prepare for the meeting, Kathleen entered the brightly lit underground rooms. She looked at the encrypted diagram again, studying the tremendous headquarters that the slans had used in the original wars.

She stared at the designs and notes, amazed at all the work one man had done while trying to protect his wife and young son. Peter Cross had sacrificed everything for them, and then Jommy's mother had also been killed. How many more sacrifices would be required? They had already paid such a high price.

Thinking of Jommy, she tried to sense him with her tendrils. Their connection was strong enough that she detected him even far away, though she couldn't capture specific thoughts. An uneasiness tingled through her, and with a gasp she understood that this was more than just a flickering contact. This was strong emotion, a powerful urgency—Jommy sent his panic out like a beacon. Or a scream!

Was he trying to contact her, or was he just afraid—or in pain? Kathleen closed her eyes to concentrate, and her tendrils quested like antennae to pick up any thought he might be sending. She caught a flash inside of her mind.

Yes, Jommy was in danger, struggling. Many men, punching him. He fought back, but more attackers came—and they had weapons. She sensed a flicker of a knife, a gleaming blade that burned a perfectly clear image in her thoughts.

Someone touched Jommy's tendrils, lifted them away . . . and then as clearly as if a siren had blasted in her ears, she felt a slash of pain as hot as a molten wire.

Unable to stop herself, Kathleen screamed. Suddenly all of Jommy's thoughts, all awareness of his presence, went black and silent. The afterimage of pain inside her head still throbbed.

"Jommy!" she cried aloud. "Jommy!"

She quested out, but received no answer. No thoughts whatsoever. Just silence.

She was completely cut off. Sobbing, she ran out of the laboratory room and up the stairs, shouting for her father, for Granny, for anyone who would come to her. As tears poured down her face and the memory of the pain continued to pound in her head, she ran into Kier Gray.

He grabbed her. "What is it? Kathleen, tell me, what happened?"

"It's Jommy. Jommy's dead!"

TWENTY-NINE

On the sheer edge of the red-stone balcony overlooking the glassed-over canyons of Mars, Jem Lorry stood with his old father. The head of the Tendrilless Authority had a calm smile on his face, as if content just to be next to his ambitious son before Jem departed to meet with President Kier Gray. He was glad of his son's apparent change of heart. To an outside observer, it might have looked like a tender father-son moment.

Jem wanted to kill him.

Even with the urgent need to cement their victory on Earth, the old man did not seem inclined to hurry. Altus was calm and confident that everything would work out exactly as it should. Jem, however, understood that things worked out only when someone with drive and vision took charge of the reins of history.

"A beautiful view, is it not, my son?" Altus said. "Look at the white rocks, the rusty cliffs, the red dust. We tendrilless have been here in Cimmerium so long, I think the need to see red has supplanted my desire for lush greenery."

Jem had always wanted to see red. Blood red.

Even though the wide Martian canyon was covered over with a transparent roof, the enclosed space was vast enough that breezes wafted up from side canyons, air currents moving about from the exchangers, filters, and processing machinery. Far below lay a bone-dry riverbed from ancient days, a ribbon of broken rocks. It seemed a very long way to fall.

"I would be happy to let the humans have this place instead of us. Let Mars be their new Botany Bay. Since you don't want me to kill them all, that seems a perfect alternative. Exile the few surviving humans here and have them scrabble tooth-and-nail for an existence."

Mildly, the old man looked at his son. "Come now, Jem, when have you ever had to fight 'tooth-and-nail' to survive? You had a comfortable life. You don't fool me with your imagined hardships."

"Imagined? I know what those people are really like. Primitive, prejudiced, easily led by propaganda. They're a danger to themselves, and they deserve the punishment that we'll impose on them. I don't know what else Kier Gray expects."

Altus seemed troubled. "You are supposed to arrange a peace, negotiate acceptable terms."

"Negotiate? Father, they are broken and defeated. They have very little leverage. We should be able to get what we want, for the good of the tendrilless."

The older man heaved a long sigh. "Perhaps you aren't the best choice to go to this summit meeting after all, Jem. I'm afraid you may not approach the matter with the same goals as the Authority."

He felt a moment of panic. "No, Father, you can count on me. You know I have the bright future of our race in my heart. I will do what's best for all of us."

Altus considered. "Maybe we should wait until we hear from Joanna Hillory before we make any brash decisions. She'll have reached Earth by now. If she's found Cross, then the strategic balance has changed."

Jem tried to control his impatience and temper. "If you were going to kill Cross, I should have been the one to go there. In fact, I can make that my priority, after I've dealt with Kier Gray and his foolish summit."

Altus scratched his beard, pursing his lips. "The more I think about it, maybe I should be the one to go talk with President Gray personally. He and I can resolve this war."

"The war is *over,* Father, even before our occupation ships arrive. Someday you'll recognize what I have accomplished and grant me the reward I deserve."

The old man patted him condescendingly on the shoulder. "Now, Jem, don't feel bad. Of course I am proud of you. You're my son. But right now I can do a better job. I'll suggest it to the Authority. I'm very sorry, son."

Jem lashed out. "If you had spent years on assignment there, cut off from your heritage, living in their squalor, you'd think differently about humans. You can't know what it was like to be among them."

The old man remained silent for a long moment. He clutched the decorative rail with his sinewy hands and leaned over the drop-off. Like a playful child, Altus worked up a mouthful of spit and let the droplet fall, watching it drift downward in the low gravity, bounced along in the air currents until finally it disappeared. Smiling, he turned back to his impatient son. "Actually, I can, Jem. You see, in my younger years I, too, served on Earth. I was part of the initial spy organization that helped set up and infiltrate the humans' Air Center."

Jem reeled backward. "You were on Earth? Impossible."

"Why is that impossible? You think me so incompetent?"

"I just didn't think you had ever set foot away from Mars. That you would—" He cut himself off before he finished his sentence. *That you would ever leave your comfortable council chair and do anything active with your life.*

"My experiences were not quite so horrific as you make yours out to be." Altus continued to gaze out at the stark cliffs, reminiscing. He actually had a *smile* on his wrinkled face. Jem wanted to strike him, to wipe off that beatific expression, but he held himself silent to hear what his father would say. "I worked among them, lived among them, talked to them. It was very difficult at first, pretending to be a mere human and knowing their unreasonable prejudices against the slans. I had to parrot their words so no one would suspect me."

"Of course you did, Father. We tendrilless hate the slans as well."

"The humans don't even know the tendrilless exist. I felt sorry for them in their ignorance. But life there wasn't so bad. We made great progress setting up newspapers and radio stations, silently taking over their communications so that we could manipulate their fears. It was easy for us to help them because we did everything so much better than a mere human could. They thought we were geniuses. The hardest part was never letting on how smart we really were."

"That's what I did," Jem said. "That's how I became the President's chief adviser."

"Yes, yes." Altus didn't sound interested at all. "I wonder if it's possible that President Gray knew who you were all along and simply didn't let on. Your mental shields are some of the best I've ever seen, but he's a smart man. Gray may have figured it out."

"Don't be ridiculous! It was because of my talent and skill that no one suspected."

"Even so, you were with *him* all that time—did you ever suspect Gray is a slan, even a rogue tendrilless? Or were his mental shields even better than your own?"

Jem scowled but didn't answer.

"At any rate, I found some things quite admirable about human society—their music, their congenial friendship, ah, and some of their gourmet foods. Nothing like what we have here on Mars. You've

blinded yourself with hate, and that is not the mark of a good diplo-
mat." Again, that annoying paternal pat on his shoulder. "You see,
Earth is where I met your mother. She was another worker in the communications towers. Oh, she was beautiful, had such a musical laugh.
She had chestnut-brown hair and large blue eyes, a delicate chin. Your
features remind me of her very much."

Jem tried to grasp what his father was saying. "My mother was
also part of the operation? She was one of the tendrilless slans sent to
infiltrate the cities?"

"No, no." Altus chuckled. "She was one of *them*, a human. She
was very sweet. I wish you could have met her."

Jem choked. "You're lying. That can't be."

"Your mother was the best thing I found on Earth, kind and caring.
She played a musical instrument, a stringed device they called a guitar,
and her voice was like gold. She and I liked to dance. We must have
spent three or four nights a week out in clubs and ballrooms. We even
won a prize once. Hmm, I think I've still got the ribbon in my quarters
somewhere. I took it with me when I left Earth after your mother died."

"This can't be!" Jem searched inside himself as if he could suddenly discover a fatal flaw, a hitherto-unsuspected weakness in his
genes.

"Oh, it is, Jem. You're only half slan, you see."

"That means I'm half *human*." His stomach roiled, and he felt as if
he was going to vomit. "I'm half human!"

"It's nothing to be ashamed of, my boy. You can't help who you
are. In fact, we can use it to our advantage after I go to Earth. Don't
worry, I'll bring you there in due time. We would seem the perfect go-
betweens in creating a new world order. You could have a good deal of
interim power. Ah, your mother would have been proud—"

In a fury, Jem whirled and struck his father in the face, making the
old man snap backward in stunned surprise. A large red mark stood
out on his left cheek. "Calm yourself! I won't stand for this sort of be-
havior."

Jem roared and grabbed his father by the collar, screaming in his
face with such force that spittle flew onto his cheeks. "You betrayed our
race. You fell in love with a weakling human. You slept with the enemy."

"She was your *mother*, Jem."

"I will never accept that." He felt cold steel within him. "And you
are no longer my father. You're a traitor. I will never let you go to
Earth in my place."

With strength fueled by adrenaline and anger, he lifted the old man. Altus seemed no more than a large rag doll in the low Martian gravity. Without taking time to think, merely following his instincts, Jem hurled his father over the guardrail and sent him falling into his beloved Martian canyon. His thin terrified wail vanished into the background breezes.

Jem stared for a long moment, shaking after what he had just done, not from horror or grief, but merely surprised at how he had reacted. The old man had certainly deserved it; he would have ruined everything. Worse, if the news got out that Jem was half human . . .

He silently vowed to keep his heritage a secret. Certainly his - father would never have told such an embarrassing fact to any of his peers. No one need ever know about his tainted blood.

He leaned over the deep, breathless drop, gathered a mouthful of saliva, and then he, too, let a long droplet of spit drop into the void. He was just full of impulsive decisions today.

Jem made his way back to the Authority chambers. It would be a long time before anyone discovered what had happened to old Altus, and by that time he would be long gone to Earth, where he would have consolidated his rule.

Inside the crystalline meeting chamber, all alone, he climbed to his father's traditional seat and lounged in the comfortable chair behind the impressive bench. Then he rang the prominent summoning tone, knowing the other Authority members would rush to the emergency meeting.

The group of old men arrived, hastily straightening their robes, donning their ceremonial caps. They looked up to see Jem Lorry sitting in the middle of their high bench and no sign of Altus anywhere. From his high position, the younger man looked down upon the other council members. "I am prepared to depart for Earth. I just wanted you to know that I'm on my way."

After today, all the tendrilless would be willing if not eager to follow him, despite the blood on his hands. The proof would be in his strength of rule. "I am going to meet with President Gray—and I will accept his surrender."

THIRTY

The pain and emptiness did not go away, but after an infinite falling moment Jommy found the strength to endure. Even as he heard the humming engines of the tendrilless scout combing the wreckage for him, searching for him, Jommy discovered a lifeline within himself: He thought of Kathleen, beautiful Kathleen, and somehow he discovered the resolve to raise his head up. To *survive*.

Sharp agony was like a spear in the back of his head. He gasped and let himself collapse breathlessly onto the rubble, struggling to hide in a dim hole. The scout ship had driven away the murderous scavengers, but he did not dare let himself fall into the hands of the tendrilless.

He could feel the biting scrape of rough stone on his cheek, discovered raw skin and a bit of blood marring the concrete debris, but that was a mere distraction, a tiny whisper compared to the bellow of hurt inside his head.

The mob had slashed his tendrils off! It was as if they had lopped the wings off a bird or pulled the fins from a fish.

When the sounds of the enemy ship finally faded, giving up the search, he got to his hands and knees and coughed, but each jarring motion, each inhaled breath, sent more thunder through his brain. He fought against passing out, and then he retched, squeezing his eyes shut. His body was wracked with tremendous waves, but he crashed through them like a small boat against a hurricane.

With the mental silence yelling inside him, he could hear the blood rushing behind his ears. But he strained to hear something else, anything else, afraid he might pick up the noises of laughing scavengers returning for him, knife-wielding Deacon and his brutal gang. How long would the tendrilless ship frighten them off? They had left him alive, but maybe he was better off dead.

Jommy bit back a moan and forced himself not to follow that line of thought. He was *still alive*. He was *still himself*, with or without his tendrils.

He opened his eyes into the fading light of dusk. The sky was a darkening blue with a scudding of clouds and finger-paint smears of smoke from the burning buildings. All of his senses—even the normal ones—were different now, blunted. He felt shut off. When he got to his feet, his balance was gone. Jommy reeled like a drunken man and then stumbled once more. He fell back onto his scraped hands, then with a grunt of effort, he stood up again, swaying but managing to remain erect.

Weaving, he made his way through the rubble, barely able to see, hoping the scout ship wouldn't return. He accidentally found shelter, the corner of a collapsed room, and he curled up behind a fallen block of structural stone, shuddering. And night fell.

He had been born a slan. All his life he had unconsciously depended on his tendrils, the way a cat used its tail for balance. Every waking moment the slender fibers in the back of his head had picked up the signals of thoughts, the endless droning babble of other people, other minds. It was like the background noise of the ocean in a coastal village, always there, soothing and comforting. He hadn't even noticed it—and now it was entirely gone.

His dreams and thoughts were like fever visions, recollections and hallucinations. Jommy remembered going to sleep when he was just a little boy. His mother had sung him lullabies, but she did more than just give him the soothing music of her voice; her comforting thoughts wove a nest around him, letting him know he was *protected*, that she would always be there for him. Everything had changed when he was nine years old—and now he was faced with an even greater shift, a handicap.

Without his tendrils, Jommy felt both blind and deaf.

Terrified of what he would find, he gingerly touched the back of his head and felt the raw stumps. The nerve endings sent a rocket of pain through him. He drew his fingertips away, saw only tiny specks of red. Though Deacon had sliced him, Jommy's slan healing powers had halted the bleeding. He was in no danger from the injury, at least.

But now what was he to do?

Next morning, after a dizzying and pain-wracked night without sleep, he picked his way forward, stumbling again. The palace wreckage shifted with an ominous patter of falling stones and sliding rubble, and he knew he could fall through at any moment.

"I am not helpless," he said aloud, then repeated it to reinforce the thought.

He blinked and looked around, trying to see in the growing dawn light. All of his senses and impressions seemed muffled, muted . . . useless. But he reminded himself that this was how normal human beings lived every day, and they managed to survive without enhanced senses or telepathic powers. Yes, he *could* smell rock dust and old sooty smoke. With his ears he *could* hear the sounds of distant aircraft cruising overhead.

But he no longer had the ability to sense Kathleen in his head. He had lost that connection with her. *Forever.*

He staggered through the rubble. The secure vault containing his disintegrator weapon was sealed again, and he had no way of defending himself. Another failure! He had come so close, but he couldn't find any means to retrieve the disintegrator now. He was too weak. He didn't know what he could do.

In all of the desperate situations he had encountered, Jommy had never felt so powerless. Previously, he had been so cocky, so sure of himself, never doubting that he would find a way out of any trouble he might encounter. Now all he could think of was to get back to the serenity of Granny's ranch, where he could be with Kathleen, where he could heal . . . though he would never be what he was before.

Disoriented and still in great pain, he could barely remember where he had hidden his car. He paused in a bombed-out street, holding on to a twisted iron girder. He squeezed his eyes shut, forcing himself to concentrate, dragging the memory to the front of his mind, until he knew which direction to go. He slumped against a scarred wall, his knees trembling.

He felt dull and listless, unaware . . . and when the sharp-edged shadow fell over him from a descending tendrilless scout ship, he leaped to his feet. He hadn't even heard it coming! The enemy had found him! Jommy was entirely exposed, out in the open. He looked around, but could find no place to hide.

The tendrilless craft's hot landing jets blasted up gravel in the debris-filled street. Jommy began to run, but he overcompensated. He didn't see a broken cinderblock at his feet, and he tripped, sprawling into the sharp shards. He got to his knees, crawled along, then lurched up so he could run again. The tendrilless scout landed directly in front of him, blocking the street.

Jommy fell backward, turned about, and tried to scramble away in the other direction. The scout ship had weapons mounted in its nose.

He was surprised the pilot didn't just open fire on him. Panic yammered through him as he heard the door open. Someone stepped out.

"Jommy," a woman's voice called. "Jommy Cross. I know that's you."

He recognized something in the timbre, the tone, though he could feel nothing, pick up no vibrations or thoughts. He turned to find a woman running down the ship's ramp, rushing toward him. Joanna Hillory.

When she reached him, her face was angry, relieved, anxious. "I've been looking for you! I drove away that mob in the palace, but then I lost you. I was just thrilled to know you were alive. I've been searching—"

He faced her, trying to look strong and brave. He thought he had already convinced her that true slans did not have to be the mortal enemies of the tendrilless, but she had been unable to stop the devastating attack. "What do you want, Joanna? Your tendrilless have followed through on their threats. Look what they've done. Look at what's happened to the Earth. Are you proud?"

"I didn't want to be part of that, Jommy, and you know it." She took his arm, helped him forward. "I couldn't stop the initial attack, but we can still do something. We can still work together."

"Good," he said bitterly, bowing his head to show her the small bloody stumps on the back of his skull. "Because I'm one of you now. I'm a tendrilless."

She led him aboard her ship, where she cleaned and bandaged his wounds, gave him metabolism enhancers, and applied healing ointments so he could recover. From her expression and her movements, Jommy could tell that she was revolted by what the mob had done to him. Though the tendrilless were perfectly happy to kill slans, this sort of abominable torture was beyond her comprehension. "Jommy, I'm so sorry."

He lay on the cot in the tiny medical alcove of her scout craft. "There's nothing you can do." Her medical packs could not grow back his tendrils. "Why did you come here after me? You should have stayed on Mars, stopped their plans."

"The Tendrilless Authority sent me to search for you. They're afraid of you, Jommy. They say you're the most dangerous man alive."

"I don't have any powers, not anymore."

"I was happy to accept the mission, Jommy. I knew I could track you down. I picked up a tiny slan signal from the area. I wasn't surprised that you came back to the ruins of the palace—otherwise I would never have found you."

"I should have stayed with my friends, helped the President."

"Do you know what they're planning? Kier Gray has requested a summit meeting, trying to put an end to the hostilities." She explained the message she had received en route. "The Authority is going to send a representative, and it's Jem Lorry. I don't trust him. He's going to set a trap, somehow."

"Lorry? I don't trust him, either," Jommy said.

He sat up, deciding he had rested enough. Driving away the remnants of his shocked sadness, he reached a brave conclusion and looked at Joanna, wondering if he could count on her, if she would support his work. Even without his tendrils, he had his mind, he had his physical strength, he had his "normal" senses.

"I am still a true slan—and I have work to do."

THIRTY-ONE

With her link to Jommy brutally severed, Kathleen felt as if she had fallen into a black hole. Grief was like tar all around her. Now she understood all too well how much pain and misery Jommy must have gone through after *she'd* been shot, after he had spent years believing she was dead.

Her whole body felt numb. She wasn't cold: just empty, lifeless, as if someone had cut a huge hole in her heart.

In Granny's ranch house, she sat at the kitchen table, and her father took a chair across from her, angry at what had happened, sympathizing with his daughter. With a clatter of dishes, the old woman rummaged in her cupboards and brought out a small china plate adorned with a goldenrod flower design. She scooped up a piece of the still-warm apple pie, added a dollop of ice cream from her icebox, and presented it to Kathleen.

Despite the delicious smells, she looked up at Granny. "I'm not hungry."

"Of course you're not. But this pie is soooo good, Granny knows you'll want to taste it. Be the first, and tell us if it's good enough to serve to those important dignitaries who are on their way."

"Jommy's dead. A piece of pie isn't going to solve my problems."

The old woman cackled. "Good food often makes things seem a whole lot better. Just like money does." She showed crooked teeth. "Besides, I'm not convinced Jommy's dead. He's awfully hard to get rid of."

"I *felt* him die." Kathleen fought back her tears.

Petty lounged against the kitchen wall, completely unsympathetic. "We're going to have to do another load of laundry if that girl keeps going through handkerchiefs." He sidled over, got himself a plate from the cupboard, and moved to the freshly cut pie.

Granny yanked it away from him. "Don't you dare." She put the pie on a high shelf.

Because her father was also a slan, even without tendrils, Kathleen could sense his thoughts and his presence, but the connection was not the same as what she'd shared with Jommy.

"I know how you feel, Kathleen. I lost my wife—your mother," he said. "Though we kept our relationship a secret. There's so much you don't know about me."

She blinked at him. "But you raised me. I know all about you. I've read your biography."

"That was just a manufactured biography. President Kier Gray had to have a completely clean slate, an untarnished reputation. The truth about me was the most classified secret in my government. I had to make sure people like *him*"—he jabbed an elbow in the direction of Petty— "would never discover who you really were. If they used that information against me, everything I was secretly working toward would fail."

"If you were so good at covering up embarrassing details, Mr. Slan President, how come you didn't just hide your brat?" Petty said.

Gray ignored him, focusing only on Kathleen. He reached out to wipe the tears from her face. "I was born without tendrils, though my parents explained my heritage. I knew about the tendrilless, knew what they were, and they prepared me for the future. They taught me how to have an absolutely impenetrable mind shield. Not even another tendrilless could sense me, unless I wanted them to.

"But when I was thirteen, my mother and father disappeared—I assumed they'd been caught, so I ran. I changed my identity and made a new life for myself . . . exactly as they had taught me to do.

"Years later, when I was a young man, I met your mother. It was an accident, but for slans there are no real accidents. I'd spent my life covering up my identity, and so had your mother. She was a true slan, with many ways of using wigs and hats and scarves. The old days of shaved heads and the Human Purity League were far behind us, and slans could get away with it now."

"Obviously we've grown too lax," Petty said.

"I met her in a flower shop. Your mother loved flowers. Her name was Rose." He smiled wistfully. "She worked there, taking care of the blossoms, removing the wilted ones, watering the plants on the shelves, using a mister on the ferns. I came in to get some flowers . . . tulips, I think, or maybe daffodils. It was springtime, and I wanted to cheer up the old widow who lived in an apartment down the hall from me."

"How sweet," Granny said.

"Fortunately, there were no other customers. When I walked in through the door and the bell jangled, your mother looked up at me. It was like an electric current passed between us. She didn't have her mind shields in place, expecting nothing. I must have been careless, too. We . . . *clicked*."

"Love at first sight?" Though she didn't realize what she was doing, Kathleen took a bite of the apple pie, letting the spicy sweetness fill her mouth.

"More than that. You know what it was like when you first encountered Jommy. Even though I was normal in all external appearances, a slan can know another unshielded slan—even a tendril-less one—instantly and instinctively. Your mother and I recognized each other for what we were. I don't think either of us breathed for a full minute. She came around the counter, setting down the flowers she'd been arranging in a vase. She went to the door of the shop, turned the lock, and drew the shade." He took a long breath. "We were married two days later."

Slans rarely needed to go through a long courtship process; they clicked like a key in a lock. "Jommy and I should have gotten married," Kathleen said.

"Rose and I lived quietly together for several years, drawing no attention to ourselves. We taught each other many things, but we didn't have other slans to interact with. We were just by ourselves. She worked in her flower shop, and I took a position in the information archives in the Ministry of Communications.

"Those were the happiest times of my life. When Rose finally got pregnant with you, we were content and satisfied. Unfortunately, because we were both slans, we couldn't risk seeking medical attention. I could pass for a normal human, but not Rose. If she went to a doctor during her pregnancy, they might run some kind of test. They might discover that the baby had tendrils. They might find out that Rose was a slan."

"So you did it all yourselves?" Kathleen asked.

"These days, home delivery using a midwife is as common as a hospital birth, especially out in the country. Because my Rose was strong, we were sure we could handle it. We read everything we could. We were ready."

His shoulders slumped. "What I didn't know, though, was that my poor Rose had terminal cancer. In retrospect, I now see a thousand little signs that I should have noticed, but we were too focused on her pregnancy. She gave birth to you, a perfectly healthy little girl, but the delivery was difficult for Rose. She barely recovered, and that was when I realized something else was terribly wrong with her. But she wouldn't let me take her to a doctor. I tended her at home, and I took care of you."

"You must have been exhausted," Kathleen said.

"I needed every ounce of my slan strength. Poor Rose lasted longer than any human would have, considering the severity of the cancer. I knew from my own diagnosis and some medical equipment that I purchased through anonymous sources that her tumors were growing and that they were inoperable. Even bringing her to a hospital would have done no good at that point. Rose would have been exposed, and surgeons aren't inclined to do their best work with a slan patient—unless they're curious and wanted to do a few experiments." Bitterness edged his tone.

"You were eighteen months old by the time your mother was near death. I begged Rose to let me take her to the hospital. There had to be some chance, though I knew in my heart there wasn't anything we could do. Finally when the pain became unbearable, she acquiesced—but she forced me into a bargain first. I dropped her off at night in the emergency room. I never gave my name or hers. She was just a 'Jane Doe.' You weren't even with me, Kathleen. They had no reason to suspect that we had a little girl.

"Over the years, Rose and I had met many kind and wonderful humans. I prayed now that whoever tended my dying wife might be a kindly nurse or an altruistic doctor, someone who would recognize her pain and help her. Though I had to go, to stay out of sight, Rose remained connected to me through her tendrils. I could sense her with our special bond. I could feel what was happening to her, though she herself had dulled her mind and body with painkillers. When the medical professionals in the emergency room discovered that she was a slan, there was quite an uproar."

"I'll bet," Petty said. "They should have called my secret police right away."

"One doctor did," Gray continued, his voice like a razor. "They gave Rose a bed, realized there was nothing they could do for her except to alleviate her pain, and so that's what they did. The secret police came, prodding her, interrogating her, attempting to rip information from her brain in her last moments of life. But she clung to the promise I'd made, and she found her own sort of peace."

"What did she make you promise?" Kathleen asked.

Gray fell silent for a long moment and swallowed twice, gathering his thoughts. "I knew she didn't have long. I took you to a conservatory, a large greenhouse filled with flowers. That was what she wanted.

"Rose regained consciousness before she died. Even without tendrils, I could sense her in my mind. I held you in my arms, little girl, and we stood among the roses, the tropical plants, the beautiful orchids. She could see them through my eyes. Despite what the secret police were doing to her, she could share my thoughts. Those were her favorite things in all the world, and even though I longed to be with my darling in her last moments, I gave her something better. I smelled the flowers, the sweet perfume that she loved so much. It's the last thing she experienced. When Rose died, it felt like a cold wind passing through my soul, and I held on to you very tightly."

In the moment of openness, Kathleen could sense that her father had lowered part of his impenetrable shield, letting her inside for the very first time. She picked up on his emotions, his bright memories, his love for her. And some of the distant, blurred recollections overlapped with her own vague memories.

Kathleen was crying. "I remember that. I remember the flowers, but I wasn't sure what they meant. It was when I was just a baby."

"It wasn't until long after that I tracked down her body. I wanted to give her a proper funeral, but the secret police had already taken her for dissection. After that day, everything changed." Gray's voice became hard now. "I decided I had to make a difference. I couldn't just allow slans like Rose, like you, to live like rats in hiding.

"Since I had discovered Rose, I knew there must be more slans, though no one guessed where they might be hiding. After I lost my parents, I had no further connection with any of the organized tendrilless. So I went to work with grim determination, all by myself. With my job in the communications ministry and with full access to the informational archives, I built a detailed and impressive history for myself. It was masterful. No one could find any flaws or mistakes. And then I launched my political career.

"I did find other slans, eventually. We arranged meetings, extended our influence, and made our plans. Because I could pass so easily among the normals, they wanted me as their champion. I built my network, manipulating, strengthening, growing. Using slan skills, nudging the thoughts of certain followers, I built a campaign organization—but I kept my personal life intensely private. No one knew about you, Kathleen.

"I won my first three elections by landslides. My career was meteoric. When many of my supporters, and even several defeated rivals (whose minds I had manipulated), supported me as a dark-horse candidate to be the next President, I felt sure I could accomplish what I needed to do."

"But what about me?" Kathleen said. "I remember someone taking care of me, an . . . uncle?"

"A kindly blind man watched over you. I paid him well," Gray said. "Either he never knew you had tendrils, or he didn't mind. You were smart enough to take care of yourself. I thought everything was set.

"But on the day of the election, in my finest hour after I had won the office of President, secret police raided the old man's home. Someone had tipped them off that he had a slan girl there. The blind man couldn't defend himself. He didn't know very much about me, but he could probably have revealed enough. Fortunately for us, I suppose, the secret police thugs killed him before they could interrogate him. They captured you—and then I had to act. It risked my political career, my best chance for changing the whole world, but I had to find a way to do both. You are my daughter, Kathleen. I had to take the chance and save you.

"As the newly sworn President, I issued a decree, announcing that in order to understand the slans and whatever threat they might pose, we needed to study them, not just react with automatic fear. I insisted that you be kept in the palace with me, where you would be safe and where, unfortunately, you would be scrutinized every moment of your life."

"Then why did you originally agree to let her be executed on her eleventh birthday?" Petty asked. "It makes no sense."

"That was a concession I had to make at the time. I had many years to work around that loophole, and as you can see, it didn't cause a problem, ultimately. But now look where we are. See how much has changed?" He reached over, picked up the fork, and took a bite of pie. Granny looked on, as if hoping for a compliment.

"I still miss my Rose. Sometimes I can hardly bear it. Even with my power as President, I'd gladly surrender it all just to have a quiet, normal life with my wife and daughter."

Petty, still pouting at the flaky pie that Granny had denied him, grumbled, "Sentimental crap."

With a swift movement, the old woman swatted him again on the back of his head.

THIRTY-TWO

Alone inside the secret slan redoubt, Anthea counted eleven skeletons. Three were sprawled on the floor; others had collapsed into piles of bones beside desks and laboratory tables. Sensing her disappointment, confusion, and uneasiness, the baby boy squirmed and began to whimper.

Anthea picked her way among the skeletons, looked at the grinning teeth, the empty eye sockets. Several of the rib cages were broken, the bones shattered and blackened. All around, she found discarded weapons, bullet casings, and empty charge packs. Black marks stained the tables, floor, and walls. Chunks had been blasted from the high rock ceiling, and bullet holes stitched a zigzag pattern across a chalkboard that hung askew.

A terrific battle had occurred here, a shoot-out—but with whom? And how long ago? Was there some sort of civil war among the slans, or had the secret police discovered this place and ambushed the hiding slans? She doubted she would ever know the answers.

She strained her ears, as if there might still be fading echoes, but she heard only the hum of buried generators. The lights were strong and steady, never flickering. The air smelled clean, though with a faint metallic odor and thankfully without any residue of the decaying bodies.

Had the skeletons been here since the days of the Slan Wars, centuries ago? She looked down at the sprawled figures, wondering if they might be the last remains of the children of Dr. Lann. She didn't think so.

She picked up one of the unusual energy weapons on the floor— a stunner?—and saw that it had been completely discharged. She couldn't use it for her own protection, should slan hunters threaten her here.

After her initial surprise, Anthea cautiously explored the large chambers, calling out, but finding no one else there. The hidden stronghold was completely empty, completely silent.

She found fresh running water and sanitary facilities, several rooms with comfortable beds, clean clothes. In a dining area she discovered a wealth of preserved packaged food. After recognizing slightly old-fashioned brands and label designs, she concluded that someone *had* occupied this place within the last few decades. The food was still good, and she ravenously ate a wrapped chocolate bar. If necessary, she could stay here a long time.

At last, feeling a warmth and contentment she hadn't experienced since Davis had rushed her to the hospital—on what she'd thought would be the happiest day of her life—Anthea realized how utterly exhausted she was. She sat in a chair and kept herself awake long enough to nurse the baby, who sucked greedily. He must have been starving as well.

Barely able to stay awake, Anthea chose one of the soft beds and took just enough time to pull out a blanket and a pillow. She lay back, cradling the baby against her, and fell asleep within moments.

Later, rested and refreshed at last, she arranged a makeshift crib for the baby and then turned to the first order of business: removing the grim reminder of the skeletons. These bones weren't just random garbage that she could sweep up and toss in a trash bin. Every one had been a person, probably an unjustly persecuted slan. She imagined that they must have died fighting, as heroes.

Finding a pair of gloves and some empty boxes, she gathered each of the remains and reverently put them in separate containers, like makeshift coffins. She didn't know what else to do. Someday, there might be a way to identify these people and bury them properly so they could rest in peace. After she had quietly tucked away each of the boxes and cleaned the dark stains, she felt drained.

Now, she could devote her full attention to investigating the place that would be her refuge during the war above. The buried complex was quite remarkable with laboratory equipment that far surpassed anything she had seen in the library archives. The tall, blocky units with spinning tape feeds and blinking lights were obviously powerful computers. Thick electrical conduits ran through the walls, distributing power from generators that must have been located in a deeper grotto.

In a separate control room, she found a throbbing device studded with crystal rods and vacuum tubes. It glowed blue-white with energy, crackling as tiny sparks discharged across electrodes and thrummed through conduits into the ceiling. A signal generator? It seemed to be sending out a pulsing message—but to whom? The system itself must have been designed by those long-ago slans, perhaps the original children of Samuel Lann, or maybe the more recent inhabitants who had died in the shoot-out. Either way, was there anyone left who could receive such a transmission? Were there still slans out in the wreckage of Centropolis? Staring at the machinery, she didn't know how to respond to the signal, how to listen to what it might be saying.

As she continued her explorations, Anthea realized that the whole underground facility had been steadily changing ever since she and the baby had arrived—powering up, *awakening*. When the Porgrave sensors had recognized the arrival of a slan, dormant systems began to come online again.

The slan scientists in this base, whoever they were, had created technology capable of detecting members of their race. Anthea realized that if such sensors had fallen into the hands of the secret police, then no slan would ever be safe. The inhabitants of this base would have given their lives to protect that invention.

In the laboratory rooms, she found neatly stacked notebooks, records signed by a slan scientist named Peter Cross. In addition to the handwritten logs, she also found a recording loop and a viewer similar to the one she had used in the library archives. She installed the reel and played it, seeing Peter Cross in person. He was a handsome man with bright eyes, dark curly hair cut short, and a high brow. He made no effort to hide the fine slan tendrils that dangled at the base of his neck.

Cross spoke at length into the recorder about complex technical matters, describing how slans were again using this ancient base, though he feared the war was over and lost, for all intents and purposes. Cross described the treasure trove of forgotten discoveries he had found here upon reopening the underground redoubt, including a series of Samuel Lann's investigations about "original memory transference" and "baseline life-recording technology."

Then Peter Cross looked directly into the imager. His blue eyes seemed to stare right out at her, and Anthea felt his words tug at her heart. "I will never stop my work," he vowed. "Not until I succeed in making a better world so that my wife and baby son no longer have to live in fear."

When the recording ended, Anthea nodded silently and solemnly to herself. "That's something we can all wish for."

THIRTY-THREE

Inside the sleek landed spacecraft, Jommy recovered, sleeping as if in a coma, then feeling weak and disoriented when he woke. Counting on Joanna's help, he tried to think of a way they could save Earth and prevent the extinction of both humans and slans. Both of them felt a sense of urgency, knowing that Jem Lorry would be meeting with President Gray soon. Worse, Joanna told him the ominous main occupation fleet from Mars would arrive within days.

As she checked her systems, Joanna glanced up to see a flash of fire as an explosive projectile came flying toward her ship. "Jommy! Someone's shooting at—" She didn't have time to complete her warning before the explosion struck the side hull. The metal plates buckled inward, and fire tore open the wall.

Jommy staggered to his feet, feeling angry and helpless. He saw the ragged scavengers outside, coming closer. "They didn't take long to creep out of their hiding holes." The looters had scavenged firearms from civil defense armories and from the cold, dead hands of civilians who had tried to defend themselves. Now they closed in on the landed tendrilless craft.

Joanna ran to her cockpit systems, struggling to power up and fire her small battery of defensive guns. Three brief shots rang out, and the bright bursts scattered the attackers outside, giving them a brief respite. Joanna got her engines activated, and the damaged ship shuddered. With a blast of rockets, the scout heaved itself a few feet off the ground.

The angry scavengers shot whatever weapons they had managed to cobble together. Before she could lift the ship out of reach, a thrown grenade took out her rear engine, causing the ship to spin. The spacecraft's rear smashed into the wall of a nearby building, bending one of her guidance fins.

Jommy gripped the back of Joanna's pilot seat for balance as the ship collapsed back to the ground, raking the street with a flare of screeching sparks. Oily black smoke poured in from the engine compartment. Joanna looked at him, stricken. "Looks like we're not taking this ship anywhere."

Though broad spiderweb cracks obscured the cockpit window, he could see tattered-looking people closing in from all sides. He recognized some of them, saw their scrapes and bruises, the angry expressions on their faces—in particular one man with sharply squared shoulders and a fresh cut on one cheek. *Deacon*. He must have recognized the scout ship that had attacked them before he and his people could finish with Jommy. . . .

Jommy reacted with instinctive loathing, and a red undertone of anger suffused his face. "That's the man who cut off my tendrils."

Deacon's gang seemed to realize that they had snared themselves big prey. Jommy imagined how the scarred gang lord would use the captured enemy craft to consolidate his power, swooping along the streets and assassinating rivals. At the front of the advancing crowd, Deacon waved his dagger in the air as he ran forward. He seemed to think nothing could harm him.

The spacecraft's remaining engine groaned and whirred. Smoke polluted the air in the compartment. "If that man wants to capture my vessel intact, he's not showing much restraint." Joanna flashed a grin as smooth as broken glass. "And I plan to show even less restraint." She opened fire with the ship's energy weapons.

The dazzling beams struck Deacon squarely in the chest, turning his entire body into a cloud of reddish mist, shattered bone, and greasy smoke. He disappeared in midshout.

The other scavengers scrambled to a halt. Four of them dropped their makeshift weapons and ran away in a panic. Another hurled an empty pistol at the side of the tendrilless ship; it struck the hull with a harmless clang. Then the whole mob vanished into the shadowy streets like cockroaches fleeing a bright light.

"They won't cause us any more trouble." A faint undertone of disappointment rode on the tendrilless woman's words.

Jommy lurched back to the engine compartment and used flame extinguishers to smother the crackling fire. Joining him to inspect the damage, Joanna shook her head. "The energy cells are cracked. The ship's ruined, completely ruined."

His brow furrowed with concern. "We can't stay here. Exposure to those cracked cells can be more hazardous than facing a desperate gang." He pulled on Joanna's arm. "I hope you didn't intend on going back to Mars anytime soon."

The woman's face showed a mixture of conflicting emotions. "I'm not returning there until we've got a viable resolution to this unnecessary war. I'm staying at your side, Jommy."

Earlier, when she had helped him escape from Cimmerium and grudgingly admitted the possibilities of his idealism, he hadn't been sure how to read her. Like many of her race, Joanna had developed tight mental blocks that kept him from sensing her innermost thoughts. But he suspected that she was more than intrigued by him, more than perplexed by his strange optimism. Even though she was aware of his bond with Kathleen, Joanna actually seemed to be in love with him. . . .

"Jommy, what were you doing at the palace? What were you searching for when that gang found you, when they cut—?" She stopped herself.

"I came to the city to find something—something vital." He reminded her of his father's disintegrator weapon, which she had previously seen him use to great effect. "I know exactly where it is. I found it. I had my hands on it—then those scavengers came." He lowered his head, then drew strength from his resolve. "Come on. We've got to retrieve it. I'm not going back to the ranch empty-handed—especially if Jem Lorry's going to pull one of his tricks."

Before abandoning the wrecked scout ship, he and Joanna stuffed supplies into a pack, though they found it difficult to see and breathe in the thickening smoke. Since he had already activated the locking mechanism on the door to the vault that held his disintegrator, he knew exactly what sort of equipment he would need. Joanna also packed two small hand weapons. Though they had once been on different sides of this conflict, he was glad to have the tendrilless woman at his side.

"Joanna, if we don't get out of this, if we can't end the tendrilless war, then I am at your mercy. You can claim me as your prize and take whatever reward or promotion that's your due. At that point, it won't matter anymore."

"It'll always matter, Jommy. You said it yourself."

He answered with a faint smile. Perhaps he truly had gotten through to her after all.

They exited the smoldering wreck and trudged away, never looking back. The scavengers could have the broken hulk with its poisonous smoke and radiation that leaked from the destroyed engines.

As sunset threw long shadows across the streets, bonfires began to blaze in cul-de-sacs and alleys. A few candles and kerosene lanterns shone behind broken windows, where people huddled around the light and warmth. It would be another dangerous and harrowing night for the survivors in Centropolis.

He and Joanna stalked toward the site of the palace, both of them sensing that unseen eyes were watching them. They clambered over stones, dodged girders and broken glass.

In twilight, they finally reached the battered vault that lay like an egg in a nest of shattered debris. When he saw dark bloodstains spattering the stones, Jommy wondered how much of it was his own.

Joanna found the discarded bottom half of the man Thompkins who had been severed in two by the slamming vault door. Untroubled, she kicked the loose legs, knocking them aside with a wet ripping sound so she could reach the vault door controls. "I wish people would pick up after themselves."

Jommy was pleased to see that his dismantled tracking device still dangled to the controls by a few loose wires. "We better open the vault door, retrieve the disintegrator, and get out of here as fast as we can. It'll be dangerous negotiating our way out of this crater in the dark."

"Especially if we have company again." She peered warily into the shadows.

Struggling to function without his tendrils, realizing now how much he had relied on them, Jommy removed the necessary equipment from his pack and installed a new power source to run the vault's pistons. His fingers felt thick and clumsy, but he managed to rig the mechanism and charge up the weary motors of the security door. Once again, the pistons hummed, and the tilted door groaned partway open until the hinges jammed.

From inside, they heard a sliding, wet thump, and Jommy realized it was the top half of Thompkins dropping the rest of the way into the vault.

Suddenly, all around them in the dimness, hundreds of bright torches appeared, surrounding the crater. In the thrown firelight, the people looked like scarecrowish trolls, a wild tribe closing in on two victims. Without saying a word, Joanna dug in her pack and withdrew her hand weapons. Gunshots rang out from the scavengers, and bullets ricocheted off the rocks next to Jommy and Joanna. One pinged off the partly opened vault door.

"This isn't going to be as easy as I thought," she said.

Painfully aware of his lost tendrils, Jommy said, "Those are either Deacon's men, or a new gang's already moved into town."

"It seems I created a job opportunity for a potential new leader."

Joanna slowly turned around, took aim at one of the capering figures, and shot him dead. Her moment of triumph was short-lived as a volley of responding shots peppered the rubble around them. She ducked behind a large chunk of concrete. "Maybe we should come back at a better time."

"Never. Not while we're this close."

A rocket-launched explosive detonated nearby, sending a spray of rock splinters and clattering pipes and broken glass. Jommy hunched behind the tilted wall of the displaced vault chamber.

Joanna looked for another target and coolly took a second shot, which sent one of the torchbearers scrambling away, his bobbing light like a drunken firefly in the darkness. She snapped at Jommy, "Get inside the vault, find what you need to find, and then climb back out. I'll hold them off as long as I can."

"Not good enough. There's no time." With his shoulder, he knocked Joanna backward through the partly opened door. She fell into the vault, and he heard her clatter among the broken shelves and scattered debris.

"What are you doing? It's dark in here!" He heard her trip and let out a gasp. "Hey, how many bodies did you leave lying around?"

Another grenade hit, exploding against the back of the vault. He heard shouting and screaming, more gunfire. A swarm of angry scavengers boiled over the rubble, coming closer. He could see their snarling faces in the torchlight.

Jommy scrambled in through the gap, hoping the door's pistons would hold just a few more seconds. Before he dropped inside, he seized the blinking device attached to the locking mechanism, then yanked it free. As he dropped down, the immensely heavy door slammed shut with a hissing groan, sealing them inside the impregnable vault in total blackness.

Next to him, he heard Joanna breathing hard. From outside, the scavengers' banging and pummeling sounded oddly distant through the thick walls.

"Well, we're safe now. We can spend the night here." His voice seemed disembodied in the rich darkness. "There's just one problem. We can't open the door from the inside."

THIRTY-FOUR

As commander of the victorious tendrilless forces, Jem Lorry had no need to disguise who he truly was. Not anymore. Now that his meddling father was out of the way, now that Jem had command of all the invading armies, he returned among the lowly humans like a conquering hero.

He came alone to the summit meeting; it was his way of showing that he did not consider President Gray or his pathetic resistance cell to be a threat. And he did not intend any "peaceful negotiations," as Altus Lorry and the Tendrilless Authority had suggested.

While his swift expedition was on its way, John Petty had transmitted a subsidiary message. "I'll guarantee your safety, Lorry. You and I both want this meeting to go the same way. Once Gray and the slans are out of the way, we can divide up the spoils."

The secret police chief was a fool to believe that, but Jem allowed him to be a fool. Petty was so good at it.

He landed his solo ship in front of Granny's ranch house, ruining part of her vegetable garden. Jem wore a full formal uniform of the tendrilless army, a dark blue shirt fastened with crystalline buttons, trousers with gold piping and crisp creases. Raising his chin, he stepped away from his ship and looked coolly at those who came to meet him. He did not bother to offer a gesture of respect to the deposed President. He had spent too many years serving Kier Gray, offering his counsel and biting back anger when his own plans were ignored. "So, Gray? I've come representing the slans."

"The *tendrilless* slans," Gray said.

Jem looked down his pointed nose. "It seems we are the only slans left."

Petty came out on the porch to stand beside the President. He looked meaningfully at Jem, who gave a slight nod, as the slan hunter seemed to expect.

When Jem spotted Kathleen Layton, he assessed her with his hungry eyes. At one time he had desired her greatly, but the shine was gone. The slan girl looked much less attractive than he remembered— her skin was pale, her cheeks sunken, her eyes red from crying. He wondered how he could ever have found her to be beautiful. Perhaps he had wanted her primarily because she was forbidden. It must have been just a passing and meaningless physical attraction.

When Granny ushered them inside her home, Jem looked around for the others he expected to be there. He could easily handle John Petty, as well as President Gray himself. But even his foolish father had recognized that Jommy Cross was one of the greatest threats. "Where's Cross?" It was a pity; he had wanted to catch all the rats in one trap.

"Jommy's dead." Kathleen used her bitter tone to slash at him, as if she blamed Jem for whatever trouble the young slan had gotten into. He wouldn't believe the death of Jommy Cross, however, until he saw the troublemaker's body with his own eyes.

Granny had set up her formal dining table, complete with a checked cloth and a vase of fresh flowers. With a clatter of dishes, she brought out small dessert plates. "My best china, for the special occasion." Granny frowned at Lorry as she served apple pie, scooping out flaky slices onto the dessert plates. "This was Jommy's favorite." She hesitated a moment, then busied herself. "I've got a pot of fresh coffee percolating. It'll be ready in a few minutes." Before she left the room, she added in a stern voice, "Mr. Lorry, I don't care how powerful you think you are, but you are a guest in Granny's house, and you will behave with respect. I don't trust anyone who invades my planet."

Lorry could barely hide his amusement. "A conqueror of a world can do whatever he likes, ma'am."

"Granny's got a shotgun in the closet if you get out of hand. Don't you forget that." She walked off into the kitchen.

Petty quickly sat down, as eager for the pie as he was for the anticipated double-cross. President Gray took a formal chair at the head of the table and gestured for Jem to sit on the opposite end.

The President still wore the same rumpled suit he'd been wearing during his imprisonment and escape. For this important conference, his protocol attendees consisted of an old woman and his daughter. Kathleen picked up a pen and pad of paper to document any treaty or agreement they negotiated. Jem found it very amusing.

Before Gray could say anything, Jem abruptly began. "We tendrilless have already conquered Earth. I agreed to come here, Mister Gray"—he intentionally refused to use the title of President—"in order to accept your surrender. There's little I can do to save your life now, but perhaps if you cooperate, I can take Kathleen Layton under my special protection." He smiled at her; she glared back.

"The tendrilless have demonstrated superior military strength," Gray admitted. "You worked secretly for years, made your plans, and then launched a surprise attack. No doubt if tendrilless write the history books, you'll portray it as a heroic effort. But there is no need for the violence and bloodshed to continue."

Jem let out a bitter laugh. "Maybe you should review the history books, Gray—the unwritten history. Refresh your memory about what true slans did to humans during the wars, and then what they did to the tendrilless."

"I already explained it to the Tendrilless Authority," Gray said in a brittle voice. "Even the tendrilless will soon begin to give birth to true slan babies again. Must you eradicate us all just for your petty vengeance?"

Thinking he had heard his name, Petty looked up and wiped pie crust crumbs from his mouth.

Jem steepled his fingers. "My father repeated some of your silly fairy tales, but I don't believe any of it. I'm sorry he couldn't be with us." He hadn't touched his pie, thinking it might be poisoned, but then he realized these people would never try such devious means. This pathetic attempt at diplomacy was their only chance. He took a bite and had to admit it was delicious.

"It sounds like you came here to argue rather than negotiate," Gray said sadly.

"I never came here to negotiate. I just wanted to look you in the face one last time before I destroyed you and took over the Earth."

Granny walked in, holding a silver pot. "Coffee, anyone?"

Jem stood, checking the time on his wrist chronometer. "Come with me outside. There's something I want you to see."

Petty jumped to his feet. He thought this was all part of the plan, but the slan hunter would soon learn differently. They would all learn.

Jem had agreed to come in a solo craft, but he had gathered a full squadron of attack ships that would even now be streaking in over this valley. He had no interest in compromises. He didn't need to make any.

As they all stepped out onto the porch, looking up in the open air, Jem could already hear the drone of approaching engines and the arrival of heavy military craft.

THIRTY-FIVE

Trapped inside the sealed vault in the palace ruins, Jommy leaned back in darkness so thick that he seemed to breathe pitch-black each time he inhaled. He could still hear the muffled noises from outside along with Joanna's increasingly urgent questions. "What were you thinking? How are we going to get out of here?"

"Would you rather have let them tear us to pieces?" he asked. The vault groaned, shifted in the rubble, then found another stable position. Temporarily.

"We had a few weapons, not to mention superior physical strength. We could have made it quite a battle. Those scavengers are cowards at heart."

"We could have killed dozens of them. This way is better. Less bloodshed."

Their voices bounced back and forth in the blackness. "Do you know how many stone-cold corpses I bumped into after you knocked me in here?"

"Two."

"Two *and a half*. I found the top portion of Mr. Legs out there. I felt his shoulders, ran my hand down his back, and then he just . . . stopped. Like one of those matinee adventure movie serials—*to be continued*."

"At least you're finding humor in the situation."

"I'd find more humor if I could have a little light and some clean rags to wipe off my hands."

Jommy worked his fingers blindly, fiddling with the small tracker device he still held in his hands. The indicator lights were like the tiny bright eyes of a green lizard. "Considering how dark it is, this is as good as a flashlight."

The first thing he could make out in the faint glow were the pale forms of the dead bodies. Joanna saw them, too. "Oh, yes—much better." Her voice was sarcastic.

They sat together listening as the noises outside gradually faded, the scavengers giving up. Jommy had known the gang members would not stay long, realizing they had no way to break into the shielded laboratory vault. Once he was sure they had gone on to search for other prey, he used the minimal light of his device and his sharp eyesight to rummage around on the floor. He pushed one of the metal shelves aside, moved scattered papers, and rolled an empty chemical bottle away.

"Looking for a deck of playing cards?" Joanna asked. "I'm pretty good at gin rummy."

As he continued to crawl on his hands and knees, he cut his palm on a shard of glass. He had to delay his search while he picked the sharp pieces from his bleeding hand and dabbed it with a rag he found. The bleeding stopped quickly. "Remind me to use your medical pack when we get out of here. No telling what toxic chemicals the secret police might have stored in this laboratory."

Joanna just groaned. "Right. *When* we get out of here."

Jommy finally found what he was looking for in the corner where the steel wall met the steel floor. His hands wrapped around a smooth cylinder that fit so familiarly within his palm. "Ah, here it is." He felt a rush of pleasure because he had succeeded without relying on his slan powers.

"Did you find a deck of cards?"

"Better. It's what we came here for in the first place. Move our packs out of the way and get behind me. I don't want you in the line of fire."

She moved up behind him, leaning close, perhaps too close. Her voice was right in his ear. "Now I see what you were thinking of all along. Does the weapon ricochet?"

"No." At least he didn't think so. He depressed the firing stud.

A misty white light lunged out like a shout of destruction. A wide chunk of the thick vault simply vanished into vapor, leaving a gaping hole that led up above the rubble. "There, I made us another door."

He gathered his pack and walked through the gap into the night, barely needing to duck his head. Outside, the stars seemed to be hiding behind a veil of clouds, but after the utter blackness of the vault, the two of them could see perfectly well. Far off in the wreckage, he could make out a few fires. The largest bonfire looked to be where Joanna's ship had crashed. No doubt the scavengers had stripped it down to a bare hulk and now used it as their camp, oblivious to the toxic fumes.

"Shall we take my car?" Jommy asked, hefting the disintegrator tube.

He unerringly led her back to the obscure alley and the half-collapsed shed under which he had camouflaged his vehicle. He and Joanna cleared the debris from the car, and she studied its battered appearance. "Looks like you've been through some rough driving."

"I didn't have time to get a wash." Using the special thumb lock he had installed, he opened the access door.

"I'll be happy enough to get out of Centropolis," Joanna said. "I had quite a head start on Jem Lorry. We should be able to get to the ranch before he tries anything."

"I wouldn't count on it. And we're going to have to do some quick explaining about you—as a tendrilless spy, you won't exactly be welcome at Granny's ranch with President Gray and John Petty."

When he sat in the driver's seat to check out the systems, a persistent droning blip caught his attention. It was part of the instrument panel he rarely used, and now he saw that the car had picked up an unexpected signal. An emergency signal.

As Joanna loaded their packs into the back, he focused the scanners, scrolling across his screen and trying to pinpoint the source. Long ago when searching for slan hideouts, he had installed specially designed systems to detect important slan broadcasts, coded Porgrave messages beyond the range of any human or tendrilless technology.

Joanna leaned in, curious about what he was doing.

Now his systems had locked on to a loud beacon. He had not heard the signal when he first drove into the city two days earlier, but now the pulsing was strong and undeniable. Some hidden slans were sending out a distress call or an announcement.

"It's the location of a slan enclave. An active one!" Tracking it, he compared the pinpoint with the car's stored guidance maps as well as the details in his own memory. Jommy grinned when he realized that the signal originated from the same place his father had marked on the secret-ink maps.

Then the astonishing signal came through the car's analytical systems, broadcasting to both Joanna and himself, a voice that Jommy vaguely recognized from his distant past. "My name is Peter Cross, a slan scientist. If you are receiving this signal, you have been identified as bearing slan characteristics in your genetic profile. We need you. Your race needs you. Please follow this signal. I hope you will find us."

Jommy swallowed hard. He knew his father had been killed when he was only six years old, but the clear voice, the encouraging words . . . "We have to go there first."

"What about the summit meeting? Jem Lorry is bound to lay a trap."

He felt an ache in his heart, thinking of Kathleen . . . and then imagining the large slan enclave, perhaps people who had known his father. "I don't think President Gray or John Petty will let their guard down for an instant." And, even with the disintegrator, he felt weak and ineffective without his tendrils.

But if he could bring back a full army of hidden slans, other weapons or technologies—then they would have a fighting chance. And the slan hideout was right here, while Granny's ranch was almost a day's dangerous journey away.

He turned to Joanna. "Help me mount the disintegrator in the nose of the car. We're going to have to do some tunneling, take the direct route."

After he and Joanna installed the disintegrator, they strapped themselves into their seats. Jommy activated the engines, turned the weapon's beam downward, then burned a glassy hole through the ground in front of him. Considering the location of the signal, he would have to go deep.

He drove forward, carving a direct passage toward the secret slan base.

THIRTY-SIX

Standing on the porch, eyes wide with betrayal, Kathleen watched the hornet shapes of deadly aircraft swoop over the line of mountains. The military ships were heavily armed, their wings steeply angled, their engines roaring. The armada looked sufficient to obliterate the entire valley.

"As I said, these negotiations are over." Jem Lorry sounded very smug, not even bothering to look at the oncoming ships. He activated a signaling device on his wrist. "I can't afford to leave you alive, Gray, to become a rallying point for any annoying resistance movement." He smiled at Petty. "And the great slan hunter is as helpless as the rest."

The ships closed the gap in seconds. Granny had already bolted back inside the ranch house, but Kathleen couldn't tear her eyes from the oncoming squadron. Projectile launchers clicked into place, and the black hollow eyes of gun barrels turned toward them.

John Petty seemed to consider the whole thing a joke. "That's not exactly true, Lorry. I knew you would try to trick me, so I played each side against the other." He shaded his eyes, then pointed to the sky. "Look at the insignia closely. Those aren't your ships after all."

Standing close to her father, Kathleen recognized the ominous symbol of a scarlet hammer against a web. "It's a secret police strike force!"

"Yes, I used the wireless to contact them while you were all asleep. I arranged for this ambush." Petty whipped out a large-caliber pistol he had hidden inside his black jacket. "Lorry, you're as dead as the rest of these people."

Jem's face contorted in disbelief as Petty's ambush force dropped a flurry of explosive bombs that pattered around the perimeter of Granny's property.

"That's just for practice. Call it an opening move." Petty held the gun steady as he backed out into the middle of the wide-open yard, where one of the smaller ships could find a landing spot and pick him up. The secret police squadron circled back, coming in for their full attack run. Petty raised his hand, signaling the pilots overhead.

Kathleen turned to her father, trying to drag him back into the house. "We can get underground. Jommy armored the house, reinforced the tunnels—"

"That won't save you. None of you has a chance against the tendrilless." Lorry began to grin. "Ah, here we are."

Over the western line of hills streaked a second swarm of ships that headed straight toward the secret police squadron. The new ships purred rather than roared, using different propulsion technology, but they looked just as deadly.

Before the secret police could retrieve Petty, the squadron spun about at the last minute to defend themselves against the oncoming enemy ships. Their large-caliber guns blasted lead projectiles through the air, stitching fiery impacts against the tendrilless attackers. One of the new ships spun out of control, its fuel tanks in flames, and crashed like a meteor into the ground.

Petty dodged out of the way of the explosion, looking just like one of Granny's panicked chickens. Angrily, the slan hunter pointed his pistol toward Jem Lorry and began taking potshots at his arch-enemy, who bolted for the corner of Granny's house, crashing through her rosebushes.

Flying in tight formation, the newly arrived tendrilless engaged the secret police ships. The invaders' weapons were hot cutting beams that gutted Petty's squadron. More explosions blasted the ground. Two secret police ships erupted in a cloud of smoke and metal debris.

Flown expertly, both sets of dogfighting ships raced and dodged like swordsmen in a deadly duel. A near miss blew off the corner of Granny's roof and mangled one of her gutters.

Kathleen grabbed her father's arm. "Come on! To the hangar shed before it's destroyed. Jommy's rocket-plane!"

Gray understood immediately. "There's no better time to learn how to fly than right now."

"Granny! Come with us!" Kathleen shouted back at the house.

The defiant old woman emerged from her home, carrying her trusty shotgun.

Gray grabbed the old woman's scrawny arm. "Hurry—it's our only chance to get out of here."

"I'm not flying in any rocket ship!" But she ran with them anyway toward the hangar shed.

Petty glared at them, seeing them flee, and he pointed his handgun. He shot twice—and missed—before he ran out of bullets. He cursed at his gun, then gestured wildly in the air, trying to direct his own ships to bombard the house. Granny turned around, swung up her shotgun, and unloaded both barrels as he dove out of the way, running around the corner of her house. Buckshot left a spreading pattern on the siding, and the slan hunter let out a satisfying yelp to show that some of the pellets must have peppered him.

"Wasn't a complete waste of two shells, then," Granny said, stopping in her tracks to plug more shells into the gun.

Kathleen and her father kept running, racing across the open yard to the hangar. Overheard, attacking aircraft swooped and circled, strafing the ground and kicking up hot divots at Granny's feet. She pointed the shotgun up at the attacking ships in the air and pulled the trigger. She didn't seem to care which side she was aiming at. "Who said you could bomb Granny's property?"

She busily cracked the stock and inserted two more shells into her shotgun while the two sides in the dogfight circled and dropped their bombs. Kathleen and Gray looked up, saw a ship roaring down toward them, bomb doors sliding open. "We'll never make it!"

Gray stopped at the hangar shed. "This structure can't stand up to a direct hit."

"You two get inside and go! Listen to Granny, now!" She shot again, and her blast peppered the underbelly of the low-flying ship. Smoke began to boil from its engines. The ship swerved, aborting its bombing run as the pilot struggled to maintain control. Opposing ships came after it, opened fire, and blasted the hull.

Granny saw she couldn't reload fast enough, and she shook her fist defiantly at the planes as the dislodged bombs fell around her. The whole yard exploded, and the crotchety old woman vanished in a splash of flames and dirt only seconds before the attacking craft crashed nearby.

Gray yanked Kathleen's arm, dragging her along. "Come on! We couldn't save her." He shoved aside the rolling metal door of the hangar shed. "But she saved us."

Jommy's sleek rocket-plane looked like a bird of prey, fully fueled and ready to go. Kathleen scrambled up the metal-runged ladder into the cockpit while her father operated the motor that ground open the corrugated metal roof. By the time he swung up beside her into the cockpit, she was already scanning the controls.

The engines coughed to life and built up power. Exhaust shot out in expanding conical plumes that boiled white inside the hangar. She studied the gauges. "Warming up. Another five seconds."

Gray disengaged the landing clamps, and the rocket-plane began to move forward, unable to contain its own energy. "We're ready to launch." He looked up from the readings. "I wish I had coordinates to tell you, Kathleen. I wish I had an idea of a safe place we could go."

"I know where to go." *Another gift from Jommy.* She reminded him about the secret slan hideout that Peter Cross had described in his notebooks. The exact directions and coordinates were burned indelibly in her mind. "Jommy would want us to go there."

She hit the launch button, and the rocket-plane burst like an arrow out of the hangar shed. They streaked away, startling the opposing squadrons of tendrilless and secret police. Below, the bombardment of the ranch continued. Over half of the ships were now knocked out of the skies and lay in smoking wreckage amid the burning conflagration of Granny's house. Even the armored walls and roof couldn't withstand it all. She saw no one alive down there.

Before any of the ships could target them, the rocket-plane raced toward freedom across the sky.

THIRTY-SEVEN

Anthea held her baby on the comfortable cot, alone but at peace. She tucked one of the dark gray blankets around her, then drifted off to sleep, dreaming about her husband.

She smiled as she dozed, wanting to stay with Davis and his infectious grin, wanting to forget all the things that had happened. She could never get the echoes of those final gunshots out of her head. With some part of her, she knew that the tiny boy had joined her like an eavesdropper in the dreams, getting to know his own father. . . .

She awoke restless. With the bright, steady lights in the underground chamber, she couldn't tell whether it was day or night outside. Maybe she would never see open daylight or breathe fresh air again.

Anthea showered and dressed, putting on a new set of clean clothes she'd found stored in bins. After being on the run, dirty and weary, she finally began to feel refreshed, able to consider the future. She and her baby might have to spend years here, live out their lives in an unknown hideout. This complex had all the necessities she and the baby could ever ask for. Except for a real life. She couldn't just surrender like that.

She found a communications monitoring room full of visiplates and speakers tuned to numerous channels. Anthea listened to emergency reports, gathering background on the attack. In the past couple of days, she had been so frantic to save her baby, on the run from slan hunters and looters, that she'd never received explanations about the unexpected war that had engulfed the Earth.

The base's sensors and radar systems had detected a much larger occupation fleet approaching from Mars. Panicked-sounding broadcasters railed about the impending slan attack, an insidious plot that had been brewing for decades if not centuries.

With all she had learned from the library archives, however, Anthea couldn't believe that the surviving slans would choose that course of action. There had to be something more behind this devastating conflict.

When she came back into the sleeping area and saw the contented baby among his blankets, she felt an odd thought echo in her mind, a soothing confidence. Though the infant didn't even know his own name, he somehow assured her that *he* was the key. Even a child, the right child, could solve such dire problems, given time. Anthea didn't know what to think, but she smiled down at her little son.

Suddenly, proximity alarms began to ring, warning systems coming alive. A grating noise ratcheted like a washboard on her nerves. Anthea didn't know what to do. The deep hideout had been discovered! Someone had hunted them down after all.

She turned away from the deafening alarms, only to see something even more incomprehensible. One of the hideout's steel-armored walls began to shimmer and grow hot, and then it melted in front of her.

With the baby safe in the other room, Anthea ran to grab one of the strange stunner weapons that she had taken from the skeletal bodies. After experimentation, she had found only one of them that still had any charge left—but she would use it to make a good accounting of herself. A last stand.

She stood bravely, holding the weapon in her trembling hands as the rest of the wall dissolved into a curtain of boiling rock and metal steam. Something large and dark came rumbling through.

THIRTY-EIGHT

With the disintegrator beam playing ahead of the car, Jommy drove into dense strata through new tunnels of his own making. A straight line down into the secret base, where he hoped to rally hundreds of surviving slans.

They followed the beacon signal, listening to the repeated recording of his father's voice. The car rumbled along fused rock, going deeper and deeper. Jommy was eager to find the underground slan society, to reunite with a whole settlement of his people and convince them to help save the Earth.

If necessary, he would act as their leader, convince them to gather their weapons—maybe they all had disintegrator tubes, like his own. Together they could rush back to the summit meeting at Granny's ranch and make a show of strength that Jem Lorry would never suspect. With sufficient persuasion, they could make the tendrilless come to terms that would allow survival for all the races of humanity.

Rarely in his life had he known so precisely where he was supposed to go. The first slan hideout he'd discovered, years ago, was full of wonders, heavy machinery, and stored records, but it was empty of the people he so desperately sought. *Somebody* had to be in the tremendous complex up ahead, since someone had activated the distress beacon. He counted on finding new allies who could help him and explain what had happened to the rest of the slan race.

Jommy broke through a thick curved wall and drove his car forward, switching off the front-mounted disintegrator weapon. If necessary, he could always collapse the tunnel behind him to seal and protect the buried redoubt again. For now, he felt this was the only way he could get to the hideout swiftly enough.

Once he drove the car into the giant underground complex, melting through the steel plates, he brought the vehicle to a halt. He and Joanna emerged from the car filled with a sense of wonder, expecting to find a large greeting party.

Instead, he faced a haggard-looking woman pointing a weapon at them. One woman. The rest of the facility seemed deserted.

Jommy stepped forward, raising his hands, trying to be calm. "You have nothing to fear from us." He took a gamble. "We're slans. This is a slan place."

The woman had hard blue eyes and an intelligent expression. Her hair was strawberry-blond, her cheekbones high, and her nose pointed. Her lips barely moved as she spoke. "Prove to me who you are."

But Jommy no longer had tendrils, and Joanna had not been born with them. "I understand your fear. My parents were both slans, and both of them were killed by the secret police. I know what it's like, whatever happened to you."

Joanna remained at his side. "Tell us what you're doing here. How did you find this place?"

Her grip on the weapon was unwavering. "I received . . . instructions. An ancient beacon calling me here."

"And so did we. I followed the signal, a homing message that comes from here. It originated with my father." He saw her expression change. "His name was Peter Cross."

"Peter Cross?" Her shoulders slumped, and she finally lowered her weapon. "And I'm Anthea . . . Anthea Stewart. I have a baby, a newborn. He's got tendrils. I don't know how, because neither my husband nor myself are slans. I don't understand it."

Jommy felt his heart swell. He stepped forward, looking at the expanse of the underground complex. "I had hoped to discover other slans here, but maybe I'll find what I need regardless."

After they had introduced themselves and briefly told their stories, Joanna busied herself in the communications room, studying the progress of the approaching occupation fleet. Meanwhile, Jommy explored the remarkable base. Each step he took through the amazing chambers and laboratory rooms filled him with awe and anticipation. He felt he could learn something important from each document or piece of machinery. Though he was disappointed to find no large settlement of hidden slans, the wealth of information was significant.

Anthea came up behind him, standing at a doorway. "I have something to show you. Something from Peter Cross."

He hadn't even noticed her watching him. He felt so helpless and blind without his tendrils. "Yes!"

She led him to the table where she had arranged a video viewer and a stack of old film loops. She activated the player and stepped back while Peter Cross gave his moving speech. Jommy listened with tears in his eyes, looking again and again at the image of a man he barely remembered. His mother had told him that her husband had been killed when Jommy was only six. Fortunately, she and the boy hadn't been with him. On the projected image, Jommy could see echoes of himself in the older man's handsome face.

The recorded voice sounded achingly familiar, much clearer than in the Porgrave transmission. "I will never stop my work," Dr. Cross said. The words struck directly at Jommy's heart. "Not until I succeed in making a better world so that my wife and baby son no longer have to live in fear."

He played each one of the recordings three times, though he had instantly memorized them. He found his father's voice and image to be strangely comforting and compelling.

Marshaling his courage and his determination, Jommy went to the boxes of bones that Anthea had gathered. She had been careful to mark the location of each body and noted any details. Jommy could only imagine the battle that had occurred here.

He stopped in front of the box that as far as he could tell contained what was left of his father. He looked down at the skull, trying to imagine the man's features. After all his searching, Jommy was finally at home, but this wasn't the home he had been looking for.

THIRTY-NINE

The pulse beacon continued to send out its insistent signal, calling any slans, but Jommy had begun to lose hope that more of his comrades would arrive.

Before he could plan his next step, he and Joanna needed to assess all the equipment and weapons available in the redoubt. How could these things help President Gray? He couldn't begin to understand the large banks of twirling disks and blinking lights, the powerful generators and the purported "life imprint" machinery that dated back to the days of the first slans. He studied his father's notes again, thought about the single disintegrator tube he possessed. Though it was a formidable weapon, it wasn't enough to take back an entire conquered planet. He needed far more help than that.

But where were all the slans?

Together, the three of them listened to the staccato radio reports and wireless bursts from small groups of survivors. They told horrific stories of human renegades and tendrilless squadrons who shot humans for the mere sport of it. As usual, everything was blamed on the "evil slans." Anthea wept, as much for her murdered husband as for the future of her baby.

Joanna tried to comfort her. "I wouldn't believe all those reports, miss. For years the tendrilless distorted and manufactured news reports. They're doing the same thing now. Notice nobody is reporting about the tendrilless? Not a single broadcast."

Jommy called them over to a large set of external screens in the monitoring room. The slow-moving force of enormous wheel-shaped battleships cruised inexorably closer, atomic-powered disks filled with armaments and tendrilless soldiers. The images were crystal clear, disturbingly close to the approaching armada. It was enough to strike cold fear into any observer.

Anthea's face was gray with dismay. "You mean the fleet that attacked us in the first place was just a . . . a warm-up exercise?"

Joanna's lips formed a bitter smile. "The tendrilless have been planning this takeover for a very long time. They didn't just want to win the battle, but to exterminate every one of their enemies." She spoke as if she no longer considered herself part of her own race.

Jommy was puzzled by another question, though. "Where are these images coming from? The tendrilless wouldn't be broadcasting this, and it's certainly not a news broadcast from out in space—" He turned dials, scanned through the available visiplates, then he smiled. "These are our own satellites, watchdog probes. The true slans must have put up a monitoring network as well! Look, these pictures are from sentry probes beyond the orbit of the Moon."

The great slow ships cruised by, filling the view, not knowing—or else not caring—that they were being observed. Each vessel looked large enough to swallow a building. The decks were marked by twinkling lights.

Joanna measured the speed and finished her calculations. "They should be here within two days. That's what the Authority projected."

"Then that's how much time we have." Anthea sounded determined rather than panicked. "What are we going to do?"

Jommy decided he would scour through all of his father's laboratory notes, maybe race back to Granny's ranch to get the rest of the journals—and bring Kathleen and President Gray with him. Perhaps all together . . .

Suddenly new alarms screeched through speakers in the underground base. He and Joanna scoured the numerous visiplates, switching to local scanners and trying to discover the source of the warning. In the past when this underground base had been fully occupied by slans, whole groups must have monitored these stations, constantly manning the hideout's defenses.

Joanna finally discovered the reason for the alarm. "It's another ship approaching, Jommy . . . high-technology configuration, an advanced model that I've never seen before."

"A secret tendrilless weapon? Another air raid?"

"It doesn't look like something the Cimmerium shipyards would build." She worked with the visiplates, trying to switch through any still-functioning cameras implanted in the city buildings, though many of the lenses were now dark, buried under the rubble of collapsed skyscrapers. "Ah, here it is!"

Finally, she locked on and increased the magnification as a silver and red ship streaked in, burning hot like a spear point just taken out of a forge. "Looks dangerous—and it's homing in on our location—no doubt about it!"

Anthea's face was both frightened and angry. "Have we been discovered?"

The image sharpened as the ship turned about and fired blazing orange retrorockets to slow its descent. As it lowered upon a pillar of fire into the ruins of the city very close to the base's access point, Jommy laughed with blessed relief. "We're not under attack! That's a rocket-plane—my rocket-plane. I left it in a hangar at Granny's ranch."

On the screen, the rocket-plane had landed, and as it cooled, the hatch opened. A thousand questions filled Jommy's mind as his heart swelled. He saw Kathleen and the President emerge and immediately guessed that something terrible had happened at the summit. He didn't know why they had come here, or what they had been through, but now they had two more allies.

He was already sprinting toward the hidden lift and its controls. "I'm going up there myself to meet them."

Safe again deep belowground, Jommy held Kathleen in his arms. The girl felt wonderful. "I thought you were dead, Jommy! Oh, I was sure of it—your thoughts were cut off. The last image was pain, such agony that I couldn't stand it! And then nothing."

When Kathleen had seen that his tendrils were sheared off, she began to sob and clung to him even more tightly. He squeezed her and tried to calm her shudders. Her tendrils were alert, able to pick up any thoughts—but he was a blank to her. He would always be a blank from now on. She still felt the emptiness, though he was right there in front of her.

But then she had looked at him with her beautiful eyes, and she kissed him. "At least you're alive, Jommy. That's better than anything I'd hoped."

Down in the redoubt, Joanna watched the reunion with proud resignation. Jommy could tell she still had deep feelings for him, but the tendrilless woman knew he would never love anyone but Kathleen.

President Gray had shadows under his eyes. He looked more defeated now than at any time since John Petty had exposed him as a slan. At least the slan hunter was no longer with them.

"I'm glad to see you alive, Jommy, but this is a bittersweet reunion, to say the least. The summit meeting was a disaster. I had hoped to find some common ground, but the tendrilless had no interest in common ground. I explained about the tendrilless slans and how all of our babies born within the next few generations will have their tendrils again."

Both Jommy and Joanna listened eagerly to the story. Anthea also responded with amazement to hear the truth about the tendrilless, that she and Davis had been among them, entirely unknowing.

"I take it Jem Lorry didn't believe you, then?" Joanna said with a smirk. "I'm not surprised—*there's* a man who embodies the worst of tendrilless prejudice. A long time ago, he and I were matched."

"What does that mean?" Kathleen asked.

"We were genetically programmed to marry each other. The Tendrilless Authority had studied our parentage, and they selected me for him, and him for me. Fortunately, we both had to complete many years of service before we were approved. While Jem infiltrated the government here, I worked with tendrilless operations in the Air Center. Fortunately, I got to know the man well enough to abhor him. Even though we supposedly had the same goals, if we'd been married, I would have killed him on our wedding night. I could not stomach Jem Lorry."

"Not many of us could," Kathleen said. "He wanted to . . . to *breed* with me as well."

"I would say he's inhuman, but he'd take that as a compliment," Gray said. He explained about Jem Lorry's treachery, and Petty's double-cross, and the attacking squadrons of tendrilless and secret police ships. "It was a massacre. We barely escaped with our lives."

"Granny's dead, Jommy." Kathleen lowered her gaze. "She went out trying to defend her home. She used her shotgun—"

Jommy hung his head. The twisted old woman had forced him to do many terrible things, but she had also saved him in her own warped way. In the last few years, as he had guided her away from corruption, she had begun to redeem herself. Some of her old personality had returned, but a large part of the goodness had remained. For better or worse, she had changed his life more than almost anyone else. "I'm sorry I wasn't there to help her. I owed her more than I gave her credit for."

Gray continued. "If you hadn't left your rocket-plane in the hangar, we would have been part of the rubble there, too. The whole ranch is destroyed. There was nothing left but burning wreckage when we flew out of there."

When Kathleen lifted her chin, she looked very brave, and Jommy loved her more than ever. "At least Lorry was a victim of his own treachery—and Petty, too. Neither of them could have survived the inferno."

Jommy could find no sadness in his heart upon hearing that news. "One less slan hunter to worry about."

Then, from outside the main chamber, they heard a rumble and a crash. Jommy spun toward the large-bore tunnel that his disintegrator had burned through the ground. A small armored vehicle with thick tires rumbled down the passage and crashed out into the middle of the base. Jommy and his companions scrambled for safety as the armored vehicle fishtailed to a halt. Jommy saw the hammer-and-web insignia of the secret police on its side.

A battered-looking John Petty kicked open the vehicle's door and barged out. He stood up, his black jacket torn and bloodied, his face smeared with soot, his hair wild. He glared at Gray and Kathleen, and when he spotted Jommy, his expression became an even more twisted look of displeasure. "Doesn't anyone *ever stay dead*?"

"Speak for yourself," Kathleen said.

The slan hunter reached inside the vehicle and dragged out another body, dumping it unceremoniously on the sealed stone floor of the hideout. As the body flopped facedown, arms sprawled out, Jommy could see that the man had been shot in the back.

It was Jem Lorry. Joanna looked at the body, but without grief.

"No, he's not a present for you," Petty said. "He's a trophy for me. Maybe I'll have him stuffed and mounted in my own base from which I'll guide the recapture of Earth—for humans. I killed Lorry while the tendrilless continued to attack the ranch. I shot him just to spite them! I grabbed one of the secret police vehicles that had already been deployed, but its driver was shot in the cross fire."

"So you just drove off?" Jommy asked.

Petty shrugged. "I expect the fighting's mostly done there, now, though I don't know who would have emerged as the winner."

"Secret police traitors or tendrilless invaders—I'm not sure I prefer either side," Gray said.

Jommy glared at the slan hunter. "How did you know to come to this base?"

Kathleen turned quickly to Jommy. "I didn't tell him. And he couldn't have read your father's notes or translated the code."

Petty seemed amused. "Why go through so much trouble? I've always known about this base. In fact, my secret police and I extracted plenty of useful things from right under your nose, President Gray."

Jommy marched toward the slan hunter, who ducked back into his armored vehicle and emerged holding a powerful pistol. "Not one step closer, Cross. I've been aware of your mind tricks all along."

"Mind tricks? You don't have to worry about those anymore," Jommy said.

Petty noticed his severed tendrils at last and let out a loud guffaw. "Well, there's a bit of poetic justice!"

Jommy would not be swayed, though. "This was my father's lab, and we learned about it from his notes and records. *So how did you know about this base?*"

Holding his weapon, the slan hunter looked at them coldly. "Yes, it was your father's lab, and that's how I know about it. *I* killed your father."

FORTY

The revelation came louder than a gunshot in Jommy's ears. A crimson static formed around his vision, closing in like thunderclouds made of boiling blood. He finally forced words out of his tight throat. "I already had plenty of reasons to hate you, John Petty, but now you've given me more than enough rationale to kill you." He stalked forward, consumed with a sick rage.

Jommy had never learned the exact circumstances of his father's death. His mother had said that he was shot in the back, but she refused to speak more of it. Jommy just remembered being on the run with her for three years as she tried to keep her little boy alive at all costs. Peter Cross had made it possible for them to survive.

"Yes, I killed him." The slan hunter swung the pistol in his right hand, aiming directly between Jommy's eyes. He found the young man's reaction to the revelation hilarious, as well as his current inability to fight back. "My secret police and I massacred all the slans in this secret base. It was one of the last mutant nests that we had to eradicate. Why do you think you found only empty enclaves in all your searches? Because my secret police knew about them all and wiped them out! We ransacked them, left a few of them as bait. Believe me, any slans still left alive after the raids—like you and your mother—were basically irrelevant to us."

Jommy took another step closer, as if Petty's weapon couldn't harm him. Gray was cooler, spoke in a harder voice. "And how exactly did you manage this, Mr. Petty? As chief of the secret police, you were working for me. Why did you not give reports to your president?"

"Oh, it must have been in a memo somewhere . . . or maybe I just forgot." He grinned. "Peter Cross knew he was hunted. All slans knew they were hunted, and we spent years trying to track their movements. We managed to kill the occasional slan loner, which gave us great publicity, but we just couldn't seem to capture one alive for a suitable interrogation." He looked at Jommy. "But we got wind of your father's movements and staged an elaborate trap. We set up an ambush with more than a hundred secret police, because we knew what a challenge he would be." Petty's eyes took on a far-off gaze as he remembered his glory days.

"When we finally spotted him, we closed in, cutting off what we thought were all of his routes of escape. Finally, when we had a good shot, I ordered one of my snipers to take him out. But you slans are fiendishly difficult to kill." He shook his head. "Cross took the bullet in his shoulder. He was bleeding badly, but he made his way into one of the tall buildings. We followed him, but he somehow got into the basement levels, then took a lift to a high floor, then ran back down a dozen flights of stairs, found a fire escape.

"At first the blood droplets made him easy to track, but his gunshot wound healed so swiftly we lost that advantage. Three of my secret police cornered him in a garage just before he was about to dash into the streets. Cross killed all three of them, broke the necks of two, stole their weapons, and shot the third. Quite impressive, actually."

"So my father got away," Jommy said, grimly pleased.

"In a sense, yes. But that was part of the plan. I was never so gullible as to believe we would actually catch him so easily."

"Easily?" Anthea cried. To a woman who had lived a normal life in Centropolis, the brutal tactics of the secret police were a revelation. "Against a hundred fully armed men?"

"Yes, easily. These are *slans* we're talking about, lady. That's why they're such a threat to our way of life."

"*Your* way of life," Joanna said with a sniff. She still looked willing to fight for Jommy, even if he did love someone else.

"What do you mean it was part of the plan?" Kathleen pressed.

Still seething, Jommy maintained his silence, looking for an opportunity to spring upon the slan hunter and disarm him.

"The sniper's bullet contained a micro-tracer. I intended for him to escape, because as wounded and frightened as he was, Cross fled to the protection of his fellow slans. Oh, he dodged us for more than a day, leaving false leads, eluding the obvious trackers that I allowed him to see. All the while, though, we had the signal so we could follow him. He went right to this laboratory base."

"Even so," Gray said, "this is a fortress. The slans held it for centuries out of the view of normal humans. You couldn't just have walked in."

Petty smiled again, waving his pistol. "That was when the second fortuitous event happened. I had decided to make a full frontal assault, even if it cost me a few hundred men. A small price to pay for eradicating the last slan nest." He shrugged. "But we didn't have to do that. Once we knew where Cross had gone underground, we were able to set up careful surveillance. After weeks of constant monitoring, a young slan, barely thirteen years old, slipped away from the hideout late one night. We'd been waiting for an opportunity exactly like that. We sprang our trap.

"We exploded a canister of sleep gas directly in front of the kid. It would have knocked out an elephant, but it barely slowed him down. His reflexes were dulled, but still he fought. We dropped electrified nets on him. More than a dozen of my slan hunters piled on to the fight. It took three more anesthetic darts to bring him down. A thirteen-year-old! We whisked the kid away to our interrogation chambers. Armored vaults, sealed self-contained rooms inside the grand palace where my scientists could do their classified work. Even President Gray didn't know about them." Petty smiled.

"Yes, we discovered one of the vaults in the rubble." Joanna Hillory gave him a cold smile. "We even found people still inside—two and a half of them, to be exact. They weren't in very good shape."

"And what did you do with this boy captive?" Gray demanded, getting back to the discussion.

"We tortured him, of course. We used every extreme interrogation technique we knew, and finally we broke the kid's will. Your father and his fellow slans didn't even know they had a traitor in their midst."

"How . . . how did you break him?" Kathleen asked. "What did you do to the poor young man?"

"We used drugs and sleep deprivation. We tested sonic pain-amplifiers. But the most effective thing was to apply raw electrical wires to his tendrils. The shock proved quite excruciating. After two days of that, the slan boy was a puddle of jelly, willing to do anything we demanded, ready to believe anything we promised him."

"You're a monster," Anthea growled.

"I'm a success story. That was exactly what my job entailed—wasn't it, Mr. President? You always turned a blind eye when it served your purposes."

Gray didn't answer.

"The traitor provided us with the access routes and security codes we needed. We staged our great assault, fifty of my most trusted slan hunters, fully armed and ready. I also had a backup plan, five hundred officers ready to come charging in the event we started to fail. But that wasn't necessary. Our young traitor did his job perfectly, opening the way for us. The slans thought they were safe, cozy in their beds, when we barged in. Ah, it was wonderful!"

Jommy didn't take his eyes from Petty, but Anthea looked around the large chamber, the burn marks and bullet holes on the walls and floor. "So you just killed them all," she said, barely a whisper.

"I won't say that it was easy. The slans put up one hell of a fight—I lost twenty of my men—but gunfire eventually brought them down." The slan hunter turned his grin toward Jommy. "I remember your father. He was hard at work in his laboratory trying to understand the antique machinery of Samuel Lann. Demonic machinery. Who knows what strange apparatus that is?" He indicated the tall humming equipment. "Cross was one of the last to fall, and I was quite impressed at how well he fought, considering he had been shot not long before."

Gray crossed his arms over his chest. "Quite an operation, Mr. Petty. How come I never heard about it?"

"I'd intended to make a grand announcement, to show the world how the slans were still hiding among us, but then I realized how much I could learn from this underground base, so I kept the operation under wraps. We removed the bodies of my men, but left the dead slans where they were. Bait. We knew the slans would come back, eventually."

"But you left all this technology here," Gray said. "Why didn't you report it?"

"We had already found plenty of slan redoubts—like the place where Jommy met Kathleen."

"Where *you* shot her dead," Jommy said.

"Oh, stop complaining about that. She's fine now. The truth is, my teams had already analyzed so many of the hideouts, we knew what to expect. My experts spent days down here studying notes, copying technology, but most of it was incomprehensible. Exactly like all the other places. Eventually I just left this place behind. The slan bodies were beginning to smell, and it was hard to concentrate on the work." His face contorted in a grimace.

"You just left them here to rot?" Kathleen was appalled.

"It helped preserve the veracity of the scene. I maintained a careful watch on the base. It was like a piece of cheese in a mousetrap, and I knew that sooner or later more slans would come." He gestured to all of them standing there. "Now look at the mice I caught! I just didn't expect that the world would end in the meantime."

Even without his tendrils, Jommy had been tempered by his ordeals, like fine steel. He squared his shoulders and looked the slan hunter in the eye. "Using traitors, and torture, and overwhelming weapons—you seem to be extremely good at beating people when you have an unfair advantage."

"I'm extremely good at *winning*. That's what counts."

"So you can't win in a fair fight, that's what you're saying?"

"It's never a fair fight against slans."

"It's a fair fight now." Jommy pressed forward so close that Petty had to step back, still holding up his gun. "My tendrils have been cut off. I have none of the mind powers you're so afraid of."

"What about your slan strength?"

"What about your own strength, Petty? You're practically twice my size. It's just me and you. Your secret police killed both of my parents. You shot Kathleen, the woman I love." He raised his fists. "Will you fight me now?"

Petty laughed yet again, but this time it had a nervous undertone. "Why on Earth should I do that? I've already won."

Joanna let out a sarcastic snort. "A strange way to define victory—your planet taken over, your government disbanded, your cities destroyed, and your secret police force wiped out, while you hide here, underground. Jommy's unarmed, and you have a gun. Yes, Petty, it sure sounds like you've won."

"I don't need a gun." With a defensive snarl, Petty set the pistol down on a lab table next to his armored vehicle. He turned back to face Jommy. "She's right, you know, much as I hate to admit it. There isn't really a point anymore. I killed Lorry, but the tendrilless are still coming. We can't fight them, and we're all going to be wiped out before long—but I'll do this for my own satisfaction." He lifted his fists, too. "I don't need anything but my bare hands to put an end to you once and for all, Jommy Cross. I am going to enjoy this—personally."

Jommy held the slan hunter's gaze. "Whenever you're ready."

They slowly circled each other. Joanna and Kathleen stepped back toward the armored car. Anthea watched warily next to Kier Gray.

Jommy knew that the chief of secret police had thorough practice in hand-to-hand fighting, while he himself had never been formally trained. However, Granny had turned him into a scrappy young man who could take care of himself. Right now he wanted nothing more than to wrap his hands around Petty's throat.

He punched, ducked as the other man swung back, then withdrew to hold up his guard. With a sneer, the slan hunter said, "Why so fancy? This isn't some formal boxing contest." Then he threw himself headlong into Jommy's abdomen, butting with enough force to knock the wind out of him.

Straining to catch his breath, Jommy pummeled him on the back. The two men grappled, broke apart again, then flung themselves upon each other. Jommy didn't have his tendrils. There was no way of using his abilities to read Petty's thoughts for a hint as to the moves his opponent might be planning. He defended himself with animal fury.

Petty crashed a fist into Jommy's left eye, and an explosion of pain made him reel backward. He shook his head to clear his vision, but his eyelid began to swell, puffing shut.

Petty slashed with an open hand and curled fingers, trying to use his nails to jab the other eye, but Jommy caught his wrist. He pulled, practically wrenching his opponent's arm out of its socket, and tumbled the other man to the floor. Shaking his head again, Jommy regained his balance. He stood back and allowed Petty to get to his feet again.

The slan hunter stood up, flexing his sore arm, and gave Jommy a curious look. "Following rules and niceties? What's your game, Cross?"

"You think fighting fair and being honorable is a game? I feel sorry for you, Mr. Petty."

That angered the slan hunter, who flung himself upon Jommy again in a flurry of pummeling fists. Several hard blows caught the young man on the shoulder, in the chest. One even glanced off his chin, but Jommy struck back, a quick rabbit punch to the middle of the man's chest, another to his abdomen. Then, as Petty tried to recover, Jommy hit him again squarely on the jaw.

The slan hunter staggered backward—and tripped on Jem Lorry's body. With his feet knocked out from under him, he sprawled flat on his back, cracking his head on the hard floor.

Jommy pounced, putting one foot on the fallen man's chest, glaring down at him. "I should just kill you, Petty. You deserve it. But I've defeated you—that's worse. It doesn't matter how long any of us lives now, because you know you've been bested by me."

The slan hunter worked his jaw as if looking for words to spit. Jommy glared at him one last time, then took his foot off the man's chest. "It's over. Nothing will bring back my parents or undo all the harm you've done, but I've made you pay."

Petty glowered as he struggled to get up, to gather his dignity. Then, moving with the swiftness of a striking rattlesnake, he reached into the lining of his tattered black jacket and yanked out a second pistol, one of the weapons favored by the secret police. "Maybe none of us will survive—but I'll certainly survive longer than you."

Only a few feet from the slan hunter and his pistol, Jommy tried to dive out of the way. The sound of gunfire was deafening inside the underground slan hideout.

Then John Petty twitched, spasmed, and slumped face first to the stone floor. His gun clattered on the ground, and his head lolled to one side. He blinked his eyes in shock. A great wound on the side of his chest pumped blood. He gasped and gurgled.

Kathleen set his other weapon back on the table. "It's what he deserved," she said matter-of-factly. "It's what he did to me."

She ran up to Jommy, throwing her arms around him and giving him a hug nearly strong enough to knock the breath out of him again.

FORTY-ONE

The gigantic tendrilless occupation fleet was still on its way. Earth didn't have a chance.

Jommy and his four companions gathered in the surveillance room to study images from small true slan sentry probes that drifted in space beyond the Moon. The bright lunar backdrop filled most of the visiplates, its barren landscape reflecting golden sunlight. The mountains and craters were scorched by unfiltered solar radiation during the half-month of day and frozen by impenetrable cold the rest of the time.

As Joanna worked to adjust the views on the visiplates, he marveled at the extreme resolution of the pictures being transmitted from so far away. It only made the heavily armed enemy fleet seem more terrifying.

"They're passing the Moon now." Joanna looked up at her companions. "That means they're ahead of schedule. They'll be here in less than a day."

"How can we possibly stop them?" Kathleen said. Gray, Anthea, and Joanna all looked just as hopeless.

Jommy wracked his brain, hoping to pull a miracle out of his hat. Even slan technology wouldn't help them now. If his father or any of the surviving slans had been capable of stopping a force so powerful, then they would never have needed to hide underground for so many years.

As rank upon rank of attack ships cruised by, huge atomic-powered wheel shapes, Anthea was more intent on the round, dark lunar craters. She leaned closer to one of the large viewing plates. "Look, something's happening on the Moon."

As the armada cruised over the stark lunar landscape, the circular gouges scooped out by ancient meteor impacts began to shift and change. Unexpected lines of orange sliced across the crater bottoms, as if the rocky floor were cracking . . . splitting apart.

Then craters all across the surface of the Moon began to glow and *open*. Joanna exclaimed, "The crater floors are artificial!" The neat fissures widened, spreading apart as camouflaged doorways to reveal a huge and mysterious complex beneath.

"Those aren't craters at all," Kathleen said. "They look like—"

"They're hangars," Jommy cried. "Hidden *hangars*."

The tendrilless occupation force reacted in a flurry to the remarkable and unexpected changes below. Their formal ranks broke apart as the gigantic atomic-powered ships took evasive action.

After the artificial crater floors yawned open, enormous warships climbed out like moray eels hidden in a coral reef. A few tendrilless ships opened fire without further provocation—and without effect. The strange vessels continued to launch by the hundreds, thousands, then tens of thousands.

Kathleen was frantic and confused. "What are those ships? Who are they?"

"This is not possible," Gray said in barely a whisper. "I never suspected!"

Jommy couldn't hide his grin. "You know who they are, Kathleen. It's no wonder even John Petty couldn't find them. No one could find them! They chose the most unexpected, the best possible hiding place. That's where they've been all these years—*the true slans*!"

After being defeated in the centuries of war, the bulk of the true slans had simply vanished. Everyone assumed that the defeated race had been wiped out, with only a few stragglers living in fear of their lives. But in reality, they had fled to the Moon, using their knowledge and ingenuity to tunnel deep underground. Looking at all the open craters, Jommy could barely comprehend the scope of their vast civilization.

"They've been busy all this time," he said with admiration in his voice.

Warship after warship launched out of the huge crater hangars, arced gracefully around in lunar orbit, and utterly overwhelmed the occupation force from Mars.

Several of the panicked tendrilless ships continued to fire, but their weapons had no effect on the exotic armor of the lunar fleet. Instead of retaliating, the true slan warships simply blocked off the invaders and prevented them from proceeding to Earth.

Joanna was both amazed and agitated. "Those slan ships can easily wipe out the tendrilless fleet. They should remove the threat. It's the obvious thing to do."

"Obvious perhaps . . . but maybe not the correct action," Gray said. "The true slans know that the tendrilless are our brothers, too."

"More like prodigal sons," Kathleen pointed out.

The lunar warships sent out energy bursts that dampened the power fields of the invading fleet, shutting down the tendrilless ships and deactivating their weapons. The entire invasion force hung silent and helpless in space. To Jommy, it seemed like a patient parent dealing with a child having a tantrum.

While the true slan ships corralled the defeated occupation fleet, several warships from the Moon streaked off at incredible speed toward Earth. The true slans' engines were obviously far superior to anything the tendrilless had used.

Even before the emissaries arrived, the leader of the true slans commandeered all transmission bands. He broadcast stern words across every radio, every communications line, every wireless set. The words boomed out, clear and final. "We demand a cessation of all hostilities. We will allow no more of this destructive war between tendrilless slans and humans. We are all bound by our common humanity, regardless of our genetic differences."

On one of the visiplates an image resolved to show a distinguished older gentleman with a silvery gray beard, a high brow, and neat hair. He stood on the command deck of one of the lunar warships. Distinctive tendrils hung plainly from the back of his neck, fine fleshy threads that extended longer than his hair. Jommy thought he looked strangely familiar, though he was sure he'd never seen the man before in his life.

"I have detected a clear signal transmitted from a primary slan base, and I will go there immediately. I wish to speak to any government representatives, any leaders who have survived this unfortunate conflict." The man leaned forward and introduced himself. "I am Commander Andrew Cross."

FORTY-TWO

While President Kier Gray prepared to face the slan delegation from the Moon, Jommy felt a knot in his stomach. He was about to meet his own grandfather.

With Jem Lorry dead on the floor, Joanna volunteered to speak for the Tendrilless Authority. President Gray was ready to tackle the rest of the negotiations himself, deciding to deal with the remnants of Petty's secret police later.

Commander Cross arrived in the underground base with ten slan emissaries. Cross wore a black military uniform with gold piping, crisp creases, and a panoply of complex awards and badges. The other delegates were a mixture of politicians, scientists, medical staff, and tactical experts. All the true slans had long, healthy-looking tendrils; secure beneath the craters of the Moon, they had never needed to hide what they were. Jommy knew instinctively that a flurry of silent thoughts must be flashing back and forth between them, but he was cut off from them all.

Commander Cross's eyes flicked from side to side, inspecting the underground laboratory and base. He extended his hand toward Gray. "Mr. President, it's a pleasure to meet you in person, at last."

Gray smiled. "Occasional messages and secret couriers aren't good enough anymore. I'm glad your people finally decided to come out in the open."

"You knew where they were?" Kathleen asked, surprised. "You knew the slan civilization existed all along? I thought all those widely publicized slan messages and the unmanned drones were fake!"

"Not all of them. I was aware that someone spoke for the true slans, but I didn't know any concrete information until now. The main population of slans remained in hiding. I was only aware of a few solitary slans, some of whom worked with me in the grand palace. Others accomplished quite a bit all by themselves." Gray shot an encouraging glance toward Jommy. "Like this young man."

Jommy drew a deep breath and stepped forward. "Commander Cross, it's my pleasure to meet you. My name is Jommy."

The older man's eyes lit up. "*Jommy Cross?* You're Peter's son. You're alive!" Throwing aside his military reserve, Cross wrapped his arms around the young man and clapped him hard on the back. "But why can't I sense you? You're a true slan, just like your mother and father—" He turned Jommy around, then looked with a sick horror at where his tendrils had been cut off. "What have they done to you? Oh, Jommy!"

As Jommy explained in a halting voice, he felt great emotions bubbling up within him, both excitement and sadness, hard determination and total exhaustion.

Cross stepped back and looked appraisingly at his grandson. "You're safe now, Jommy. You're all safe." His lips quirked in a smile. "As you might have noticed, we've brought enough reinforcements to see that everyone behaves. Our ships will root out any last tendrilless resistance and stop the continued destruction."

"But what took you so long?" Kathleen asked. "The tendrilless attacked days ago. Most of our cities are already ruined."

Andrew Cross hung his head. "I am ashamed that we didn't take action sooner. We slans are much longer-lived than normal humans, and after so many generations, so many centuries, hiding has unfortunately become a habit for us.

"Centuries ago, after the great breach between the tendrilless and the true slans, we went underground in our complex on the Moon. We faced many difficulties in those first few years. Lunar resources are scarce. We had to manufacture water and air, scavenge metal from meteorites beneath the craters. While the original wars had knocked Earth's civilization back to a level from many centuries before, we were able to build our base and develop our technology. If the humans had known we were hiding on the Moon, they would have devoted every resource to a space program. Nothing like an enemy to focus the attention of a government! So we maintained a low profile.

"Recently, when the tendrilless war started, we watched by tapping into news broadcasts and wireless transmissions. We had known for some time that the tendrilless were infiltrating your political systems and your communications, but still we did not act.

"Some true slans insisted on letting the factions hammer it out for themselves. They insisted that we shouldn't get involved, that we had no debt to either side. When the great air strikes began and your cities fell, those same isolationist slans wanted to let you all destroy yourselves while we remained safe on the Moon. They were willing to abandon any true slans remaining on Earth." He hung his head. "I knew that my son Peter and his wife had been killed long ago. We thought the same thing had happened to you, too, Jommy."

Jommy felt a lump in his throat.

"A large group of dissenters—including myself—demanded that we take measures to save our human and tendrilless stepbrothers. Sadly, we were outvoted. But when we detected the clear distress signal emanating from the base here, I had the leverage I needed. I showed the proof, called for another vote, and my isolationist opponents backed down. That was when we launched our raids."

"What distress signal?" Anthea asked, carrying her infant in her arms. His tendrils waved in the air, as if he could sense the other slans in the chamber. "Is that what my baby and I triggered when we found this empty place?"

"It was just you and your baby? The base was empty?" Commander Cross said, amazed. "You did it yourselves? Only two of you?" The slan delegates, the scientists and politicians, looked up at her. Cross's disbelief began as a chuckle, then grew to full laughter.

"What's so funny?" Anthea asked.

"I argued that there must be a whole enclave of true slans. Hundreds if not thousands! I convinced the isolationists that we'd have an entire resistance movement here, ready to go."

"You do have a resistance movement," Jommy said. "The five of us."

The commander grinned. "And if you're anything like your father, Jommy, I should not underestimate you."

Gray motioned for the slan emissaries to sit at a long conference table in the underground chamber. Anthea, who was the most familiar with the layout and the stored items in the secret base, found food and drinks for them, then went to nurse her baby.

"Now this is the way a summit meeting is supposed to be," Kathleen said with a bittersweet smile. "I miss Granny and her apple pie, though."

Jommy felt a pang, trying not to keep a score of how much he had lost in recent days.

Commander Cross laid out his plans, which were already set in motion. "We will certainly encounter hot spots of tendrilless activity for some time yet, even without Jem Lorry to provoke them. Some of the invaders will still fight, but it's a lost cause. They will realize that eventually. I just hope we can impose peace before too many others die."

"We'll be a long time counting all the casualties," Gray said. "The people—slans, tendrilless, *and humans*—require strong leadership. They need to see that we are united and intent on rebuilding."

"The tendrilless will never stop fighting," Joanna pointed out. "They can hide so easily among humans."

Cross gave a mysterious smile. "After this day is over, they shouldn't be much of a problem. I guarantee they won't have any further interest in killing slans. They'll have nothing to complain about." To his astonished audience, he and the slan scientists explained what was at that moment happening in Cimmerium.

A squadron of advanced technological vessels had already launched from the Moon toward Mars—research probes bearing a new sort of transmitter, a ray generator developed by slan geneticists.

"What kind of rays?" Kathleen asked.

One scientist, a man named Dr. Philcroft, said in an awed whisper, "*Mutation* rays!"

Anthea was the one who piped up. "Mutation rays? Like the ones Dr. Lann supposedly used to create the first slans? But that was just propaganda—no truth to it at all. I've studied the tapes and records in the archives. Slans were a natural mutation."

"We know, but it doesn't have to be that way. In our lunar base we had many centuries to expand our medical science. What was originally imagined as a wild rumor, we were able to turn into reality. Slan geneticists did indeed create a device that would do exactly what the ignorant mobs had accused Dr. Lann of doing. Recall that the tendrilless hated us in the first place because they felt we had denied them their rightful powers. Thus, we found a means to activate the latent genetics frozen in the tendrilless slans. They always had the potential within them, but it was masked. Within a few generations their children would be born with tendrils anyway. So, we just accelerated that schedule."

Commander Cross picked up the story. "We fitted our scientific ships with transmitters to disperse the mutation rays widely, and those vessels are flying over the glass ceilings of Cimmerium even now. Every tendrilless soldier in the occupation ships has already been exposed." He grinned. "The results should be quite readily apparent."

"You mean the tendrilless on Mars are even now—?" Jommy tried to fit all the pieces together.

"Yes. The mutation rays are engendering the growth of tendrils. The Tendrilless Authority and all the people remaining in Cimmerium are rubbing the backs of their heads and finding quite a surprise. Everyone aboard the occupation ships is doing the same. They're all true slans now."

Jommy pictured what must be happening in the Martian city and aboard the giant wheel-shaped vessels. Tiny strands would emerge from the backs of their heads, growing like fine antennae. The former tendrilless would suddenly be able to pick up each other's thoughts—and what chaos that would cause! But the newly awakened tendrilless wouldn't know how to use their new skills. It would be a cacophony in their heads and an uproar in Cimmerium.

Kathleen shook her head wryly. "If Jem Lorry were still alive, I can just imagine the expression on his face as he transformed into one of his most hated enemies."

"And he would suddenly know just what everyone else thought of him," Joanna added.

"So, you see, there is no longer any need for conflict because the two parties can't tell each other apart," Cross concluded.

Jommy touched the back of his head, gathered the courage to ask his question. "And what about me? Can you regrow my tendrils? Can I be a normal slan again?"

His grandfather shook his head sadly. "Alas, there are no genetics to be triggered in you, Jommy. The mutation rays won't do anything to you, or to humans."

"We don't know how to convert humans yet, but the key is at hand, I'm sure." Philcroft looked at one of the other slan doctors, who nodded.

Kier Gray responded with a tired smile. "People can always find a reason for conflict, Commander, but you've just removed one of the largest ones."

Joanna looked from the military commander to the slan scientist. "You mean . . . I won't have to be tendrilless anymore, either? You can transform me as well?" She scratched the back of her head as if searching for delicate tendrils there. "I'll know what it's like?"

"You have the genes," Dr. Philcroft said. "All tendrilless slans do."

Anthea was also intrigued, holding up her baby. "Even those of us who didn't know we were tendrilless slans."

While the political delegates worked with President Gray to hammer out the details of an interim government, Commander Cross sat with Jommy and Kathleen.

"I miss your father terribly," the older man said. "He was such a brave and brilliant young man. Peter and your mother insisted on staying on Earth even though we could have brought them—and you—to safety on the Moon. But Peter was too dedicated to his work, and your mother refused to leave him. She clung to her hope. They both wanted to make a better world for you." Commander Cross shook his head. "I'm so sorry that I couldn't keep them safe, that I couldn't protect *you*, Jommy. I can't imagine what it must be like to lose your tendrils." His voice quavered.

"I survived," Jommy said, sitting straight, "and I'll continue to survive. Those tendrils defined what other people thought of me, but they didn't define *me*."

"What was Jommy's father working on that was so important down here?" Kathleen asked. "We have his disintegrator weapon, and we read many of his journals and lab notes."

"Peter was laying the groundwork for the return of the real slans and the conversion of the tendrilless, but he knew it wouldn't be easy. He understood that slans had to defend themselves in the meantime, which is why he invented that horribly destructive disintegrator. He was a good man, Jommy."

Jommy smiled. "I remember that much."

Anthea walked in holding the baby boy. Commander Cross looked at her, his tendrils raised and waving; he seemed to be in contact with the infant.

"That child is a sign that the waiting is over. More and more true slan children will be born again. This is the start of a new order, a new hope." His brow furrowed. "But that baby is so young, what psychologists call a *tabula rasa*—a blank slate or empty vessel, just waiting to be filled."

Anthea kissed the baby's pink forehead. "Maybe he's waiting for a safe and happy life."

Suddenly the scientists shouted from across the underground chamber. Dr. Philcroft's voice rang out clearly. "Commander Cross, come quickly! And Jommy, you, too—this is important. You'll never believe what we found!"

FORTY-THREE

Inside one of the underground medical labs, the slan scientists had discovered equipment they had not expected to find away from the lunar complex.

"This is some of the best slan medical technology that we've developed," said Philcroft. "Peter Cross, or someone with him, must have built them according to our early designs. And the machines are still operational."

Kier Gray had also come running, hearing the urgency in the scientists' voices. "That's the same sort of technology we used to save my daughter." He gave Kathleen's shoulder a warm squeeze. "Otherwise she would never have survived the bullet wound in her head. But with a slan miracle device like this, we brought her back. I was sure the only such machine on Earth was destroyed when the tendrilless leveled the palace."

"I saw the tendrilless use that technology in Cimmerium, too. They reconstructed a woman with a severe head injury." Jommy looked at Dr. Philcroft. "But why the sense of urgency? You called us in here—"

Philcroft blinked his eyes. "Don't you see? It's a *reconstruction* device." Clinically, the doctor touched Jommy's head, turned him around to inspect the scabbed-over ends of his severed tendrils. "We can use it to grow your tendrils back." The other slan doctors agreed. "Given this equipment, it should be a simple enough procedure."

Kathleen threw her arms around Jommy. He had not dared to hope, had not even imagined a miraculous solution. "I'm ready right now," he said. "Let's not delay."

The reclining medical chair had armrests and an array of probes, mirrors, crystals, and a dishlike metal cap that lowered over Jommy's skull. It looked like a bizarre torture device that John Petty might have created.

Dr. Philcroft adjusted the equipment. "Just lean back. We've already run diagnostics, so there's nothing to worry about. You'll hear a pulsing sound and feel a tingling. I doubt it'll hurt . . . much."

"It could never hurt as much as when they cut my tendrils off." He closed his eyes, and Kathleen took his hand.

The slan medical specialists discussed the various settings and readings; the machine was already powered up. Lights blinked furiously, and the crystals glimmered. Jommy could indeed feel throbbing transmission pulses like tiny electric ants crawling over the back of his head and inside his brain. He imagined his cells dividing furiously, healing, growing. The reconstruction device worked with incredible speed.

"I see them!" Kathleen cried. "It's working."

As the seconds passed, the room illumination seemed to grow brighter to Jommy, and every background noise became clearer and sharper. Moment by moment, his senses increased by orders of magnitude. The new-grown tendrils spread out, questing, drinking in impressions.

Philcroft and his companions clucked excitedly among themselves. Then a shift happened in Jommy's mind, and he felt his primary sensory input starting to come from the back of his head. Suddenly, beginning as a whisper that grew to a roar, he could hear other thoughts, fresh impressions.

And there, like a bright light at the end of the tunnel, he found Kathleen's mind and her heart. They were connected again, mentally reunited at last. He felt a surge of love.

Philcroft switched off the machines, and Jommy sat up, breathless. He was healed—aware, and alive, and *intact*. He gingerly touched his tendrils, then Kathleen's. He climbed out of the chair and drew a deep breath. "Despite all the misery and prejudice I experienced because of these tendrils, I'm certainly glad to have them back!"

For the rest of the day, President Gray, Commander Cross, and Joanna Hillory made joint announcements to the public at large. The three of them worked carefully to reassure the survivors in the cities. They described their plans for rebuilding Earth and creating a bright future for everyone, with peace among the races.

Meanwhile, now that Jommy's tendrils had been healed, the slan scientists were intrigued by the rest of Dr. Lann's ancient equipment, which had been installed so long ago down here in the secret base.

They devoted their studies to understanding the brain-pattern records and mental storage devices, mounting intact data spools on the bulky generators. "Even we haven't concocted innovations like this." Dr. Philcroft ran his finger along the transparent covering that shielded a set of spinning information disks.

Anthea Stewart, feeling safe but somewhat lost, took care of her baby and tried to plan ahead. She entered the research room, watching Philcroft and his unsuccessful attempts to activate the strange, ancient device. When Anthea brought the infant close to the great machine's embedded detectors, though, the data disks began spinning faster, lights flashed. The machinery hummed with furious energy.

Philcroft cried out to his partners. "Did you do that?"

"I didn't touch a single switch! It responded by itself."

"It can't activate spontaneously—there must have been some trigger." Then the men looked over at Anthea.

"I didn't do anything!" She set the baby down in his blanket to keep him safe from the machinery. His tiny tendrils were questing in the air as the old machinery spun and buzzed.

"The sensors detected a new presence," Philcroft said. "It's the baby."

Anthea remembered how the Porgrave signal in the library archives had activated because of her baby, how the whole underground base and its locator beacon had awakened from dormancy when she had carried the child inside.

The pulsing continued. The slan doctors rubbed their own heads. "Can you feel it? A targeted transmission, but I can't understand it."

Suddenly, the machinery stopped, the data disks halted, the lights went dark on the control panels.

"Did it short out?" Philcroft said.

"No, I think . . . I think it was just finished."

Anthea glanced back down at her baby—and to her astonishment he lifted his head and looked around with hungry curiosity. Using his small hands, he propped himself up, sitting in his blankets. His tiny lips curved in an amazingly adult smile.

Then, in a perfect voice, he said, "The memory storage and transference worked perfectly. *I am Samuel Lann!*"